Atop Gods' Peak

By Finn Douglas

For my father,

who has always supported me.

For my mother,

may she rest in peace.

Table of Contents

Preface and Acknowledgements 4
PROLOGUE 5
Upon A Fateful Night 11
First Journey 22
The Man with Frozen Eyes 31
Mentor and Student 41
Man and Beast 50
Departure 60
Mark of the Raven 70
The Cavernous City 78
Movements Like Flowing Water 90
The Blades of Iora 102
The Stones 114
The Man of Darkness 123
The Power of Emotion 138
Poems of the Void 150
Connected Through Tragedy 159
The Power of Command 171
The Pie 186
March for the Mountain 202
Morality 218
Ascension 240
Atop Gods' Peak 264
Descent 283
EPILOGUE 302
About the Author 306

Preface and Acknowledgements

Hello and thank you for picking up *Atop Gods' Peak*! This book has been a year in the making, and countless years in the crucible of my imagination. It has been a long, and surprisingly difficult road. Who could've thought writing a book was a lot of work? Not me when I started. However! You hold in your hands the culmination of my effort, my pride and joy. I sincerely hope you enjoy reading this book as much as I enjoyed writing it!

First off, I'd like to thank my Creative Writing teacher, Peter Suruda, for helping me through the entire year I was in the process of writing this book. He has dedicated more time, effort and love to this book than I ever expected, and I am truly honored. Next, my parents. Thank you to my father and mother, for never giving up on me, and always being ready to support me. I would also like to thank one of my closest friends, Brooke Mosby, for keeping me sane this year and helping me through every issue I encountered in my life.

For alpha readers! Thank you to Eric Douglas, Rick Almquist, Naima Zida, Devan Shults, Preston Lyman, Daniel Collin, Michael Turpin and a few others who requested their names not be included here.

Lastly, something a bit... unconventional. I'd like to thank some music artists who stayed in my ear the whole time I was writing this. First off, I'm a big fan of 80s' city pop, so I'd like to thank Tatsuro Yamashita, Anri, 1986 Omega Tribe, Masayoshi Takanaka and Kingo Hamada. For a lot of the action scenes, I wrote with a lot of metal and violin music. The main metal artists were Avenged Sevenfold, Periphery, Sleep Token, Gojira, Disturbed, Zeal and Ardor, and Trivium. My violin needs were met with Eternal Eclipse, Elephant Music, Secession Studios, Yasunori Nishiki, Rok Nardin and Brian Delgado.

With that, please enjoy the book!

PROLOGUE

Serena Helphain

The energy around me swelled as a bolt of orange fire burned the tips off my waist length raven colored hair. I whirled to the side in a graceful spin and flicked my wrist upwards, the energy around me trembling in anticipation. With a push of my will, a large spike of ice burst from the white-stone tiled floor and speared through a boy who looked my age.

Deep crimson poured down the length of my spike as I walked over to the boy. He was the last of his small group. He pleaded at me in a dying voice, "Please... you won't get away with this... the church will stop you!"

Energy coalesced floating just above my hand in the form of a rough, jagged, frozen dagger. I walked past the dying boy without giving him another glance and flicked my wrist again at the boy. The dagger streaked out and with a sound of flesh tearing, took his life.

I sighed and pulled back my hair into a ponytail, tying it with a thin piece of black string. The blood of the group of white-robed acolytes had splattered across my tight-fitting black cloth clothes that accentuated my form. I rubbed at the black leather plates covering my breasts and waist, trying to rub the blood off to no avail. My outfit was a stark contrast to everything else in this damned temple. Everywhere you looked was the same pearly white stone tile and carvings. The only ounce of color you could find was the runic energy conducting metal, bronze.

"Damned kids *had* to get blood on my new armor." I muttered to myself as I walked over to the corpse of another white-robed boy. I pulled a white stone ring with bronze trim from his dead fingers and held it up to the light, examining the eloquent runes engraved on it. I slid over my slender ring finger, and it adjusted, shifting in size until it fit.

I hiked up a flight of stairs, pumping the energy of the world around me into my legs in the form of a spectral shell. A smile twitched at my lips as the wind whistled around me, each step taking me higher than most average people could jump.

My feet gracefully touched the ground as I came to a halt in a pearly white hallway that stretched to my left and right. Ahead, was another staircase, which at this point I was tired of climbing. I walked down the hallway to the left and stepped up to the first stone slab of a door. It was more of a stone slab with bronze runes and inlays spiderwebbing across its surface. I pressed the ring I had picked up from the acolyte earlier into a ring of bronze runes and they flared to life with a white glow. Slowly and soundlessly, the stone slab slid away. A glowing crystal light ringed with runes hung from the ceiling, illuminating the white storage closet filled with different metals and stones in an orange light.

I sighed and shut the door. I wasn't some petty thief; I didn't need their riches. My goal was much higher. Each room in this hallway proved more disappointing than the last, storage closet after storage closet. Finally, I walked to the other end of the hallway and kicked the last door with a burst of energy. To my surprise, cracks spread across its surface. I followed up with an energy-infused punch, blowing the door to pieces.

Five burly clean-shaven men with short, cropped hair stood drenched in sweat. One was pinned to the ground by another in the center of a poorly made ring outlined with spilled spices. Everyone froze in surprise beneath the swaying crystal lantern that lit the storage room. Before the man pinned to the floor could react, I pulsed energy into my aura, forming smooth gauntlets of light around my arms. I let it flow to the rest of my body, giving myself a spectral shell. With a flick of my wrist, the cold air in the room surged beneath the base of the man's skull and a spike of ice the size of my hand burst through his throat with a spray of crimson.

He gurgled and wailed as the life drained from him.

Next.

One of the spectators charged at me with an energy-infused jab. I tilted my head to the side and felt the wind whistle as his fist rocketed by my ear. Cold air and energy coalesced in my palm into a familiar icy dagger, which I rapidly plunged into his sweaty skin. Blood poured from the several stab wounds, and he stumbled backwards in bewilderment, but too slow. I spun into a sweeping kick and he fell backwards as I flicked my wrist. With a satisfying wet crunch, he fell onto the ice spike I had just summoned.

With their size it was a battle of evasion. The man who had pinned the other down swung a hook at my head. I dodged backwards, only to watch in annoyance as he feinted the blow into a jet of fire. I let my footing slip out from under me and fell to the ground on my back and the fire barely roared past my face.

A pillar of ice met my back and carried me forwards at high speed in an arc towards the man's head. I spun in air, wrapped my legs around his neck, locked them behind his head and in one fluid motion, twisted with all my weight. Despite his daunting size, he spun along with me. We both crashed to the ground on our backs, and I pulsed energy into my legs to keep him from breaking my leglock. I summoned another dagger above his head and willed it to crash down on his neck. Deep red splattered the plates of my armor once more.

I clicked my tongue in annoyance. *Next.*

The remaining two charged me at the same time. A smart move. The first threw a spinning kick at my throat, his foot trailing a green aura. The other blasted a wave of sharp earthen shrapnel at my navel. I bolstered my aura with as much willpower as I could muster and raised my arm to block the kick. The shrapnel dug into the aura protecting my navel but got no farther than the surface. I smirked as the man's kick met my braced forearm with a crack. He looked at me in surprise as the girl half his size stopped his kick.

My fist rocketed upwards and into his knee, shattering his aura and his kneecap. He howled in pain and dropped to the ground with tears falling like waterfalls. The other swung a fist clad in earth in a hook at my head which I deftly leaped over. I flipped in air and came down in a kick on the man with a broken kneecap's throat, crushing his windpipe.

He heaved as he desperately tried to breathe and looked up at me, bug-eyed as his life slipped away. I looked back to my last opponent as he thrust another punch at my head. I leaned back, just out of reach of his punch, and felt the wind rustle my hair. I grabbed his wrist as he tried to pull back his punch and yanked him towards me. My fingers wrapped around his throat and the cold energy I had built released. He stared at me in shock as his neck froze instantly, and his head snapped from his body like an icicle.

I smiled slightly.

Without another glance to the training room, I turned and left, my hair swaying behind me. I walked quickly back to the staircase and began to cycle energy into my body from the air around me before forming a misty aura around my legs. With a powerful kick, I flew up the staircase in a streak of black.

After a few powerful, launching steps, I cleared the top of the staircase. To my left was a large open-air balcony that beautifully showed the stars of the night sky. To my right was a small dining area. Between the two, another staircase. I sighed, *how many staircases can this place have?* I thought to myself.

I dispersed my aura and walked towards the balcony. A figure became apparent in the starlight as I stepped closer, a large man in white robes embroidered with gold. I stood next to him, "The stars are gorgeous tonight." I looked over the sweeping elevated plateau covered in mountains and snow that was collectively named Mount Iora.

Without looking to me the man spoke in a deep voice, "Indeed." He turned to me. "What are you doing up so late, acolyte? Rest is important—" His eyes widened when he noticed my black skin-tight suit.

I smirked. "Had to look?" Before he could react, I kicked his kneecap with a pulse of energy —overextending his knee— grabbed him by the neck and tossed him over the edge. His white robe rapidly dropped into the dark shadow of the mountain as he fell hundreds of feet.

I smiled as I looked out across my home, taking a deep breath of the fresh mountain air. The mountain of Iora was a strange place. It was a raised plateau of land that went high enough to constantly gather snow and was covered in mountains that easily breached the clouds. My eyes drifted towards the clearing I knew lay in the distance, fond memories of my brother and father floated to the surface of my mind. The deep green leaves of the trees and the powdery whites of the perpetual snow always brought a smile to my face.

After a long, hard look out at the gorgeous night, I turned away. Each step I took, my smile died a little. I bounced up the steps reaching new heights with each push of energy off the white tiled floor.

After a short climb up a staircase, I reached a wide-open space with four doorways. One was a large, grand staircase that seemed to descend infinitely downwards. The one opposite one to the staircase I had climbed descended towards the other side of the mountain I had neglected. Finally, the last was a wide-open archway that led to a cylindrical room with a circular floor lined with bronze runes that caught the light of the crystal runelights mounted to the walls.

I pulsed energy through my body and vaulted myself forwards into the room, quickly whipping around to check for any unsuspecting acolytes. I swept my raven hair from my eyes and let the energy fade from my aura into an azure mist as I relaxed from the sight of an empty room.

I strode into the cylindrical room and pulsed energy down through my feet, into the bronze inlayed in the floor. The sounds of gears and mechanisms clanking filled the chamber as the floor began to rise. Slowly, blinding light began to trickle through the archway above. My stomach dropped in anticipation, and I called the energies of the world around me into my protective aura.

As the platform ground to a halt, a searing pain filled my body. I cried out and fell to the ground on my hands and knees. My channels erupted like lava flowed through them. My consciousness began to fade as I released everything I had eaten that day in a spray of bile. I desperately clawed my hand towards the archway filled with blinding light.

Find me.

CHAPTER ONE

Upon A Fateful Night

Reynolds Helphain

It was the middle of the night, the moon bathing my bed in its soothing silver light. The wind pushed itself into my room from under the window, lashing me with its frigid bursts. I sat straight up in bed drenched in sweat. My heart pounded in my chest like thunder. Every muscle in my body felt tense and my mind was spinning.

What was that? I thought to myself. The dream had felt so vivid, but there was no way it couldn't be more than what it was: a dream.

A searing pressure emanating from my sternum burst to life, like I had been speared through the chest with molten lava. I clenched my teeth as my face contorted into a grimace, tears running down my face and onto my grey tunic. It was time. A godly entity was burning them into my chest with an ethereal quill. I struggled to try and make sense of the runes as they formed through my teary vision. *Apheon, Celphen, Rugand, Yildaar.* Most of the runes were unreadable and unfamiliar to me, however the ones I could read were tied to the thunder god, Yildaar. As the last rune formed in the center, the pain began to fade. Even being barely able to see through my tears, I already knew exactly what rune that was. *Helphain,* my family name.

After I rubbed the tears from my eyes, I pulled back my shoulder-length, middle parted, jet-black hair and lifted off my tear-stained tunic, dropping it next to me on the rough fiber sheets of my bed. I looked down and saw what looked like a series of complex, interconnecting tattoos on my sternum. I grinned.

I pulled myself from my bed, slowly and carefully to make no noise. *Find me.* The words were lodged in my brain tighter than an arrow in flesh. I opened the door to my room, beginning to quietly work my way down the hall and towards study. I slowly slid the door open, careful not to step on the notoriously creaky floorboards.

The room had a shelf on the left wall that spanned floor to ceiling, filled to the brim with strange vials of liquid and different materials used for elixirs. On the far side was a desk of roughly cut cedar. Finally, and most importantly, on the right was a waist-high, decrepit bookshelf filled with tomes and random trinkets on top.

I scanned the dusty bookshelves for anything useful. *That dream can wait until morning,* I thought to myself, *I'll need to talk to father about it.* With that, I tried my best to focus on the new and exciting runes that had burned themselves into my skin.

I sifted through the tomes and eventually picked one on reading runic markings and sat down at the desk. After combing through the book for what felt like hours, I finally managed to gain a small understanding of my own runes. My father had forbidden me and my sister from studying these tomes when we were younger, saying they were, "Too complex," and that we should, "focus on strengthening our bodies."

I scoffed quietly as I skimmed, thinking back. *What a load of garbage.*

The large central mark was my family crest, which contained my bloodline's unique abilities. This book had no notes on what it did, so I ignored it for now. However, the other runes were much clearer. The marks directly ringing my crest were apparently the runes that allowed me to store the primordial energies of the world. Lastly the complex runes sporadically ringing the previous ring determined which form of energy I could manipulate, which in my case was lightning.

After finding what I was looking for in my initial book, I exchanged it for another, thinner book of basic training techniques and began flipping through. I stopped on a random page and began to follow its instructions.

I lifted myself from my chair and onto the floor, settling into a meditative position. I held out my hand in front of me, clearing my mind. I visualized raw power flowing into me from all around. A warm feeling began to grow in my chest, not the agonizing pain from earlier, but something more tranquil. Slowly, the heat built as I gathered the energy inside me. When it felt like it could burn through my skin and disperse, I imagined the energy flowing through my body like a river. The warmth began to dissipate as it flowed down my veins. I grit my teeth as every ounce of my body the energy touched felt like it was exploding.

I could feel the internal workings of my body changing, becoming less of a man and more of a conduit of the world. Deep grooves were carved everywhere the energy touched, forming channels to guide the energy through me. I could feel my hands numbing from pain as I focused the energy into my palms, almost begging to be let out.

Concentrating even harder, I willed the energy to flow out and into the world. I watched in awe as tiny particles seeped from my skin and formed into ribbons of dim light. I tightened my jaw from the strain as I put all my power into trying to coalesce this raw power into a ball. I watched as they slowly drifted together, then promptly dispersed back into nothing. A frown tugged at my face as the fatigue tugged at my body. It felt like every part of me was being dragged down by an inescapable force. I slumped back down on the uncomfortable floorboards and drifted into a deep slumber.

. . .

Golden rays of the morning sun streamed through the window, illuminating the muscular middle-aged man standing over me. My father stared at me with a devilish grin painted on his well-defined, clean-shaven face, his eyes almost gleaming with happiness. He leaned in, peering down at my chest and inspecting my dark runes. He flashed me another gleeful grin and said in an excited voice, "Morning son!"

Groaning, I started to sit up and muttered back, "Hey..."

His ecstatic voice rose in volume as he got closer, eyes almost twinkling like stars, he replied, "Looks like your runes formed, right on time!"

I lifted myself to my feet, my dad straightening as well, "Yeah, yeah," I murmured, blinking the exhaustion out of my eyes, "How about we talk about the runes *after* breakfast."

"Alright, kid" my dad said. He scratched his messy, spikey brown hair before practically launching himself down the hallway to the kitchen. I chuckled softly as I heard the floorboards creak with his vanishing footsteps. I stepped out into the now sunlit hallway and drowsily walked towards the main area of the house.

This room was just like the rest of the house, rough, battered and made of poorly hand-cut planks. On the right side was the dining table and kitchen -where my dad was shuffling around- the left had a small stone fireplace that looked as if hadn't been used in millennia and accompanying it was a very contrastingly well-worn, fiber couch. I sat down at the table and felt the chair protest my weight. I watched my dad fly through the kitchen like a hurricane, things flying out of the cabinets and onto the counter as he prepared to cook. I let my mind wander to my dream as he went.

His runes flared from beneath his tunic as his energy flowed from his hand and formed a small fireball. It danced around his palm, lighting the fire in the stove as he shot me a grin filled with pride for his affinity in pyromancy. I rolled my eyes. He threw the ingredients he had chosen into a pan and began to cook.

After he had finished concocting this strange dish, he brought over two make-shift plates and sat down at the end of the table. We ate in silence for a moment and after mulling over how to bring up the dream, I spoke, "Hey father," I pushed my strange food around my plate, "I had a dream... about Serena. It felt... different."

He looked up from his food and chewed his mouthful before speaking. "What do you mean?"

"Do you know where she went on her expedition? Did she ever tell you about it?" I looked out the window, past the deep green, snowcapped trees and out towards the mountains in the distance.

He sighed, his energy fading slightly. "She never told me about it. Claimed it was 'uneventful.' But I mean, you saw her. She didn't look the same, did she?"

I shook my head, my black hair falling in my eyes. "No. I was going to check on her down in the Lower Greens when I enrolled at the academy, but... this dream was definitely something of a vision."

He tilted his head to the side slightly, raising an eyebrow. "What're you, a fortune teller? A vision?" He sighed and jokingly slumped over the table. "I knew it. I shouldn't have dropped you when you were a baby."

"I'm serious, father." I pushed my hair back behind my ears. "It was like I was in her body. She killed... so many people. Maybe that's why she seemed so different."

"That could've changed her. I don't think it'd change her that much." He locked eyes with me, suddenly more serious. "What else happened?"

I leaned back and absentmindedly tapped my foot. "At the end she was in a lot of pain. It was like her channels were attacking her own body."

He frowned. "I've never heard of something like that before." He scratched his chin. "I'm guessing you're going to go to the same place for your expedition?"

I nodded slowly. "I think so." I stood from the table. "I don't know what I'll find, even if I find nothing at all, at least I'll be stronger for the academy."

He nodded, stood up, and walked over to the kitchen. "That's true," he replied as he dropped the wooden plate in the sink. "Why don't we go outside and do some quick exercises before you leave?"

I grabbed my own plate and mimicked him. "Yeah. That sounds good." I smiled slightly as I tried to push the thoughts of my sister away. I had practiced combat with both my father and sister for countless moon cycles, it was what I was confident in the most. *Finally, I might get to wipe that smug look off his face.* I thought eagerly, but I knew this would be very different from times we'd sparred before. He'd hold back much less now, that I was sure of.

He grabbed a large brown bag from the closet and strode towards the door, opened it and headed into the cold. I followed him and walked towards the poorly made door in long strides. As I opened the door, I was hit with a wave of frosty air. I stepped out into the large clearing in front of our house, taking in the snow-covered ground and the scent of the ancient trees.

My nerves tingled as they adjusted to the thin, frigid mountain wind. I swept my gaze ahead of me and over the edge of a cliff, smiling. I took in the stunning surroundings. I could see for miles, sweeping hills, crystal lakes, rivers curving into the distant sunrise, sprawling forests and small villages. But most impressive of all was the large stone-walled city that almost felt like it was sparkling in the distance, the key to my future and the start of a new chapter of my life. I took a deep breath, savoring the moment. Everything looked gorgeous in the golden light.

My father stood at a small rectangular table with strange training equipment and peculiar artifacts I didn't understand laid out. I walked over to him, the soft, powdery snow crunching underneath my worn boots. He turned to face me, the golden rays of morning light making his features stand out even more, contrasting the dark forest around us. His short dark brown hair fell in spikes just above his brows. "Before you embark on your epic, splendid, amazing journey of epic proportions... I will test you," he told me in a dramatic, booming voice that echoed through the forest.

"What're we starting with" I rolled my eyes.

He stood up very straight, his face dropped into an icy mask, his gaze shifting from caring and soft, to piercing and powerful. He then began to speak in a high-strung voice. "Well, if I were to talk in terms of the academy: Runic Knowledge 101, Energy Manipulation Basics and Diversified Melee Combat."

After a few seconds passed his face finally cracked from his deadpan face and he smiled brightly as we both broke into chuckles. After we finished laughing, I replied, "Gods I hope they don't talk like that."

"Welp, guess you better start praying," His voice morphed from a joking tone back to normal. "For now, I'm only going to show you the basics of using your energy, as its pretty intuitive. Other than that, I think a little... father-son duel is in order." A smug smile spread across his face, as if he could taste victory already.

"Oh?" I cocked an eyebrow, "Try it old man." With that remark I could almost see the flames of competition sparking to life in his eyes. He picked up two wooden swords from the table and tossed one to me. I caught it out of the air, bringing it up to eye level to inspect it. It followed the standard longsword design of the capital city, a long blade, medium handle size, with a curved guard sparsely decorated with different runes that were foreign to me. I gripped the handle tighter as we began to walk towards opposite ends of the circular clearing, the rough wood texture of the handle scraping against my callused hands.

As I reached the forested edge of the clearing, I flourished my sword in a stylistic manner and took an offensive stance facing my father. His runes flared from beneath his tunic as he shot a small orb into the air and took his stance. The ball exploded with a loud bang. We began. We crept towards the middle. I focused on my breathing, the sound of the crunching snow and his presence, drowning everything else out. The snow almost exploded around his feet as he pushed off the ground, hurtling towards me, winding back a swing.

My eyes widened as I raised my sword to parry, but it was too little too late. He was already swinging before I could move my sword for the complete motion. It felt like my sword had been hit by a tree, knocking my arm to the side, and sending me whirling back. Before I could regain my balance and try to recover, his fist slammed into my chest sending me reeling. My eyes bulged as I stumbled back. I tripped over a rock and my back slammed into the ground. I laid in the snow, coughing from the sheer impact of that *dampened* hit.

Just like this morning, when my eyes fluttered open, there he was, peering down at me but this time with satisfaction in his eyes.

"Hey!" he said cheerfully, "How's defeat treating you?"

"Shut it," I groaned weakly, raising my arm and sluggishly swinging at him with my empty hand. He laughed as he grabbed my half-formed fist out of the air and tugged me up to my feet. I stumbled around for a moment before regaining my balance and he let go of my arm. I wrapped my fingers around the now ice-cold handle of my training sword and tugged it out of the snow, resting it over my shoulder.

"At least this old man can still whoop your ass" he mocked, "Maybe if you hadn't acted *so* confident, I wouldn't have used a little energy."

"Cheating old man," I muttered under my breath before responding, "either fight me *fairly*," I glared at him. "Or show me how to use my runes."

"Runes it is!" he replied, his smile fading just a little. We walked over to the old table where all the strange things were, and he started fiddling with the objects.

Lighting a fire under a small pot, he began to toss brightly colored plants and herbs into the pot. He slowly stirred them together before letting them sit still as the water inside shifted in color. Next, he grabbed a few pieces of what seemed like jewelry with deep runes carved into the various metals and tossed them in my direction. The flying metal that was probably worth more than this house caught the light as they soared haphazardly in every direction. I stumbled around trying to catch the various trinkets.

Once he finished brewing the strange concoction, he bottled it up in a small wooden flask and handed that to me as well. He instructed me to move towards the center of the ring we had just fought in and to wait for him there. I began to don all the trinkets and artifacts my father told me to. *I wonder if this is what it's like being a noble*, I smiled to myself, preparing for him to come instruct me again.

He glanced from piece of jewelry and back at my disheveled clothes and face from flying into the snow. He stifled a chuckle and began to talk about what each trinket did, "The gold necklace you have will limit the amount of energy you can use at once, so we don't have a repeat of whatever training you tried last night," he explained with a wry smile, "The rings you have on each hand help you focus the energy into specific limbs. Finally, this mixture will reduce the pain from channeling energy for extended periods as well as allow your body to temporarily hold a little bit more."

After a brief explanation of the form he was going to teach me, I drank the tincture and he backed away, signaling me to begin the exercise. Feet planted firmly in the snow, shoulder width apart, I clasped my hands before me in a praying motion and shut my eyes. I cleared my mind of everything around me, the cold, the birds, the wind, the sounds of swaying trees all faded to nothingness. Just as the relentless void began to clasp my mind, filling it with doubt, I began to see golden motes like stars flowing from everywhere and yet nowhere at all. They coalesced into a stream and flowed inward, touching my runes and making every cell in my body feel like it was humming.

I opened my eyes and released my focus. My runes were glowing faintly with the power I had just gathered. The runic light reflected in my eyes felt as if it was reflecting into my soul, filling me with sparkling courage. I began to concentrate again. Entering the all-consuming void in my mind once more, I began to visualize just like the night before, the energy flowing down from my runes and into my hands. This time the energy didn't burn as it ran through my body. It felt more like bathing in warm water. I split my hands, both tingled with the warmth of my newfound strength. Slowly, I raised them into a combat stance and opened my eyes.

I started to walk towards a tree, but the second my concentration shifted from my energy, so did the warmth in my hands and body. A golden steam rose from my hands as the power I had just accumulated turned to a luminescent cloud. I turned and looked at my dad. He was just leaning against a tree, watching me intently. He gave me a small nod, as if to say to try again.

Repeating the same form as before, I felt my runes slowly being filled with golden power. I once again willed it into my arms, feeling it flow like honey. This time I focused on trying to keep the energy in me as I moved. It was as if I was trying to keep a swarm of bees in a net, requiring every single bit of my willpower and focus to make sure nothing escaped. The rings on my hands began to glow a faint, dull blue. The second they activated it felt like my net suddenly became a blanket, requiring much less attention to hold in the energy.

Still concentrating on my flowing energy, I raised my arms once more and swung at the tree with a right hook. As my fist collided into the tree with surprisingly little pain, the bark caved and cracked. The entire tree shook as dark birds cawed, and snow rained from high in the branches. Golden steam rose from the impact, my energy completely dispersed from my hands and into the trunk. Fatigue tugged at my chest and arms, but I hardly cared. I was buzzing with excitement.

My dad walked over while clapping, a grin on his face. "Nice hook, kid. I'd hate to be that tree right now," His grin broadened as he continued, "Only problem is... I'm willing to bet you have almost no energy left."

"I've got a sliver of energy left." I lied with a thin smile. "But I'm not that fatigued. I could probably keep going."

"That's good! Your reserves must be as large as your sister's then." He smiled sadly. Serena was an abnormality, almost a monster in terms of raw talent with energy.

My excitement dimmed. "I hope so." As my father turned to go back towards the table full of artifacts, a thought entered my mind. "I did have a question, actually."

"Oh?" He stopped and turned back. "Go ahead. Lay it on me."

"That stance you had me do; do I have to do it every time?" I placed my hands together again as a demonstration.

He chuckled. "Well, no. You *can*, sure. It's a technique that helps the mind associate an action with gathering energy. It can make it easier, but in the long run, it'll hinder you." He flashed me a smile. "Anyway, follow me back to the house. We're just about ready to wrap up." With that, he skittered away.

I rolled my eyes.

CHAPTER TWO

First Journey

Reynolds Helphain

After my father had packed everything up and stored it back in the house, he came out with a different, simple bag that was packed full. With the flick of his wrist, he tossed it to me. I shot him an inquisitive look before opening it up to view its contents. Inside was an old fiber mat, some warm clothes, a few heating rune stones, a crude but sharp wooden dagger, a few books, various other survival supplies and about one week's worth of food.

I smiled. "Already? I've barely learned how to manifest my energy." I shot him a sly smile.

My father chuckled deeply and gave me a smile. "This *is* what you wanted after all. I imagine it will be a tough journey. Don't think just because Serena could do it, you can too. You can always wait a little longer."

I grimaced in annoyance, but he was right. She had a talent beyond belief, before she could even fully read her runes, she had the ability to freeze ponds with a flick of a wrist, and to call spikes from the ground with little effort. She was a true prodigy. She had come back from her quest distant, detached, cold and monstrously powerful. It'd been six moon cycles since she left for the capital, and we had yet to hear from her, unsure if she realized her dream.

I steeled my resolve and gave him a confident grin. "Even if I'm not a monster like her, after six cycles without hearing from her, the way she had come back, and now with this dream... I can't afford not to find a way."

He smirked. "People with talent are nothing in the face of those with determination. Only by enduring hell will you truly realize your full potential," he said before continuing with a wink, "and Rey, these forests have been protected by the barrier crystals for countless cycles. Everything is probably too scared to leave its tiny cave and come near. Maybe when you get back you can teach your old man a thing or two you've learned."

I put on my new bag and smiled at him. I started to walk away, with each step my heart swelled with excitement. I turned around, sprinting back to my father one last time. I felt his tree trunk arms wrap around me as I took in the feeling of his embrace, savoring every moment as if it could be the last. "I love you, Gaelin." I smiled at him.

"I love you too, Rey. Good luck out there."

With that, I trekked away, the sun rising behind me cast my long shadow into the trees. Even from miles away it was obvious which cliff I needed to travel to. Jutting out of the side of a mountain was a large icy shelf.

Hiking through this forest was quite peaceful, the rhythmic crunch of the snowy ground under my boots, the birds chirping in the morning sky, a nearby creek flowing with the sound of rushing water and trees that seemed to spread off in every direction. The occasional Froezinx stuck its furry head out of the snowy mounds. Its blue eyes scanned the area before disappearing into the snowy dunes once more.

After walking for what felt like hours, I arrived at a creek. Waves of fatigue flooded my legs, and they screamed to buckle. I slowly and painfully set myself down on a large rock on the bank of the creek, to let myself take a well-deserved rest. After collecting my thoughts for a minute, I swept my eyes over my surroundings.

The large creek looked as if it were flowing crystal, sparkling and flowing smoothly. Reflected in the rapid water was the jagged rocky edge of the creek, filled with gravel and large rocks that defended the ground around it like walls of a castle. Stretching over the creek was a large fallen tree, branches strewn everywhere, and decomposing roots torn from the ground long ago.

I watched as a nimble Froezinx emerged from the snow nearby and snatched up a branch. It was about the size of an adult's shoe, covered in fuzzy white fur with a puffy black tail. The most discernable features, however, were its unique markings on its forehead. Small black diamonds connected by straight, rigid lines. It turned to look at me with blue eyes that looked like faceted crystals. It made a chittering noise and dove into a large snowy mound.

I pulled a leather waterskin from my pack and dipped it in the frigid, sparkling water. After a quick swig, I reattached it to my pack and moved towards the fallen tree. I placed a foot on its rotting, snow-covered trunk and cautiously pressed more of my weight onto it. Under my full weight I could feel its old, rotted trunk creak and bend slightly. I carefully balanced and began to cross the log, the snow under each step slipped into the creek and was washed away.

After the short balancing act, I hopped down from the log on the other side with a crunch. Suddenly the sound of rope snapping filled the air around me. The world seemed to have crawled to a snail's pace as I dived from where I was, watching a grid pattern being torn from the snow.

I shot up from the ground and fumbled at my side until I drew my wooden dagger. Adrenaline pumped through my body and my senses felt like they had been struck by lightning. My eyes darted in every direction for danger, only to settle on a net made of thick metal cable. Glowing runes covered the inside and bathed everything in a faint, pale icy glow.

I slowly relaxed as I double-checked for danger and found none. As I sheathed my dagger, a tree caught my eye. I ran my gloved fingers through the deep claw marks and anxiety bloomed in my chest. They seemed old, but you could never be sure. My eyes swept across the area and found more clawed trees until they settled upon a cave on the side of a nearby hill. I backed away from the clawed trees and glowing net. After backing away around fifty paces, I turned and jogged toward the cave.

The cave seemed normal enough, with a large, rough opening full of stalagmites and sharp rocks that slowly receded into darkness. Normally I would have just jumped in to explore, but this time was different. As I stumbled through the darkness, it felt like my limbs grew heavier with every step. After a minute or two of walking, every footfall felt as if I was slowly being crushed by a boulder. I drew closer and closer, every instinct in my body told me to stop, but I couldn't, my curiosity burned brighter than ever in my chest.

I took step after step, feeling as if my very clothes wanted to anchor me to the ground. The deeper I went, the more my eyes adjusted and the more my excitement died. It was just jagged rocks and rough stone on all sides. There was almost nothing unnatural about it, rocky walls and hanging stalagmites. I slowed to a halt, my breath coming out in deep, panting heaves as I reached the center of a rough circular area. Against the wall opposite the way I had come was a pile of shattered, broken boulders and rocks that seemed to block off the rest of the cave.

Each step I took toward the pile made me feel like I was being crushed exponentially. The aura of whatever was past those boulders almost brought me to my knees from simply being near it. Sweat stung my eyes as I tried to get closer and closer. My lungs tightened, until my knees finally buckled, and I collapsed onto the floor, convulsing. I could feel the fatigue of trying to stand up to such a horrifying pressure in my entire body, weighing me down. I desperately tried to crawl away in a series of feeble attempts. My mouth flapped open and closed as I struggled to draw in air. Slowly and desperately, I clawed far enough away to take a deep, long breath.

I hacked and coughed, finally able to breathe after being crushed like an ant. I slowly dragged myself off the ground and towards the opening of the cave, where I could see clearly. My sister had told me a long time ago that pressure could only be resisted by bolstering yourself with energy, and I planned to do just that.

I swung my bag off my shoulder and onto the ground as I began to dig around inside. Finally, I found the book I was looking for and began to flip through until I found an incantation for gathering the earth energy around me, *"Sacred Earth Cultivation Art: No. 5"* Following the instructions from the text, I rose to my feet and moved myself into a stance for hand-to-hand combat.

I closed my eyes and let my mind begin to recede into the void of concentration. Even though my eyes were closed, I could see as if they were open. I stood on a black lake that rippled and reflected light that wasn't there. I turned and looked in every direction, the void seemingly stretching everywhere. I slowly began to chant.

Tyleus, lord of the earth and ground, I, a humble mortal who treads upon your domain, beg of you to give me but a fraction of your energy. Allow the ground to rise around me, to fill me with the might of stone and the sturdiness of steel!

It seemed nothing had changed, until large pillars of stone began to jut out of the black lake of my mind around me in a ring. As they slowed to a halt, crystals burst from the sides of each pillar and webbed together, trapping me inside. Slowly, a green ball coalesced before me from nothing but wisps of light. I reached out, touching the orb tentatively with my fingers. The second I made contact it streamed into my hand and disappeared. Every energy channel in my body burned as this newfound energy dispersed through my body.

Dust swirled together out of the void, forming large boulders and glowing crystals. The rocks and gems fused together to form something of an almost ape being. I could feel the raw, unadulterated energy that was stored in its deep emerald eyes. It stood almost double my height, much stronger and heavier.

Prove your worth. A voice boomed in my mind.

The rocks that formed its body ground together as it lumbered toward me in an aggressive, prideful strut. In any other scenario, I would run away without a second thought, but we were in *my* mind. I was entirely calm, the movement of its body sent invisible ripples through the void straight into my mind. Its every move was clear without having to even look in its direction.

As it reached me, it swiped at me with a speeding, rough movement. The world seemed to slow as I felt its movement's trajectory the second it swung. I leapt up, over where the speeding arm would be. In one fluid motion, I thrust my arm down and planted my hand on its moving arm as I vaulted over the swing. It stumbled back in surprise as I landed on its back and began to flail, trying to knock me away. I slammed my fists into the back of its head, one punch after another. My knuckles bled and pain racked my brain, but I kept slamming my fists into its stone skull. With one final heavy blow, I reached a large crystal in its skull, but I was too late.

Distracted by my own assault, I hadn't noticed the ripples of a fist rocketing towards me. Its boulder of a fist hammered me in the side. With a sickening crunch I felt my side compact as if every nerve in my side was melting. The world spun around me as I flickered in and out of consciousness. A metallic taste filled my mouth as I began to stand, now several paces away. My feet trembled and my organs burned from the pieces of bone that splintered through them.

I scanned with blurry vision for my opponent and found it lumbering at me from across the arena. I stumbled forward, trying to call upon the energy I knew flowed around me. I focused as hard as the pain would allow me, almost begging the energy in my mind to listen to me and bend this world in my mind to my will. The concentration I could muster barely nudged the energy around me, but it would hopefully be enough.

I gave it a task I thought would be simple, to mend. I imagined my bones fusing back together and muscles weaving to what they were. Nothing happened. I thought desperately back to the diagrams of human bodies I had studied. A spike of pain rammed itself into my temple as I focused as hard as I could on weaving the energy in the correct places. The tiny amount of energy I could muster ever so slightly began to reweave my body. This process spread warmth to every bit of bone and muscle that was touched by the mending energy. Now all I had to do was stall.

I hobbled away from the massive ape; each step threatened my concentration as pain arced from every bone in my body. Luckily for me, stone wasn't a very maneuverable or fast element to have a body made of. After we had circled the arena a few times, I spun on my heel and pushed the pain down. I didn't know what would happen if I died, but I had no choice but to fight.

I strode toward the golem on freshly healed bones and prepared myself to dodge another catastrophic hit. It swiped at me once more and immediately tried to follow it up with an uppercut. Weaving out of the first hit, I stepped back and grabbed its arm on the upswing. Desperately clinging to the rising stone, I used it to propel myself into the air. I twisted in the air and came down on its back once more. I wouldn't make the mistake of relying on just brute force this time.

I grabbed the gem embedded in its head and tried to *pull* the energy from deep inside. I pictured the energy flowing from the crystal and into my soul. Runes intertwined my hand and the gem as I felt the golem's energy trickle into my own. *Not enough!* I thought in a panic as I cursed under my breath. I roared as I put every ounce of my will into pulling the energy from the beast's head. The trickle erupted into a tidal wave as I felt my channels burn and protest from the sudden intake of energy.

I felt the ripples in my mind of its fist moving and quickly released the gem. I bounced off its back and dropped into a roll in one fluid movement as the fist blurred past where I was before. I sprung back to my feet on the dark lake of my mindscape and forced the void that was my mind to push any excess energy I was leaking into a shell around my body. In the real world, forming an aura like this takes much more concentration and skill. However, since we were in my mind, I could bend the rules a bit. Slowly the energy stuck to my skin and crystallized in a suit of armor forged of pure power.

I turned and faced my opponent and a smile tugged at my lips. Now that I was covered in a powerful aura my confidence soared. Every step pushed me off the ground with enough power to give me airtime, sending me flying like an arrow at the gorilla. The gorilla jabbed at my chest in a lightning-quick motion as I approached. The void rippled in advance, and I knew what was coming. Thankfully for my aura, the speed of its blow wasn't enough to catch me off guard.

I met the jab with a sidestep and a jab of my own to its elbow. The stone arm blew to pieces as fragments and dust flew in every direction. Not wasting any time, I leapt off the ground through the dust and delivered a powerful kick to the center of its head. With a deafening crack, it blew apart into pieces and sent dust billowing in every direction. As the dust spread and settled, a green glow grew brighter.

Where the massive stone primate's chest had been, a single glowing green rune floated and emanated waves of powerful energy. I reached out and felt warmth dance at my fingertips. I let it absorb sink through my skin and settle in my body. Nothing changed. The stone arena and ape that the incantation had formed in my mental void began to fade into dust slowly as I let out a sigh.

One step closer, Serena, I thought to myself with a smile. With that, I closed my eyes and pulled my mind from my mental void, back into the real world.

. . .

I opened my eyes and looked around the cave to thankfully find nothing had changed. *Shouldn't have left yourself unguarded and in the middle of nowhere, idiot!* I cursed myself in my mind. I probed at my runes with my mind to see if anything had changed, and to my delight, found something new. A warm, powerful rune felt as if it was tugging ever so slightly at the world around me.

I willed the energy to soak into my body. The warm, addicting feeling of power flooding my very cells began to intensify and grow in potency. I closed my eyes once more and felt the flow of the energy in my veins. I reached out in my mind towards the power in my runes. With a mental tug, I willed it to surround and fill my channels. As I began to feel it circulate, I began trying keep the energy from floating too far from my body, similar to what I used against the ape. A thin mist of glowing golden energy floated above my skin. Slowly but surely, it dispersed with each passing second.

Despite my mental fatigue, I decided to attempt to enter the pressure again, knowing full well how reckless it was. *I need the strength to find her.* I closed my eyes and relaxed my muscles. I began to focus again, concentrating on the energy flowing through me and began to stabilize the mist. With a push of willpower, I tightened it against my skin and clothes. I quickly reached into the field of pressure as I opened my eyes. My heart pounded. Nothing happened. Only a slight amount of pressure surrounded my forearm. A moment later my misty energy completely leaked out, and the strength was sapped from my arm in a matter of moments.

I was absolutely thrilled. My face flushed as a wide grin grew on my face. I had managed to control my energy —even for just a moment— to move within powerful pressure. I proudly walked towards my bag and slumped down against an uncomfortable rock wall. After I shifted around for comfort to no avail, I grabbed some of the bread from my rations and took a big bite. Its dry taste was bland enough to make me never want another bit. I struggled to get the piece of stale bread down into my stomach and groaned as it did. I wrapped my fingers around my leather flask, drank a small amount of the chilly water and put everything back in my bag. I shivered slightly and rubbed my goosebump-covered arms. I gave the mouth of a cave a long gaze and a sense of dread crept into my heart as I saw the speeding winds.

I need a fire, I thought with a sigh. Slowly, I picked myself up and faced the roaring winds.

CHAPTER THREE

The Man with Frozen Eyes

Reynolds Helphain

The wind had picked up to the point where the falling snow obstructed all sight, only a sheet of shifting white. *That's going to sting,* I thought to myself with a sigh. I found a flat section of the ground to sit down on and began to strengthen my body. I closed my eyes and pulled energy from the earth around me. Slowly the flow began to taper as the earth incantation began to lose strength. Warmth crept into my body as I cycled energy. I pushed and pulled with all my willpower as I molded an aura.

The energy traveled through me with a new level of speed. It seeped from my skin in a golden mist, glowing and heating the air around me. I focused as hard as I could and willed the energy to stop after traveling a tiny distance from my skin, to form a strengthening barrier. The energy began to slow until it halted slightly above my skin, ever so slightly seeping through this mental barrier and dispersing. Slowly it gathered until I had a very thin, almost gelatinous glow sticking to my skin.

Feeling the energy clad to my skin, warming me, I stood up and began to step out into the maelstrom of snow. I could hardly feel the cold wind against my skin. Slowly but surely, I marched blindly into the snowstorm. By the time I had found a dead, standing tree, my skin was pink and the aura around me had thinned drastically. I focused on my right arm, willing the gelatinous aura to thin in non-crucial places. With a push, I gathered the energy into my fist. Within a few seconds of transferring the energy away from the rest of my body, it felt as if my skin was burning from the freezing winds. I wound back my fist and slammed it into the trunk, feeling it shudder and quake under the weight of my blow. I slammed my fist into it again and again, the gathered energy diminishing with each strike. The bark splintered apart along with the wood of the trunk in satisfying crunches as I hammered it.

As the tree began to fall, I transferred the energy back out of my fist and into the rest of the aura surrounding my body. Even just with the small amount of time I had thinned it, my skin had turned a bright red and had gone numb. With a cacophony of deafening crackling and crunching, the tree fell, slamming into the snow with a loud thud. I struggled to jog over to a couple of its branches and snapped them off before hurrying back to the cave.

I stumbled through the cave's mouth and dispersed my aura back into my body with little success. I watched sadly as most of the energy I had gathered floated away like mist. With a sigh, I broke the branches into smaller pieces of kindling and tossed them onto the rocky ground. They clattered and echoed through the cave as I piled them together close to the mouth of the cave. My exhausted feet dragged across the ground as I walked towards my bag, and after rummaging around for a moment, pulled out one of the heating runestones my dad had prepared for me.

It was a rough disc of dark gray rock with a ring of small runes that circled a larger rune on one face. I channeled the remaining energy from my aura into the stone, feeling it spark with heat as energy entered the runes. The runes quickly burst to life with a bright orange glow and began to tremble and hum in my hand. I tossed it into the pile of kindling, and it rapidly lit itself ablaze as the runestone met the wood.

I laid out the old fiber mat next to the fire and took a seat. I took a deep breath and looked out of the mouth of the cave. It was the middle of the night, the sounds of the crackling fire clashed with the rushing wind outside in an almost soothing way. *Nobody is coming through that storm.* I closed my eyes and began to meditate and cycle my energy as I sunk back to my void of concentration.

. . .

I released my meditation and let my inner thoughts fade away, sliding back into my physical body. My cycle of training completely exhausted me in almost every way, leaving me ravenous as a beast. I divided my food even more and sadly lifted it to eye level. After a sad look at my rapidly draining food supplies, I took a bite of the stale bread I had allowed myself. I groaned as I felt myself become dehydrated almost instantly as it absorbed all the moisture from my mouth.

After finishing my bread, I began to prepare to fall into another deep meditation. Just as I was about to sit down, I noticed the faint figure of a man slowly approaching my cave through the snowstorm with a cloak billowing out behind him. I grabbed my bag and ducked behind a stalactite. My hand shook as I pulled my wood knife from its sheath, and I prepared myself for whatever came next.

A man in dark leather armor wrapped in a blindingly white cloak stepped into the cave with a commanding presence. His light, faintly glowing blue eyes darted around the room with chilling pressure. As he slowly turned to survey the whole room, the blade of his longsword caught the light and sent a chill down my spine. He grimaced as he shifted his weight and looked directly at where I was hiding.

"I know you're there," the man said in a smooth, deep voice. I stepped out slowly, my grip on my dagger tight enough that my knuckles went white. "Put that toy down," he slowly ordered as he motioned at my dagger with his longsword.

I slowly put my dagger down on the cold stone floor and raised my hands slowly. "Hello," I said in a low, cautious voice. "What are you doing here?"

"Saw the light and figured I'd find shelter here." He said in a wavering but softer voice, his icy eyes peering at me with suspicion and a hint of curiosity.

"I'm Rey. I come from a small cabin about a day's hike from here." I smiled weakly, still terrified.

He grimaced and wavered slightly before grabbing onto a nearby stalactite, then said, "Well Rey, I'm Hundri, and it's my humble opinion that you go home, gather your things, and seek protection under a clan."

Confusion settled in my mind, and I timidly asked, "What, why? I haven't seen a hint of danger in ages."

He lowered his sword slightly and leaned against the cave wall as he began to explain in a slow voice, "This part of Mount Iora is a little more dangerous than you might realize. The clans have ordered— actually, do you know what the clans are?"

I cocked my head to the side slightly. "No, I haven't."

I watched his eyebrows rise slowly as his face shifted from a pained expression to one of mild surprise, "None? Not even the Optyr clan?" He whistled softly. "Your people must be more ignorant than I could've imagined. I'm surprised."

I scratched my head in thought, trying to no avail to remember the name Optyr. "Well, the area where I'm from is rather secluded and about as far north as you can get." The second I said the word north, his face drained slightly.

"You're not from *that* part of the north, right?"

I raised an eyebrow inquisitively. "What do you mean?"

He gestured slightly, "Near a cliff, sweeping view of the Lower Greens, demigod nearby." I nodded and he sighed. "Of *course* you are. Well, the Optyr clan has generally decreed that area forbidden."

"Forbidden? Why?"

"Not sure really. It was decreed only a few years ago. Apparently, there's some fearsome monster who lives in this area but..." He gave me a pointed look, "Clearly not."

Annoyance bubbled in my chest, but he was right. We would be too weak to stop something truly powerful. "Well," I sighed, releasing my annoyance in long exhale. "That would explain why I haven't even heard of the clans."

He relaxed his face a little. "Just forget it for now. By the way, why are you hunkered down here if you have a cabin not far from here? Couldn't you just walk back?"

"I need to head south." I clenched my fist and stared down at it, my voice quavering ever so slightly "Not only that, but I'm too weak to protect the people I care about. I can't afford to be weak any longer."

He looked at me with a new-found respect in his eyes and sheathed his sword before saying, "That's an admirable goal. Travelling out here will either make you tough as steel," He cracked a small smile, "or bury you beneath the freezing snow. On the topic of freezing, would you help me over to the fire, I think I'm going to start freezing to death soon."

I chuckled, walked over to him and felt him wrap his arm over my shoulders. I moved him over to the fire and sat him down on the fiber mat before walking over to my bag. I rummaged around until I found the medical supplies and pulled them out. With a light flick of the wrist, I tossed him a roll of bandages and walked to the other side of the fire from him. I slowly lowered myself onto the rough fiber mat and groaned in satisfaction. It had been a long day of standing.

"Thanks." His eyes flicked up to my clothes. "How are you not freezing?"

I looked down at the simple, thick grey tunic I wore as well as my loose black pants. I shrugged. "Not sure. Never really gotten cold easily," I gestured out to the whistling wind, "I'd freeze to death out there for sure, but without crazy weather, I don't usually get too cold."

He studied my face for a moment. "Huh." He shrugged as well. After a few moments, he pulled back the hood of his cloak before unclasping either side and letting the thick fabric fall to the ground. He had piercing blue eyes that rested under a mess of wavy black hair that stopped just above his eyebrows. He had a chiseled chin sparsely decorated with scars that were masked by thick black stubble stained with blood.

His blood-stained, dark leather plates clattered to the ground as he unstrapped them from his upper body, revealing in the firelight his lean, muscular form. Even the dark clothes he wore under his armor were damp with blood.

He unstrapped a wrecked leather thigh plate on his right side, revealing a large gash in his leg. The dark brown pants he wore over the gash were shredded and covered in dark red dried blood. He unraveled the bandage roll and wrapped the wound. Once he was done wrapping the massive wound, he began to wrap smaller cuts around his body.

I gave him another inquisitive look, "You don't have any elixirs?"

He frowned slightly. "I do," He pulled a small, faceted vial filled with a deep green liquid from his belt and swirled the liquid inside before continuing, "For some reason they don't seem to work."

I furrowed my brow in confusion. "I've never read about something like that. You have any healing techniques?"

He looked up from his newly wrapped wounds, his blue eyes met mine and after a moment of consideration, he answered, "No, I'm not a life mage. My blessing from Iora lets me use the power of ice."

The air began to chill as the moisture around us flowed into the palm of his hand. A pale blue glow began to emanate from where the moisture gathered and slowly began to take shape. A moment later he held a small ball of ice.

"Interesting." He tossed me the ball and I held it for a moment before setting it down. "My element is supposedly lightning, but I haven't been able to manage getting as much as a spark."

He chuckled quietly and spoke again, "I'm not surprised. Training with energy is a long, arduous road. Especially if you try to figure everything out on your own. The rune passed through your family may be of some use, depending on what it is. I know mine was." His irises began to brighten until they brightly shone an icy blue. I squinted as I took a closer look. Upon closer inspection, I could make out small, glowing white runes circling his pupil. "The 'Eyes of God' as my people call it."

He glanced at me again before continuing with a hint of sorrow in his voice. "As you probably know, family crests are inherited to different degrees. I was both lucky and unlucky with the strength of my eyes." He sighed before continuing, "Remember this: despite what you may believe, power will only chain you down if you want to use it for the good of others. I don't mean use it selfishly, but be wary of what you tie yourself up in."

I smiled weakly. "Well, I plan to use whatever meager power I have for the sake of my family. Guess I'm destined to be chained down then, right?"

He gave me a long, unreadable look before he took a long deep breath. In a puff of visible steam from the cold, he let out an exasperated sigh. "Family, huh?" He smiled slightly.

"Yeah?"

"Whatever you use your power for, make sure you're satisfied with what you do."

A wild idea crossed my mind and a grin pulled itself onto my face. "I have something to use my power for that I think would be satisfying."

He raised an eyebrow. "That being?"

I continued, "I'm going to come with you as somewhat of a partner and along the way, maybe you can teach me a thing or two. If you don't think I'm ready, you can test me all you want."

After a moment of hesitation, a grin broke out across his face. He patted the ground next to him on the mat, motioning me to sit next to him. Glowing icy runes began to flow out of his palm, forming into complex strings and circles.

I sat down next to him, and he gave me an instruction, "Go ahead and enter your mental void. I don't know if you call it something different, but hopefully you understand what I mean."

I nodded with a chuckle and closed my eyes. As the world began to flicker away, I felt his palm press against my forehead. Warmth spreading across my forehead and began to permeate my very mind.

. . .

The world around me turned into swirling clouds of dust as they were blown away in an incorporeal wind. I stood on the calm pool of water that made up my consciousness, a never-ending lake of inky darkness. My jaw dropped. Hundri waved at me from a few paces away and began to walk towards me slowly. *How is he in here?* I thought in bewilderment. He slowly spun around as he walked, taking in the endless nothingness before turning to me and whistling in admiration.

"This mental void sure is... a void." He cocked an eyebrow at me before he continued, "Some of the children in my clan have a recreation of their home, or a safe place in here but yours is simply a lake of just... pure darkness."

"I mean, I could try to create something in here." I shrugged and said in a joking tone, "I've always had a strong imagination."

He chuckled slightly. "Sure, go ahead."

He watched me expectantly as I extended my arm and pictured a spear. The depths of my mind responded immediately, the darkness at my feet weaved together into tendrils and into a cocoon of darkness. Slowly, the tendrils of void uncoiled, revealing a simple, undetailed spear. Before it could fall, I snatched it out of the air.

Hundri's eyebrows shot up. "Strong imagination indeed. That was certainly impressive. Most novices can't control a single thing here for a lack of a few things; maturity, concentration and will. To put it simply: age. The reason most people find something that makes them feel safe in their void is because of an automatic reaction from the simple fear of the unknown."

"So, what sets us apart then?" I replied, "If I am that much of a novice, of course."

A smile spread across his face before he extended his hands once more, a web of runes glowed to life in his palm. "I can put *my* ideas into *your* head."

The runes spread across his hands pulsed brightly, and in an instant, the world was flooded with light. Suddenly, I wasn't standing on nothingness anymore. I stood in a simple living room that was much nicer than my own. The room had creamy white wallpaper and was highlighted with dark brown wooden accents. It projected a sense of coziness from each piece of furniture, from the worn furniture to the brown fur blanket strewn on the floor. A cool breeze swept through large, floor to ceiling glass windows with fluttering white curtains blocking the view of whatever lay outside.

As I began to walk towards the tall windows, the seams of reality began to tear. Inky black cracks formed across every surface, even suspended in the air. They began to destroy everything. Everything seemed to fall away into nothingness, and slowly the world faded back to the dark reality of my mental void. Hundri stood a few feet away with an obnoxious grin.

"Alright, now that's out of the way, what can *you* do?" He stepped back a few paces and gestured for me to demonstrate.

I clasped my hands together and concentrated. With a push of willpower, my runes flared as they began to gather the energy around us until they were humming and glowing a golden color. I released my now clammy hands and I looked at Hundri. He shook his head slowly in disappointment. I clenched my jaw and focused until my face was covered in sweat and my teeth were pressed together hard enough to crack a stone.

I began to let energy out, focused entirely on limiting how much would be released and how far out of my body it would travel. After what felt like hours, my body was covered in a thin layer of rippling energy that jiggled with every movement.

I slowly pushed the condensed energy into the aura surrounding my feet and with a cocky grin, shot towards him. The rippling dark lake below me blurred slightly, almost like I was flying. The ethereal wind whistled in my ears and filled me with ecstasy. My stomach dropped and my ecstasy was whisked away as I quickly realized that in my haste to prove myself, I had poorly planned this jump.

As I began to approach Hundri, my foot caught the ground. I spun and fell, sending massive ripples through the surface of the dark lake below. After I had rolled to a stop, I picked myself up and looked up to Hundri, who stood a few paces away. I admired my dispersing aura with newfound appreciation. *Good thing that my aura absorbed that impact, or I was probably dead.*

Hundri took a few steps towards me and shot me a look I couldn't decipher. "Well, your energy gathering skills are novice at best. I would consider you past novice when you can gather energy while moving, without that cumbersome hand sign." He sighed and squatted beside me. "The amount of both time and effort it took you to construct that flimsy aura definitely need work. I would've given you some credit for that leap, until you slammed into the ground and almost broke your leg." He poked the kneecap of the leg that had hit the ground the hardest and a scream tore itself from my lips. "However, you're not the worst I've seen. The best teacher is experience. With me, you're going to get *plenty*."

I dryly muttered, "You remind me of my father."

He chuckled before continuing, "While I'm healing, I'm going to give you a new training regimen. Think of this as a true test of your potential. When my healing is done, if you can show me, you're ready, I'll bring you with me back to my city."

CHAPTER FOUR

Mentor and Student

Reynolds Helphain

Once my leg had healed and I agreed to accept his training, he began to explain his new training model for me, "Since I've already healed a little, it should only take me from anywhere between a week to two weeks to heal my leg enough to hike. In the meantime, here's what I recommend you do. First, you should practice cycling energy in from around you, throughout your body, and out again. Do that in the morning for at least three hours. Next, focus on your aura. Two hours of constant forming and reforming as well as another two hours of trying to hold it steady on your body while you move. Later in the day you will spar in normal combat with me in your mental space."

I nodded my head slightly before several questions floated into my head, "That sounds... brutal honestly." He nodded. "I am curious though; why aren't we working with my element?"

He scratched his stubble as he answered, "For a few reasons, mainly being that you need a strong foundation on the basics before you can try anything else. Other than that, simply because I'm not a lightning elementalist. I've only studied ice magic, which probably won't transfer well."

"That makes sense. Any tips for basic aura techniques or just basic techniques in general then?"

He smiled proudly, "Perhaps rephrase that with 'teacher' at the end, and I'll spread my sagely knowledge." I shot him a playful glare and he threw up his hands in surrender, "Alright fine! I didn't think it'd be too much to expect a little respect from my first student, but it's not important."

He cleared his throat. "Well, just in case you don't know basic energy theory, I'll touch on that." He raised his index finger to the sky, "First, opening your gates can be accomplished with one of three methods: incantations, willpower, or artifacts. Incantations are the easiest to use and quite powerful, however they are also the slowest and the easiest to fail with. Sheer willpower is the best in my opinion. It requires just a quick thought to open your gates, however it does require much more training, unlike simply memorizing and reading incantations. This is part of the reason so many mages use grimoires or tomes; to simply avoid memorizing." He shook his head. "Lazy bastards. Anyway, artifacts are completely different; they are something like... disposable shortcuts. They have runes and incantations inscribed on them that can do a variety of things that would take mages hours in a matter of minutes. The downside is that they are expensive and can be destroyed, essentially crippling the mage."

I pondered a moment before responding, "Alright then, willpower seems like it's the best way, and only practical way I can train at the moment, so I'll work on that. Any advice?"

He laughed sheepishly. "Well... on the topic of gathering energy and cycling, there's not a lot of advice to give besides just practice. Aura is a different story though. I recommend you think of aura like you are deliberately forging it into place rather than just letting it seep out and flow like a liquid. Imagine letting out small bursts of energy out in specific spots and trying to shape them into an overlapping sheet of scales. Think of scale mail, if you know what that is."

I sighed and began to focus on trying to form one of the scales Hundri had described. I lifted my hand to eye level and focused on the backside of it. Warmth began to radiate down from my torso, like a fire spreading through my veins. I pictured the scale as hard possible in the core of my mind and I watched as the energy slowly responded to my thoughts. Golden motes of light leaked out from my skin. Slowly they flowed together in strips and bands, weaving together to form a scale.

After a few moments of concentration, the energy stopped flowing out and slowly finished constructing itself into a gelatinous scale.

Annoyance bit my mind as I watched the scale wobble on the back of my hand. I steeled my mind and sweat beaded up again as it slowly crystalized into a rock-hard scale.

I looked up at Hundri and gave him a big, confident, gleeful grin. He nodded slowly while giving me an equally slow clap. "Congratulations on making... a single scale!" I shot him a glare. "In all seriousness though, that single scale looks good. Much better than that worthless aura you made earlier. Now how about you try making a gauntlet of them?"

I gave him a quick nod before focusing once more. The rest of the energy in my warm runes on my sternum flowed out and into the back of my hand. Slowly my chest grew colder as the energy moved. It floated out of my skin in a misty haze and floated just above the skin for a moment before coalescing into the shape of scales. They began to form and solidify with each passing moment as they continued to resemble scales more.

Once they finished forming, they immediately hardened, almost entirely skipping the strange gelatinous stage. After the entire process was done, a small patch of around twenty scales were fused to the back of my hand. I felt waves of accomplishment wash over me as I stared down at the group of scales I had made.

Hundri beckoned me closer as he drew his broadsword and prepared to strike the back of my hand. With a grunt, he swung downwards. It plummeted down in a powerful slash and with a sharp ringing noise, it slammed into the back of my scaled hand. The aura had chipped from the powerful impact and my hand now shook slightly, but I stood firm. I stared in wonder at the scales that still sparkled with golden light. They were so much easier to create it was almost unreal. I willed the energy to retract into my body and watched in fascination as they unraveled into strips and strands of light that seeped below my skin.

"They're amazing, aren't they?" Hundri asked with a smirk on his face, "Eventually you can do something like this." The air around him shimmered for a second before a wave of glowing, semi-transparent scales washed over his body from the neck down before they faded into invisibility. I could still feel the waves of frigid energy pulsing out of him, despite the aura being hidden. My sweat began to freeze, and my body shook from the rapid drop in temperature. Before I could say a word, the temperature returned to normal as he retracted his aura.

"Alright, next up how about a duel?" He smirked and extended his hand, palm up. "If we do use weapons, I will need a sword that won't kill you."

"Let's do it," I said with a smile.

"So, what'll it be, unarmed or with a weapon of choice? It's up to you, I don't really mind." Hundri asked as he paced in a circle on the dark lake, his movements rippling into my mind.

"Let's go with an armed battle, my swordsmanship feels a bit rusty at the moment." I extended my arm to the right and willed the void to respond to my commands. A chilling, wet feeling filled my hand as tendrils of the void lake below writhed, slowly intertwining into a dull, steel longsword. I flicked my wrist in Hundri's direction, and another sword pulled itself from the void. We both brandished our swords and stared at each other with intensity. I slowly spun my sword in my right hand before dropping into a low combat stance. He did the same. His armor and the sword he had clipped to his belt both disintegrated into motes of light as he gave me a firm nod to signal his readiness. I nodded in return and started the duel.

We circled each other for a few seconds, watching and waiting. Suddenly Hundri lurched into a full sprint, bearing down on me at full speed. I mimicked him and began to sprint, the distance between us closed within a matter of seconds. Upon reaching each other I grabbed the handle of my sword with both hands swung downward with all my might. Our two swords met in a flash of brilliant orange sparks as his blade flashed upward to parry mine. Not wasting a moment after the parry, he immediately swept my blade to the side and swiped in a beautiful arc at my right side.

I pushed myself backwards as his sword cut the air just in front of my torso. As soon as his sword flew by, I pivoted and pushed off the ground into a lunge, closing the distance instantly. I slashed wide at his right side, waiting for him to attempt a parry. The second he lowered his sword to parry; I stopped the swing short, feinting. I pivoted my torso and slammed my fist into his cheek with as much force as I could muster.

He stumbled back, repeatedly blinking as he struggled to get his bearings. Slowly, a grin formed across his face. "That was a solid feint. You're more adept at swordplay than I thought. That being said, I think I can get a little more serious now."

With that warning, he bounded at me once more. Each step he took, his grin grew. His sword blurred into a thrusting motion as he reached me. The ripples reached me before my brain could process his move. Thankfully my instincts kicked in as I sidestepped the jab, whirling around for a slice at his legs. Before I could truly start the motion, his leg blurred in a pivot and slammed the side of my chest with a roundhouse kick. I crumpled as the blow hit me. I grimaced as daggers of pain shot through my side and knocked the breath out of me. I gasped and heaved as I rolled a few paces away on the dark lake of the void.

I pushed myself off the ground and to my knees, coughing as I regained my breath. A flash of light blurred towards me, and I immediately dropped to the ground in a roll. Despite the throbbing pain, I pushed myself up onto one knee, only to find Hundri standing over me with a smirk on his face. He winked at me and extended a helping hand, "Good try." I groaned and grabbed his hand, the thick calluses of his hand rubbing against my own as he yanked me to my feet.

I stumbled around for a moment —still a bit woozy— before I found my balance. I turned to Hundri and something was clearly wrong. His form was flickering in and out of existence, the molecules of his body ripped away in a blue mist, before partially reforming.

I started to open my mouth to express my concern and confusion, but he put his hand up to stop me. He gave his disintegrating hand a sidelong glance before he spoke, "It appears I don't have much time left here. It's not easy manifesting yourself in someone else's mind, contrary to what you may believe."

I sighed. "Who could've guessed! Anyway, I'll meet you outside." He gave me a small wave before getting ripped apart into glowing azure particles, carried away on an ethereal wind. The flecks of his form twirled away into the all-absorbing night of the void, twinkling like stars as they disappeared. I let myself slip away from the void and felt a deep tug in my gut as the world began to form around me once more.

My feet itched. The mat beneath me came first, then the rest of the world slowly began to come back into focus. The crackle of the dwindling fire crackled, its heat crashing over me like waves. Wind buffeted the cave with enough force to tear off my arm, contrasting the crisp fire with dull whistling. I turned to Hundri who was slumped against the wall and watched as his fingers danced in the air. Light traced the tip of his index finger while he drew runes and weaved them into complicated strings. They slowly floated apart before disintegrating into particles. Upon him noticing my return from my mental void, he paused and gave me a tight, pained smile before going back to painting runes in the air.

I stood up slowly and stretched my arms with a groan. After I finished my stretches, I used the remainder of my energy to forge my scales. After around twenty seconds, I felt it finish forming into a full coating around my index finger. I descended into the cave until I began to feel the pressure of whatever laid those crumbled rocks. I extended my index finger, and creeped farther in. The closer I got, the greater my nausea became, everything in my body felt weak except that finger. I stared at it in mild awe as it withstood the pressure. Slowly the energy tugged away from my finger as the pressure dragged it downwards. I waited for a few minutes and excitedly came to the conclusion that even just this was enough to resist the indomitable pressure. I briskly backed away and withdrew the scaly finger plates back into my runes.

After a quick hike back up the cave and to Hundri, a curiosity began to tug at my mind. I sat back down across from him, the dimly burning, hot oranges clashed against the cool blues of his eyes with beautiful contrast. "Hey, Hundri, do you know what that pressure is coming from?"

His luminous eyes turned to look at me for a moment before he stared deeper into the cave. After a few seconds of what seemed like studying something, he turned his gaze back to me and replied, "From what I can tell, it's some sort of enchanted beast, nothing too strong" After a moment of consideration, his eyes seemed to shine even brighter with eccentricity, "I have a *perfect* idea! How about when I'm healed enough to move, if you can kill that beast, I'll give you a powerful reward. How's that sound?"

A goofy grin pulled against my lips as conflicted emotions tore at my brain. The fear of whatever lay in the depths of this cave had taken root deep within my mind and it pushed me desperately to turn him down, that my task was impossible. In contrast, my insatiable lust for growth and strength whispered to me that I should believe in myself, that the payoff would be enormous. After a moment of deliberation, I grinned wide. The risk was worth the reward.

"Alright. I'll do it," I said firmly. The more I thought about it, the more I realized just how insignificant I was. If something that was supposedly 'nothing too strong' was making me fall to my knees from simply being near it, just how weak was I? Even after pushing this fear deep into my mind, I could still feel it gnawing at my confidence.

"Great. I'm sure you'll manage." he said in a sincere voice before he gave me a small smile and returned to forming floating runes. With the fire of my ambition newly stoked, I grabbed some nearby loose rocks and descended into the cave once more.

As I approached the crumbled wall once more, I began to leave small rocks on the ground as markers for different levels of pressure. Once I hit the limit of where I could stand without falling, —about ten paces in— I placed the rest of them in a small pile. I closed my eyes and focused. Slowly but surely, I gathered as much energy as possible. After what felt like an eternity, I let the gates in my body open as the addicting sensation of power trickled to every inch of my body. I slowly walked five more steps before the pressure finally stopped me.

I thought back to the hand-to-hand combat training I had done with my dad and my sister. Emotions and memories bubbled to the surface of my mind as I began to train. Every movement I had honed over years of sparring should've shot out like a bolt of lightning, and yet they each seemed more like they were flailing wildly under the pressure. My punches were sluggish and weak even my kicks almost sent me off balance every time I lifted my foot from the ground.

A perfect place to train.

. . .

I stood there for hours. My fists carved through the air as I practiced the movements again and again, only stopping for the occasional bite of bread. The light that once danced on the walls from the fire above had long died out, and Hundri was fast asleep. With energy coursing through my veins, even my senses seemed improved. Moonlight beamed through cracks in the ceiling and the sweat on my forehead sparkled like jewels that slowly ran downwards as I finished the last few of my movements.

After training here for even a few hours, I could feel an enormous difference. Even with my aura retracted, I could walk past my previous limit. I trained until my training set was quick and precise before moving a few paces deeper. After repeating this practice countless times, was making good progress. With a smile, I looked at the boulder wall. *I'm coming for you,* I thought with a smile.

The ground beneath my boots crunched as I stepped on small rocks and pebbles while exiting the pressure of the beast. I slowly walked over to where the fire had been, now only a pile of ash remained. The blizzard outside still raged, effectively hiding this entire area from any potential attackers. In the mouth of the cave was a line of five small banners placed into the ground. Normally I would've been intrigued enough to take a look, but exhaustion tugged me down towards the mat.

Hundri was sprawled out over roughly half the mat and was wrapped in his cloak for warmth. I laid down on the mat next to him, the rough fibers grating against my back. I rolled away from him so we were back-to-back and let my eyes wander. My mind raced as I thought about how crazy my day had been so far. So much had happened. As I struggled to contain the excitement inside me, I shut my eyes, and attempted to sleep.

CHAPTER FIVE

Man and Beast

Reynolds Helphain

Every day since Hundri arrived had grown more torturous with the passage of time. The same grueling routine from sunup to sundown. Wake up before the sun rises, absorb and cycle, practice weaving aura, and duel Hundri.

A slow rocking sensation had slowly lulled me from my blissful dreams, pulling me back to reality where I was to fight my most challenging battle yet. I raised my hand to block the harsh golden sunlight that blinded me as my eyes slowly opened. Hundri knelt at my side, shaking with decreasing fervor as he saw my eyes open. I groaned as I pulled myself up from my ratty mat and pushed Hundri aside.

He cracked a small smile and said, "Well, well, well look who finally decided to get up!" I rolled my eyes as I stood up and began to stretch. A satisfying warmth spread from each joint that popped and every muscle that was pulled. My eyes drifted around our makeshift camp, the fire from the night before was now reduced to dark charcoal and most of my materials had been packed away in the bag I had brought.

I gestured towards the bag, "I'm guessing you've healed enough to travel?" My heart pounded as he nodded. The moment to prove myself had come. Filled with both excitement and fear, a nervous smirk spread across his face. After an exaggerated stretch, he started walking deeper into the cave. I took one last long look at our little campsite and the great forest beyond the mouth of the cave. I finally tore my gaze away and jogged after him.

Slowly the deeper parts of the cave came into view as my eyes adjusted to the dark room. Hundri stood facing the pile of boulders and ran his hand across the across the stone while he waited for me. He gave me a quick glance, "Ready?"

I gave him a thumbs up, "Ready." He turned back to the wall and raised his hand up to eye level. The air trembled ever so slightly as he pulsed energy into his hand. Chills rushed through me and every instinct in my body told me to be on guard as I watched a thin layer of azure energy weave itself into existence around his raised arm.

He strode over to the wall of crumbled stone and pulled back his arm. His fist slammed into the stone like a cannon. The noise boomed and echoed through the cave room as tiny pieces of stone rained from the ceiling. The ground shook as the boulders crumbled to the floor in a cacophony of crashes. Through the billowing dust, the glow of Hundri's fist faded back below his skin in strips of light. He gave me a firm smile and a nod before turning back towards the fire. I steeled my will and forced my body to stop quivering. This was the best chance I had to grow, and I wasn't going to waste it. I clenched my fists until my knuckles went white and walked past him, into the unknown below.

The farther I walked, the darker it got. Each step resounded deep into the cave no matter how hard I tried to stay quiet. After what felt like hours, light creeped into view once more. Small white specks that cast an ethereal glow lazed around the tunnel as they drifted around aimlessly. Almost entranced, I reached out toward one of the chunks of light and felt the electrifying tingle of pure, condensed primordial energy. I slowly grasped it in my hand and felt the energy seep into me with a soothing heat. I drew my hand through the air as I walked, grabbing at the flecks of light as I walked deeper. It was mesmerizing to watch them morph and change as they sunk into my flesh.

The tunnel had begun to taper slowly before it suddenly turned into what seemed to be a larger room. I peeked around the jagged corner and took in the sight of a large white bear lying in the center of the large cavern. Wisps of ethereal light emanated from its fur and danced through the air before they split into the familiar white flecks I'd seen before. Its soft snores echoed in the cave as if they were right behind me despite its distance. It occasionally moved in its sleep; its legs scraped across the rough, rocky floor ever so slightly as it hibernated.

Slowly, I backed away from the entrance to the cave and grabbed at the wisps of light, filling myself with raw energy. I glanced down at my hands and watched as the new energy I had absorbed coalesced into countless small scales. I waited a few seconds and forced them to spread out until I had very poor looking scale mail that wrapped my hands. Once the ethereal light finished hardening like gems, I creeped out around the corner.

As I slinked through the cave and avoided loose rocks or anything that made noise, I took in the majesty of the beast before me. It was twice the size of Hundri and I put together, covered in almost silvery white fur that shone like the moon and with long glowing patterns of runes etched into its body. The tiny bits of energy spiraled around it as it slept, each time it breathed, the fleck of light pulsed brightly. With a loud clattering noise, the blood rushed from my face as I froze.

A rock bounced from where I was standing. I watched in horror as it clattered across the floor before bumping into its paw. My eyes darted upward towards its head, praying it was still asleep. An eye the size of my palm stared back at me. It shone like crystal as it stared me down. A low growl filled the cave as it pulled itself to its feet. I stared up at the bear as my stomach dropped. With a slow exhale, I steeled my nerves with a hard glare.

We stared at each other for a moment as sweat rolled down my forehead. It studied me for a moment before its gaze settled on my energy-coated hands. Its jowls pulled back as it felt the waves of energy pulsing from my body. It pushed off the ground with its hind legs, lunging at me with its paws in an arc to crush my fragile body.

With a pump of energy to my legs, I pushed off the ground as hard as I could. I desperately fumbled and twisted through the air as I landed behind an outcropping of large stalagmites. I grimaced in pain as the loose rocks on the ground dug into my chest with my rough landing. I ignored the new scrapes and small cuts on my chest as I glanced back at where I was standing before.

Light caught the claws of the bear's giant paw as it swiped at me again. My blood went cold. I took a deep breath and pushed off the ground slightly, sidestepping the swing. The stalagmites to my side crumbled as the bear's claw sheared them in half in a cloud of dust. I quickly pivoted and returned a quick punch to the back of its paw under the veil of the cloud.

I expected to feel the crack of bone under my aura-coated fist but was met with a dissatisfying lack of damage. The bear lunged again, the back of its paw slamming into my torso. Bile and blood flew from my mouth as I slammed into the wall of the cave. I grimaced as an explosion of pain erupted from my rib cage. My teeth ground together as I pushed past the pain and pulled myself to my feet.

I raised my eyes to meet the bear's. My stomach dropped as reality washed over me. I was nothing. There wasn't the faintest hint of fear in its eyes. I was nothing more than another stupid human who had dared to challenge it. I wasn't even strong enough to be considered a threat. A grin spread across my face. *Time to get clever.* I broke my gaze away and turned away from the bear in a sprint.

An idea sparked into my mind. I changed course towards the stalagmites and reached for the tiny flecks of light, gathering the energy inside as I ran. The bear's paws thundered against the stone behind me as I ran, growing closer and closer with every passing second. By the time I reached a thin stalagmite, it was almost on top of me. I swung swiftly in a punch at the stalagmite's base and grabbed the broken chunk out of the air. My senses screamed at me as I felt the bear's breath on my neck. I deftly rolled to the side. A gust of wind blew my hair around wildly as I popped to my feet. The bear's paw stood atop a pile of rubble I assumed to be the remains of the stalagmites. Its crystalline eyes glared at me ferociously as it growled again.

The bear broke into a charge once more, launching a flurry of swipes from every direction. I dropped the stalagmite as I ducked and weaved each blow. My stomach sank as a blow finally caught me off balance. I quickly threw my arms up in a panicked defense. Its claws swiped through my aura like a knife through cloth, leaving me with nothing but scraps on each hand to fight back with.

When the blows finally came to an end, I let out a guttural roar and grabbed the javelin-like stalagmite from the ground. My pounding steps echoed through the cave as I sprinted into a leap. Energy rushed from my runes and flowed into my arms as I drove the rocky point into the bear's shoulder. With a squelch, the stalagmite pierced into beast's hide and sunk deep into its body. The feeling of bones cracking as it went deeper and deeper filled my mind with sick satisfaction. With an agony-filled cry the bear craned its neck to reach me on its back. It snapped its jaws to no avail as I dropped below its slobbering jowls with hard impact.

With a quick push off the ground, I dashed backward and conjured the last of my remaining energy to reform the scaled gauntlets. The bear stumbled backwards as it pawed and bit at the stalagmite implanted in its shoulder before turning back to me with fire in its eyes. A shiver went down my spine. It was furious.

A voice in my head screamed at me to run. Its anger was palpable as energy began to coalesce in a reddish glow. Waves of energy even stronger than when it had been hibernating washed over the room.

My heart thundered and sweat dripped into my eyes, yet I couldn't move.

Its muscles seemed to bulge and harden. The stone in its shoulder shattered as its muscles grew and tightened. The flow of blood that soaked its fur slowed as it began to heal my devastating blow. The runes circling its torso blazed to life and created an almost audible hum as it prepared to lunge.

The loose stones and debris on the ground bounced as it flung himself at me with a hulking leap. Its massive paws slammed into my arms as I moved them into a defensive stance. The partially formed scales on my hands cracked and splintered under the unbelievable weight and strength of its paws as I dropped to my knees. I cried out in pain as the bones in my forearms began to crack as well.

I glared up at the bear with tears in my eyes. It continued to apply more and more strength to the paw I was desperately blocking. My teeth scraped together as I roared and pushed back with all my might. Pain bloomed from my fractured arms and wiped my mind clean. It pulled its paw away as it released the unrelenting pressure. As I got my regained my bearings from the wave of pain, the claws of its other paw slashed across my chest. Crimson sprayed in three arcs as heat bloomed in my chest.

I stumbled backward in shock. The gashes on my chest pumped out blood. I desperately moved energy down to my chest and sloppily applied it to the gashes to slow the bleeding. My energy reserves began to pump themselves dry as I desperately tried to keep myself alive. I began to feel the blood loss slow ever so slightly as the energy clogged the cuts. With a hateful gaze locked on the bear, I dropped into a combat stance for one, final stand.

With my teeth grit and blood rising in throat, I tightened my fist. I infused my dwindling energy into my fist and rushed toward the bear. The bear's swipes and jabs crushed the ground around me as I dashed between each blow, ducking and weaving. All that remained in my mind was victory.

With a hap-hazard pulse of energy, I launched myself onto the head of the bear. Its eyes widened in surprise as I wound back my energy-charged fist. A large vicious smile spread across my face as I thrusted my arm through its red gelatinous aura, and into its squishy eyeball. I thrust deep through its eye, into its skull and wrapped my hand around its almost rope-like optical nerve. With one final push from my feet, I leaped off of its head and pulled its eye out on my way down.

I yanked on the long rope of torn, sinewy meat and brain that connected to its head. With a sickening squelch, the rope snapped. It roared in pain one final time as blood sprayed out in every direction. Deep crimson painted the room and I with the scent of iron. The bear keeled over. Its limbs went limp, and they flopped to the ground, splayed out in every direction. I rubbed the blood from my eyes and stood still for a moment. Pain throbbed from my cracked arms and fatigue pulled at every limb in my body. I took long, heaving breaths and despite the pain, walked over to its hulking corpse. A satisfied smile spread across my face even with the torrent of pain inside me.

Every step I took closer to its crimson-painted corpse made one of the runes on my chest burn like the sun. By the time I had reached the bear's chest, it was glowing bright enough that I could see it through my bloodstained tunic. My family crest. As if my muscles guided my cracked arm on their own, I reached out towards the bear's runes. My hand sunk into the wet fur of the large beast and touched the warm glowing runes beneath.

A pressure began to build in my forehead and grew with each passing second until it became unbearable. I fell to my knees, wailing. I desperately clasped my hands over my head and rocked back and forth on the ground. My screams echoed across the room as the pressure grew to a point where I thought my head was going to burst. The unfamiliar images flashed through my mind, random images that flowed together into a complex web. With one final scream of fear, confusion and pain, my vision faded to black.

. . .

Slowly, the world came back into view. I felt the bear's slick fur on the back of my neck as I pushed myself to my feet. The flecks of light illuminating the cave were gone, the darkness only fought back by glowing runes that were freshly burned into my clavicle. I quickly looked back at the bear as the light from the unfamiliar runes faded. I was too slow. Endless darkness swallowed me on all sides.

I fumbled through the dark until I found my way to the entrance of the cave. I stumbled over rocks and stalagmites with almost every step. By the fifth time my shoulder met the floor, I decided to rethink my approach. I pushed my questions out of my mind and concentrated the miniscule amount of energy I had left into a bright ball that floated just above the tip of my index finger. After what felt like a minute, a small ball of light bathed the tiny area around me in golden light.

After I formed the light, finding my way out of the cave was substantially easier. With each step I took, I had to push back the pain of what felt like broken ribs. Every jab of pain wiped my mind clean and sent bile rising in my throat. Its sharp, sour taste felt like it was burning my chest and throat.

After a short, but painful hike, I emerged from the crumbled boulder wall. The silhouette of Hundri sat still against the harsh light shining from the mouth of the cave. As he heard my approach, his eyes fluttered open. His glowing irises flicked up to meet my gaze.

"I take it you were successful?" His eyes flicked across my body, taking in the amount of blood soaked into my clothes.

I noticed his gaze on the blood and winced before saying, "This was mostly the bear's." I gestured to the blood. "The beast in that cave was this giant white bear. Ripped its eye out. Also do you really expect me to believe that behemoth was weak?"

A small smile spread across his face before realizing that I was genuinely upset, then he quickly masked it. "It *is* weak, just maybe not to your standards. The system my people use to rank these enchanted creatures would've probably placed it somewhere near the top of the lowest grade."

"You should have at least warned me about what I was getting myself into." My voice echoed through the cave, startling even Hundri a little.

"Hey, calm down a little. I wouldn't have thrown you at it if I didn't think you could've won." He raised his hands in a calming gesture, "And look! You did win. I bet you learned a lot because of it."

I sat in silence for a second, fuming. Even though anger bubbled deep inside, I knew he was right, as much as I hated to admit it.

"Besides that, what's that new rune on your chest?" His eyes could've burned holes in my chest with the intensity he was staring at my runes.

After a moment of consideration, I pushed my anger away and replied with a wince of pain, "Honestly, I don't know. After I killed the bear, my family crest began to glow, my hand moved on its own and touched the bear's runes, and I blacked out. Fragments of memories flowed into my brain, then... these were on my chest. "

"Well, it definitely doesn't feel like your energy. Whatever runes that bear had are probably what are now on your chest." After a deep breath, he beckoned me over and motioned for me to take his hands.

His glowing eyes flared with brightness as the rough callouses of his hands began to cool. Slowly, a weak, impotent energy began to fill up my runes. I frowned. "This feels... different," I gave him an inquisitive look. "Why is that?"

He scratched his stubble as he thought for a moment. "My energy is of the ice aspect. Since you use lightning energy, any energy I give you will feel weak and dull."

"Huh." I said matter-of-factly. "Well should I give it a try then?"

He nodded. "Go ahead. I'll stop you if anything goes wrong."

The unfamiliar cold energy spread into the rune as it began to glow a deep red. My face began to flush as every tiny negative thought in my head started to grow and fester. My teeth ground together as my anger permeated every inch of my body. Every insignificant moment and problem growing into flames of rage. My fists clenched as I let energy flow into my hands. The energy felt different, violent and unpredictable. It slowly coiled and writhed out of my palm like agitated snakes as I bolstered my hands. My pain faded away as energy from all around me flowed unhindered into my body.

Once my hand was wrapped in my now crimson-tinged aura, I screamed in frustration at the world, my sister, and most of all Hundri, for sending me on a death mission. My aura seemed to bubble and hum with every heartbeat. Without thinking I leapt into the air and thrust my fist at Hundri.

He sighed and he effortlessly sidestepped the punch. I slammed into the ground shoulder first. Bile rose in my throat. I slowly picked myself up and glared at Hundri.

"That wasn't my fault," He remarked as he shrugged and gave me a little smile, "How about we talk about this when you wake up?" Before I had the chance to process what he said, something slammed into the back of my neck, and the world went dark.

CHAPTER SIX

Departure

Reynolds Helphain

    I blinked awake. The fire had new wood and was blazing next to me; however, the light was drowned out due to a new morning sun that shined through the cave's entrance. I slowly pushed myself up from my poorly made bedroll with a groan and looked down. My torso was now wrapped in bloodied bandages and the sharp pain of my broken rib was gone. Slowly, I picked myself up, despite every inch of my body aching faintly. I trudged down the cave and saw Hundri tightly wrapping some of the bear's fur into a roll.

    "How'd you heal me?" I called down.

He held up an empty faceted vial. "Still had one. Couldn't use it on myself, so figured I should use it on my student. Body might ache for a while. You were pretty beat up. A wonder you didn't die of blood loss."

    "Thank you, Hundri." I gestured to the bear's fur. "You skinned the bear?"

    "Any part of an enchanted beast tends to be great conductor for artifacts. I was thinking of getting this made into a cape or a cloak for you. Afterall, I did promise you a reward if you remember." he replied as he precisely rolled the bear's fur.

    I pushed the thoughts of the bear out of my head and continued to slowly descend the cave before asking Hundri the main thought on my mind, "So, what happened with the bear's rune? My memory is a little foggy."

"You went a little berserk. You seemed *really* mad and tried to attack a punch my way," Before I could respond, he shot me a tiny smile, "Don't worry, your broken bones and exhaustion kept it from being stronger than a toddler flailing."

I bit back a snarky remark and replied, "Interesting." I gestured down at the rune. "I can still feel some of its... hate still residing in me."

Hundri paused, his brow furrowed for a moment in concern, "Honestly, I've never heard of anyone taking an enchanted beast's runes before. I'd say it could be a side effect of your first time using it, coupled with your inexperience. But tell me if it happens again. Just to be safe, let's leave this rune for emergencies." He strode over to my bag, picked up the bedrolls, a few other supplies I had taken out, and his newly cut furs, then shoved them all inside.

I walked up the cave to join him and watched him stomp out the fire. "Where are we off to?"

"Home." He turned to look at me with a small grin, "A city called Anhalt." He gestured to the bag and gestured for me to carry it. I sighed, leaned over and grabbed the strap of the bag. I grunted as it hardly lifted off the ground even when I lifted with all my strength. I opened the bag to see a pile of large rocks at the bottom.

I glared at Hundri, "Do we *need* these *rocks?* Or can I throw them out?" I said in a dead-pan voice.

"No, not at all." He smiled widely. "However, you *do* need the training, don't you? So, go ahead and summon that flimsy whole-body aura you had when we first met."

I groaned at his response before concentrating on my aura. After a minute or two, a squishy aura surrounded me with soothing warmth and filled me with strength. I reached down and attempted to lift the bag again. This time I was able to sling it over my shoulder with little difficulty. Even despite the aura, I still felt the strain in my aching arms, back and knees.

I set down the bag and concentrated once more, hardening and strengthening the crucial areas for heavy lifting. For the last time, I hoisted up the bag and slung it over my shoulder, this time, comfortably. I shot Hundri an exasperated glance and nodded that I was ready to go.

Hundri stepped into the slow gusts of the dying storm and beckoned me after him. I adjusted the bag on my shoulders and took my first step out into the daylight in days. The snow crunched softly under my boots as I was blinded by the sun. I squinted for a moment, waiting for my vision to come back before I marched after Hundri.

The wind had died down since I was in the forest last, but it wasn't gone entirely. Barely visible blades of wind slashed at my aura as we trudged out of the cave. Every step we took I had to shift my aura to patch holes as the wind ripped at it. Hundri raised his arm and pointed toward the peaks of nearby mountains, and we continued hiking through the snow.

Our footsteps disappeared behind us as the wind swept up the snow in frosty gales. Time blurred, what felt like hours of exhausting trekking turned out to only be a few minutes. Every time I looked behind us, I was dismayed to still have the cave in sight.

Once the wind thinned enough to be able to hear Hundri's footsteps, I called out, "Hey Hundri!"

His hair blew softly in the wind as he turned to me and slowed to match my pace. "What is it?"

"Tell me about your city. I'd love to know a bit about it before we get there."

Hundri pushed branches out of the way and waited for me to catch up before answering. "Well, my city, Anhalt, lays deep inside a mountain we call Mount Luceat."

"Which one is that?"

"The second tallest mountain in the area. The tallest one we use for prayer, it's a sort of holy place for my people."

"Oh really? That's actually where I'm headed."

He looked over his shoulder at me, his glowing eyes locked with mine, "Interesting. Why are you heading there?"

I grimaced softly, thoughts of my vision reappearing. "I'm hoping to find something about a lost family member," I said solemnly.

Hundri studied my face and went silent for a moment. The only sound around us was the was the crunch of the snow beneath our boots and the soft noises of the wind as it whistled by. After a few minutes of arduous hiking, Hundri slowed down again to match my pace. "Anhalt is a great city. It's widely considered the trade hub or just the general capital of mount Iora. People and tribes from all over this snowy hell come to our city to participate in trade."

"Anhalt must be giant right? To be big enough to be considered a capital, it must be impressive."

"Yeah, it's huge." Fondness crept into his voice, "I've explored every corner and street of that city. Lived there my whole life. I'll show you some of my favorite spots when we arrive. It's a wonder how secure they keep it despite the number of people who pass through every day."

The wind began to pick up and the branches began to sway. As I opened my mouth to ask another question, snow fell from the branches above and landed on my face. Through the frigid powder I could saw Hundri turn around to stare at me. A smile danced across his lips as he began to chortle at my snow-blanketed head and shoulders.

Ignoring the stinging pain, I sputtered the snow out of my mouth and dusted it off my face, compacting it into a ball. "Shut it Hundri", I groaned at him as I chucked the frosty ball at him. Before the ball could make a satisfying hit to his smug face, it stopped in the air.

His smug face grew into a devilish grin as I felt pulses of energy emanate from him. Slowly, I looked around. Tens of flying snowballs surrounded me at every angle. I threw up my hands. "I concede." I chuckled a little before affirming it once more. "You win. Let's just keep walking."

With one final chuckle from him, the snowballs fell, and we began our trek once more. He suppressed his smile from before and continued, "Well, the city is high above the ground in the depths of a mountain. It was built centuries ago in a massive cavern. It's pretty much entirely enclosed."

A question fluttered into my mind, "Wait, then how do you get into the city? Do your people have some sort of teleportation magic?"

"Calm down, calm down. I'm getting there." A small smile formed upon his lips as he explained, "my people have massive platforms that ride on rails and can carry hundreds of people. They float using the power of charged crystals and are guided by long rails."

The thought of giant platforms carrying people in and out of a mountain was foreign to me yet made my heartbeat faster in excitement. "How do you guys manage the security of the city if some of these platforms are made to carry hundreds of people?"

"Well obviously we have methods of checking people coming into the city. The civilian entrance requires you to pay a fee *and* we check all of your belongings to make sure you aren't smuggling anything dangerous. There are also merchant entrances and military entrances, which we will be taking as I *am* a captain after all."

A smirk tugged at my lips, "Why be a captain if you don't enjoy the perks right? I bet you can get in and out easily that high up." Hundri's chuckles echoed through the now darkening forest before he recomposed himself, but before he could get a remark in, another question bubbled up in my mind. "Have the defenses ever failed? It seems like you have the makings for an impenetrable fortress with something like that."

Hundri's face darkened as a palpable tension filled the air, his anger almost tangible. The feeling coiled around my body, it began to crush my lungs and reduced my walk to a stumble under the weight of his emotion. Just as quickly as it had come, it stopped. As I stood up, I felt Hundri's strong hands pulling me back to my feet.

"Sorry about that. Bit of a tough topic for me. I lost something important to me the only time that our security failed."

Guilt bloomed in my chest as my gaze fell. "I'm sorry Hundri, I didn't know."

"It's fine. It was a major point in my people's history and culture now, so it's worth touching on before we get there." His sorrow-filled eyes locked with mine for a moment, "The only attack we have had on Anhalt was from a group we call the Raven's Wings. They're a terrifying group of master mages and assassins who normally move like shadows. Until that attack, we thought they were just a myth. They wear jet-black hooded cloaks covered in feathers from an enchanted beast that shimmer like obsidian. Under their cloaks, they wear some sort of partial plate armor that ripples and hums at the touch. The main identifier, however, is the twisted bird-like mask they wear. They all use different forms of spellcraft, and different weapons made of the metal as their armor."

I studied his face for a moment, the pain of thinking about these Wings was written all over him. I softened my voice from my usual crass tone. "What did they take from you Hundri?"

He hesitated. "My father. He was one of the three great heroes that fought back the Wing that our attacked Anhalt. It took all three of their lives to fight off one Wing, even as sad as that sounds their names will go down in our history; Uyl, Juku and my father, Halvor."

Time crept by at a snail's pace. A feeling of awkwardness sat between us as I gave Hundri time to process how he was feeling. We had begun to hike up the nearest mountain. The jagged rocks sunk into my shoddy boots as we hiked before falling out with the next step. With the sunlight fading, the jagged stone of the mountain became a menacing shade of grey.

Now that he had recomposed himself, Hundri found a flat clearing and instructed me to set up camp before walking over to a nearby tree. I set down my bag and began laying out a fire pit and an area to sleep. With a soft hum, his sword began to shimmer with a luminescent azure. With a few quick slashes, the tree fell to the ground. A moment later his sword flashed away again, splitting the log into firewood. I tossed the wood into a small ring of stones I had laid out and looked back at Hundri.

I called over to him, "Try the little stones with runes on them in my bag." He nodded back and grabbed the palm-sized rock from my bag. After inspecting it for a moment, he injected energy into it. The runes glowed a bright orange as they sparked to life and the stone was tossed into the wood. Slowly, the fire grew. Bathed in orange light, me and Hundri both sat down on my ratty mat.

Hundri turned to look me in the eyes. "If you wouldn't mind, I'd like to perform a ritual of my people with you." He noticed the obvious confusion in my face, "It's a kind of rite for after you've killed a powerful beast like that bear."

I thought about it for a second before nodding in agreement. He reached into a pocket deep in his cloak and grabbed out a small glowing gem. Even my dull senses could feel the pulses of energy the gem released.

"While you were sleeping, I spent a few hours forming the beast's dwindling energy into this gem. I want you to absorb the energy inside. My people believe there can only be absolute victory." His eyes looked deep into mine, studying my expressions to see if I would agree. I reached out tentatively and slowly pulled the gem towards me. The faceted edges of the gem dug into my hand as I clenched it. I imagined the energy inside, the bear's power. I could feel it thrashing around in the gem. Golden runes formed and floated between the gem and my fingertips. Once the golden light of the transfer faded, it felt like something clicked in my head. My runes burned as they seemed to grow ever so slightly across my skin. I slowly unclenched my hands and watched the gem crumble to dust as the fragments floated through my fingertips.

Hundri nodded in response to seeing the gem crumble away. "Good job. Most people don't get it on their first try and it has to be transferred to them from another."

"I can't imagine that's true." I studied my hands for a moment. "It's simple," we both said in unison. "Just imagine the energy transferring from the gem to your hand." We both burst into chuckles and the sound echoed through the trees as we slowed to a stop.

A thought bubbled to my mind, "I've been meaning to ask, why are you out here by the way? I don't imagine its standard practice for a captain of Anhalt to be out in the wilderness alone and wandering into random caves."

He cracked his knuckles and pondered for a second, clearly unsure how much he wanted to tell me. "Well, I was moving a battalion of around a hundred soldiers towards a sighting of a... fugitive." Energy pulsed through the air with malice. "A few nights before we were supposed to arrive, he got the drop on us. By the time I was awoken, half the battalion was already dead from the blade of one man. While I was still getting my senses and thoughts together, he attacked me. I lost. When I woke up again, I was in a pool of blood, some my own, some my comrades." His face darkened as he recalled the events. "Nobody but me survived. I hobbled away as far as I could get before finding shelter."

His face shifted to an unreadable mask as I tried to study him. "I'm sorry Hundri. I'm guessing you have to tell your people now?"

He nodded in response before shuffling around with his half of the mat. "Who else is going to tell them?" He forced a tight-lipped smile before changing the subject, "Well, it would be a good idea for us to get some rest tonight. We've got another day of trudging through the snow tomorrow."

I agreed with him, and we wished each other a good night's sleep. I laid down on the bedroll and felt him stand up. I propped my head up on one hand and watched him trace the edge of the camp with a set of small wooden flags. With a pulse of energy, he returned to the mat. We laid back-to-back to preserve warmth in the freezing tundra. Once I felt the rising and falling of his chest on my back, I sat up. Slowly, I closed my eyes and let the world crumble away around me.

My eyes opened to the comforting yet eerie darkness of the void. Slowly I rose to my feet and looked around. My eyes drifted as I studied the empty space. Something strange caught the corner of my eye; a glowing white ball that floated aimlessly through the void. I sprinted over to it and reached out. As my fingers met its surface, the light was gone as if it was never there. Slowly I looked around once more, and my blood ran cold. Standing before me, was the bear I had killed.

It towered over me; this time constructed by ethereal golden wisps of light. I slowly walked around it, inspecting each transparent patch of golden fur. I could see the energy pumping through its body like veins as it coursed to every part of its body. When I circled back around to the front of the bear, I tapped it on the forehead, curious if it was alive. As my fingers touched its warm golden fur, a shock shot through my body, as if something had connected to the bear in my mind.

The bear's gem-like eyes creeped open and stared deep into my eyes. Its mouth opened. My legs slammed the murky void as I shot backwards into a fighting stance. "Is this... death?" the bear's eerily human voice echoed through my mind.

"You... can understand me?" I slowly asked as I eyed its every move.

The bear slowly nodded, "How strange." It looked throughout the void before continuing, "why did you summon me?"

I pondered the bear's question for a moment, why *did I summon it? A better question is* how *I summoned it.* "I'm not sure, I wasn't even aware I could do this. It's new to me." I slowly dropped my fighting stance.

"Odd. If you have no use for me, I shall depart." Its large wise eyes gazed at me. It was an eerily strange feeling to hear an enchanted beast speak in the human tongue. I had only heard of talking beasts in stories.

Unsure if I would be able to summon it again, I decided to ask it one more question. "One last thing," I gestured down to the rune I got from the bear, "what is this?"

"It allows the user to apply and grow their hatred to amplify their abilities. I advise against using it lightly. The growth of that anger will remain for a long time. Each time you use the rune, you will grow closer to myself." With those last words, the bear turned to a golden mist and drifted back into a compact glowing ball. The ball slowly twirled and danced away into the void.

As it disappeared into the distance, I thought back to something Hundri said about my mindscape when we first met. I clenched my fingers into a fist. I slowly extended my arm. I turned my hand to be palm up and extended my fingers in one fluid movement. The void almost felt like it was shaking with a low resonating hum that filled my mind. Out of the liquid-like void, stone bricks seeped up from the depths. After a moment, a full, almost house-like structure about the size of my room sat before me. I walked up to its dark wooden door and stepped inside.

The stone walls were drenched in a cool, pale blue light from crystals the size of my hand lining the walls with bronze fixtures. To the right of the door was an average bed with white fluffy sheets. To the left, was the same desk from the study in my home. As per usual it was covered in books. I picked one up and felt the roughly bound leather cover brush across my fingertips as I flipped to a random page. Each page was covered with unintelligible writing, aside from a few phrases I could specifically remember from this book. I set it down and looked at one of the two other objects in this room. Above the desk was a small case with a crimson book beautifully inlayed with gold, my family crest in the center.

I lifted the hefty book out of its case. I flipped to the first page, now realizing why it was unfamiliar to me, even in my own mind. The contained a detailed drawing of the bear I had just killed. The page hummed as I dragged my fingers across the diagram. The page warmed under my fingertips and began to glow. The bears consciousness began to awaken as the light began to coalesce.

I withdrew my hand from the diagram and the glow died. The rest of the page was covered in details about the bear, physical characteristics, behavior and information on its runic abilities. After studying the page for a moment, I put it back in its case. The final object in the room, a chest, was filled with the murky darkness of the void. Objects floated to the surface as I willed them into existence. I closed the lid of the chest and stepped out of the room.

Now that I had done a little more exploration, I pulled myself from the depths of my mind. My eyes opened to reality. Hundri lay next to me, asleep. The fire had died down quite a bit, its blazing embers still shined bright. I laid back next to Hundri and stared up at the full moon. The stars glittered high above the treetops, the wind and rustling of branches slowly lulling me to sleep.

CHAPTER SEVEN

Mark of the Raven

Reynolds Helphain

As soon as Hundri awoke he shook me awake and we began to clean the camp. The mat was tossed back into the bag and the fire kicked to ash. Finally, Hundri's runes flared and the snow around us thinned. Slowly, it shifted and covered any traces that we had been there.

After Hundri's display of magic, I decided to ask him about something on my mind, "Hey Hundri, what were those flags you put out before we went to sleep for the night? I noticed you used them back in the cave too."

"Oh, they're a form of barrier magic," seeing I wasn't satisfied with that answer he continued while we began to trudge into the woods, "it basically made a perimeter of sensitive energy that would wake me up if something large enough disturbed it. A large, consistent spell like that normally takes a lot of concentration, that's why its stored in that series of flags."

I nodded slowly, "That makes sense. Would you show me how to do that at some point?"

"Possibly, but it will not be for a while. It needs you to have a strong base with your energy control. I personally learned how to use them a few months after I could consistently manifest my element."

I ducked under a branch heavy with snow, "Alright, after I manage to use my element like that, you'll teach me?"

He let out a sigh, "Fine. Though that will take a while in itself. Next time we reach a somewhat flat area we can try to work on that. Sound good?"

"Great! Thanks, Hundri." I shot him a smile and began to bulk up my aura. Over the hours of hiking with ridiculous amounts of weight, I had gained a much stronger hold over my aura. I no longer had to dedicate so much concentration for such a gelatinous form. Reinforcing the firmer areas and repairing the aura as it was damaged were now the main things that took concentration.

Step after step, we plodded through the snow. The snowy trees thinned as we climbed higher. Just as the number of trees began to thin, we reached a long stone brick path stretching up the mountain. The rough stone grinded against my boots as we began to traverse the path. On either side of the path lay destroyed statues and idols, fragments of what used to be runic lights lay around them in shattered pieces.

"What happened here?" I asked as we walked down the increasingly ruined path.

"Bandits probably," his voice dripped with hatred and disgust, "the bastards destroyed the statues of our leaders and even had the audacity to steal the energy inside the crystals used to light my people's way."

His anger felt almost tangible as we walked in silence for a moment. "I'm sorry Hundri. I'm sure you will get the chance to make them pay when the time is right." He nodded in response before I asked another question, "Speaking of lighting the way, mind enlightening me on where we're going? I don't remember you mentioning your city having a path like this."

"You're half right. We aren't going to the city yet, it's too far to travel to on foot. I'm going to teach you how to use one of our platforms."

"One of the ones you mentioned yesterday?"

"Exactly right. This one is going to take us directly to Anhalt." His voice was filled with pride at his people's accomplishment. "These are masterpieces of engineering; each one taking cycles to build and even longer to fine tune for safety. They're powerful enough to move many soldiers across this mountain in days."

"Well, I can't wait to see one. How much farther to the top—" I was cut short by the sight of a large stone gateway carved into the side of the cliff. Hundri glanced over and smirked slightly at the sight of my dropped jaw. The door was at least double the size of my house if it was flipped on its side.

The surface of the door was covered in carved memorials of great people. Three stone knights with dark metal eyes stood on either side of the door with one who stood atop the archway. Their massive grey bodies and faces were intricately detailed, the level of care each was given was apparent.

They stood with their massive stone swords pointed upwards towards the heavens, as if challenging the gods themselves. On the surface of the door seemed to be some sort of underworld depicted. Carvings of monsters and hell-spawn roamed the spiky landscape. Above the destroyed ground of the underworld was a swirling cloudy storm, with countless giant beings casting bolts of power down upon the monsters below them.

Hundri walked past me and towards a small pedestal to the right of me. I walked over to join him as he pulled a small chain necklace with a small metal cube off his neck. His energy seeped into the sharp edges, and with the few quiet whirs and clicks of gears, the metal folded apart and revealed a small white glowing cube in the center. He pressed the glowing necklace into the pedestal and the air seemed to tremble.

With a loud rumbling, large bronze lines in the ground, door and pedestal —almost like veins— began to glow a deep blue. The massive stone door slowly began to open, the more it opened, the more visible the massive gears inside were. The small cube Hundri used to open the path ahead folded back up and he put it around his neck once more. As we walked closer, I could feel the vibrations from the door opening in my bones, even the pebbles on the ground began to bounce.

The inside was nothing like I expected, and clearly not what Hundri expected either. The stench of iron filled the air. The dark stone walls and white tiled ground were painted with splashes and pools of dark crimson. Hundri's face curled up as his eyes widened. The ground was covered in hundreds of mangled corpses. Torn flesh, destroyed armor, and missing limbs were everywhere, even in the thick, dark wooden beams that supported the shadowed ceiling. Hundri's teeth ground together, and his knuckles were white as we slowly stepped over bodies. Each was more gruesome than the last.

Even without looking at Hundri, I could feel his anger. His energy was leaking out of him like a hurricane. The sheer force and pressure of his aura was enough to almost shred mine to pieces. I had to push everything deep into my mind and purely focus on keeping my aura stable. Despite my best efforts, the torrent of power almost doubled me over.

As I stumbled and struggled to stay on my feet, I pleaded, "Hundri...," I said weakly, "please, your energy... I don't think I can take much more."

Hundri looked over and his face relaxed slightly, "Oh Gods, sorry. I lost my grip for a second." With that, his energy stopped flowing out and I was able to regain my footing. I nodded weakly before my eyes caught something that stood out resting on the ground. My feet trembled as I struggled over to the object. I raised it up to the light and could almost see a vein in Hundri's forehead pop. In my hand was a shimmering dark feather that caught the light and reflected back a spectrum of colors. I looked at Hundri grimly and held out the feather.

Hundri's face looked as if he was going to explode. His hatred for the feather was so powerful it could've burned right through it. He took several deep breaths, before putting it in the bag. "This is bad," A grim look spread across his face, masking his seething rage, "If the Wings are back, we are in a bad place. Especially with this damn *monster* wandering around."

We slowly walked through the piles of corpses to find any shred of information, but to no avail. The only conclusive evidence we could find in this horde of corpses was the feather. After what felt like hours of searching through mangled bodies, we walked over to the floating platform. "We should hurry to the city. Now that we've seen this, we can't wait any longer. I *must* warn them."

"So how do I use this?" I walked over to a pedestal carved out of a dark wood with four bronze prongs at the top that connected to a glowing blue spherical crystal. My fingers gingerly touched the top of the orb. A soft hum emanated from where I touched as I traced the orb's top.

I jumped in surprise as Hundri yanked the bag off my shoulder, breaking me from the orb's entrancement. "Try putting some energy into it" Hundri suggested gruffly. I touched the top again, but this time pumped a tiny amount of energy into the orb. Small glowing blue runes floated from under my fingers and flowed down the engraved bronze inlays that detailed the wood. The sound of gears clanking and parts moving filled the air. Three large bronze discs with glowing crystals extended from the platform. Two on either side, in line with the rails, and one on the bottom. The whirring began to grow louder as the three discs began to spin. By the time they reached full speed, a small bubble to shield us from the elements had already formed. The orb began to pulse rapidly. With one final tap on the top, it rocketed out of the station and down the tracks.

I gazed out of the bubble in awe, the scenery flew by in a blur as we raced through the landscape. Hundri sat down next to our bag and beckoned me away from the gorgeous scenery. I sat down on the cold, white polished stone across from Hundri. He raised his right hand, palm facing the sky and we watched as a jagged ball of ice formed. "Elemental manifestation is challenging," He looked at me dead in the eyes, any hint of humor dead, "Don't be embarrassed if you don't get it right away, most people don't."

I nodded in response; I'd heard stories from my father about him forming his first flame so I knew that it could take a lot of training. Especially being able to use it consistently or in combat. I cleared my throat, uncomfortable in his agitated aura "Uh, well do you have any tips?"

"What really helped me to form ice for the first time was connecting it to me and my personality. Freezing in the wilderness, the sting of snow on my bare skin, the times I've had to make cold, harsh decisions. Times where I've pushed all emotion away to make the right calls. Thinking about the aspects of ice, what makes it distinct and unique. Understanding is the most important part. See if you can connect events like that."

My eyes dropped down to my hands. I felt the warmth of energy leaving the runes on my sternum as I pushed it through my chest, down my arms and into my fingertips. Slowly the heat built in my fingertips.

I drowned out the sounds around me until the only sound left was my breathing. Lightning. A volatile stream of godly power. Cracking the sky in deafening booms with each strike. Powerful enough to destroy buildings. An ever-changing current of power from the heavens. It was a mysterious, volatile power. The most everyone knew was its godly nature.

As I pondered the nature of lightning, I began to feel the energy coil in my fingertips. It streamed together, forming the beginnings of volatile arcs. Once they began to writhe hundreds of snakes beneath my skin, I pushed.

Nothing happened. I pushed again; nothing. Each time I tried to push the energy out, it felt more resistant to obeying my commands. Just as I was ready to give up in frustration, something clicked; lightning is *volatile*. Lightning is erratic. Lightning doesn't want to listen. No, lightning wanted to flow and destroy uninhibited. Slowly, I released my control over the writhing energy.

With a soft hum, a different set of runes on my chest began to glow with soft golden light beneath my tunic. With a quiet crackle, a small arc of golden voltaic energy flowed between my index finger and thumb. Then it was gone.

A wild grin spread across my face as a giddy feeling filled my body. I looked up at Hundri, who was smiling ever so slightly. "I'm impressed. Of course, it gets easier as you keep using your elemental abilities, but for now it will just manifest as probably just small sparks."

"Thank you Hundri," I gazed up at him sincerely, "I'm going to keep training while we ride."

His smile died a little, "Sounds good. I think I'm going to get some shut eye in the corner." With a small wave, he grabbed the mat from our bag, and laid down. After a few moments, his breath fell into a rhythm as he drifted off into sleep.

I pushed Hundri out of my mind. I rose from my seated position as my boots squeaked against the polished stone. My slow rhythmic breaths dominated my mind as I pushed away my surroundings. I felt my internal gates slide open as an influx of energy infused itself with my body. After my runes had reached the maximum energy they could store, I pushed outward. The newly absorbed energy began to dance across my skin in tiny arcs.

I began to practice the three-step plan I had developed for training. Push energy out, form the energy into scales, then temper and harden them. By the time scales coated both my arms completely, I could taste the salt of my sweat in my mouth. I formed more and more until I could barely stand.

My fists sluggishly flailed through the air despite the physical enhancement, as if I was swinging through honey. My runes burned like a brand had been pressed into my chest, each movement eliciting a wince from my tight lips. Finally, when it felt like I was on the verge of unconsciousness, I broke down the scales. To keep me standing I infused it into my shaking knees, while the rest I channeled into my hands.

I clasped my hands together, before imagining the voltaic energy sparking together beneath my flesh. I released the energy from my control and allowed it to arc between my fingers. A spike of pain drove itself deep into my temples as the energy arced out. Thousands of points of sharp tingling pressure danced across my hands while I pulled them apart.

I clenched my teeth. The spike of pain in my forehead grew exponentially as I pulled my hands apart. Finally, as it grew unbearable, my hands got too far apart, and the flow of electricity stopped. I slumped over and supported my now sweat-drenched body with my hands braced on my knees. Rough, jagged pants escaped my throat as I heaved for the air I hadn't realized I wasn't breathing.

I knew I couldn't stop there. I pushed the pain that danced across my limbs and runes out of my head. I honed my mind and began to focus again. Minutes passed as I cleared my mind. Once I found peace, I began to suck the ambient energy around me into my runes, as if I was breathing.

When it felt like my runes were brimming with power, I stood up again and winced from my exhausted limbs. I shakily walked to the other side of the moving platform. Just in case something went wrong, I didn't want Hundri too close.

I wiped the sweat from my brows and extended my arms. I slowly dropped into a stance similar to one used for hand-to-hand combat. Slowly, I let the energy inside me leak out and into the rune I obtained from the bear. I split my mind, half of it focusing on keeping a weak, but steady trickle to the bear's rune and the other half focusing on gathering energy in my hands.

The energy violently spiked and writhed. As I felt my energy taking shape inside me, I felt something else growing. My face began to flush as I felt my aggression grow. I focused my new-found anger into the energy within my hands. Slowly, my hatred and destructive will were imparted into the crackling energy. Pain flared in my hand and tears dripped from my eyes. The energy began to tear itself free of my hand.

My face drained with fear. I couldn't stop it. With a deafening crack, I felt the energy leave my body in a single moment. A white-hot heat blasted from my right hand as a flash of red-tinged golden lightning exploded outward. It cracked the air like glass and exploded against the bubble that surrounded the platform.

I watched in horror as a crack began to snake outward from where the bolt collided. It slowly spread into a spider-web-like shape. Suddenly, the orb atop the pedestal flashed red as beams of light shot out from it, tracing the cracks. Almost as quickly as it had formed, the crack filled itself with energy and disappeared without a trace.

Letting out a sigh, I felt my adrenaline subsiding. My legs grew weaker as I hobbled over to the mat next to Hundri. My stability faltered as I keeled over the worn surface, and I crashed down on my back. Without a second thought, I let exhaustion overtake me.

CHAPTER EIGHT

The Cavernous City

Reynolds Helphain

My eyes shot open. My body flailed as I searched my surroundings, my eyes wide and my heart beating like a drum. We had begun too rapidly slow down. I caught my breath before standing up and looking at Hundri. His eyes locked with mine and a smile tugged at the corners of his lips as he tried to hide his amusement.

"Good morning my dear *somewhat of a partner*," he said in a teasing voice.

I rubbed the exhaustion from my eyes and stood up. My muscles ached. "Good morning to you Hundri," I grumbled as I stretched, glaring at him from under my mess of hair. I pulled it back behind my ears and adjusted it so no tiny strands would get in my face before walking over to him. "It seems we're slowing down."

"You would be correct," he said cheerfully, pointing toward a rapidly approaching mountain at the end of the track. "That's Mount Luceat. I imagine we'll be there shortly. How was the training?"

I exhaled heavily and chuckled nervously before answering, "Well, I can comfortably maintain scales up to about halfway up my upper arm, I'm able to make lightning spanning about an inch or two," My voice faltered for a second. "I-I also used the rune I got from the bear with my lightning and... well... almost destroyed the bubble."

Hundri stared. He didn't even say a word for a moment, just looked at me. "That rune must be much more powerful than I thought then. Energy, depending on your degree of connection to it, responds strongest to two things: emotion and intent. If that rune utilizes hatred, it *should* greatly increase the control you have." He closed his eyes for a minute and tapped his foot against the polished stone rhythmically. "I was right. It seems like you don't have the control you need for that rune yet."

I could feel he was right. If I focused on the rune, it still felt foreign, like a new limb had been grafted onto me. "Where do you think I should begin if I want to master it?"

"Honestly, I have no clue." His eyes met mine. "Everybody's path to mastery is different. Especially depending on what you're mastering." After a moment of consideration, he answered again, "I would advise introspection. Explore your mental void more. Find yourself."

A shadow loomed over us as we slowed to a crawl. "Well, that will have to wait for later, because it looks like we're here." I kneeled over, pumping energy into my shoulders and back as I lifted the hefty bag and slung it over my shoulders. I grimaced as my muscles ached and my channels burned. Both overused.

The shadow cast from the maw of the cave swallowed us, the only thing visible as my eyes adjusted to the sudden darkness were Hundri's piercing luminescent eyes and the softly glowing bubble. Slowly, I began to see.

We were in an area that was a mix between a natural cave and an imposing, well-designed chamber. The ceiling was jagged with stalactites and each wall of the cave was covered with massive bronze supports. The floor was a well-polished dark grey stone, with curving and twisting inlays of bronze. The far wall was man made, built into the side of the cave with large stone bricks that were larger than any bricks I had seen before. They constructed into an ominous blockade that felt like a fortress. Glowing crystals secured with bronze brackets bathed the room in golden light, filling the space with an odd warm, cozy feeling despite its size.

Hundri and I strode off the platform and onto the dark stone. Our well-worn boots squeaked against the polished rock as we walked toward a decorated dais in the center of the room. Intricate statues depicting three knights stood with their palms cupped, perfectly shaped for something square to be placed between them.

Each knight was very different in appearance. One wore armor decorated with orange gems, curved horns rising from his helmet and fire ringing his feet. On his back was a large, detailed curved great sword resembling the claw of a beast. Another was highlighted with glowing green gems. This one wore armored battle robes with very minimal armor and levitated off the ground slightly. The cloth of their robes billowed behind him in a dramatic fashion. He wore no helmet, which revealed a wild spiky haircut, a sharp chin, and glowing eyes. On his forehead glowed a complex rune formation. The final knight wore simple armor with white pearlescent gems embedded across his body. His armor was practical and lacked decoration. It had nothing ornate or unique besides the strange gems. At his side was a blade with a hilt carved like hawk's wings.

Like before, Hundri's pendant unfolded into the glowing crystal, and he inserted it in the socket. A soft hum began to reverberate from the gems as the knight's armor blazed to life. The room was bathed in colorful light as a cacophony of horrendous clanking noises filled the room. Gears hidden within the wall spun and clanked as a large door slid into the ground.

I got over my awe and turned to Hundri. "Are these," I gestured to the knights, "the three heroes?"

He nodded solemnly before he gestured to the one in the simple armor adorned with glowing pearlescent gems. "That one was my father; Halvor." He ran his fingers across the glowing crystals before recoiling into a tight fist. "He was a great warrior, and a better man." He paused for a moment, his face slowly dropping into sadness. "He had a strange branch of pure energy instead of an elemental affinity. Nobody could understand his powers. Only that the gems on his armor focused and controlled it."

As much as I wanted to ask more questions, I could tell by Hundri's pained face that it wasn't the time. I began to walk away from the dais and felt Hundri catch up to me as we walked through the large doorway.

Past the doorway was a long hallway. It was wide, almost large enough to be considered a street, with dark wooden columns lit by glowing crystals. The floor was the same polished grey stone as the cavern before.

The walls were engraved with geometric patterns inlayed with bronze that seemed to stretch the length of the hall.

After walking through the hallway for many minutes, we saw our first people. Another door sat at the edge of the hall and was also decorated with geometric bronze inlay. On either side of the door stood a man and a woman in full armor without the helmet. The one on the right was a tall, lean, middle-aged man with short blonde hair, soft features and dark hazel eyes. The rightmost guard looked as if she wasn't much older than me, with soft features and dark brown hair spilling in curling locks that stopped just below her shoulders.

As we approached from the shadows of the hallway, their hands shot down and they drew their swords with practiced efficiency. Energy pulsed through the air, disrupting the aura I was using to carry our bag. The man's baritone voice filled the hallway. "Name and identification."

Hundri's icy glowing eyes locked with the armored man. "Captain Hundri Traegan and my... somewhat of a partner..." He looked at me, gesturing to introduce myself.

I cleared my voice and locked eyes with the man, then looked towards the woman. Her gaze never left Hundri, not even acknowledging my presence. I stood up a bit straighter. "Reynolds Helphain." The man responded with a curt nod and the woman continued to ignore me before they both sheathed their swords.

My agitation was shoved away and bottled up in my mind as the female guard began to open her mouth. "Welcome back— "

"Yes, formalities aside I have urgent information for the council," Hundri interjected.

The woman's face twitched slightly as Hundri cut her off. "As I was saying, Captain Traegan, Grand Commander Ronhelm will be pleased you are still alive." Hundri's face tightened slightly at the mention of the name Ronhelm.

The guards gave him a small bow before one of them inputted their pendant into a slot on the wall. With a rumbling, the door slid open, and light spilled out. "This is a military entrance, so we're entering through the military district," Hundri whispered to me as I looked around in awe at my surroundings.

We walked out of the doorway and into a large semi-circle with many doors identical to the one we came from that lined the curved edge. The only differing feature was the glowing number above each door. The straight edge of the semi-circle was home to barracks and military buildings. They were made of the same rough, dark stone and dark brown wood from trees in the surrounding area. The most beautiful part, however, was the ceiling. More appropriately, the *sky*. An entrancing sea of mystical glowing dust masked the spiky roof of the cave. They swirled like nebulas in the sky and shifted in the sky. Each cloud of blue and purple flowed together and mixed as they bathed everything in beautiful colored light.

I stood frozen. The dust swirling and dancing through the air high above took my breath away. When I finally responded, it was so quiet I had to repeat myself for Hundri to hear. "It's beautiful..."

He looked at me and tried to suppress a smile, but it still obviously danced on his face. "That's what most people think when they see it for the first time. C'mon, I've got a lot to show you."

I struggled to take my eyes off the beautiful ceiling. With great effort my eyes finally lowered to take in the rest of the scenery as we walked. People in combat robes and partial armor marched laps around the semi-circle. We weaved through groups of soldiers who were spending time with groups of friends, moving boxes, transporting materials and weapons, or simply lounging around.

The scenery rushed by in a blur as we hustled through the tumult. Everything we saw was surprising and exciting. Mages cast large elemental spells, sparks flew from duels and large decorated statues towered over the bustling streets. Finally, Hundri led me to a large imposing building. It had a tall, black tiled pointed top, a tall portico supported with rectangular wooden beams, a dark stone floor and ceiling, and brilliant white walls. Bronze fixtures with glowing runelights and bronze decorative inlays traced the walls of the building in beautiful swirling patterns. In the front was a memorial that consisted of towering, dark metal statues of the three heroes.

We walked up a tall flight of stairs before walking inside the imposing building. It immediately opened into a wide, massive, cylindrical chamber. People in lavish robes strode back and forth between different hallways that branched in different directions. Another set of metal statues of the three heroes once again stood at attention in this room, swords pointed to a massive golden chandelier that hung from the ceiling. The domed ceiling was painted with an exquisite painting of what I assumed to be the gods resting upon different thrones constructed from their respective elements.

We strode down a hallway to the left, and found ourselves in a winding, empty hallway decorated with long murals that told a complex history. Finally, we reached a dead end. Hundri extended his hand and his azure energy formed complicated runes at each fingertip. After they all finished forming, the five runes swirled together in the palm of his hand. A soft hum filled the air as I watched him press the newly formed glyph to the wall.

To my surprise, the wall began to bend under the force of his arm pressing the wall. It warped and shifted as the energy spread into the wall. Just as suddenly as it began, the wall finished warping. A simple door of dark metal sat before me. "Illusion magic," Hundri remarked after seeing my look of surprise. "Comes from light magic. Pretty rare."

"What's behind the door?" I muttered, still taken aback after seeing a solid wall warp like dough.

Hundri's lips formed a small smirk, "Grand Commander Ronhelm and the rest of the military heads." With that, Hundri pushed open the door ever so slightly and the sound of loud chatter filled my ears. Hundri turned back to look at me, "I'm going to talk to Ronhelm about what we've found and about my battalion." He patted down his body before finding what he was looking for. Hundri grabbed my arm, raised it and opened my palm. He placed a cold flat medallion in the shape of an eye with an azure crystal iris into my hand.

"What's this for?" I turned it over to find an inscription and address on the back. *Hell's Pavilion, where the damned drink their last. 4500 Halvor RD, room five.*

"It's a bar and meeting place for adventurers. It's where my friends and I used to drink our hearts away when I was still atop the adventuring world. Go there and look for my friends. They'll be able to tell you're with me from the energy that medallion gives off." He turned and began to walk through the now fading doorway before calling back, "I'll come find you when I'm done here."

And with that, the doorway ceased to exist. All that remained was the dead-end wall. My footsteps echoed through the hall as I strode down the hallway again and took the time to examine the murals as I walked. I slowly began to gloss over the murals on my sides as I walked. They grew repetitive, despite their beauty. Paintings of warfare and bloodshed depicted a gruesome history that seemed to repeat itself over and over. Grow, build, fight and repeat into infinity. Only one thing seemed to pull my eye in this hallway of warfare.

Just before I reached the point where this particular hallway ended, there was an event of godly proportion depicted. Like the door I had seen before, it depicted the crack and spiky world filled with monsters and hell spawn. The swirling reds, the billowing grey smoke and the brightly colored figures in the sky created a powerful picture. As the mural continued, I noticed the appearance of titles on the pieces.

I stopped before one that caught my eye and read the title, "Iora's Gift." The piece depicted a golden-haired woman with shining blue eyes in a loose white dress standing on the edge of a cloud with her arm outstretched. Below her, a massive mountain of ice drew itself from the ground, impaling and eviscerating countless monsters below.

A shiver went down my spine. I shook the gory imagery from my head and walked towards the end of the hall. The sounds of people surrounded me as I walked back through the main chamber and towards the busy streets. I stepped out of the imposing building and walked aimlessly as I searched for any indication of where I was.

The streets were pristine and elegant. Made from a white stone that was well kept and high quality enough to not even dull in shine after thousands of people had walked upon it. Each person I walked by on the street exuded an aura of power. I could tell that each one could crush me should I step out of line. Even the vendors who sold various bits and bobs on the streets were strong.

As I walked, I cared increasingly less about finding the place Hundri to find. Each stall on the road was filled to the brim with complex and interesting wares that caught my eye. Magical, runic jewelry. Massive, imposing great swords that looked like they should've belonged to the Gods themselves. Something eye-catching was never far from sight.

I stopped at an artifact store and watched an old man with a fine combed white beard put on a simple silver ring with a blue gem as its highlight. With a quick pulse of energy, a grid of dark blue hexagonal panels of light formed floating above his palm.

His voice croaked out loudly across the small party of armored onlookers, "Anyone care to try their luck at breaking this grade five shield? If you can break it, I'll give you half off your next purchase!" It was quiet for a moment before a man with short, spiky, rigid, and gelled hair stepped forwards. He wore loose fitting pants with leather plates, and two metal pauldrons connected by leather straps across his chest. Runes that he displayed proudly on his almost entirely bare muscular chest flared to life as rocks on the ground bounced to life.

They flew up with a hum and formed a bulky coating around his hands. "Sorry gramps," the man exclaimed as he pulled back his fist. With a thunderous boom, the stone gauntlet snapped through the air and impacted the shield. Dust flew up into the crowd causing a fit of coughs from even people simply passing by. As the dust cleared, sounds of surprise shot up around the group. The shield held. The old man stood there effortlessly as the shield flickered and repaired the massive crack along its surface.

"Anyone else want to try?" The merchant winked at the crowd. Waves of applause and murmurs of excitement about the ring exploded outwards as they clamored forwards. The man with the earthen gauntlet's face flushed red as he stormed off, muttering curses as he went.

With a small chuckle I turned away from the stall and began to survey the street once more. After walking for a while, I found a crossroads marked with a sign that was luckily in my language. *Halvor road! Finally.* I walked down the almost empty street, taking in the sights of each pristine building and piece of art.

Every building was made of stark contrasting colors: white marbled stone, dark sleek stone and dark brown stained wood. The road eventually opened into a large circular hub. In the middle laid a massive fountain that reflected the gorgeous colors of the magic above. It was filled with shirtless teenagers that looked about my age who stood knee deep in the water. They practiced movements resembling combat stances as their runes glowed a dark blue. The water around them moved and churned in different, unnatural ways that seemed to correspond to their flowing palms.

I'm going to have to ask Hundri about these later. I thought to myself as I strode past the training soldiers. My eyes settled on a bench, and I strode over towards it. I sat down on the cool, masterfully crafted and decorated bars of the bench as my eyes wandered across the plaza.

Off-duty soldiers and adventurers strolled with people, idly talking to each other as they entered and excited different places. Everything blurred together as I watched everyone fall into the same patterns. Even still, they were fun to watch. The only things that stood out were the gorgeous swirling nebulas of the ceiling and the people practicing in the fountain.

Somehow, the way they moved was even more mesmerizing than the magical sky. Each bend and curve in their bodies and arms pushed the water in beautiful patterns. They were all drenched in sweat and fountain water from hours of practice. When I had first arrived, they had been just pushing and pulling the water on the surface, but as time progressed, they began to step up the intensity.

Streams and orbs of water rose from the surface and struggled to keep their shape the higher they got. The spectrum of talent and skill was wide and varied. Some created perfect orbs that didn't lose a drop of water and took hardly any effort, while others were struggling to raise their collapsing orb above the surface. The instructor stood on the wide rim of the fountain with at least ten orbs rapidly spinning behind him. With the flick of his wrist, a ball would fly out from behind him and arc toward a student practicing. The student would then have to either redirect or deflect the orb. Even the students who could perfectly maintain their orbs struggled to handle the oncoming assault.

A ball of water zipped toward an almost entirely dry girl, and she rotated her body to be parallel with the orb's path. She held one arm extended to keep her own orb steady while her other arm twirled in a mesmerizing movement. As the orb was about to hit her now outstretched palm, she drew it into an arc from her head to her waist before thrusting her hand outward in a palm strike.

The water blasted back toward the instructor. To nobody's surprise, the instructor effortlessly swatted at the stream of water, and it burst into tiny droplets and mist. The teacher called out to his students, "Alright, I think that's enough for today's class. Everyone may return home now. I will see you all again in the next few rotations. Get some rest."

Damn, there goes my entertainment.

As the class dispersed, I took my attention back to the sky, losing myself in its rhythmic motions. Memories began to bubble to the surface of my mind. Dinners with my sister and my father, the sting of the snow on my face as we dueled late into the night, reading the few books we owned for hours next to a crackling fire. Longing for the simpler times of the past swelled in my chest.

Before I could think much more about her, an unfamiliar feminine voice began to speak next to me. "Lost in thought, are we?"

To my right on the bench sat one of the students my age. She had auburn hair pulled back into a ponytail to keep the majority of her hair out of her eyes. She had sharp features and a hard jawline that was covered in unblemished skin. Her eyes were a dark brown and looked down at me slightly due to her being slightly taller than me. Her apparel was clearly workout oriented. She wore a small tight-fitting shirt to cover her slender form, leaving her defined muscles exposed below. She also wore loose baggy pants and what looked to be the soles of boots tied to her feet.

With a sheepish smile, I met her eyes. "Yeah, it's my first time in Anhalt. Whatever magic is up there is spectacular... never seen anything like it."

She tilted her head up and looked up at the ceiling. A mixture of purple and blue light reflected through her eyes. After a moment of silence, she looked back down at me. "What's your name?"

"Reynolds, friends call me Rey,"

"I'm Abigail." She smiled warmly at me. "So, what are you doing in Anhalt? Especially the military district." Her eyes swept over me, "You don't really look... military."

I chuckled in return. "Wow okay, I see how it is." I responded in a teasing tone.

She laughed as well, "Well I'm sorry but you really don't. Do you even have your runes yet?"

My voice raised in pitch, mildly insulted, "Yes! Obviously. It'd be weird for me to be in the military district if I couldn't even use my energy."

She nodded in agreement, "Yeah that's true. People who can't use energy are practically useless, after all."

With a smile I continued, "To answer your previous question, I met someone in the military who has become a sort of mentor to me. He went to go complete some official business, so I was left with some time to kill before I met back up with him."

"Huh well that's interesting. What's your mentor raised your rune's strength rating to?"

"Strength rating? Did you forget I'm not from around here?"

She chuckled slightly, "Ah sorry, I did. It's pretty straight forward. It's simply a system used to measure your ability to fight using your runes."

"Interesting, what are you then?"

She touched her bottom lip with her index finger, thinking for a second before she explained, "Well, there's many levels. It starts at bronze, where most children are, then above that is silver, and above that is gold. Each level of power gets wider the higher you climb. The farthest you can go with bronze may take you two weeks, while gold could take you cycles to reach the highest level. Me personally, I'm only recently pushing the boundary of bronze into silver."

"That's a little confusing. I don't really know how to tell you where I'm at then."

"Well, there's two steps in the process. I can help you get a rough estimate if you want."

"Oh, I'd appreciate that actually. I feel like it'd probably be valuable information to have in a city ruled by strength." I chuckled slightly, "I can *feel* strength oozing off people in the streets even if they're just merchants."

She laughed as well, "You need to be strong if you're not planning on getting robbed by just about anyone. The first thing to do is inspect your runes." She smirked slightly and tapped her just above her breasts where her intricate runes lay. Blood flushed my cheeks as I quickly turned away.

Hearty laughter filled my ears as I turned away from her, looking anywhere but her direction. After her laughter stopped, I turned back to her, my cheeks still burning. I met her eyes as she stared down at me with an almost sadistic glint in her eyes. She made no effort to hide her smile as she continued, "Don't worry, I'll be the one inspecting your runes."

"Somehow that makes me more uneasy." I muttered in response, causing another good laugh from her.

"Don't worry, I'll be gentle." She murmured as she placed a finger on my chest.

"Oh shut up!" I shot back despite my burning cheeks.

She snickered quietly. "In all seriousness though, all need is to glance over some of your runes and kick you around in a sparring match."

A smile formed at my lips, "Alright. Let's do it then."

CHAPTER NINE

Movements Like Flowing Water

Reynolds Helphain

I had followed her to a private training room within a large academy that was given to her because she was apparently a student with high potential. The room was a grey rocky cave with smoothed walls and ceilings to appear man-made. It was brightly lit with the same orange glowing crystals I had seen mounted in bronze everywhere. In the center of the room was a mat imbedded into the ground, made of tightly woven fibers. The edges of the chamber were lined with benches, chests and large troughs of water which I guessed were to practice her water magic.

I sat across from her on a wooden bench, facing her. My shirt was off, revealing my lean muscular torso. My cheeks burned brighter than the sun. Her hands gingerly danced across my runes, and I bit back laughter as the tickling sensation spread across my skin.

"Well, from my very limited knowledge, what I would say is that you're pretty new to bronze. I wouldn't be surprised if you got your runes a few weeks ago."

I chuckled. "You'd be right about that."

She raised an eyebrow but said nothing as she continued to study my runes. "There's one thing that doesn't make sense." She flicked the rune I had gotten from the bear, and I twitched slightly. "I've never seen something like this before."

"Yeah, it's a long story. Anyways! I had a quick question for you."

Her eyes flicked up to meet mine. "What is it?"

"What is the obsession with bronze? Everything is made with it, and you all even named rank in your strength rating system after it."

She looked at me in surprise for a moment, silent. "You really are clueless." She smiled. "Bronze conducts energy very well. It's the metal that can transfer energy the fastest, and with the least energy lost."

I sighed. "Well, that should've been obvious. Thanks anyway."

"It's okay! I don't mind if you're a little slow." She smirked.

"Oh, you'll find out how quick I am when I beat you into the floor." I glared at her. "Let's get to the sparring part."

She grinned wildly and nodded in return. I hurriedly put on my shirt as my blush faded. We both walked to opposite sides of the large mat and took fighting stances. "Rey, since you're apparently *so* new to Anhalt, I'm guessing you don't know our sparring customs, right?"

"No. I doubt they are that unique."

"Well, I'm sure you've heard it before, but our military likes the phrase 'absolute victory' a lot. For most duels you can go all out, as long as you don't kill or permanently injure someone. It's only over when someone can't fight anymore, or when one person yields. A big thing is though, don't use any spells that you don't have the power to stop. Recklessly using a powerful spell could, well, I'm sure you understand despite how slow you are."

My face twitched slightly at her last comment and my brow furrowed slightly in worry. "That... that seems a little over the top don't you think? Don't people get hurt pretty often then?"

"Sadly, yes. But that's just how it is. Strength is respect and power in our society. Be careful who you duel."

I shot her a smile and a raised eyebrow, "Should I be dueling you then?"

"Don't worry! There's a good chance I'll listen if you tell me to stop." She cracked her knuckles and winked at me. "If you ask nicely, that is. Let's get started."

Slowly, I let the energy build up in my runes until they quietly hummed. My confidence had greatly increased in forming scales. The improvement was apparent. The tempering stage had been removed from the process and the scales formed already hardened now. They also took much less concentration to hold. Even the forming time had gone down to only half a minute to cover my hands.

Looking up at her, I noticed the impatient look in her eye, "Sorry, takes me a minute to get prepared."

Abigail sighed, "This is just embarrassing."

Annoyance flared in my mind as I strengthened my legs. I leaped forward, closing the distance in five steps. I took a right hook at her head, letting the energy that coated my arms carry my punch forward with devastating force. "I'll show you embarrassment!" I grunted.

"Still pretty embarrassing," She weaved, grabbed my wrist and pulled me toward her, "but not the worst I've seen." Her other hand shimmered with energy as her right palm slammed into my chest, sending me rolling into the mat, back where I had begun.

I groaned and stood back up, "It's okay to pull your punches, you know." We began to circle each other, and I used this opportunity to form more scales beneath my tunic.

"Where's the fun in that!" she said cheerfully before she shifted into a strange stance I'd never seen before and did a pulling motion with her right arm. It had openings all over, yet for some reason, my instincts screamed that it was impenetrable. A memory clicked into place. She had used it while I was watching her at the fountain. My instincts screamed. My head whipped around over my shoulder, just in time to see a bolt of water flying towards my back.

I let my instincts take over. I quickly side stepped to the right. It narrowly missed and flew into her palm where it hovered in an orb. Her runes blazed blue beneath her tunic. It wrapped around her wrist like a bracelet before she dashed at me. Our arms and legs flew in flurries of blows as we blocked, parried and dodged. Sweat rolled down my brow as I was slowly pushed backwards. I was losing ground, and quickly. A knowing smile danced on her lips as we brawled.

Annoyance trickled into my heart as I began to channel increasing amounts of energy into my blows. I swung ferociously with my left arm, and as she pivoted to block it, I feinted my blow and swung around in a powerful, energy infused roundhouse kick. She quickly dropped her arm to block, but not fast enough.

With a satisfying thud she skidded a few feet away. "Nice kick. I'm sure you know I let that happen though. All part of the test!"

A breathless chuckle escaped me as I wheezed out, "Sure... you... did..." I pushed the exhaustion out of my mind and split my focus. I began to concentrate on lightning, the raw voltaic energy from the heavens. I willed the energy in my hand to take shape, slowly charging beneath my skin and deep in my channels.

My veins and muscles themselves ached and burned from the constant movement of energy in our heated duel. I clenched my teeth as the pressure in my hand built to a painful degree. By the time I looked up, she had multiple orbs of water floating behind her back. She leaped at me in a flying kick with frightening speed. With a pulse of energy, bolts of water arced out in a barrage as she soared towards me. I dashed to meet her and weaved the first bolt before getting hit square in the chest by four others.

Dull pain shot up from all over my upper body. A grimace escaped as I pushed past the pain, weaving to the left of her kick. My arm jetted straight toward her now open side. In a quick motion she moved her arm into position to block. Unable to change my trajectory, I released the electric charge inside my palm.

With a loud pop and a crack, she flew backward, the shimmering gauntlet of energy she had formed was almost shattered and smoking. My aura fared no better, it sizzled and bubbled as it slowly disintegrated back into particles.

A sharp whistle escaped her lips as she examined the gauntlet. "Now that, that is a good hit," she said in a teasing voice.

I ignored her and focused once more on gathering energy. Before I could gather enough to fully repair all the scales, she was upon me once more. I crossed my arms as her fist slammed into my defense. My guard was blasted apart as I reeled backward and struggled to find my footing. Before I could, another jab shattered the scales under my shirt, barely missing my solar plexus. With a smirk, her hand arced upward and grabbed the collar of my shirt.

Her energy imbued arms lifted me easily off the ground as I flailed desperately. I repeatedly slammed her spectral-gauntlet-clad forearm with my fists to no avail. Each hit felt like impacting a solid wall.

She smiled at me. "It will only hurt more if you keep struggling."

"I don't... go down... that easily," I panted out as my flailing grew weaker.

"Well, should've asked nicely." She threw a punch and slammed my stomach. Gagging and coughing, nausea began to overtake me. "Do you yield?"

My vision swam. I looked into her once warm brown eyes that now stared back cold as ice. "I-I... I yield," I sputtered out. I felt her grip release and the world spun as I slammed into the mat.

I lay on the ground, wheezing for a moment as the pain subsided and my vision returned. I rolled onto my back and stared up at the rocky ceiling. My muscles ached as I pushed myself up to a sitting position to catch my breath. Abigail was now sitting on one of the benches. Water lazily floated through the air and into her mouth. Her eyes met mine. "Thirsty?" As I opened my mouth to respond, a ball of water the size of my head slammed into my face. My back hit the mat again from the impact. Slowly, I sat back up, glaring at her as I wiped the droplets out of my eyes.

Ignoring her guffawing laughter, I stood up. I slowly hobbled over to the bench she was sitting on and collapsed next to her. "How'd I do?"

"In terms of your energy control, your aura was there. Though it was a bit flimsy, it seemed to hold up without much focus. Your gathering of energy is almost embarrassing, and your elemental control seemed pretty, well, uncontrolled."

"You could've taken my arm off if I was weaker. Adding on the fact that you only used it once and it was a sizable uncontrolled attack, you have very little to no control. I will give you credit however in your hand-to-hand combat. You're pretty solid there. I would say your energy and elemental prowess are low bronze for sure, but your hand-to-hand combat is better than most bronze fighters I've seen."

"Thanks," I grumbled back, "What do you even get out of these?"

I sat back up and looked her in the eyes and listened to her explanation, "Anhalt is a city ruled by strength, so almost everything. From popularity to military status," I perked up as a question floated to my mind, "To winning petty arguments, that rating is the single most important thing you can have."

"What rating would a captain be then?" My mind drifted to Hundri and the times he had used magic.

She raised an eyebrow. "Captains all have to be high silver, most of them are gold. Why do you ask?"

I stared deep into her eyes, studying the obvious curiosity plastered on her face. "Curiosity," I responded simply in an attempt to not reveal too much. "Speaking of curiosity, how do you use your element so smoothly?"

"You might've guessed," with a flick of her wrist, water rose from one of the troughs, "but creating something from pure energy is much harder than manipulating something that already is there. All though, that isn't much of an option for you, is it?"

With a sigh, I slumped backwards. "Yeah, I suppose you're right."

"Anyway Mr. Curious, weren't you supposed to be going somewhere?"

"Damn it!" I exclaimed loudly. I had completely lost track of time. I groaned and pulled myself off the bench in a hurry. My rushed footsteps echoed through the room as I jogged towards the door and threw it open. I had no clue where I was, and no clue how to get back to where I was.

I put on my most charming smile and turned back around slowly, "Hey Abigail..." I sang. "Would you mind helping me find my way back?"

"Yeah, yeah, sure." She pushed herself off the bench and strode over to me. Her hands wrapped around the edge of the door and held it open. She gestured me through. "Ladies first," she said with an almost believably genuine smile.

"Very funny," my voice dripped with sarcasm as I stood firm. We stared at each other for a moment.

"Would a lady do this?" Before I could react, her foot was pressed against my abs. With a sudden push, I stumbled through the doorway. She glanced down as I pulled myself to my feet and locked eyes with my glare. With a chuckle, she walked past and patted my head, "Suck it up. Look in the mirror, your hair is almost below your shoulders."

"Whatever," I grumbled back as I looked around. We were in a long hallway we had taken to get to her training room, each side lined with doors that lead to private training rooms. The architecture and materials were the same as the streets outside, dark stone, dark wood, and bright marble. Tall arches lined with bronze held up a chiseled, detailed ceiling bathed in cool white light from hanging runelights.

We walked in silence for a minute, the only sound was the squeaking of our feet against the floor. As a corner came into view at the end of the hall, a young man came around ahead of us. He strutted confidently towards us and carried himself with an arrogant aura. His clean-cut swept-back black hair bounced with every step and his blazing amber eyes starkly contrasted with his silver-trimmed deep navy uniform. It was clearly tailored to him, looking almost as sharp as his jawline.

"Ahh Abigail, you should know it's against academy policy to bring..." His voice shifted into one of almost disgust, "commoners this deep into the academy, even worse the private training rooms."

I glanced between his pompous glare and Abigail's twitching face. "Kayne," The agitation in her voice was apparent, "Why don't you go back to practicing your little party tricks in your room, so I don't have to ruin a perfectly nice hallway."

His face contorted in mock surprise, "My, my, was that a threat Abigail? I'm hurt! Do I need to report this to the headmaster?"

"Go ahead," she snarled, "I don't have time to kiss your wealthy ass like everyone else. Maybe if you had the balls to challenge me to a duel you could prove your money wasn't the only thing you were good for."

With that last remark, Abigail grabbed me by the arm and pulled me forward. Kayne sneered back at us as we went. Abigail opened the exit of the private training wing and pulled us both into a large empty lobby area.

Even though we had passed through it earlier, it was still astonishingly eye catching. It was a tall cylindrical room with a large domed roof that was covered in bronze inlay depicting vines and leaves. In the center sat a large, ornate spiral staircase. Different seating areas with large, padded chairs, couches and coffee tables ringed the banister of the deep steps. Two other hallways stretched out on opposite ends that bustled with people in different colored uniforms. Large stone signs hung above each door to signify the purpose of each room. Ignoring the hallways full of people, we descended the tall staircase. After a short trip down the large staircase, we found a side exit that led to the street.

Once we were no longer surrounded by her peers, I built the nerve to speak. "So, who was that lovely Kayne guy? He seemed like a real gem."

A bitter chuckle left her lips. "The pompous rich kid of a noble family. I sort of do hope he challenges me to a duel so I can wipe that smug smile from his face, though there would be a lot of drama. We're considered opposite 'rising stars' among the new class."

We pushed open the door and walked into a back alley. "What do you mean opposites? Besides the fact that he's a pompous ass and a bully," I paused for a second and smirked, "Although with how you just kicked my ass you might as well be a bully."

Her laugh was drowned out as we stepped onto the street, "Mostly because of our styles of fighting and upbringings. I come from a poor family, a commoner family as he would say. I earned my spot at this academy, unlike him who paid off the board." She clenched her fists for a moment before slowly letting them go limp at her sides. "His fighting style is to run like a scared child and throw countless ranged attacks. I don't think I've ever seen him fighting hand to hand. The core of it though is probably because I'm a water elementalist and he specializes in fire."

"Well, I can definitely see how that would make you opposites," I said with a chuckle. "Is that why you called his magic party tricks?"

"Exactly. Fire is all flash and bright attention-grabbing attacks, while water has a subtle beauty to it. The way it flows and changes, gentle yet still powerful. It's a very flexible element, making it very intuitive to manipulate."

I watched in amusement with a small smile as she walked and talked about the essence of water. Her eyes seemed to sparkle as she talked about it, her passion apparent. The more she described the subtleties and nature of her element, the more I realized why she was so proficient in water; she was almost an embodiment of those traits. She was beautifully fluid and persistent.

The way she talked about how simple and straight forward it was for her element to manifest spurred envy in my heart. "I wish my element was that natural to use. Lightning is so erratic and volatile. To actually use it I have to let go of controlling it and just let it flow out."

She frowned slightly, "You shouldn't let go of control of your element. If you put too much energy into an attack and can't control it, you'll end up hurting someone you care about or worse." She raised her forearm.

"I know I shouldn't let go of control," I sighed again, "But I'm really unsure how to control it otherwise."

She walked in silence for a moment as her index finger traveled to her lips. "I'm not sure how much this will help as it's something water elementalists use, but maybe don't try to control it. Just try loosely guiding it. Precise control is something usually gold mages and rarely some silvers can accomplish, but for bronze it's better to think of it like you're pushing it in the right direction rather than managing every aspect of it."

A smile spread slowly as I processed her words, "Somehow, that makes sense for lightning too. I'll try to focus on guidance more next time. Thank you."

Her warm smile reflected the swirling nebulas of the sky, "Of course! Anytime Rey." I smiled back and we walked in silence for a moment before taking a turn back into the large circular plaza.

Most of the people had left, only a few couples and drunk friends now stumbled about. "Well Abigail, I'm going to go do what I actually came here for now but thank you for the fun afternoon."

"Yeah! Thank you too Rey, we should do this again sometime. I'd love to teach you another lesson." She smiled mischievously and handed me a small metal card with runes engraved into it.

"What's this?" I examined the unfamiliar runes for a moment before pushing an inkling of energy into the card. The runes shifted and warped into a small picture of her with information about her next to it. "Never mind, I think I get it now, Ms. Depthart."

She shot me one more smile before turning away, her auburn hair swaying in rhythm with her hips as she walked away. As I turned, I heard her call back to me, "I'll be here tomorrow training if you want to watch again!"

I tried to suppress my smile and walked towards the fountain in the center of the plaza. My reflection stared back at me from the crystalline water. The exhaustion was obvious on my face from days of over-exertion and pushing myself to my limits. I leaned down and cupped water into my hands, letting the cold liquid splash against my face.

I wiped the water off my face with the shoulder of my tunic and began to search for the Hell's Pavilion. The stores and establishments around the plaza were clearly high end. Each restaurant sold food that smelled like slices of heaven. The artifacts stores and equipment stores were also clearly very well known, with equipment bejeweled in glowing energy crystals and adorned with pieces from different beasts.

Each place appeared to be exquisite at what they were but infuriatingly lacked the one thing I was looking for: any connection to Hell's Pavilion. That is, until I found a small artifact store with a large crystalline eye on its sign. I opened the door and stepped inside. Instantly I was overcome with the scent of old books, grease and burned objects.

Every wall was packed full of various baubles and trinkets. There were rows of glass cases with beautiful jewelry, shelves of various potions, tinctures and racks of magical tools. At the far end was a large, paneled counter where a young man stood. Behind him was an open doorway with shelves of books and tools, clearly a workspace for making artifacts.

The young man's voice interrupted my thoughts, "Hello! Welcome to the Tuldrin Emporium!" He swept back his volumetric black hair. "Is there anything I can help you with?"

I walked up to the table and gave him a tight-lipped smile before handing him the medallion Hundri had entrusted me. "Does this look familiar to you?"

He pulled glasses out of his white-collared dress shirt pocket and inspected the medallion. The outer edge of the lenses flared brightly for a moment as he examined the crystalline iris. After a moment he folded up the glasses and placed them back in his pocket.

A wide smile formed on his handsome face. "Welcome to Hell's Pavilion, live well and fight hard." With a click of a button under his table, the empty wall next to the workshop door slid downward, revealing a stone staircase that descended into blackness.

"Thank you," I gave him a curt nod and began to walk towards the steps.

He gave me a tight bow and adjusted his tight black pants. "A pleasure."

CHAPTER TEN

The Blades of Iora

Reynolds Helphain

As I descended the dimly lit dungeon-like staircase, I was alone with the pattering of my footsteps. I shivered. After the quick downwards spiral, I came to a large ornate door. It was a large black slab of dull metal, accented with bronze geometric lines and a large slot shaped like an eye. After fishing around in my pocket for a moment, I retrieved the gold metal medallion. With a click and a hum, it slotted into place.

The bronze glowed a bright azure for a moment as the door began to pull itself apart. The medallion dropped back into my hand as the last bits of the dark stone pulled themselves into the wall, revealing the room beyond.

It was clearly an area for the higher-class members of society. I stepped out into the dimly lit room and took in everything around me. The sound of quiet string instruments and horns crept into my ears along with the murmurs of quiet conversations from the bar to my left. There were surprisingly few people, some sat or stood at the tall bar drinking, while the other few sat at tables by the musicians quietly enjoying a various meal.

The ceiling and walls were supported with large dark stained wood that hung dim orange crystals. The light reflected playfully in the bottles behind the bar as I walked past the quietly talking men and women in various sets of armor. I looked around for Hundri but found nobody.

With a sigh I leaned against the bar and waited for the bar tender to come over. I closed my eyes and took a long breath through my nose;

the scent of booze and beer created a unique atmosphere that felt somehow nostalgic.

The man sitting next to me clapped a hand on my back. "Aye! Welcome in, boy."

I turned to the portly man as he withdrew his extremely muscular arm. "Thanks." I sighed.

"So, yer with Halvor's boy, ye?" He swept his only glowing orange eye over me. The other milky eye stared listlessly into nothingness.

I looked at the grey-haired man in surprise as he adjusted the hair from his eyes and retied a bun on the back of his head. "How did you—"

"Not important." He grinned and took a sip of the amber liquid in his wooden mug. "Name's Orlin. Blacksmith."

"I'm Rey. Hundri's..." I looked at the ceiling, pondering. "Apprentice?"

He nodded slowly. "He can pick em' good."

"What do you mean?"

He grinned wider and pointed at his eye. "A gift. Anyway, cause yer here for Hundri, he's back thata way." He gestured with his thumb towards a hallway.

I nodded. "Thanks, Orlin."

He grunted and went back to drinking.

I walked through the empty center of the large room and into the hallway until I reached the fifth door. It resembled the door I had seen at the front, and I immediately knew what to do. I pressed the medallion into the socket as the cold metal beneath my fingertips began to heat.

With a flare of azure light and a click, the door pulled itself apart. the medallion. I let the medallion drop into my hand and walked into the room. The second the door reformed, green runes along the inside of the door frame flared with light. I climbed a small staircase and found myself in a similarly constructed room with Hundri and a group of people staring at me.

They sat in a booth around a beautifully carved table on a large U-shaped couch, drinks in hand. Above them hung a warmly glowing bronze chandelier, dimly illuminating a bar against one wall and a rack of random trinkets, armor and weapons on the other.

I cleared my throat, clenched my fists and introduced myself, "Hello, I'm Reynolds Helphain. Hundri's apprentice—" I was cut off as they all clambered out of the couch and cheered drunkenly.

A portly man with unruly ginger hair and puffy cheeks wrapped his thick arms around my waist, squeezing the air from my lungs. His gruff voice filled my ears as he talked with unnecessary volume, "Ayyy! Welcome to the family Rey!"

The stench of alcohol made me recoil slightly as I stepped backwards and responded weakly, "Yeah. Thanks."

A small woman pushed him away so she could get a look at me, her eyes racing across me, seemingly taking in every detail. I took a step back instinctively. She wore a simple black loose-fitting tunic that hid most of her robust body. Her blue baggy pants rustled as she took another step closer, and the clasp of her dark leather belt caught the light. Her vibrant emerald eyes swept over me from beneath well-kept, wavy golden hair the contrasted a silver chain necklace around her neck.

"Sorry about him," She rolled her eyes, "He likes to meet new people." She was clearly less intoxicated from the way her words flowed with elegance. She shook her head in disapproval at the portly man, who's head drooped slightly in response. "That lovable man is Ogland, my husband. I am Yaldrie. The voice of reason." She gestured to the rest of the group, "Go on, introduce yourselves."

I recognized the first man. Before he could open his mouth to introduce himself, I cut him off, "Let me guess, earth mage? And a fist fighter?"

His eyes widened on his alcohol-flushed face as he took another sip from his wooden mug, "How'd... you guess?" he slurred out.

I mischievous smile tugged at my lips, "Old man. Grade five shield."

His face flushed brighter. He cleared his throat and introduced himself before any of his group members could ask about how I knew about his element and fighting style. "My name... Gods' above what is my name? Right, Hello, I'm Ralteir."

"And voice of idiocrasy," Yaldrie cut in.

"Shut it!" he yelled back, inciting howling laughter from everyone present. A smile tugged at my lips.

A slender girl who didn't look much older than myself walked up to me slowly, a bun of jet-black hair on her head jostled with every step. Her soul-piercing golden eyes met mine and she smiled. "Hey! I'm Syre and I'm the range specialist of the team. I get the feeling we're going to get along *really* well." She waggled her eyebrows at me as she took another sip of booze. I stared at her for a moment, confused at her drunken nonsense.

Before I could give it more thought, Hundri stepped up and slapped her on the back of the head. "Gods above Syre! Control yourself!"

She cried out in pain, "Hey! Hey! I'm sorry, okay?" she dropped her voice to a mutter "You're no fun." Hundri smacked her on the back of the head again and she simply glared up at him as Hundri introduced himself.

"Hey Rey, as you probably could tell, I'm Hundri and am this wild group's leader," I nodded in response and looked towards the next person.

A slender man glanced up at me as he brushed chin length, messy brown hair from his eyes. "Hello. I'm Kai. I specialize in artificing."

Syre answered my unasked question as she wrapped a firm arm around my shoulder, "Rey don't worry about him. He gets nervous when he meets new people, especially when he's drunk. Come and sit with me, have a drink."

"Well nice to meet you all. I'm in your hands from now on."

Cheers went up around the group as they celebrated their new member. Once all the noise had died down and we had sat back down, Hundri spoke, "So kid," his luminescent eyes flicked across my body, "Why do I see another person's energy signature on you, hm?"

Confusion struck me like a horse before ideas burst to life in my head. "Wait Hundri, you can *see* energy?" He nodded in response. I sat in silence for a moment, flabbergasted. After I finished processing my thoughts, I stumbled over my words as I answered. "I was out with a girl, that's probably why you see those."

He raised his eyebrows and whistled, "Okay so on your first date, she what? Beat you relentlessly with magic? I didn't know you were into that kind of thing."

I groaned and rubbed the bridge of my nose, "First off it wasn't a date, I just met her, and we sparred. Nothing like what you're thinking." Everyone except Syre groaned.

Syre gave me smile but said nothing.

I tried to steer the drunken lunatics away from their horribly misguided thoughts by asking them random questions as I shifted uncomfortably on the couch. "Does our group have a name?"

As if he had been lit up like a lightbulb, Ralteir spoke, "Well, we go by..." He paused for dramatic effect, "The Stone—"

Ogland loudly interrupted him, "Absolutely not! Yer the only damned stone mage in this team. Yer *also* the one who got us stuck with our current name! We can't change it after all these damned moon cycles." Everyone nodded in agreement besides Ralteir.

"I still feel like Stoneshapers is cooler," Ralteir muttered.

Ogland's voice boomed out once more, "Nobody but you can shape stone! How does it make any sense?" Ralteir went quiet once more, clearly dejected. "And you shoulda thought of that cycles ago!"

"Speaking of elements, what do you all use?" I asked the group, once again trying to stop the entropy of the conversation.

Hundri spoke up first, "The *coolest* element of them all," He paused, waiting for someone to laugh at his pun, only to be met with deadpan stares, "Ice. Get it? Cool? Ice?" Everyone remained deadpan and we quietly moved on to the next person.

Ogland spoke up next, "Fire," he said simply.

Then Yaldrie, "One of the two wind mages in this disorganized team"

Syre chimed in next, "I'm the other wind mage of the group."

After her was Kai, "My element doesn't matter. I'm not really a combatant, so I use things I make."

Once they had all gone, Syre returned my question, "What about you Rey? Hundri didn't tell us yet."

"I use lightning."

"Oh wow!" exclaimed Yaldrie. "I heard those are pretty rare!"

To everyone's surprise, Syre hadn't said a word. She only sat there smiling at me, making it obvious she had something to say. I sighed, "Just say it, Syre."

"I'm sure you can keep things... *electrifying*." Groans shot up around the group.

I ignored Syre's comment and addressed Yaldrie, "How rare are lightning mages? I know they're uncommon, but I didn't think they were *that* rare."

Yaldrie thought for a second, "Well... if you look at Anhalt's population of around ten thousand, there's maybe... four hundred lightning mages? Compared to earth mages, there's definitely over a thousand of them. The rarest elemental affinity though is gravity, there's probably only ten or less in Anhalt. One of them gets to boss Hundri here around on a daily basis."

Hundri groaned in annoyance, "Damn Ronhelm to the void! He hasn't given me a *real* assignment in ages! Hunting that fugitive was the first *real* assignment he had given me in *cycles*. I swear because of Halvor they won't let me do anything *real*. All because of those God forsaken stones."

"Stones?" I thought back to the statue of Halvor and slowly began to connect the dots.

Hundri groaned again, "Yeah! They are these *supposedly* special rocks that my father found. Nobody knows what they truly even do, even my father wouldn't tell me. All anyone knows is they're strong. If I die, I think they're *scared* nobody will be able to use the power of Anhalt's greatest heroes."

We all went silent for a moment before Ogland spoke, "A heavy burden to bear." After a moment, he raised his mug, "To Halvor!"

"To Halvor!" everyone echoed as they gulped down more of the amber liquid in their mugs.

"Oh! I forgot to pour you a drink lad," Ogland exclaimed as he began to stand from the table.

Quickly, I gestured him to sit back down, "Honestly, I'm not sure drinking is the best idea right now." I glanced at Syre.

Ogland followed my gaze and chuckled, "Aye, likely for the best then. No telling what *some* of these people might do,"

Syre's eyes widened as she realized we were talking about her, "Hey! I'm just making friends!"

"Really Syre?" He stared seriously at her, "Don't remember you treating *us* like that all those cycles ago, eh?"

She glared up at him for a moment, "Whatever."

Syre and Ogland tapped their mugs together and finished off the liquid inside. While those two slurped down their alcohol, Yaldrie spoke up, "Well Rey, Hundri here told us you already managed to take down your first enchanted beast, and alone even!"

I nodded, "Yeah. It was this big white bear."

Kai's eyes seemed to light up and he began to talk almost too fast to understand, "Impressive! Did you manage to get its pelt?"

Taken aback from his sudden enthusiasm, I slowly answered, "Well, Hundri should still have it."

Hundri grunted and slowly got up from the table and grabbed a bag from the wall. With a tug, he pulled the white bear's pelt out of its leather depths. Kai dashed from the table as well, eagerly snatching the tightly rolled pelt from Hundri.

"Make a cloak out of it if you can, Kai." I called over. He nodded in response without looking, almost salivating over the bear's fur.

"How'd you take care of such a large beast if you're... well," Yaldrie hesitated, unable to find the right words.

I laughed at her attempt to be polite, "The word you're probably looking for is weak." She chuckled nervously but made no effort to correct me. "It wasn't too hard to kill," I lied. "I used the terrain around me to make it easier, using stalagmites like spears to pierce its hide. Finished it by ripping out its eye from deep inside it."

They nodded and cheered, throwing up their mugs. "Ay lad, using the terrain as an advantage is the mark of a warrior alright." Ogland slurred out after trying to take a sip of his now empty mug. He growled at his mug and hurled it across the room, and it clattered into the corner.

"Thanks, Ogland," I chuckled. It was obvious these people were close friends and had been through hell and back together. From the depths of my thoughts, I noticed Ogland starting to tip over.

I shot my arm out and caught his head before it reached the hard wood of the table. His beard tickled my hand as I jostled his head to keep him awake. My head swiveled to look at Hundri and I gave him a slightly concerned look.

Hundri nodded and his voice boomed out over the group, "Okay guys. I think it's time to call it a night, poor Ogland can't handle the booze anymore and you guys won't be up for tomorrow's training if you all are complaining about hangovers."

They all groaned and began to file out. Their steps swayed as they walked out from around the table, which only proved my point. Before they left, they each grabbed their weapons, armor and other belongings from the walls.

Hundri pulled the same simple longsword he had when we met from the wall and clipped it to his belt. He slung the backpack over one of his shoulders and covered it with a dark cyan cloak.

Ogland pulled a massive sword almost the size of his body off the wall. In a fluid motion, he slung the impossibly large hunk of metal over his shoulder and onto his back. It had hundreds of tiny runes running down the wide flat of the blade that eventually touched a large orange gem on the inward curving hilt. Other than the great sword, Ogland had no other possessions to carry with him.

His wife, Yaldrie, put on a deep forest green cloak and grabbed a tall, old wooden staff. Its thick wooden prongs held a glowing green gem at the top with small runes running along the length of the wood.

Syre grabbed a small rod-like handle that was covered in runes. With a flourish, a large combat knife caught the light as she spun it into a leather sheath on her lower back. She then began to strap leather plates and guards all over her tight black clothes.

Kai and Ralteir didn't have anything to grab. They seemingly wore everything they needed. Ralteir wore leather fingerless gloves, with iron studs on the knuckles, small metal plates and pauldrons for protection. Kai wore nothing that seemed battle related at all, only a sharp dress shirt, stylish pants, many rings, watches, jewelry and a belt covered in pouches.

One by one, they all filed out and bid us goodbye until it was only Hundri and I in the room. "Well kid, what'd you think of my friends?"

I smiled, "They're fun. They all seemed pretty strong too, I don't think I could beat a single one."

Hundri laughed, "Yeah, they're some of the strongest people I know."

"Let's get you home old man. You need to be ready for training tomorrow as well." I watched him attentively, ready to support him if need be. As we approached, the door pulled itself apart and clicked shut behind us as we stepped into the quiet hallway. As we stepped out into the main room, I paused, and I swept the room for Orlin. The musicians had begun to pack up and the bartender was in the process of ushering the few remaining drunkards out of the bar. Orlin was nowhere in sight.

"What's wrong?" Hundri turned to me, noticing I had stopped.

"I was looking for someone. They left." I caught up and we continued forwards.

Hundri gave me a sly grin. "Was it the girl?"

"No," I chuckled. "An old guy. Said he was a friend of your father's."

His smile faded slightly. "Ah. Old Orlin. He's a good man."

"He seemed like it."

As we walked past, the bartender bowed slightly and Hundri nodded in response. We ascended the dungeon-like stairs and popped out into the trinket store. Before we reached the door to leave, Hundri handed me a small golden coin and whispered in my ear, "Toss that to the young man who let you in."

I turned around and flicked the coin in the direction of the counter. With a cut nod, he called to us as we stepped through the door, "Thank you! Come again Sir Traegan and...?"

I shot him a smile, "Reynolds Helphain." With that, we stepped back into the plaza. The sky's light had died down to a dim mix of purples and blues, with pin pricks of white light that emulated faint stars. We walked into the now dimly lit streets, each squeak of our boots echoing through the vacant houses.

The once bustling streets had thinned to only the occasional wanderer. Most of the people we walked past were stumbling through the dark, tripping over themselves in a drunken stupor as they tried to find a way home. Occasionally groups of guards would stroll past on patrol and gave salutes to Hundri if they noticed him, which he returned.

After countless turns and what felt like hours of walking, we reached a door. It was a relatively average building compared to the rest of the buildings I'd seen on Halvor road with similar design. It was around three floors tall with large balconies extending on the front of each floor.

I opened the front door and entered the lobby. Paintings of beautiful mountains and landscapes hung on the white walls above couches and furniture to relax in. Against the wall opposite the entrance was a door labeled as the entrance to the stairs.

We hurried through the empty lobby and up two flights of stairs, where we found a locked door labeled, "Hulgarth,"

I raised an eyebrow and look at Hundri, "Are you sure you live here?"

He smiled slightly, "It's for anonymity. I'm a bit famous you see."

He pressed his pendant into a small indent in the wall and with a click the door swung open. I walked inside with Hundri and immediately felt like something was wrong.

He flopped onto a nearby couch, sank into its cushions and began snoring. I sighed and looked around Hundri's living room. The room was eerily familiar, down to the wallpaper and the furniture. The walls had a plain white wallpaper with dark wooden accents. It was a small space with a couch facing a long knee-height table with a blanket folded on it, a rack for guests to put their coats on and some paintings along the walls in between doorways to different rooms.

I had seen it all before, in Hundri's mind.

I grabbed the blanket from the table and laid It over Hundri's sleeping form. I cracked open the first of three doors, finding a bland hallway with a few doors. Ignoring that section of his home, I opened the second door. The cold refreshing air of the cavernous city washed over me as I stepped out onto the balcony.

The cool air filled my lungs as I gasped at the gorgeous view. The city stretched on for what looked like eternity, and the swirling mosaic of a sky cast dim gorgeous light over the jagged tiled roofs of the buildings. Taken aback by the view, I sat down on a firm long chair. The weight of my exhaustion crashed down with the weight of my body onto the cushions as my eyes grew heavy. My thoughts and desires started to fade along with my consciousness as the depths of sleep pulled my mind. Struggling proved pointless. I let myself go into the void.

CHAPTER ELEVEN

The Stones

Reynolds Helphain

    The sounds of the bustling streets filled my ears as I rose from the chair in a haze. The sky's brightness had returned, painting the white marble into shades of deep blue and violet all around me. I looked over the balcony, watching hundreds of people move through the streets like water in a stream. Each person wove to and from place to place in a chaotic harmony.

    I walked away from the edge of balcony and felt the cool metal handle of the door in my hand as I swung it open. The scent of grease and weapon polish filled my nose as I entered Hundri's home once more. The hinges of the door creaked as I stepped back into the hallway that I chose not to explore the night before. I followed the scent into the first door on my left and found Hundri hunched over a large table polishing an ornate sword.

    Oblivious to my entry to the room, he took a large swig from a large leather waterskin next to him. Slowly, he sheathed the sword and examined it for a moment. I sat in silence while I leaned against the frame of the door, watching him work.

    He stood from the table and placed the sword on a rack with tens of swords and bladed weapons. As he massaged his forehead, he walked over to a stand with armor on the opposite wall. His eyes flicked over its sparking steel surface in admiration.

    My jaw went slack. I recognized that armor. Sitting plainly and clearly in this room with no protection was Halvor's armor and sword. It was a simple suit of armor with detailed runes and glyphs hammered into its plates. Ever shifting and moving pearlescent stones lay embedded in the backs of the gauntlets, pauldrons, breastplate, and thigh-guards.

Clenched in the gauntlets of the armor was Halvor's sword. It was in a sheath of black leather, with detailed silver inlays running along the length of the scabbard. Where the sheath touched the hilt of the sword, glowing blue runes blazed brightly, casting a faint ethereal glow over the armor. The hilt was shaped like the wings of a falcon, with hundreds of tiny runes running through the grooves of its feathers. The handle was also wrapped in the same dark leather, capped off with the head of a falcon as the pommel.

I could hear Hundri's gruff voice, but it was slowly reduced to a dull murmur. Something whispered in my mind in a language I couldn't understand. Before I could realize it, I felt myself moving towards the armor. As much as I tried, I couldn't control myself. Hundri turned to me and gave me a smile. His mouth moved up and down, but no sound escaped it, only more whispering. His brow furrowed in confusion, and he began to stand as I reached outward and touched one of the pearlescent stones.

I blinked. Sweat rolled down my face in a salty stream. A weight pulled at my chest as I slowly looked around and watched Hundri disperse into colored specks. I yanked my hand away from the stones as fast as my body allowed. My labored breath came out in frantic pants as the room around me began to crumble away. The walls crumbled into dust and were whisked away revealing only a sea of endless rippling darkness.

As the building around me blew away in an incorporeal wind, I ran. Each step on the dark void felt like I was moving through honey. It reflected a light that did not exist, making each step ripple outward as if it was water. From behind me, I heard a quiet squelch. My blood ran cold, and my breath froze in my chest.

I slowly turned around. It felt as if a thousand rocks were strapped to my body and every instinct screamed to run. Not a foot away floated a massive eye. I leaped backward in a panic and felt its piercing gaze track me as I landed a few feet away. All around me squelching noises began to resound through the void. Every direction I looked my gaze was met with a massive eye staring back. Then the voices began to come from every direction.

He is not ready...

Cast him to depths...

A walking catastrophe...

Unworthy...

Impure...

A guttural scream escaped me as inky black arms reached from the all-consuming sea of darkness below me. Their icy grasp pulled me downward and to my knees as the eyes leered. I frantically swung at my arms as I willed energy to protect me to no avail. The world ignored me. Where the inky abyss wrapped my limbs, numbness spread. Dread filled my mind.

Slowly, the will to move was torn away.

I stretched my hand to the dark sky as my head began to descend through the veil of liquid darkness. A final prayer escaped me. I opened my eyes within the depths, only to find a true void. Nothing, no points of reference to look for. No liquid floor. Once again, the eyes flew open all around me.

A soft, yet authoritative woman's voice boomed into the recesses of my mind, *You. Time runs out. Claim your birthright. Fight.*

I opened my mouth to scream, but no sound came out. I glared back at the massive eyes. More arms began to coalesce around me, flying to me from the murky darkness. Their claw-like fingers dug into every bit of my flesh. Another soundless scream escaped my lips, burning pressure arced out from each wound. Tears tried to run down my face but floated away in the void as each throb of my heart sent waves of molten pain across my body.

For those within you, in memory and spirit, you must fight. Remember.

Memories flashed through my mind, Serena, Hundri, my father, playing in the snow, climbing cliffs with my sister, and my father reading dusty books in the study. With one final mute scream, my mind slipped away.

. . .

My head throbbed and my ears rang. The world seemed to be moving in slow motion as I fell in an ungraceful arc towards the ground. My vision flickered in and out of darkness as my mind returned from the nightmarish mindscape. My body fell into Hundri's arms as he lunged to catch me, saving my head from slamming into the polished wooden floorboards.

Hundri leaned me against a simplistic yet high quality drawer next to Halvor's armor, his mouth moved, but all sound was drowned out. I groaned as I slowly sat myself up so my back wouldn't jab into the smooth metal handles. The ringing dulled down and allowed me to finally understand Hundri.

"Hey! Kid! Are you okay? You almost really hurt yourself! What happened?" His voice was filled with worry.

I rubbed my temples in an attempt to quell the spikes of pain hammering my brain but was given no relief. "I'm fine," I muttered. "How long was I out?"

His brows creased in worry and confusion, "Out? It looked like you tripped on nothing and couldn't move. Did something happen?"

"I—" A chill ran down my spine, I could almost feel the cold grip of the ethereal hands wrapping around my neck. "I went to some sort of void. Hundreds of eyes stared at me, whispering in my ears as they wrapped ethereal hands around me and pulled me down into the depths."

A range of emotions flashed across his face as he processed the information, I had given him. "What did they say to you? And that happened when you touched the white stone right?"

"It's kind of a blur. When I touched the stone, they told me I wasn't ready for something and that I had a birthright to fight for, whatever that means," my voice shuddered as I recalled the words of the voices.

I looked up at the stones and my stomach dropped. They were all gone. He followed my gaze and shot upwards. "Where did they go?" He looked down at me frantically. "What did you *do*?"

"I..." I stuttered. "I'm just as confused as you are."

He slumped down to the floor with me. "I don't understand..." He looked at the ceiling, as if in silent prayer. He sighed, long and hard. "I'm sorry you had to go through that Rey. I..." he hesitated for a second, "On every front, I'm just as lost as yourself."

"It's alright. I think I'm going to take a walk to clear my head. Before that though, care to show off your collection?" I gave him a weak smile to hide how much it had rattled me.

He nodded, stood up and offered me a helping hand. I wrapped my hand around his, feeling the rough callouses in his palm as he practically threw me off the floor. I looked at grooves where the stones had been in Halvor's armor once more before turning toward Hundri.

He lifted a sword off the rack and walked toward me. It flew for a moment as he tossed it to me. The simple scabbard was wrapped in a rough black leather, with silver on either end. I unsheathed the blade and placed the scabbard on the table to my left. It flourished in a beautiful arc through the air, its blade was reflective to a mirror finish. The only thing that caught the light was a thin line of runes running up the length of the blade. It had a simple cross guard in the form of a beveled, simple piece of metal. The handle was simply wrapped in bands of leather, and it was capped off at the pommel with a silver dome.

My curiosity over the runes along the blade got the better of me. Both my hands wrapped the handle as I pushed energy into the blade. The energy began to race down the length of the blade and toward the runes, but before it could reach them it began to dissipate back into the air. I ignored my frustration, released a hand from its handle and pushed energy into my fingertips. They pressed against the cold metal of the blade and ran along the runes. A trail of energy seeped into the runic markings as I dragged them along the length.

With a hum, the runes sparked to life with a green glow for a moment and the edges began to whistle. I slashed the sword and was surprised at the lack of resistance the air offered my blade. A moment later, the enchantment was gone, the sword returned to its non-magical state.

"What's this blade called?" I asked, my eyes still locked on the runes as I tried to understand the complex marks.

Hundri grinned in response, "That one was one of my father's favorites, the Sword of Whistling Winds. Although it's not the original, only a recreation, it's still very powerful."

I sheathed the sword again and tossed it back to him. "The engraving was interesting; wind magic I assume?"

He nodded in response before striding back over to the rack of weapons, "Which of these do you want to see next?"

The floorboards creaked slightly under my feet as I walked next to him and began to survey the swords. Each one was greatly different, no two alike. None truly pulled my interest as my eyes flew over them until I spotted a small, black dagger. I picked it up and pulled it out of its simple dark leather sheath and examined it.

Its handle seemed to be wrapped in durable, worn bandages with a black metal pommel and a jagged guard. Along the guard ran silver inlays in the shape of feathers and situated in the center was a small purple gem. It had a long onyx blade, and instead of runes running along its flat, it had long grooves that looked akin to veins.

I hesitated and stared down at its blade as its crystalline structure seemed to shift slightly every second. "Is this- Is this the knife of the Wings?"

He nodded solemnly and I put it back in its sheath. The only noise in the room was the soft sound of the blade running along the inside of the leather. I placed it back on the shelf and moved on to other weapons. Once more, I found myself uninterested by the blades, each one blander than the last.

Hundri's voice penetrated my thoughts, "Hey kid, want me to help pick you a sword that you can keep?" I stared at him for a moment, shocked that he would let me keep a blade of this quality. "Don't worry, it won't be from the *nice* display case." He pressed on a panel of the wall, and another rack of less fancy swords slid out.

He glanced at me and seemed to be measuring me with his eyes. The swords rattled slightly as he ran his hands over the pommels until he settled on one. He picked up a longsword and handed it to me. It was similar to the others, simple with no real decorative flair. I pulled it from the sheath and flourished it through the air. I could feel the balance was perfect for my height as I did a few practice slashes and movements.

It clicked back into the scabbard as I looked over to Hundri, "So I can keep this one?"

He smiled and nodded back. "Yeah, go ahead kid." I ran the scabbard through a ring in my belt, securing it on my left hip. I practiced drawing the sword and sheathing it so I would be ready at a moment's notice.

"Thank you, Hundri." I smiled warmly at him before looking back at my sword. "I think I'm going to take a walk for a bit. I'll come find you guys later tonight."

His smile waned. "Sounds good. Go back to the military district exits, you'll find us near there if you wander a bit." After a short pause he reached into his pocket and pulled out a few silver coins. "And here, take these." He dropped the cold metal pieces into my open palm.

I shoved them in my pocket and walked to the door of the room and wrapped my fingers around the cold metal of the handle. "I'll be safe. Thanks again for the sword and coins."

With that, I stepped out of the room and closed the door behind me. I took a deep breath and strode down the hallway, staring at the ceiling blankly. I couldn't stop thinking about those stones, that armor, his sword. *What does it all mean?* I thought to myself. I hoped some magical answer would float to the surface, but none came.

I passed the living room, out the front door and back into the stairwell. My footsteps echoed on the chiseled stone stairs as I descended. Before I knew it, I was out in the street again. A mix of vile and intoxicating aromas overwhelmed my nose, comical quantities of fruity perfume, grease, weapon polish, and people who hadn't bathed in weeks. With no real direction, I began to walk down the street. My shoulders brushed passed cloaks, armor and all sorts of battle-ready garments as I looked once more for Halvor road.

In this district, each shop was vastly different. Between the design, materials and wares, every store felt unique. Some shops were brick and stone buildings built into larger complexes, while others were simply tents or boxes covered with awnings. None were interesting enough to truly pull my attention away from looking for directions. That was until I heard the ringing of a hammer.

I bumped into the black-cloaked man in front of me and stumbled backwards. He seemed unfazed, as if I had walked into a solid wall. Slowly, he turned to face me. To my surprise a scrawny looking man with trimmed black hair, amethyst eyes and sharp handsome features met my gaze. He glared down at me for a moment before turning back to watch something with a crowd of onlookers that blocked the street.

I weaved through the crowd. A familiar behemoth of a man who was almost entirely pure muscle slammed an ornate hammer onto a slab of red-hot metal in the shape of a sword. Each slam of his hammer kicked up sparks.

From my left, a burly man spoke, "I can't believe I get to watch the great smith Orlin forge another masterpiece!"

I smiled as he quenched the blade and pulled back his long scraggly silver hair into a bun. My feet scraped the pavement as I leaned over toward the burly man, "What are some works of his I might've heard of?"

He leaned towards me and lowered his voice slightly, "They say that he forged the weapons for the four great heroes."

He lifted the blade out and let the shimmering liquid flow off its golden blade. A cheer came from the crowd as they began to walk on now that the forging of the blade was apparently completed. After seeing Halvor's sword, I was truly impressed with his work.

The stagnant wall of onlookers returned to a flowing and pulsing tumult. His face twitched up into a slight smile as his glowing eye locked onto me before he turned back and returned to the innards of the smithy.

I moved with the streams of people, looking for familiar landmarks. As I walked my steps fell into a rhythm. They carried me across the large smooth stones with an almost silent squeak. Music filled my ears and the alluring aroma of expertly cooked food swept over me as I passed restaurants and cafés.

Each thing I passed looked increasingly more interesting, to the point where I wished I could delay my quest to look around at all the magic wares. I had no clue how long I would be staying in Anhalt, but I was already forming a long list of things to see and places to go. Absentmindedly I walked the streets, watching the mystic sky.

To my surprise, my body guided me where I wanted to go. Everything started to look more familiar as it clicked with my memory. With one more turn, the street opened into the massive plaza from before.

CHAPTER TWELVE

The Man of Darkness

Reynolds Helphain

Compared to when I arrived in the late afternoon the day before, it was completely different in the early hours of the morning. Hundreds of people wandered around the giant circle, playing games, enjoying music, and shopping in the stores lining the edges.

I pushed myself through the crowd and found the bench I had sat on the day before. I took a seat once more and closed my eyes. Something about the darkness was unnerving and eerie. I didn't feel safe in the dark anymore. I felt goosebumps rise on the back of my neck as I shuddered at the thought of those eyes.

I opened my eyes. A startled noise —something akin to a scream escaped me— as Abigail's warm eyes suddenly were right before me. "Hi!" She sang as she suppressed a laugh and pulled away.

My heart pounded. After a moment, I steadied my breath. "Good Gods Abigail, good morning." I stood up from the bench and met her gaze again.

"And good morning to you too," she said as an evil smile broke out across her face. She once again had her auburn hair tied back and wore a simple tight-fitting tunic and baggy pants. "Do you want to do a bit more training and sparring today? I'd *love* to win again."

A soft sigh left my lips, "Maybe if you taught me a bit more, I'd be able to give you a fair fight."

She softly chuckled as she grabbed me by the wrist, "Alright then, let's get to it."

With an unnatural amount of strength, she began to yank me down a street. I yelped in mock pain, "Hey, hey!" I called after her, "I can walk myself you know!"

She loosened her grip and let me catch up. "Well Rey," she glanced over at me with a smile before continuing, "Anything in particular you want to learn today? Also, I don't know if I mentioned this already, but nice sword." She tapped the scabbard on my hip.

I brushed my hand against the cold metal of the pommel as I responded, "Thanks. And honestly, I just need to work on every aspect of controlling my energy. My combat skills are fine, but the difference energy control makes is apparently huge."

"Sure!" She tried to suppress an evil smile but to no avail, "We can try dueling with swords if you want."

I sighed once again. "Let me guess, you're even better with a sword?"

"Maybe," she sang, now freely grinning devilishly.

We turned down another corner and the scenery got more familiar with each step. "I don't think you really know how to do much with lightning elementalists, but do you know anything I could do to strengthen my control?"

"I don't know. Just practice more."

"Well that much is obvious," I laughed.

The distant ringing of a hammer brought a question to my mind, "I know this is a little random, but you know the smith named Orlin?"

Her smile fell as she touched her lower lip in thought, "Ah, yeah. He used to be employed by the military council directly to make their weapons, many of the weapons used by the greatest heroes were made by him."

My brows furrowed slightly as my voice took an inquisitive tone, "Then... I don't understand how he could be working in such a low-end looking smithy in public. Doesn't feel like a legendary smith should have those conditions."

"Well," she paused, "Its rumored that all of his works come out beautiful and powerful, but he always scraps them. It's also rumored that he forged a cursed sword named Volay."

My eyebrows lifted, "A cursed sword? What's it's curse?"

Her face shifted into an unreadable mask as a slight edge crept into her voice, "Nobody is really sure the full scope of its abilities. Its runes engraved *themselves* into the blade when it was forged and even the most skilled artificers couldn't read them. From what we know, it's hard to discern the user's abilities from the abilities the sword itself provides."

"It's *still* being used?" I stopped in place for a second, stunned. "I thought cursed blades were so unstable they usually maimed or killed their users. How long has this thing been in use for?"

"The wielder of Volay has been on the loose for fifteen cycles. Nobody has been able to stop his rampage. He wanders from city to city, up and down this massive mountain massacring battalions and armies alike." Her knuckles went white. "Even butchering villages."

I scratched my light stubble as I thought and cleared my throat, "And what kind of elemental magic does he use?"

"That's the scariest part; he doesn't use an element. It's thought that he was either a rare person who wasn't born with an element, but nobody knows." She swallowed "It's scary to even say, but an already powerful warrior might have synergized with one of the least understood weapons in decades."

She was right about how scary that was. Orlin possibly created the tool of the greatest monster in cycles. It made sense why he lost so much status. "What does he look like then? I'd prefer to avoid running into him."

She chuckled weakly. "He has long dark gray hair, brilliant glowing white eyes that look devoid of life, a large, curved sword that's made of an onyx black metal and a glowing white crystal blade. People call him the Hollow Blade."

"I'll keep a lookout and pray to Yildaar I never meet him." A small smile danced on my lips. "All though it could be pretty exciting to clash swords with one of the strongest men alive."

Abigail rolled her eyes, "You're hopeless."

"You can't tell me you wouldn't *jump* at the opportunity to battle the wielder of Volay," I said between laughs.

Her face dropped behind an unreadable mask again. "Yeah. What I wouldn't give..."

I frowned slightly as I met her eyes and could almost see the lust for battle deep within. We turned another corner and reached the door we had come out of the previous day.

She rattled with the handle and tried to open the back entrance. After a second of frustration, she face-palmed herself and slipped a medallion into a carved slot in the doorframe. The door slid backwards on its bronze hinges and revealed the staircase from the day before.

Our footsteps echoed as we walked up the ornate wood and stone staircase. Before long, we reached the top and found ourselves before another door. She directed me out of the way and opened it slightly. Her hair danced as she quickly took a look either way before giving me a nod. "It's clear," she muttered toward me before she began to jog towards the door to the training rooms.

I quickly followed her through and down the hallway. The mild scent of sweat filled my nostrils more and more as I took steps into her training room. "Did you train here again last night?"

She raised an eyebrow slightly as she walked past me, her hair gently brushed my face as she passed. "Yeah, helps me process my thoughts I guess,"

I didn't want to push her, so I chose not to mention it, "I certainly wish I had that habit."

She chuckled softly and walked to the center of the mat and patted the ground in front of her. "Come here and sit down already. You wanted help, right?"

I dejectedly grumbled, "Yeah... yeah. Alright," as I walked over to her and sat down. We were face to face once again and her annoyingly smug grin got under my skin slightly.

"Here, can I enter your mind for a minute? I'm a little curious of all that goes on up in that crazy head of yours."

I tapped my forehead, "Go ahead, come on in."

I was met with a blank stare of confusion in return. "What? Mental connections are done with one of these." She lifted a small black chain with elegant runes carved into each link.

Now it was my turn to be confused, "What are *you* talking about? I've had someone enter my mind and I've never seen a chain like that before."

Her eyes lit up in surprise and she touched a finger to her lips, "You must've met someone powerful then. Who was it?"

"I'm not sure really, just a man in the mountains," I lied.

She cocked an eyebrow, "Why would you let some random person into your mind? Are you stupid?"

"I have no clue how to protect my mind from something like that so he just kind of appeared."

"Interesting... well with how strong you are, I'm surprised you're alive and are in one piece" She wrapped the black chain around her wrist, then mine. "That aside, are you ready?"

I gave her a short nod. The cool metal links began to heat up as energy coursed through them and the runes began to shine a bright white.

Her eyes rolled back in her head, and she went limp. A moment later, I followed suit.

. . .

Were my eyes open? I wasn't sure. The darkness was pure around me. I focused my mind and concentrated on the space around me, its shape, its form. Everything about it. With a push of energy, it was back to the same world of liquid darkness I had entered with Hundri, aside from the shack that sat in the distance.

With a swirl of darkness, Abigail appeared across from me and looked the same as the outside world, besides the chain was wrapped around her wrist instead of linking us. "Nice shack," she jabbed with a smile.

I rolled my eyes in response. "What are we here for anyway?"

"Well for me, I always grasped the fundamentals better in my mental space," she paused, "And I want to try something."

Warmth spread in my chest like a blanket as I filled my runes with energy. "Sure, what's first then?"

"First," she began to pace around me in a circle, "Were going to need a sword. Do you know how to form things in your mind? It's usually a subconscious process but it can be done—" I extended my hand and felt the void respond to my intent, and as effortlessly as I would tear a leaf, a wooden sword identical to the ones my father and I had used formed in my palm.

She froze for a second and stared at the sword. After a moment she recovered and tapped the wooden blade, almost to check if it was real. "Tha-that was unexpected, I won't lie."

My laugh echoed through the empty space around us. "So, what should I do with this sword?" I gave it a few practice swings before meeting her gaze.

"Before we do anything with the sword, would you touch the chain around your wrist for me?" I did as she instructed and felt the polished metal against my fingertips. The runes were almost white hot, yet I felt no pain. Something spread into my mind, nothing I could put into words, yet something that felt so natural it had been there my whole life. Instinct.

I let this new instinct guide the energy through the blade. The energy flowed through my sword arm, and I felt the potential brimming at my fingertips. Darkness surrounded me as I shut my eyes. I focused solely on her guidance and let the energy dance through my hand.

Something clicked. I already treated my sword as an extension of my body, so what held me back from protecting it like I would protect myself?

I pushed energy into the fibers of the wood and through the core of the sword. The energy crackled and resisted as it almost threatened to blow the sword apart from the inside. To my surprise, it was easier to control than I had thought. With another push, I let the energy seep out from the blade and form an aura. A thin golden shimmer of mist appeared around the blade.

I swung the sword and was surprised at the simplicity of the skill, "Is this so easy only because I know my way around a sword?"

She nodded. "The stronger connection you feel to the weapon and the more you understand it, the more you can treat it like a limb."

I had been treating the sword like an object, not a part of me. This new realization spread the wonderful warmth of realization through my chest. "This is probably the best you can get without training, try cheating a little since we're in your mind."

The void began to aid me as I allowed it. It tempered the shimmering mist into a solid glowing edge of light around the blade that hummed as I swung it, "Interesting! I'll have to keep working at this then. How much of a difference does it make?"

"As you've seen, difference in aura control can make a fight one sided and weapon aura is a huge part of that." She gestured in front of her and almost ordered, "Lend me a blade? Metal."

I swiped my hand in her at her feet and the void coalesced into an almost identical sword to Hundri's. She twirled it in her hands and examined it, before giving me another order, "Hit my metal sword with your wooden one,"

I shrugged in mild surprise before I took a stance and released a blow onto her blade. To my genuine and now total shock, her blade split in two. It was a clean and effortless cut, as if I had cut through nothing but the air.

The blade felt as if it could cut through space itself and that intoxicating thought riddled my mind with excitement. "Wow..." I muttered as I stared at its glowing edges as they faded back into specks, the sword aura now relinquished. Abigail nodded approvingly. "What's next?"

"Hmmm," She touched her lip once again, "Well before we go back to the real world, why don't you show me around your..." She gestured towards the lone structure in the darkness, "your shack?"

The shack grew closer as I laughed and began to walk towards it, "Sure, why not. I doubt you'll find anything interesting, but why not."

"Structures like these in our mind signify how well we can control our energy and give shape to our thoughts," She knocked on the door in a joking matter before practically kicking in the door to my shack.

I clicked my tongue and raised my eyebrows. "Wow," I sang. "You seem to be lacking manners. You didn't even wait for a response."

She rolled her eyes, "When have you known *me* to be *courteous?*"

A chuckle left my lips, "Fair enough." After I let her take a glance around the room, I continued, "Is it as glamorous as you imagined?"

"Just about."

"Really now?" I cocked an eyebrow. "Well take a look around then."

She promptly began to search the room for anything of interest. Naturally, she went to the place I predicted first, the decorated tome in a case above the desk. She opened the case and effortlessly flipped through the book. "Wow!" She sang. "These are fantastic notes on Maegellan Frost Bears." To both of our surprise, the name she had spoken began to write itself at the top of the page. "What... what is this book?" She gave me an inquisitive look.

I scratched the top of my head nervously, "It's linked to my family crest."

"Interesting!" She flipped to the next page in the book and was disappointed to find a blank page. Finally, she peeled her eyes up from the book and curiously asked, "What does your family crest do anyway?" I hesitated for a moment, and she immediately picked up on my reluctance, "I would tell you mine, but my family never talks about it. We're told as kids never to touch it, that it was cursed. Anyway... yours is?"

She looked at me expectantly and her brown eyes dug into my soul. "Don't look at me like that." I said in an exasperated voice. I sighed and decided not to press the topic of her own crest. "Mine seemed to have let me take the runes of a bear I killed, but I don't know if I can use it again." I pointed at the book in her hands, "That book has loose information on the bear."

Her eyes lit up brighter than something flammable near a fire mage. "What's the bear's rune do then? Nobody really knows what magical beast's abilities are for sure, but now you can learn!"

I chuckled at her enthusiasm and touched the rune on my chest. "It increases the strength of my aura a substantial amount, but also makes me pretty unstable."

She tilted her head slightly as she looked down at the book again. "What do you mean by unstable?"

"Specifically, it amplifies anger, and I'm worried the change could be *permanent* so I only use it in emergencies."

She looked up again, the disappointment she wouldn't get to see it in action evident. "Makes sense I guess," she muttered as she put the hefty tome back in the polished case. "It's probably because your brain is incompatible with the magic, or your mental control is weak."

"Weak you say?" I waved my hands and a perfect replica of the Hell's Pavilion medallion swirled into existence from the inky blackness.

With a flick of my wrist, the void consumed it. She glared at me. "Ugh, true. Then those runes are probably incompatible with our bodies, which would make sense."

I nodded solemnly. "I need to find a different one to use, but I'm still not sure the limits of what I can take. Like if I can take them from *people*, or even better, if I can use other elements with it."

She laughed quietly and looked around again. "As amazing as that would be, since it's not your normal element, you would use *much* more energy for conversion."

"Conversion?"

She sighed. "Yes Rey, conversion. Since it's not your natural element, your body has to spend much more energy to use incompatible runes."

"Ah!" I turned away quickly and chuckled. "Of course! *That* conversion. I knew about that, of course."

I slowly turned back to see her giving me a skeptical eyebrow raise. "Uh-huh."

She bent over and began to rummage through a chest in the corner while I thought of wilder ideas. "So, what if I could even take runes off weapons! Maybe then I could use the powers of something like Volay on my own! Or, or maybe I could imbue its powers into something else! There's so much potential."

She looked up and gave me a small smile before turning back to the chest. "Well, we can always try stuff if you want," she called out, her voice echoing through the chest as her head was almost entirely within it. Abigail's head popped out a moment later, hair slightly crazed. She let her long hair out of her ponytail before retying it neatly. "Okay, I'm done tearing your little place apart, let's go back out and get into the fun stuff."

I matched her devilish smile with a weak grin, "Yeah, lets."

Her fingers wrapped around the chain on her wrist and tugged. It slowly unwound and the runes dimmed. She gave me a wink, "See you in a second," and with that, her body went limp. Tendrils of darkness writhed out from the darkness below and began to wrap around her.

I watched in horror as her limp body was pulled downward and submerged into the darkness below. *What in Yildaar's name?* I thought in a panicked rush. This was new. This hadn't happened with Hundri.

Where her body had sunk into the depths, two eyes and a mouth formed. They leered up at me with an unsettling malevolence. A voice filled my brain directly, *Hey.*

I stared down at it in horror watching as a version of myself made of pure inky dark liquid dragged itself from the darkness. It looked as if my liquid silhouette stood before me. Its figure and build matched mine identically. It leaned close to me and whispered in my mind again, *Hey.*

My voice caught in my throat as my heart pounded like a drum. *Kill her. Her power is better off with us.*

Something churned in my chest. A nauseating feeling spread through me as I glared at its insane grin. My fingers trembled at my side, and I slowly clenched them into a fist. The tiniest amount of energy formed into an aura around my knuckles. *Get out of my head!* I screamed back in my thoughts and threw a right hook at its head.

It caught my punch perfectly and threw me to the ground. A maniacal laugh echoed through my head, *You're pathetic.*

I growled and pushed myself off the ground, my fist soared into an uppercut as I rose. It slammed into its chin with enough force to break the average person's jaw, but to no avail. As if I had hit brick; it stopped in place and began to slowly sink into the shadowy figure.

I swallowed and my heart was loud in my ears. I flailed relentlessly in a pitiful attempt to escape as I was slowly dragged into my silhouette. The liquid void had swallowed up to my forearm, yet still I persisted. My other fist slammed into its temple and began to be swallowed as well.

A matter of moments later, it was swallowing my shoulders as well as my strength to keep fighting. I went limp as the darkness wrapped my head. A chilling void surrounded me within the being and its demonic voice crept into my mind, *Kill her Rev. Consume her power.*

I screamed, yet no sound escaped my lungs. I was met with only unforgiving silence as I drowned in the liquid abyss.

. . .

I woke. I was suddenly back in the real world. I looked up from where I was sitting and searched for Abigail, who was rummaging through a cabinet full of wooden sparring weapons. Light pain shot out in my eye as salty sweat that I wasn't aware of dribbled down.

She turned to look at it. The cabinets clicked shut and she walked over. "Welcome back." Abigail extended a helping hand down towards me.

My heart sank. Behind her was the shadowy figure I had seen in my mind. *Kill her.* My blood ran cold and instinct took over. I pulled her down to me by the wrist as fast as I could. She landed in my arms with a yelp, but the figure was gone. The only thing left was my pounding heart and Abigail on my chest.

She pulled her face from my chest and onto her hands and knees. My face burned red as hers floated close enough to feel her breath. My heart pounded. She smiled down at me, "Hey." After she studied my flushed face for another moment, soaking in my expression before she pushed herself off. "So, what was that about?"

I laid there for a moment with my ears on fire. "I-I," I hesitated. I had no clue how I could explain what I saw without sounding insane. "I don't know. Sorry," I muttered.

She furrowed her brow slightly. "It's all good, Rey." I clasped my hand around hers and she pulled me to my feet. After a second of studying my face, she began to talk again, "Are you okay? You seem a bit rattled, and not just from me."

"I'm fine," I groaned out as I stretched my back. Spots danced in my vision as I rubbed drowsiness from my eyes and adjusted my pants.

My eyes flew open to find a wooden sword flying directly at my face. I grabbed it out of the air right before it was able to hit me and flourished it on my side to adjust to the weight.

She pointed her wooden cutlass at my longsword. "Try your sword aura on it, but don't sharpen it."

I gathered energy for a minute then sent it up my arm and the rest of my body, letting the power flow until it was pleasantly warm. Scales of light grew out in a defensive layer in patches around my fists and vital points. I pressed my intent into the energy in my hands and let it fill the handle of the sparring tool first. As if it was my arm, the energy ran down the center of the sword and tapered into a point.

With mild difficulty, I released the energy from the core of the blade and let it form the shimmering mist. It hummed almost imperceivably as I twirled it in my hands. I shook off any thoughts of that entity and focused on the task at hand, kicking her ass.

Like the day before, we began to circle each other on the mat. "Ready to go?" she sang as she pointed the point of her weapon at my throat.

"Ready as I'll ever be," I grinned and dropped into my familiar combat stance. The mat creaked against its supports as we charged towards each other smiling ear to ear. Her sword arced diagonally at my right shoulder and with a quick pivot I stepped around the cut, shouldering her in the chest.

She stumbled backwards slightly with grace as she positioned her blade to protect from any attacks to her upper body. Unluckily for her, I noticed her guard and began to drop into a low sweep.

With a startling rush of cold, a small ball of water blasted my cheeks and the form of my kick faltered as I fell onto my tailbone. Her sword flew through the air at my leg as she regained her footing. I ignored the water that distorted my vision and desperately rolled away.

A tiny spark of pain burst on my thigh as her dulled blade grazed me. My face twitched slightly in pain as she snickered, "So close."

She stepped backwards and regained her form as I got on my feet. My rough hands swiped across my eyes clearing the water. "That was dirty," I spat in mild frustration.

Her shoulders rose and fell in a shrug. "If you aren't fighting dirty you aren't truly fighting."

I raced to find a witty comeback to no avail. Instead, I dashed forward. *She's right, I should push my limits, right?* I thought to myself as I strengthened my grip on my sword.

I gritted my teeth and focused on my sword's aura. I reached for each particle with my mind and focused on the nature of the way the energy coalesced. My head began to ache under the strain of shifting the formed aura's shape. The edge of my blade sparked and hissed as it danced towards Abigail's sword.

Our swords slammed into each other. I smirked while I waited for the shock to give me an opening. She widened her eyes in mock pain before meeting my gaze, "Cute trick." Confusion racked my mind. That allowed her fist to cleanly impact my left cheek.

I stumbled backwards and tried to regain my balance, only to be met with another fist that slammed my wrist. My sword clattered to the ground as she pressed her foot into my sternum. With a powerful push, I felt my back sink into the mat, the point of her shimmering wooden blade pressed to my neck.

Her hair swayed as she shook her head disapprovingly, "You know wood isn't great at transferring electricity, right? Plus, I sucked the moisture out of the blade anyway just in case."

I raised my arms in defeat and sighed. "Good match." My fingers wrapped around her warm wrist as she hauled me to my feet.

"That move would've worked if we were using real swords," I complained.

"Yeah, if you used more electricity, sure." She smirked at me. "Let's try that again."

I laughed, "Alright, I hope you know I won't stop until I get a solid blow on you."

"Deal." We took our positions again, wooden blade in hand and with a roar, I charged.

CHAPTER THIRTEEN

The Power of Emotion

Reynolds Helphain

My feet dragged against the polished stone of the street below me as I walked to the place where Hundri had designated. My body was battered and worn out from hours of sparring. My bones and veins ached from the constant channeling of energy; every inch of my body felt like fire was running across it.

I had lost track of time and the magical mist in the sky was already beginning to dim but it had been worth it. I had a few new tricks to show Hundri next time we sparred. The streets had thinned since earlier that day. My mind drifted as I walked. *I hope Serena is okay,* I thought sadly as I walked.

It had been cycles since I had heard about her. My last memory of her was a strange one. She had seemed so... melancholic and apathetic towards leaving, despite how excited she had been weeks before. I felt a deep longing paired with unrelenting concern in my chest. Each memory I recalled of good times with her made it more painful.

A gentle hand wrapped around my shoulder. "You okay hun?" The voice of a croaking old lady permeated my ears.

I blinked rapidly, and to my surprise, found cold tears running across my cheek. "Oh- yes, I'm fine."

"Here, have this." An old lady with a polished wooden cane ringed in bronze runes took a step towards me. She wore a heavy brown robe over a crimson blouse. Her silvery white hair was tied in a bun that slightly pulled back the creases on her face. Sitting on her shoulder was a black cat with a white underbelly that led up to its lower jaw and amber eyes. A bead of sweat dripped down my brow as the cat met my gaze.

She reached into her robes and handed me a small bronze plate chiseled with the image of a woman. She pressed it into my palm, its cold, firm metal surface made my hand tingle slightly. I looked down to study it, "May the icon of Iora bless you." She smiled warmly at me with her few remaining teeth.

I smiled back. "Thank you." As I turned away and dabbed at my eyes, I studied the metal plate. The unfamiliar, poorly hammered engraving of a woman with her hair in a bun stared back at me. She was surrounded by what looked like falling snow, though it was hard to be sure with the quality. I sighed and slipped it into a pocket.

I shook my head to clear the thoughts of my sister, the strange old lady and the icon. Instead, I focused on finding my way to the place Hundri had mentioned we would meet. After a while of walking aimlessly through different markets and streets, I found my second distraction.

The entrancing smell of seasoned meat filled my nose and forced my stomach to growl almost as loud as the bear I had killed. I hadn't even realized I was hungry.

A thick armed man with a portly stomach waggled his eyebrows at me from inside the stand. "Kinda sounds to me like somebody's hungry, eh?" He called over to me.

With a sigh, I approached him. He was sitting on a worn mat under an even more worn awning. Sticks of meat sizzled on a small metal grate supported over a row of glowing red crystals. His girthy fingers wrapped around a small, pointed stick and shoved it through a row of meat. "That's gonna cost ya a silver."

I grabbed a silver out of my pocket and placed it into his now outstretched other hand. He grinned with yellowing teeth and handed me the stick of meat. "Thank you for the food," I muttered as I walked away, meat in hand. I took a bite.

The meat tore away from the stick and the flavor burst through my mouth. I let out a quiet groan of satisfaction as I enjoyed the first piece of real food since I had left my home. The speed I tore through the meat was astonishing; one moment it was there, the next, it was in my mouth.

A thought crossed my mind and I quickly turned around. As I approached the meat vendor, I fished in my pocket for the icon. "One last thing, do you know what this is?" I showed him the icon.

He scratched his chin and leaned closer. "Hmmmm." He raised an eyebrow and leaned back. "Church of Iora loves em. Icons of their goddess." He tapped the metal. "That's her."

I looked at the woman in the metal once again. "That's Iora?"

He nodded. "Aye."

"I swear she looked different. Strange."

He leaned back on a pillow behind him. "Aye, she did. They changed her looks a few cycles back."

I slipped the icon back in my pocket. "Well, thank you."

"No problem." He flashed me a smile. "Want more meat?"

"No, thank you."

With food in my belly, a renewed energy filled me. I pushed the confusion from my mind and began to look for the training building in the military district that Hundri had mentioned. The fun part of being lost was all the unique things I could find, from beautiful statues to kids playing in streams under small bridges. Even when I assumed the sun was going down, the city was surprisingly full of life. Bars, shops, art and much more were everywhere I turned in the city.

Eventually, however, my little adventure came to an end as I recognized landmarks and began to hone in on where Hundri was. The military district was unlike the others, which was expected. It was clearly focused on efficiency, with many large streets that connected all parts of the city to barracks and different military housings. The occasional statue and carving were placed into the sides and corners of the dark buildings, leaving the area mostly bland and imposing.

The streets in this part of town were almost empty in the later hours of the night. As I walked from building to building, I eventually stopped a short woman to ask her for directions. She wore simple grey and white robes that stood out brilliantly in the night. She stumbled through the street with a stack of books.

"Do you know where I could find Captain Traegan?" I asked as I lowered my voice slightly, so as not to wake people who could be sleeping.

She pushed a lock of short brown hair out from behind her glasses and looked up at me with sea-green eyes. "Oh Captain Traegan?" She seemed a little confused but pointed towards the end of the street, "If you go to the end of the street and turn right, it will be the first building on your left. He's training right now though. I don't know if it's the best idea to interrupt that."

I gave her a little smile, "Thank you for the directions." I could smell burning wood and sweat as I got closer to the building. I climbed the short stone staircase up to the large wooden door and wrapped my fingers around the rough metal handle. With little effort, I began to swing the door open, the muffled sounds of combat grew to a loud cacophony of swords clashing, people talking and spells flying.

The door slammed shut behind me. All the members of the blades of Iora were present doing different things. Ralteir and Yaldrie were in the arena circling each other, clearly at the start of a fight. Hundri and Kai were standing just outside the large sandy ring with a stack of small papers on a wooden slate. Ogland sat off to the side with Syre in meditative poses and their hands linked by the same chain Abigail and I had used.

Not wanting to bother Ogland and Syre, I walked over to Hundri. As I expected, he sensed my approach and turned to look at me, "Welcome back, you sure took your time."

"Met up with a friend and sparred most of the day. Learned a few new tricks. What's going on here?" I looked at Ralteir and Yaldrie again. What those two were doing was obvious, what I wanted was some clarification on what Kai and him were doing.

He raised an eyebrow at my comment about sparring but said nothing about it, "Never mind that. How're you feeling?"

I frowned. "Fine. Nothing unusual if that's what you mean."

"Are you sure?" He scratched his chin in thought. "Nothing strange? Unusual?"

I shook my head. Lying felt terrible, but whatever was going on, I could handle it myself. No need to make him worry. "No, sorry."

He sighed and turned back to the fight and gestured with his right arm. "Me and Kai have put little artifacts on Ralteir and Yaldrie to measure their power."

It was my turn to cock an eyebrow, "'Little artifacts', huh?"

"Hey, Kai's the one who made them I have no clue how they work," he retorted.

I chuckled, "Fair enough."

Kai shot me a look, "Time to be quiet. They're about to start,"

I muttered an apology, but it was quickly drowned out as Kai rung a large bell and began to yell, "Alright, as per usual sparring and dueling rules, no killing, no maiming, keep everything blunt and avoid vital points. Other than that, try not to destroy the building so we don't have to pay for any repairs."

With another ring of a bell, they began to fight. The ground around Ralteir's feet kicked up and encased the soles of his boots before sliding him across the ground at breakneck speeds. Stone gauntlets with glowing runes formed around his clenched fists and he took a swing at Yaldrie.

Unluckily for him, in a gust of wind, Yaldrie dashed backwards just out of his reach. She chanted slightly for a moment as glowing green runes formed and floated around her wrists. Within moments, they formed into tiny spinning balls of wind and rocketed at Ralteir. His reaction speed lagged slightly. He threw his right arm into a block and roughly pivoted his torso to reduce the area he could be hit.

The orbs slammed into his gauntlet and drilled into the stone as they faded away. He skidded backwards with dust kicking up in clouds behind him. He wasted no time as he dropped back into a run and was carried forwards, runes gathered at his fingertips with whispers.

Yaldrie stomped the ground, and with an explosion of dust and wind, she soared upward. Her boots glowed a faint green as tiny bronze runes lining the bottom ignited and began to gather the wind beneath her. With her fall drastically slowed, she began to gather energy around once more.

Over the sounds of magic and high winds I thought I heard a stream of curses from Ralteir. I chuckled softly. The ground bulged under his feet as two large pillars of rock blasted him upwards. Glowing orange runes sprung to life around his fist as he thrusted towards the still distant Yaldrie.

The arena bulged again as many boulders at least twice the size of my head rocketed out. They hurtled past Ralteir on a collision course with Yaldrie who was already prepared. She pulled her staff off her back and twirled it in front of her before swinging it in a wide arc at Ralteir and the boulders.

A visible blast of wind tore from the crystal at the tip of the staff and slammed its targets. Ralteir grimaced as the wind crashed into his chest and slowed him down substantially. It was apparent that he no longer had the speed to reach Yaldrie, but he ignored that fact and thrust his arms out towards two of the boulders that were crashing downwards. He clenched his fists and the rocks burst apart into fragments that flew towards his fists.

His left gauntlet merged with the flying boulder shards and connected to his right hand. His now very bulbous hand rocketed outward and stretched to reach Yaldrie's foot. To her surprise and mine, it barely managed to connect and wrap around her shin. A devilish grin spread across his face, "Eat this you coward!" he screamed as he flicked his long earthen arm downwards and slammed her into the floor with an explosion of dust.

The floor beneath me shook slightly and I shot Hundri a concerned glance, "Are you sure she's okay?"

He didn't respond, his eyes were fixed on the arena with furrowed brows. The dust began to settle as Ralteir landed without a hint of grace as the ground adjusted to make his fall painless. To Ralteir's and my own surprise, the dust suddenly began to swirl and clear. Yaldrie stood where the dust had obscured, battered and bruised but still standing. "Well," her voice cut through the air, "If we're going to get more serious, then allow me to have some fun as well."

She twirled her staff once more and tapped the base to the ground. Nothing happened. Ralteir's eyes darted around the battlefield to no avail. Eventually, he looked upward, but was too late. A massive gust of wind slammed into Ralteir's chest and flattened him to the ground. The stone gauntlets he wore on his fist cracked apart as he lost control over the spell and rolled onto his side.

He heaved, trying to get his breath back as Yaldrie walked over to him. With her boot, she rolled him over onto his back again. "Done yet?" she asked, her voice clearly tired.

Ralteir's face morphed into an ecstatic grin, "Not even." He slapped the ground with an open palm and a stone pillar shot out of the ground and tried to wrap around her arm. She dashed backwards and sliced the thin pillar in two with a blade of wind from her staff.

Yaldrie began to sprint left and formed barrages of wind orbs. Almost immediately, Ralteir began to chant. They rocketed through the air towards Ralteir, only to be stopped short by a wall of earth just thick enough to absorb the impact. A boulder flew straight up from the wall Ralteir stood behind. With a spin and a kick, it was sent hurtling at Yaldrie.

She gathered power in the tip of her staff and released it in an explosive blast that shattered the boulder. Ralteir flew through the billowing cloud of dust clad in earthen gauntlets and plates of armor. His rocky fist slammed her in the chest and before she had time to react, he grabbed her by the shoulder and kneed her in the gut.

She stumbled back and desperately flicked the tip of her staff upward, sending a loose rock into his stone chestplate where it shattered uselessly. He dusted off where it hit and glared at her. "You know my own rocks don't work against me."

A laugh escaped her despite her clear disadvantage. "All or nothing. I guess that's how it is." Glowing runes began to form on the back of her hands and grew more complicated with each passing second. His eyes flicked down to the runes and the fear on his face was apparent as he noticed they were forming into glyphs. He shed the armor and rocketed towards her. She dashed back, slipped something into her ears, and released the fully formed glyph.

Its effects were clear almost immediately. Every sound from around her was amplified one hundred-fold. Yaldrie clapped her hands together and a deafening boom rocked the arena. I winced and covered my ears as they began to ring from the sound. Ralteir stumbled backwards and seemed to have screamed, though none of us were able to hear it.

Yaldrie took full advantage of that moment and burst forward, the wind accelerating her. She dropped into a kick that swept Ralteir's legs and sent him sprawling onto his back, while he covered his ringing ears with his hands. With a flourish, she pressed the jagged gem against Ralteir's throat. My hearing began to return, and I could just barely hear the words, "Do you yield?"

"Ugh!" grumbled Ralteir, "You win." She twirled her staff once more and stylishly put it on her back before she offered him her hand. He reluctantly grabbed her hand and was pulled to his feet. They walked towards me, Hundri and Kai. Ralteir and Yaldrie began to talk quietly as they walked backward before Ralteir turned around and started repairing the arena.

Yaldrie reached us and before I could get a word out, Kai grabbed her by the hand, "My *dearest* friend Yaldrie, would you do me the honor of explaining that sound move to me? I didn't realize that was able to be done with wind."

She chuckled, "Of course Kai. How did your little measuring things do?"

He inspected his papers, thought for a moment, then answered, "From my observations of just the battle itself, we can obviously say Yaldrie is a ranged fighter and Ralteir, a close-range fighter." He looked up and saw our disappointed expressions and smiled nervously, "B-but that's not all! The average power of Yaldrie's spells was quite high. Ralteir's spells were a little below Yaldrie's." She smiled brightly. "However, Ralteir's physical hits were around the same strength as Yaldrie's magical ones." Her smile faded.

Ralteir called over from the arena and obviously had been eavesdropping, "Hey I was pulling my punches! Guess we know who's stronger."

Yaldrie rolled her eyes and I took that as my opportunity to interject, "That sound clap was amazing!"

She smiled warmly, "Thank you, Rey. I've wondered if it was possible for cycles now and finally had a breakthrough. I'm happy you all got to witness that."

I glanced over at the meditating people and chuckled, "Besides them of course."

We laughed together for a moment. "Well, what are you here for? Could you be fighting someone today?"

I looked over at Hundri who was standing quietly next to me. "Yeah, what am I doing here Hundri?"

"Well, I was *planning* on having you fight Ralteir, but he might not be in the best condition for it, so I'll let you take your pick of who to fight. We'll all hold back of course. Can't beat you *too* hard." He flashed me a quick smile, "You can fight me if you want."

I pondered who to fight for a moment. "Actually, I do want to fight Ralteir still. I'm not in peak condition either, but I think I can put up a good fight."

Hundri's voiced echoed over to Ralteir as he looked behind him, "Hey buddy, are you okay enough to fight the kid?"

An unsettling smile spread across his face, "Oh yeah, I got this man,"

Hundri turned back to me, "Well there's your answer." He smiled.

I turned my attention to Kai who was scribbling on his paper, "Oh yeah, Kai, is the cloak done?"

A look of mixed confusion and annoyance grew on his face. "What do you think? You gave me it last night. Plus, why would you such a nice piece of equipment on a sparring match with *Ralteir* of all people."

A small sigh escaped me, "Fair, fair. You do realize the cloak will *probably* get blood on it right?"

His brow crinkled at that remark, "Don't even remind me," he groaned. "Anyway, I'll give it to you in the next five rotations of the sun. Come here for a second." He placed a few metal discs with glowing gems all over my body, then gave me a thumbs up. "You know the rules of a sparring right?"

I nodded, "I've had a brief explanation."

"Good, then make sure to be extra loud if you need to yield."

With that, Ralteir and I walked to the opposite sides of the arena. He looked me dead in the eyes and cracked his knuckles and neck. I did the same and loosened up my battered limbs. Lastly, I let the energy around me gravitate into my body and prepared for a tough fight despite my injuries. *At least it'll be good practice,* I thought to justify this terrible choice.

After a bit of concentration, warm scales formed over my hands like gauntlets as well as over my chest and back. I wish I could've used my new sword, but I wasn't sure I had the control I needed to dull the blade with energy. He did the same but put a layer of rock over the energy. "Ready to get started Ralteir?"

"Oh yeah, let's do this." He smiled. I had hoped that watching the previous match would give me some sort of advantage against him but his first move was something unexpected. His palm touched the ground before I could see the runes hovering in front of it. My feet sunk into the ground as tendrils of rough earth began to slither up my legs.

I coursed energy through my arms as fast I could and tried to free my legs. I was too late. He was already right in front of me, the ground having carried him like a comet. My last choice was to try to throw my arms up in a cross guard as his now stone-clad hand impacted me in the gut.

A howl of pain tore from my lips as I was lifted out of the earthen shackles by the force of the impact. It was a wonder my ribs didn't snap. Another explosion of dull pain slammed my left pec so hard it felt like my heart was beating a second time. My mind dulled and my vision spun as I felt Ralteir wrap his hands around my forearm and flip me over his body.

My back slammed into the ground and a spiderweb of cracks exploded outward. My vision slipped in and out. I caught glimpses of a boulder forming above my chest and Ralteir's smile as he began to speak. "Is that... it?"

Anger flared in my chest, and in a moment of foolishness, I let the energy flow into the bear's rune on my chest without restraint. Energy began to pour into me uncontrollably as every nerve in my body burned like fire. My vision came back into focus and the pain of his blows dulled until they had completely subsided. I pulled myself to my feet and locked eyes with Ralteir, who was suddenly farther away. His hands and gauntlets danced with prepared runes.

I began to sprint at Ralteir, and the room blurred. My fist collided with his open palm as he caught my punch and his gauntlet cracked. "Now *that's* a punch," he growled.

A snarl exploded out of me as I feinted with a punch to his gut— which he fell for— and swung at his face with an unintentionally lightning charged punch. He could barely react in time, a stone helmet with glowing amber crystals for eyes formed from his chestplate just before my fist could dent his face. The lightning exploded across his helmet and carved deep grooves into its surface that revealed his glaring eye.

"That could've killed me!" his voice echoed out from his angular helmet. The helmet crumbled apart and infused itself into the back of his chestplate. His gauntlet began to be covered in even more runes as he reformed it into a longsword. I saw Hundri begin to run toward us and the energy around us began to be pulled towards him.

Without a second thought I charged towards Ralteir and ignored the danger of a blade. I closed the gap between us, and he thrusted his sword at my chest. I weaved just past it and slammed the flat of the blade with my open palm. With a loud crack, lightning exploded across the flat of the sword and its weak stone blade blew apart into dust. His eyes widened in fear and a less-than-sane ear-to-ear smile spread across my face.

I swung my crackling fist at his now exposed head in a deadly thrust. Just before I could get the final hit, an explosion of ice sent us flying. My head hit the cracked ground, and the world suddenly went black.

CHAPTER FOURTEEN

Poems of the Void

Reynolds Helphain

At first, I felt nothing. It was like any other morning, only I was in an unfamiliar bed and was staring up at a ceiling that wasn't my own. The first true difference came when I tried to move my arm to rub my eyes. Fiery waves of pain exploded in my arm and sent streams of tears down my face. I gnashed my teeth together as hard as I could in an attempt to block the screams of pain that tore at me from deep inside.

Only then did I begin to feel what had happened to the rest of my body. Every inch of my skin emanated a searing pain that made my thoughts fuzzy. Hundri burst into the room at the sounds of my pain and rushed to the side of my bed.

Slowly the pain relented and dulled to a weak throb as I let my muscles go limp. I sucked in cool air with a deep breath and investigated Hundri's cold eyes. "What... happened to me?" I wheezed.

"You and Ralteir both got a little too into the fight. Fought with more strength than you should've." He rubbed the bridge of his nose and stood up a little straighter. "I know you are injured but," his voice rose in volume to a yell, "What were you thinking?! It's a miracle you didn't kill each other! You have no control over that power yet and no control over yourself when it gives you a taste of that strength!"

I couldn't meet his eyes any longer, the weight of my actions and the guilt I felt were too much. "I lost control," I muttered, "I was in so much pain from Ralteir kicking me around that I just... gave in to my emotions."

I glanced up at him and he kneeled down to look me in the eyes, with a deep sigh he continued, "I'm sorry. I shouldn't have yelled at you like that. It's easy to get emotional like you did, but it's paramount you get control over that power before you let it out like that. If this happened when you were stronger, you could've killed all of us and more." He paused for a second, "I'm just glad you're ok. I think we're going to avoid any more sparring of that intensity for a while, okay?"

I didn't let my surprise show on my face and warmly smiled back. "Thank you Hundri, I won't let it happen again." After a moment of silence, I added one more thing, "I've got to ask though... how'd I fight?"

He smiled and gave me a wink, "Let me get Kai."

As he was beginning to stand, a thought floated to my mind, "Hundri, was it even within the rules for him to hit that hard? I thought I was going to die."

He stopped and let his weight creak back into the chair. "It was. As long as he doesn't kill or permanently damage you, what he did to you is perfectly fine. Besides you hit just as hard." He sighed deeply, "I'd understand if you held a grudge against him. He should've pulled his punches against you. I'll talk to him."

The look in his eyes spoke to what he was saying. I could see the conflicting emotions in him. The love for his friends, the teachings he'd had all his life, and the worry for his student all warring within him.

"Hundri..." I hesitated, "It's okay. It's not your fault. Don't worry, next time I'll wipe the floor with him." I forced a smile on my face despite the pain. For Hundri's sake.

He gave me a weak grin, "Yeah, I'm sure you will." He placed a firm hand on my shoulder which sent a wave of pain across my body and weakened my smile. He quickly withdrew his hand, "Sorry about that."

We both laughed for a moment. He stood up and walked to the door, looked back, then left and closed it behind him. His footsteps receded slowly until I was left in deafening silence. It was entirely empty aside from a glowing orange crystal hanging from the ceiling, the bed I was in and a small bedside table with a wooden cup of water.

I took a deep breath and closed my eyes. In the darkness, I began to feel the power floating all around me. I tried slowly and let it ever so slightly pour into me. The energy traveled through my body and before it could get stopped and held in my runes, it went right out.

Panic filled me. *Are my runes damaged? Am I crippled?* I pushed those thoughts out of my mind. Before I could dwell on it any longer, five sets of footsteps approached. I let the world return to view just in time to see the door swing open and most of the members of the Blades of Iora spill in.

Kai weaved through the group and spoke first. "That was a wild fight, Rey. Would you like to see the information I recorded from my measuring tools?"

My voice cracked slightly as I began to talk which elicited scattered repressed chuckles. My face flushed slightly. "Yeah,"

He smiled and began to read off his papers, "Well, Ralteir's blows were much higher than when he fought Yaldrie. You didn't manage to get a punch off before you had that power spike, but the energy in your arm when you were trying to free yourself would've at least warranted a decent punch." I whistled slightly and let him continue. "After you started losing control, your average power jumped to substantially to close to Ralteir's normal strength."

Hundri slowly clapped in the back of the group and Yaldrie spoke up with worry all over her face, "That's impressive... but I worry about the cost. You seemed angry; *too* angry."

"I lost control. The anger, the rage, the hate, the spite..." I grimaced, "It's more than I can handle, even if the power it gives is intoxicating."

She gave me a sad smile and stepped back to let Kai talk again. "You greatly overworked your runes and runic channels in your body.

Essentially, they were pumped full of more energy than they could currently handle. They were greatly expanded and carved out in almost an instant. Now they're extremely sensitive, raw and not tempered. Overall, it will have made your channels better at transporting larger amounts of energy, but their control will be weaker and the risk of dying from this much overuse was way too high. Another question, where did you get those runes? I haven't seen those before."

I gave Hundri a quick uncertain glance which he returned with a slight nod. "Well, it's my family crest, it lets me—"

Suddenly Syre popped out of the group with such force that her black hair swayed violently behind her. "Wow! That's a cool family crest!" she said with great excitement in her voice.

I stared blankly at her. "I wasn't done talking..."

She smiled weakly and shifted awkwardly, "A-ah, sorry about that. Please keep going."

"All good," I chuckled, "As I was saying, from what I've gathered, it let me take the runes of the bear I killed."

It was silent for a moment before Kai spoke again, "That... that is some strong power. How many at a time can you hold?"

"Honestly, I'm not sure. I don't even know the rules regarding what I can take runes from and what I can't."

"Well that certainly explains why it seems to be a power not built for a human." He scratched his head slightly and seemed to enter a world of thought.

Hundri chuckled quietly, "Alright guys let's get out of his hair for now. The boy needs some rest." A chorus of telling me to feel better and get well soon went up from the group as they shuffled out of the room and left just me and Hundri. "Try to get some sleep kid, I'll come check on you in the morning."

A weak smile tugged at my lips, "Thanks. Goodnight, Hundri."

"Goodnight Rey." The door clicked shut behind him.

I was once more alone in my thoughts. There was nothing I could do except sleep or just wallow in my own pain, and nothing good could come of that. My eyes slowly shut, and I relinquished myself to the darkness.

. . .

The cold liquid of the void rippled against my body in even, rhythmic pulses. I arose from the dark sea, back in the void of my mind. I turned to my right towards the small shack would've been, only to see a small house that *resembled* the previously decrepit building, only now refurbished and larger.

I opened the rough wooden door and entered the stone building. The door swung open with a soft creak and revealed a cleaned up, higher class version of the sole room that had been in the shack before. Same bookshelf, desk, chest and crystal lights. Now, however, there was a new door to the right of the chest.

The book in the case seemed different, however. A low hum filled the air around it and rattled the glass of the case. I grabbed the small cold metal handle of the case and swung open the glass door. The gold inlayed in the crimson cover had grown more extravagant and complicated. As I ran my hand across its bumpy leather surface, glowing white runes formed floating over my family crest on the cover.

I absentmindedly read and muttered the words on the cover, "Svaldir," the void around me seemed to tremble for a moment at the word. Suddenly, the book disintegrated into flecks of light and was whisked away in an ethereal wind. I didn't understand where it had gone, or why, so I repeated the word.

With a soft hum, tendrils of light rapidly coalesced into the same tome I had been holding a moment ago. I smiled faintly. *I need to try this in the real world.* I flipped open to the front page and noticed the short paragraph about the rune I had obtained grew in size.

I began to mutter under my breath as I read, "The runic ability of the Maegellan Frost Bear is an emotional spike spawned from rage that greatly boosts the user's strength at the cost of control. This ability seems to not be made for mankind in any regard. Our bodies are strained greatly by full use, and the rage it induces seemingly degrades the mind."

After quickly flipping through the book's worn and yellowing parchment pages, I murmured Svaldir and watched the book disintegrate once more. I walked towards the new door and my hands wrapped around the thick metal handle. With a light tug, it creaked open, revealing a dimly lit hallway made of large stone bricks.

My footsteps were the only sounds as I walked down the hall. After a few steps, I came to a trio of doors, one on the left wall, one on the right and one at the very end. The two on the walls were simple wooden doors, while the one at the end of the wall was less of a door and more of a giant stone slab covered in runes and figures.

My attention immediately was drawn to the slab, the detailed picture and runes were nothing I recognized or understood. Each time I looked at the runes and images my focus shifted away, keeping me from gathering any true meaning from it. I pushed and pulled on the stone to try and open it, but it didn't budge.

With a sigh, I gave up and opened the door to the left. It was just like my bedroom back home, the bed, the chest in the corner, even the window led to the same view I had seen countless times. My boots creaked against the wooden boards of the floor as I shuffled through the bursts of frigid wind. A feeling of deep longing seemed to pull me towards my bed. My back hit the rough fabric sheets of my bed and a laugh trickled out of me. I had never imagined something so uncomfortable could bring me so much comfort.

I pulled myself back up to my feet and smiled at the room around me. Every detail was perfect. I thought of telling my father of my adventures as memories of him telling me stories in this very room flashed through my mind.

The old wooden window closed fully with a small push downwards, but the chill of the cold mountain wind remained in the air. I walked back towards the door I had entered with a faint smile on my face. It was nice to see where I had come from. It was almost like I could see the memories dancing around the room like ghosts, me, my sister and my father all passed out on my bed.

I shut the door behind me and stepped into the dark stone hallway once more. My hand ran across the course metal doorknob as I pushed it gently open. The space beyond the door was a fuzzy, unfocused mix of light and color. I jerked my head to the side. A wedge of pain jutted through my temples. Slowly, I turned back to look into the undefined mass. Instead, I found a replica of Abigail's training room in front of me.

The mat creaked below my boots as I walked into the center of the room to look around. Everything from the cave-like ceiling to the troughs of water that lined the edges for her elemental magic was the same as the real world. Unlike reality, there was a rack of swords on the wall opposite the door I had entered. They were the same wooden swords I had used time and again with my father.

After wandering around the room for a few minutes and exploring every crack and crevice, boredom seeped into my mind. I turned back towards the more interesting unknown in this place: the stone slab. The mat warped and bent as I jogged across its surface towards the hallway.

It seemed to have the same effect as this room when I first entered it, the same inability to focus on the details even though I could make out the general form. The door slammed shut behind me and echoed throughout the small stone corridor. I squinted intently at the slab hoping for any sort of change, but none came. I tried everything I could think of, I tried getting closer, different angles and even getting farther away. And still, nothing.

Frustrated and running out of things to try, I grabbed one of the bronze brackets that held the crystal lighting gem and yanked. As I expected, it didn't budge. I tried the next best thing, even though I wasn't sure it would be healthy for my physical form. I focused my mental image of a glowing crystal filled with energy and let the void do the rest of the work. Dark tendrils from the shadows and cracks in the stone swirled around above my palm.

The tendrils of darkness began to retreat to the shadows and light began to slip through their multi-layered shroud. A smaller, more handheld version of the crystal shined from my palm with a warm light. I clutched it tightly in my palm and held it up towards the stone slab. As the crystal got closer to the wall, it slowly became more in focus. Runic words glowed faintly as the energized crystal's light washed over them.

I struggled to read the words. They kept coming in and out of focus as I had to lean forwards to decipher them, which moved the crystal. I grew annoyed as my reading was continually interrupted by my shifting perception. Eventually, I gave up and focused on my new problem, holding this godforsaken gem still.

Instead of trying a simple solution like willing a stand for it into existence, I tried something that could have bigger implications. I leaned on a memory I had hoped to never have to think of again. I pictured the horrifying form, the feeling and the presence of the hands that drowned me in the void.

I felt a chill run down my spine as I remembered the eyes looking at me, almost taunting me as I was dragged beneath the surface. I felt powerless again.

I watched in regret and horror as the void shifted to my command. Out of the cracks in the stone stretched a set of impossibly dark fingers that reached towards the sky. Slowly and steadily, they rose from the ground until the entire arm was formed. I shuddered at the sight of it, in all its terrifying glory. I slowly extended my arm with the crystal. I had half expected it to grab me by the wrist and start to pull me under again but was pleasantly surprised as it brought the gem close enough to focus the runes.

Atop gods' peak

When all is bleak

With resolve in thy soul

Fight death's toll

What lies within is pure

Through trial, I must endure.

None of it made sense to me. I was left with more questions than answers. In the center of the stone slab was a small indent the size of a berry. I desperately looked for anything that would give me a hint of what this meant. I leaned against the wall and watched the arm melt into the shadows along with the glowing crystal. I leaned against the wall and began to let myself slide to floor but quickly stopped as a spark of inspiration flared to life.

I furrowed my brow at the door as I moved to be standing parallel to it. If I couldn't use energy, I had one last trick in here. I closed my eyes and watched ethereal tendrils of darkness grow from the darkness around me before hardening into pointed tips.

I thrust my palm forward and watched the spiked tendrils soar into the slab. They stopped motionless just before touching the surface. Slowly, they crumbled to bits and were swallowed by the runes on the stone.

At least I know I can do that now, I thought in disappointment. My bottom dropped to the ground as I lowered myself into a squat. *Why would there be something in my mind I didn't remember or understand?* It didn't make sense. The uncomfortable and uneven flooring pressed into my back as I laid down. I could feel the exhaustion catching up to me as my eyes slowly drooped to a close and my thoughts slowed.

CHAPTER FIFTEEN

Connected Through Tragedy

Reynolds Helphain

The scent of fresh fruit wafted into my nostrils as I peacefully was brought from my sleep back to the real world. Yaldrie sat on the side of the bed next to me with a small plate of delicious-looking fruit and bread. I sat myself up with a surprising lack of pain and yawned. "Hello Yaldrie,"

She smiled at me, "Hey Rey! I'm glad you're awake. How're you feeling?"

"I don't know," the slab of stone in my mind still plagued my thoughts, "Better for sure."

I rubbed my eyes and saw Yaldrie's smile grow. "That's really good Rey! I'd be a *bit* concerned if you didn't feel better after sleeping for three days."

I stared at her blankly for a second. "Three..." a feeling of unease washed over me. "Three days?"

"Yeah. Four if you count the night after the fight with Ralteir." She looked at me with concern, "Most people who strain their runes like that feel exhausted for days. We weren't surprised."

My stomach grumbled with the force of an earthquake, and I let out a sheepish laugh. "Well... that makes sense after three days."

She chuckled and held the platter of suddenly more appealing food close to my nose. Before I knew it, my mouth was watering. I grabbed a slice of apple and popped it into my mouth. I groaned quietly as chewed. Yaldrie stifled a chuckle and watched as I grossly shoveled the food into my mouth. My cheeks bulged like a chipmunk with each handful of bread and apple that were stuffed in my gullet.

"Sorry," I mumbled almost unintelligibly through mouthfuls of food. With a loud burp, I finished my plate. The soft mattress sank beneath me as I flopped backwards, "Since I'm feeling better, am I good to walk around the city?"

"Are you sure you're able to?" Her surprise was evident on her face, "Do you want me to get Hundri?"

A lock of hair flopped into my vision as I nodded, "Yes, please. Thank you."

I pushed the dark strands out of my eyes as I watched her stand up and run her hands across the sheets where she had been sitting to smooth them. "He'll be right in." And with that, she briskly opened the door, walked out of the room, and shut it with a light gust of wind.

My feet swung towards the ground and dangled just above the planks as I moved to a sitting position. I examined my body which had newly wrapped bandages covering the parts where Ralteir had hit me. Curses danced around my mind as I thought of what to say to him. I barely felt the rough texture of the planks as I placed my weight on the soles of my calloused feet.

My head felt inexplicably heavy as I rose to my feet. Everything lost focus as I stumbled around and lost my balance. Instinctively, my arm shot out and wrapped my fingers around the smooth wooden edge of the table. Slowly everything came back into focus. *Lightheaded? Seriously?* It made sense, I'd been motionless for several days.

I released my grip on the table and stared down at my rough hand. *Svaldir,* I thought with a push of energy to my hand. Nothing. Not even energy flowed as I pressed my runes with my will. "*Svaldir,*" I murmured aloud with another attempt at a wave of energy. I don't know what I had expected, this was the real world, I can't just create something out of nothing.

"Soul?" Hundri asked inquisitively from behind me. I hadn't even noticed him come in.

My hand dropped to my side as I turned to him, "Nothing, don't worry about it." He was wearing a black tunic with cyan embroidery, long beige pants and a belt with a sword hanging from it. "And don't you clean up well."

He nodded with a small smile, "Since it looks like you're feeling better, want to take a stroll?"

"Sounds good. First though, do you have any sort of clothes I can wear?" I gestured down at my shirt and pants which looked like they had been mauled by an animal. "The tears in my clothes earlier looked cool, but this is just a little much."

He laughed and opened a chest that had been hidden at the foot of my bed, "Lucky for you, I came prepared." He pulled out a set of clothes and tossed them to me. I haphazardly caught each piece and set them down.

I stared at Hundri and waited for him to leave, which he seemed to not understand. "I'm going to change. Would you mind, you know... leaving?"

"Right! Sorry." He laughed and closed the door behind him on his way out.

I started to pull off my shirt, but it tore and fell apart with barely a tug. At least it was off. A small curiosity gnawed at the back of my mind as to who put on my bandages. A chuckle quietly left me as I pictured a big guy like Ogland applying bandages.

The shirt was of a bright white fabric and fit me perfectly. The pants were of the same material, only darker in color. With the pants was a thick rope acting as a belt that I embarrassingly struggled to tie with shaking hands. Also resting at the foot of the bed was the sword Hundri had given me. Fortunately, it still had the straps and rings that hung the blade from my belt.

I reattached my blade to my new rope belt and opened the door to find Hundri leaning against the stone wall to my left. He pushed himself off the wall and turned to me before glancing at my attire. "Looking sharp."

I stared at him, deadpan. "They're your clothes."

He smiled, "I know."

I rolled my eyes and surveyed our location. I was still in the training building and sparring arena I had seen a few days prior. The arena Ralteir and I had sparred in was already repaired. *He's probably already awake. I barely scratched him.* Hundri began to walk towards the exit and beckoned me towards him.

"Say Hundri," I caught up to him. "Why can't I infuse energy in my body? I can feel the energy brimming in my runes, but it just won't listen to me."

His large hands tapped my sternum. "Syre placed a seal on your runes for the time being. It should wear off sometime today."

Several thoughts burst into my mind which I echoed to Hundri, "I didn't realize it was possible to seal energy like that. Why did you need to?"

His handsome features darkened, "While you were sleeping, sometimes your energy would leak from your recently damaged runes and spread into your already sore body. With no control over your energy, you started flailing and screaming in pain."

"What? I don't remember that at all." I ran my hand along my other arm, almost longing for the feel of raw power flowing through me. "How can she seal magic anyway?"

He opened the door into the desolate and dim morning streets of the military district. I smiled at the refreshing chilly, early-morning mountain air as it washed over me. I gestured to Hundri to lead, and he started to walk down the street to the left. His eyes met mine and reflected dim orange light as the misty magic above blazed the colors of a sunrise.

"She's from an allied hunting tribe that lives near the foot of the mountain. Our people trade furs and meats with them regularly in return for protection from neighboring tribes. They are well versed in archery and seals which they commonly use as traps." He paused for a moment as we took a corner and exited the military district into a more populated street. "Her parents taught her the bow and seals before sending her up to Anhalt to be trained by our renowned academies."

"I can understand imbuing a spell into a seal, but to seal energy itself? I've never read about that before."

"It gets much harder the stronger the rune she's trying to seal. She couldn't seal one of my runes, and even if she could, it would only be for a few minutes." He cracked me a grin, "Your runes are much more simple."

I rolled my eyes again. "What happened with the academy then? She should be old enough to enroll right?"

His face darkened slightly. "She did enroll a few cycles back. She was the star student, excelling in both magic theory and combat. The only problem was her attitude. She was belligerent and crass to professors and students alike."

Reminds me of someone, a smile tugged at my lips with the thought. "I can't imagine being a bit difficult could be *that* terrible."

He grimaced, "Well, not terrible enough to get her kicked out all the way, no. A professor made a joke about her family that she... took very seriously."

"Oh." I could read between the lines. It was a wonder she was still free.

We turned down another street filled with the fragrance of apples. We weaved past the morning workers setting up booths of fruit with nods of respect as we continued down the street.

I let the dark conversation rest and asked another question on my mind, "So, where are we going Hundri?"

"We're going to get a loaf of *the* best bread I've ever had. Been going there since I was younger than you and always liked to get the first warm pieces they make." His face morphed into one of bliss at just the thought. He looked over at me, "I hope you're hungry."

My stomach grumbled again in response and we both burst into hearty chuckles. "That sounds great Hundri." We walked in silence for a while, and I stared up at the tapestry of weaving light above us. It was still my favorite part about this city, more than the architecture and even more than the people I had met here. There was something so captivating about its swirling patterns.

Hundri pulled my attention back. "Hey Rey, I know I asked earlier, but why are you *really* out here? Why not live a peaceful life instead of one of brutality and endless fighting?"

I locked eyes with him for a moment, surprised by the depth of his question. "I—" I hesitated; memories of my beloved older sister flashed through my mind. "I fear for my sister. We had a dream of being royal knights far away and since she was older than me, she got to pursue our dream before I could even start." I looked down at the stone tiles as we turned another corner, and my voice began to break. "She had much more talent than I do." I paused for a moment, thinking back to my vision before deciding I would sound insane if I spoke of it aloud. "My family hasn't heard from her in so long that I worry for her. I need to tell her so much—"

I was shaken from my increasingly distraught thoughts by Hundri's strong hand on my shoulder. "I'm sure she's okay kid." He pulled me into his embrace. For a reason I couldn't understand, I felt my eyes begin to sting as I pressed against his chest. Tears rolled down my cheeks. I heaved for a moment in his arms before pushing myself away.

I wiped my face as I smiled at Hundri. "Thank you." I murmured, still sniffling slightly.

After a few minutes of walking, he tried to lighten the mood. "So, who do you think would be stronger now, me or your sister?"

I chuckled, "You could probably give her a challenge."

"She can't be *that* strong."

"You know that snowball trick you did when we were hiking to Anhalt? She could do that after she came back from her own expedition. That was two weeks after she awakened."

Hundri stopped walking and stared blankly at me which elicited a fit of guffawing laughter from deep inside. "I don't believe you, that's *insane*." He shook his head in disbelief as he caught up to me.

"It's true. She was even stronger than my father."

Hundri turned to look at me, deadpan. "I have never met either of these people. You realize that right? Saying she's stronger than your father doesn't mean a thing to me."

I chuckled weakly. "That's true," We rounded another corner onto a street that smelled of melting butter and rising bread. I let the fragrance fill every corner of my nose as I relished the atmosphere of this street.

Hundri's lightly scarred face turned to look at me, amusement plastered plain to see. "Already smell the bread, huh?"

I locked eyes with him, "Bliss." I made a sweeping gesture with my arms, "This is the smell of bliss."

He cracked into a smile, "Yeah." We stood still and let the slowly increasing flow of people speed up around us.

"We should probably get moving if we want to get the fresh bread, right?"

Hundri nodded and began to hurry me down twists and turns until we reached a small brick building supported by wooden pillars on the corners with a wooden sign hanging over the door that read, "Rythe's Bread."

"Is this it?" I rapped my knuckles against the rough wooden beam and was met with a strangely hollow echo. My shoulder pressed against the rough brick as I leaned against it.

He smiled and gazed at the polished wooden door with swirling patterns of dark iron. "Yeah. I'll be right back with your bread."

The door swung open with a light push, and he went into the warmly lit room filled with the scent of bread. The smell washed out into the street for a moment and filled my mouth with dripping saliva. My stomach grumbled as I slumped to the ground and closed my eyes.

Surrounded by the darkness of my closed eyes, I tried to squeeze the tiniest amount energy from my runes. I pictured my energy as a lake and the seal like a dam. With a push, I forced a few drops slowly but surely through cracks around the edge of my mental dam. With an electrifying pulse, I felt my perception shift. Something I had been missing since I woke up. My sense of energy.

As if the lights had suddenly been turned on in a dark room, energy flickered in my mind. The streams of light faded as I opened my eyes, reminding me that they were nothing more than illusions. After letting the energy wash over me, a strange feeling in the back of my mind began to itch. It was just shy of being painful, but still constantly pulled my attention.

I tried my best to ignore it and was thoroughly distracted when a set of knuckles stopped itself just shy of caving my face in. I flailed in my sitting position pathetically late and was met with a cacophony of laughter. *Abigail.*

Sure enough, she stood bent over right in front of me. I scrambled to my feet and quickly ran my eyes over her. She was wearing a fluffy off-white blouse that contrasted her auburn ponytail, a brown beast-hide jacket lined with runes and tight blue pants that highlighted her form. Around her waist was a thin leather belt hanging a longsword from her left hip.

She extended a hand which I gratefully accepted and was yanked to my feet. "Hey Rey!" She wrapped her arms around me in a hug. "I hadn't seen you in a few days and started to worry a little." Her flowery smell clashed beautifully with the smell of the bread as I sat in her arms for a moment, stunned.

I opened my mouth to respond but my lips flapped uselessly. "I-I'm okay." Once my brain had begun to work again, I let her go and pulled back my shirt, revealing the bandages.

Her eyebrow raised as she stared at the cloth wrappings. "You lost that bad, huh?"

I chuckled weakly. "It was pretty even actually." I scratched the back of my neck nervously. "I had to use the rune I got from that bear though."

Worry filled her eyes again as her eyebrows pressed ever so slightly together. "Rey...," She hesitated. "Please be careful, okay?"

Once again, I was taken aback by her concern, and I gave her the only response I could muster, a weak nod. After an awkward moment of silence, we both began to talk over each other in a garbled unintelligible mess of overlapping words. We both paused for a moment and laughed.

I smiled at her and gestured for her to go first, which she did. "So, what are you doing here this early anyway?" She brushed one of the few loose locks of hair not restrained in a ponytail out of her eyes as she locked my gaze.

I pointed my thumb back at Rythe's Bread, "My mentor wanted to take me to get fresh bread. What're you doing out here."

She inhaled the smell of fresh bread wafting out through the windows of nearby bread stores and smiled. "Same for me almost. My mother sent me out to go get some bread for a special dinner tonight."

I gestured toward the building I was leaning against once again, "Is this your favorite bakery as well?"

She shrugged. "Not particularly. Just saw your sorry ass sitting there and decided to say hello."

Before I could think of a witty retort, the door to my left swung open and Hundri stepped back out into the street. Hundri opened his mouth to say something that was undoubtedly a clever or snide remark but quickly closed it when his eyes settled on Abigail. His face shifted into an impassive stare as they locked eyes.

Abigail's face darkened and her hand dropped to her sword, her voice now sharper than its blade, "Hundri. Funny running into you here."

Hundri responded, suddenly cold and dispassionate, "Abigail."

Confusion rocked my mind, but I shoved those feelings and thoughts aside and interjected myself between the two. "Woah, hey guys. Hundri, Abigail, what's going on here?"

They both looked at me with a hint of surprise in their eyes and Abigail asked first, "How do you know him?" Her voice was still cold and sharp.

I looked her in the eyes and tried to read her emotions but would've had better luck trying to find emotion in a statue. "He's my mentor."

Her face twitched slightly, "This... *man* is your mentor?"

"Yes," I responded slowly. "What's that to you?"

Her mouth curled back in anger but before she could talk, Hundri spoke. "You know her, Rey?"

I shifted my gaze to Hundri who was as unreadable as Abigail. "Yeah, she's the girl I've been sparring with."

His face tightened ever so slightly, "So that's why the energy on you seemed so familiar. Deptheart family."

Questions bloomed in my mind over and over in an endless stream until I couldn't resist asking one, "What happened between the two of you?"

Abigail glared up at Hundri. "Why don't you ask your *mentor*." She spat.

Hundri remained ice cold. "Her mother and father used to be members of the blades of Iora. Back when we were still a fresh group." Each word seemed to make Abigail more hateful, "We were attacked by the Hollow Blade. The battle was in a village and each time our blades clashed, bystanders died. I made the choice to pull out. We were extremely overwhelmed and outmatched. Abigail's parents refused to leave, so I made the best choice for the team,"

Abigail's voice cracked with emotion, "The best choice for the team? You left them to die! How could that be the best choice?" Energy leaked from her body and placed a tangible pressure on her words. "If you had stayed, maybe they could've won. Maybe—" She choked back tears. "Maybe my dad would still be alive. He sacrificed himself for that village and my mom. He was selfless. A *real* hero." As she spat the last few words, I could see a wisp of sorrow swirl in Hundri's eyes.

He let his impassive mask slip for a moment, "Abigail... I hoped you would understand after all this time." He took a deep breath. "I've said this time and time again. I didn't have a real choice. Your parents *chose* to stay. If we stayed, we *all* would have died. I—" This time it was Hundri's turn to choke back tears. "I-I, tried to tell them we didn't stand a chance. They refused to let the people die. Maybe I *am* selfish but you're right. Your parents are real heroes. I just wanted to protect as many of my friends as I could."

I was left speechless. I struggled to open my mouth to form my next words but decided that I had no place to speak in this. Instead, I just watched Abigail's face. She was at as much of a loss for words as I was. Her mouth opened and closed as she tried to find what to say but struggled with the obvious range of emotions that played out on her face. After what felt like hours, a single tear rolled down her face.

Instead of addressing Hundri, she looked at me and it was clear she just wanted to run away as fast as she could. "Come find me later." Her voice quivered, "We need to talk." With that, she turned away and hurried in the other direction.

CHAPTER SIXTEEN

The Power of Command

Reynolds Helphain

I turned back to Hundri, who now faced away from me and up at the mystic sky. He breathed deeply before slowly turning back to me. The moment I met his gaze I saw something deep in his eyes- no, his spirit- looked broken. What looked back from behind his now messy hair wasn't the great warrior I was used to seeing, but a man. A vulnerable, human man.

I faltered, "Hundri are you..." My brows creased in concern. "Are you alright? What was that?"

His shoulders drooped slightly as if the shame of his actions were a physical weight suddenly placed upon him. "I..." His gaze dropped and he started to walk down the street. "Hearing the kid of some of my closest friends so angry at me like that... her hate and sadness it... I don't know what to do. I hadn't seen her in so long. I'd forgotten."

"Did you really... leave them behind?"

He winced at the question and his gaze dropped to the stone tiles below us. "I did."

That couldn't be true. I refused to believe it. There had to be more to the story. I couldn't picture Hundri ever leaving someone behind... but I hadn't known Hundri all those cycles ago. He *had* run from the Hollow Blade *again* right before I met him. But was that the same? I didn't know.

We walked in silence down the twisting streets. I couldn't find the words to express my questions. After walking for what felt like hours in silence, we reached a large stone archway formed into a wall of dark stone. The archway was chipped and old, with a runic engraving that read, "Memories of old, promises of new."

"Is this... a graveyard?" Hundri cut me off with a piercing look filled with sorrow. A chill ran down my spine. I flinched back and my gaze bolted down to the tile below.

Hundri patted me on the shoulder. "Sorry kid, just wait here for me. I need to attend to something."

With that, he walked through the archway into what looked like a dreamy forest. I leaned against the arch and let my thoughts wander. After a few minutes, I let my curiosity get the better of me and I began to slip into the graveyard, placing the bread atop the stone brick wall.

It was a grim place. Every area felt as if it radiated a depressing aura. Grey-green grass spread out on every side with weapons planted in the soil, which I assumed was the marker of each warrior. It was dimly lit by floating balls of light and the sky above was pitch black. Trees occasionally decorated the desolate field.

I walked over to the nearest ball of light and inspected it. At its core was a small glowing crystal surrounded by a bronze cage etched with glowing green runes that spun quickly. It felt as if I was walking through a gloomy dream as I wandered through the field. The dim lights that floated aimlessly painted each weapon and plaque I passed with a dreamlike light.

My eyes danced across the field of weapons until I finally stopped on a figure in the distance that kneeled before a grave beneath a tree. *Hundri.* I slowly crept towards him and tried to stay out of sight. *I hope this seal prevents him from feeling my presence.* It was my running theory that if I didn't have any energy leaving, entering, or even in my body that Hundri's godly sight wouldn't be able to find me.

I ducked into the cover of the tree behind him and slowly peeked around the trunk. He knelt before a beautiful, curved silver sword with a gold hilt that was engraved with runes in a pattern reminiscent of the tide. I didn't need to read the plaque to know who this belonged to. *Deptheart family.* What I truly didn't expect to find at the grave of this fallen warrior, was the sounds of a broken man sobbing.

Between sobs I could barely make out the occasional words, "Kael... I'm sorry. I wish I stayed... I *should've* stayed." He wiped his face before continuing, "Your daughter hates me now. I... I don't know what to do. Madrigal despises me too... How can I make this right...? I never... I never meant for this to happen."

I shouldn't have come. I felt the weight of guilt settling on my shoulders as I pulled myself out of earshot. I peeled myself away from the tree slowly at first in an attempt to sneak back to the entrance. Eventually, I deserted my feeble attempt at stealth and broke into a sprint. I weaved and hopped over weapons as I ran, the realization that I was completely lost slowly settling on my heart.

I collapsed in the grass and caught my breath. My chest rose and fell in heaving breaths. A chuckle echoed across the grass from deep inside me. *I forgot how tiring running without energy is.* I felt bad about overhearing Hundri's grief. I would never be able to tell him I heard that without him feeling like I betrayed his trust, so I decided that what I heard would stay a secret locked deep inside.

After laying in the soft green grass for what felt like an eternity, I pushed myself up and tried to find my bearings once more. A random idea popped into my head. What if the lights had another purpose? I grabbed a nearby floating light construct and closed my eyes, pushing my will into it. As I test, I put everything I knew about the Deptheart into the bronze structure. It spun faster and faster as I released it until it began to speed off towards a lone tree in the distance.

I reached out for another nearby orb of light. With a push from deep in my mind, I directed it to find the exit. It stood still for a moment, spinning wildly. My heart sank, *did it not work?* Suddenly, it rocketed off and relief filled me. My feet pounded against the grassy soil as I ran after it, the archway slowly coming into focus.

Within a few minutes of running, I made it back out of the grim graveyard and hopefully Hundri would be none the wiser. My chest rose and fell rapidly as I collapsed against the stone arch of the doorway. I ran my hands across my forehead and wiped away the freshly beading sweat. I forgot just how much of a difference controlling energy could make.

After a few minutes of just sitting around, I decided to meditate. The darkness enveloped me as I closed my eyes and focused on the runes marking my chest. I let my senses wash over the runes in my mind's eye, taking in every detail until I found the seal. It didn't take long for it to become apparent. As I tried to push energy in or out, a glowing green glyph became more tangible just above my runes. It floated like a spider with webs of light stretching to each of my runes and encased them in smaller runes.

I'd never broken, or even seen a seal like this so I tried everything I could think of. I tried the simplest thing I could think of first which was to overload the seal. Sweat beaded on my head once again as I pushed my will into the energy in my runes. I pictured the same drop of energy flowing from around the edges of the seal only on a greater scale.

Only then did I question if this was a good idea. Energy leaked into the rest of my body at exponential rates, the familiar warmth twisting my concentrated face into a smile. The seal began to crack, and the glowing glyph began to flicker in and out as its strands broke. With a feeling akin to someone lifting a weight from my chest, the seal dissipated.

I stood up with a smile on my face as I let my power smoothly cycle through my body. My newly widened channels could transfer a decent amount more energy much faster than ever before and the difference was night and day. I raised my right arm up to eye level and focused my energy into my fingertips. I could almost see the subdermal glow as I allowed it to spread out across my skin in a scaled aura.

After a few seconds, a familiar shifting gauntlet of light wrapped my hands. My smile broadened. It felt good to have control again. I dissolved the gauntlets and let the power flow back into my body.

Before I had the chance to try anything else with my newly reforged energy channels, footsteps behind me drew my attention. I turned to see Hundri's glowing eyes were now puffy and red around his glowing pupils. He looked gaunt and broken. After a moment, he recomposed himself and stood up straight. He cleared his voice and began to speak, "Hey Rey," his voice cracked, and he cleared his throat again, "Looks like you got rid of the seal on your runes. Are you feeling better already?"

I looked at him sympathetically. "Yeah, I've literally had *days* of sleep to heal." I paused for a moment. "Are you okay Hundri?"

His eyes drooped to the ground for a second. "Yeah. I am not really in the mood to talk about it though."

I nodded and softly responded, "Alright."

We began to walk down the street away from the graveyard but made it less than fifty feet before we were stopped. Two men in steel armor glowing with multicolored runes stepped into our path blocking our way. The first man to speak had short blond hair that hung just above his brown eyes. "Captain Traegan, you and your mercenary group's presence is required by Grand Commander Ronhelm."

Hundri grimaced and before he could speak, the other man who had short spikey brown hair and chestnut eyes continued "You know Ronhelm doesn't like to be kept waiting. We've already sent for the other members of your team. Please follow us."

"Guess you get to meet Ronhelm," Hundri muttered disdainfully in my general direction.

. . .

We had followed the two knights back into the military district and to the building Hundri had originally been called to, which I was informed was aptly named the Military Command Center. The knights activated the same glyph in the wall and the doorway formed just as it had the first time. They peeled off and stood on either side, directing us inward.

The room we entered was made of the same polished dark stone as the rest of the building with giant wooden beams as support. In the center was a large circular table made of crystallized azure energy that projected a map of the mountain hovering just above the surface. Around the room were a few other doorways, maps, chests, racks of weapons and strange magical devices I didn't recognize.

Sitting around the table in beautifully carved, cushioned stone chairs were the Blades of Iora and a man I didn't recognize. He was imposing to say the least. He wore dark, almost black plated armor that was covered in golden trim. Inlayed in the shoulder plates, chestplate and across the surface of the armor were deep amethyst colored energy crystals that swirled and pulsed with his breathing. The purples and blues of the room's light clashed on his tanned, worn skin. He wore his dark brown hair short and neatly trimmed and spiked, with a sharp thin beard befitting a king. At his waist was a similarly colored and forged sword that emanated an aura almost as frightening as Ronhelm itself.

His voice deep and smooth voice called toward me and Hundri with an oppressive weight. "Welcome. Take a seat."

We walked towards the empty chairs and were about to take a seat when Ronhelm flicked a gauntlet covered hand and the chairs slid backwards as if pulled by an invisible string. I looked at Hundri who seemed to think this was perfectly normal. I had forgotten Ronhelm controlled gravity. I swallowed my fear and any pride I may have had and sat down. With a beckoning motion, Ronhelm pulled the chairs towards the table. It felt... wrong. Something inside me hated the feeling that Ronhelm had a massive spectral hand throwing me around like a doll.

Yaldrie shot me a sympathetic look that I almost didn't catch as my interest in the glowing map swallowed my attention. It looked as if it had been painted onto the world with brushstrokes of light and energy. I slowly extended my arm and touched an ethereal mountain. My fingers effortlessly slid through the construct of light as if it wasn't there.

This time, Ronhelm shot me a look like he was going to scold a child for playing with something he shouldn't have which, granted, was exactly what was happening. I felt even my soul recoil at his stern glare, and I quickly shot back to attention in my chair.

Ronhelm's smooth voice washed over the room, "Allow me to formally begin this meeting. Blades of Iora, welcome." We all nodded weakly and opened our mouths to match his greeting, but Ronhelm continued talking. "I have called you here to send you on a mission. And before you ask, I know it's unusual to send a group technically made of mostly civilians on a military operation. However, we have our reasons."

Hundri spoke up with as much courage as he could muster in the half second Ronhelm inhaled, "What *are* your reasons? Wouldn't it be better to avoid sending them and to use a trained team?"

A muscle twitched on Ronhelm's face, which normally would mean nothing to anyone had he been anybody but Ronhelm. The air of the room changed. Everyone was on edge. As if nothing was wrong, Ronhelm's buttery smooth voice filled the room once more. "We *would* prefer to use a group of military personnel instead of a... rag-tag group of mercenaries," each person in the Blades obviously quivered in annoyance but had to let it slide as he kept talking, "but because you all are led by the *great* Hundri Traegan, you're the most reliable group of mercenaries we can find. The reason we reach out for mercenaries at all is much more dire."

He gestured toward the map and a circle of runes inlayed on a ring blazed to life in the same azure color as the map. As if it was listening to his thoughts, the map zoomed in greatly to a mountain that looked all too familiar to me. My destination. "Mount Eiona," Ronhelm spoke again, "As some of you may be aware, we have had great resistance from a bandit group who has occupied the mountain. We suspect they are backed by either a powerful clan or some greater power."

A green light in the shape of a circle blinked to life at the base of the mountain which seemed to be connected to a rail system similar to the one Hundri and I had used. Ronhelm's armored finger pointed at the green indicator as he explained, "This is the entry point of Mount Eiona. As most of you know, this is a common place of prayer. We've made it to about here without too much resistance." A second marker appeared, this time a glowing red X, "We've been slowly increasing the strength of the parties we've sent to gauge their strength, and none have returned. However, they have locked the platform on their side of the rail, so travel has gotten more difficult. We think your team should be able to take it back for us."

The response across the group was mixed. Hundri's face told two stories. His brows furrowed in concern and his eyes blazed with excitement. Yaldrie and Ogland bickered quietly while Ralteir beamed at the map like it was a gift from a god. Syre shared in some of Ralteir's excitement but was slightly more composed. Kai didn't even look like he was listening. He had a strange mechanical bronze monocle with runes blazing around the edges of the lens and was wearing a matching piece of equipment on his hand that looked like a mechanical skeleton which he was using to study the table.

I didn't know what to think. Technically I wasn't even a member of the Blades of Iora and was nowhere close to their strength, but I couldn't help but think with excitement that this offer extended to me too. It was risky, but the gain... was it worth it? Sure, it'd take me exactly where I needed to go, but I might have to fight trained, bloody thirsty warriors. I might have to *kill* someone. The thought made me sick. I could *die*. My mind raced at the possibilities. A small part of me hoped this wasn't up to me.

Hundri was the first to speak, slowly at first, "What do we know about the enemy forces?"

A broad smile pulled itself onto Ronhelm's face. It felt unnatural as if his face was made to scowl. "You'll be heading out tomorrow morning. We don't know much but—"

Hundri cut him off, "We haven't agreed to go yet."

The scowl I felt should've rested on Ronhelm's face formed as the smile died. He laughed and my blood went cold. "I don't think you understand." His eyes began to slowly glow purple. "I wasn't asking." My body grew heavier with each passing moment until I felt as if was going to be crushed under my own weight. The weapons on the nearby racks shook and strained against their supports and the Blades of Iora slumped over as well, aside from Hundri. Stone pieces and dust fell from the ceiling as it started to bend downward under the pressure of Ronhelm's will and my mouth gaped open and closed as I pleaded for air.

As if it was never there, the pressure suddenly disappeared, and it felt like I could breathe again. I heaved in breaths along with the other red-faced blades of Iora. Even Hundri looked strained as he slightly slumped and rested his weight against the table. Ronhelm hadn't even stood. *What a monster.* I thought fearfully.

Slowly Hundri regained his composure, albeit much faster than anyone else at the table. "F-fine..." He heaved. "But you didn't answer... my previous question." Hundri coughed so loud with such force that I thought he was about to explode.

Ronhelm chuckled for a moment as if Hundri had told a joke. "Ah, I suppose you're right." He flicked his hand at the map and it scoped inwards again on the mountain, now displaying a network of tunnels and rooms that stretched through it like veins. He pointed at the bottom where the veins intersected and continued talking, "This here is where the bulk of their fortifications seems to be."

He highlighted a few pathways and kept talking. "We've managed to break through and go up these pathways a few times. The room at the bottom has at least fifteen to twenty guards that range from low steel to low gold. The later pathways we've explored have had dwindling numbers. Usually, the hallways only have a pair of guards patrolling with the individual chambers having more depending on the room." A few side rooms lit up.

Hundri nodded slowly, clearly processing. Everyone else sat quietly, clearly uncomfortable to talk before Ronhelm. "That sounds possible. What do we know about their leader?"

The luminescent map faded away and settled back into runes engraved in the glowing crystal table. It had been obstructed previously, but now that I could see the runic scripture that created these images, I was floored. It had to be the most complex set of glyphs I had ever seen. Hundreds if not thousands of circles and strings of runes weaved together to create a beautiful tapestry of magic text.

Only a few moments later did they all flare back to life and project floating runes that shifted into lines of light in the shape of a person. Floating above the table was a model of a blank person. "We have heard from scout and reconnaissance teams that he's a large man who wears furs and leather plates, seemingly a berserker of some kind." As Ronhelm described him, the floating, luminescent man began to shift. Its muscles grew defined and larger with large plates of fur and leather protecting his new body.

"From other descriptions, he has a large scar over his left eye. His weapon of choice is a pair of enchanted knuckledusters which share his element, flame." The details he described shifted into reality, including a ring of flickering spectral fire at its feet.

Hundri's face creased in concern. "Do we have any gauge on what his strength rating should be?"

Ronhelm paused for a second and stared deep into Hundri's eyes, their cool colored luminescent pupils clashing with a fearsome intensity. "We believe," Ronhelm sighed, "That he's about on par with you, Hundri."

The room was silent for a moment as everyone processed that alarming information. Hundri spoke slowly at first, "Someone... my level? You know I'm halfway through gold, right? Are you sure he's going to be on par with me? What's his family crest? What about my team, they can't handle—"

Ronhelm cut him off with a stern look, "I know you're worried. It's been a while since you've had an opponent at your level. Everyone in Anhalt is much stronger or much weaker." Ronhelm continued answering Hundri and the Blade's questions –who had just found the courage to speak– but something caught my mind.

How much stronger is much stronger? Is gold not the strongest? The thought burned at my mind worse than any fire.

Every hair on my neck stood up and my blood felt as if it stopped. I looked up, wrenched from my thoughts to see Ronhelm looking directly at me. "You," he said while looking in my direction. "What is it? I can feel your curiosity."

My mouth flapped open and closed, unable to process the thoughts I had into sounds under the weight of his gaze. Finally, I got the words out. "You said there are people much stronger than Hundri. I thought gold was the strongest." I paused then quickly added out of fear, "Please forgive my insolence Grand Commander."

A small, almost unnoticeable smile tugged at his lips. "Gold is not the strongest, no. Rarely do people reach the top of gold, but for people who are extraordinary, there are tiers beyond. After gold comes diamond, then legend, then demigod."

I couldn't resist asking the question on the tip of my tongue, despite Hundri's look that told me not to. "And how strong are you?" I blurted out, stumbling over the words.

His tiny smile grew to a full grin which once again looked out of place. "Halfway to legend. I could level this building with a thought."

I summoned all my courage and glared at him. I steadied my voice, "Then why aren't you doing this? No point in risking the lives, right?"

"Aye, he makes a good point," Ogland added weakly.

Ronhelm sighed and leaned back in his ornate chair. "If it were more severe, I would. My *presence* in this city is a deterrent for crime, raids and the like. I also have other work to attend to here."

As if suddenly tuning into the conversation, Kai spoke, "And we have no choice but to go on this... suicide mission?"

A muscle twitched in Ronhelm's face once again. "As I said before, you have an obligation to your city and people to serve at our call."

Everyone was clearly uncomfortable. Everyone except for Ralteir. "We have permission to beat them to a pulp, right?" The excitement in his voice was unnerving.

"Of course. The more completely we eradicate them, the better." Ralteir's excitement grew.

Kai spoke next, "What kind of reward do you have to offer us for completing this arduous task?"

Ronhelm's face was back to a scowl as he sighed once more and rubbed the bridge of his nose. "We can arrange an artifact or two from Anhalt's treasury befitting the difficulty of the mission to be given to each member of the team upon completion."

The mood greatly lifted, and I could almost see excitement brimming in every person. The only person who still looked concerned was Hundri. "Ronhelm, I have one request to make."

The Grand Commander's eyes flicked up to Hundri with a chilling intensity. "And that is?"

"Let this one," He gestured to me, "Stay behind."

A torrent of mixed emotions sprung to life in me. This could be my only chance to make it to Mount Eiona but was it worth the risk? Before I could finish thinking my thoughts were cut short.

"Why?" Ronhelm said simply.

"He's bronze! What is he going to do against steels? Be a meat shield?" Hundri's agitation grew with every word and for some reason so did mine. It was nice to see he cared, but for some reason his doubts still stung.

"He also is affiliated with your group. If I let one of you stay, I have no confidence you will keep an oath to complete the mission." He gave me a small smile. "Even if he is just bronze, its plausible that he kills a steel or two. Great experience." The weight of his energy crept into his voice, "He goes."

Syre straightened from a slouch in her chair and spoke up while she ignored his forceful tone, "What if we all swore through blood to complete the mission? In exchange, you let him stay."

Ronhelm scrunched his nose in disgust. "A blood oath? How barbaric. I was going to require all to form a different form of contract but if a blood oath is what you are all comfortable with, it is more simple and effective." His gaze shifted to me. "Then I leave the choice to you."

My heart pounded in my chest. Around me every one of the Blades searched for my eyes but I let my gaze settle on Hundri. Indecision riddled my mind like a swarm of bees and clouded my thoughts. Hundri smiled and gave me an almost imperceivable nod.

With that tiny gesture, the fog lifted from my thoughts. The Blades had pushed back against a monumental man to give me a choice, an exit. If I wanted to catch up to my sister, I had to take the hardest path and every shortcut I could. A smile tugged at my lips. I let my eyes lock with Ronhelm's. "I'm going."

A wide, unnatural grin formed on his face as he boomed out loud chuckles. "Alright," He met my eyes again. "I like you. I can see the fires of determination blazing behind those eyes."

I said nothing, only meeting his gaze. Hundri and the rest of the Blades looked mildly stunned to hear both my answer and Ronhelm's affection. Only then did I notice a fuzzy tension in my mind. I had forgotten to breathe. I slowly pulled in air and felt my thoughts clear again.

We all sat in silence. Nobody dared to challenge his authority. Nobody dared to do so much as breathe, aside from me. After another moment, Ronhelm spoke again, "You should all prepare yourselves and anything you want to bring. I will send men to collect you early tomorrow morning and you will ship out on a lift. Is that clear?"

Everyone muttered and choked out an agreement of some form, but in the slew of responses not a single one was understandable. Ronhelm flicked his armored hand in our direction. "Dismissed," he commanded before he began to change the display on the table.

We slowly stood up and shuffled towards the door. With the sound of shifting parts and the glow of magic circles, it disassembled itself into a doorway and we piled out. When it finally clicked shut behind us, I could finally breathe freely, as if the air around Ronhelm was heavy. I took a deep breath.

The guards on either side of the door gave us strange glances as we all took deep breaths with relieved looks on our faces. The only one with an ounce of composure was Hundri. He looked almost the same as normal, calmly breathing as if nothing had changed. After everyone had a moment to collect themselves, we hurried down the hallway we had come from and away from prying ears.

"What... was that..." I huffed as I leaned against a wall to catch my breath.

Hundri smoothed his shirt and swept the hallway for anybody listening before he spoke, "Either Ronhelm just sent us to die, or we become heroes. Nothing really in the middle."

"If he only *could* be as strong as you, shouldn't we have the advantage with all of us here?" I asked.

Ogland cut in, "Aye, but if ya think about it, he will have numbers as well. We got no clue what kinda techniques he could be usin'. It's risky."

Hundri nodded in response. "As much as I would like to pretend it's an option *not* to go, Ronhelm made it pretty clear that we didn't have another choice. Personally, I'd rather die fighting for my people than die because I was too scared to fight."

Under my breath I mumbled, "And I'd like to not die." Laughter blanketed the group as everyone heard my comment. I quickly added, "But from where I stand, its risky. If it'll take me another step higher," I paused, "*damn* the risk."

A cheer went up from the group and Hundri slapped me on the shoulder a little too hard. "All right team," Hundri raised his voice. "Everyone get your affairs in order. We should meet at the gates before sunset else Ronhelm sends people for us."

Everyone nodded and began to split off down the hallway and out of the building, but I turned to Hundri. Before I could open my mouth to speak, Hundri cut me off. "Go see Abigail. With the risk this mission holds, you may not see her for a long time, if ever again." I nodded and bid Hundri goodbye for now. With a turn, I was off to find Abigail.

CHAPTER SEVENTEEN

The Pie

Reynolds Helphain

The sky had started to dim by the time I found Abigail. She was sitting on the rim of a fountain, weaving water between her hands with a placid look on her face. I hoped she wasn't upset with me, but knowing her, she probably was. The streets had begun to thin as the light above dimmed.

She sensed my approach and looked me in the eye. To my surprise, what stared back at me wasn't angry, or sad. It radiated an emptiness that seemed all too familiar to me for a reason I couldn't explain. I listened to my instincts and wrapped my arms around her in a tight embrace.

Time seemed to stand still as I felt the warmth of her chest rise and fall against mine. She heaved silently as tiny droplets spilled onto my shoulder. Slowly, her voice began to leak out, tiny sobs muffled by the fabric of my shirt. I let my hand run over the top of her head and slowly rubbed. We sat there for what felt like hours without saying a word. No words needed to be said. Guilt gripped me like a fist. I had no good news to tell her.

After an eternity, she wiped her eyes and pulled herself back. "Sorry," she mumbled in a broken voice.

"It's okay." I smiled at her warmly. "Sometimes we all need a shoulder to cry on."

She smiled back. "Yeah."

"Are you okay?"

She shifted uncomfortably. "I'll be okay. Let's talk about something else, okay? I don't want you to think of me like *that*."

"Alright," I gestured to the street with a loose flick of my arm. "Feel like taking a walk?"

She nodded and began to walk. I quickly fell in line, and we strolled through the streets, lost in our own thoughts. After walking in silence for a few minutes, I decided to give her the news. "Hey Abigail, I wanted to get this out of the way sooner rather than later." She shot me a confused look. "I am going on a mission with Hundri soon. To Eiona. I don't know how long I'll be gone, but I promise I'll see you first thing when I come back, okay?"

She slowed and something in her face shuddered with emotion. After a moment, she spoke. "You better come back." Her eyes went to the ground as she quietly added, "I just don't want to lose anyone else..."

I slowed with her for a moment, stunned. I smiled at her with as much confidence as I could muster as feelings of dread, self-doubt and guilt clenched my soul like a vice. "I'll be back and better than ever. When I'm back, I'll floor you in a duel."

She looked up at me sad eyes. "You promise?"

Every ounce of my heart told me to stay. My brain rationalized with the fact that I could never get another chance for growth like this again. Indecision riddled every part of me like holes in cheese. With the same confident smile, I placed a hand on her shoulder. "I swear." Guilt clenched me, but I had no other choice.

We walked in silence again. It felt like every step we didn't speak, the harder it became to force out a word. After walking for a bit, I finally mustered the courage to ask something, anything. "So... anything unique about your sword?" It was a stupid question and every breath she didn't answer made me feel even more stupid.

She brightened with an obvious air of pride and placed a hand on the grip of the sword on her hip. "This was my mother's old weapon. We don't have enough money to buy anything new or fancy as we have to pay tuition for the academy." A rune flared to life where the sword touched the scabbard, and she slid it out enough to see a circle of runes on the blade. "It's seen many, many battles. The circle here is pretty basic, it just allows for water energy to flow through the blade easier." She tapped an inner ring on the circle. "Fun trick with it though, if you stop pushing energy into specifically this part of the circle when its full of energy, it will all cascade out the tip in a short-range burst."

I stared in minor awe, it was nowhere near as powerful as the swords Hundri had shown me, but it was still very impressive. Magic tools and mechanics were something I hadn't even dreamed of seeing myself, and from what I had read in books, I didn't think they would be commonplace either. "That's awesome. What was the runic light I saw before you drew the blade?"

"Ah that! Here," She fumbled around the scabbard on her waist until it came off and she handed it to me. "Try drawing it."

I placed my hand on the grip firmly and tugged lightly. Nothing. After a few seconds of waiting, I dripped energy into my hands and yanked. Nothing. Abigail snorted and I shot her a look of annoyance which only caused her to laugh harder. After a few more unsuccessful attempts I handed it back. "So, I take it its sealed in there until you activate a hidden circle?"

She winked. "Something like that. It's scripted to only open with Deptheart family energy. For anyone below gold, it would be impossible to draw this sword."

"Oh, why can gold people get around it?"

"Why do you think?" She stared blankly at me and spoke again before I could open my mouth. "They have so much raw power that the runes physically cannot hold the sword in."

"Gods..." I muttered. "Well good thing most gold people probably have their own high-grade weapons. No need to steal one from someone almost steel."

She nodded in agreement before asking about the sword on my hip. "How about you? Any special story for your blade?"

I chuckled, embarrassed. "My sword is as standard as it gets." I drew the blade and held it before me. The already sparce people walking down the street began to hurry away and avoid me. I could feel strange glances from all over, peering at me and my sword.

Abigail chuckled weakly and whispered, "Maybe put the sword away. While Anhalt does allow people to carry weapons, nobody draws them unless they're looking for a fight."

My heart dropped and I quickly sheathed it as my face flushed red. "Sorry." I muttered before clearing my voice. "But as I was saying, it's got no special history that I know of. It's just a sword."

"Makes sense," She smiled, and her tone shifted slightly, "Good for someone like you. Nothing special for a first sword."

I raised an eyebrow, "Someone like me? What's that supposed to mean?"

Her smile grew more and more devious. "Ah... what was the word again...? Ah yes! *Weakling.*"

I scoffed. "You know you aren't that much stronger than me, right?"

She slung her arm over my shoulder. "Fair point. We can be weaklings together then."

A smile danced on my lips as my face heated. "Yeah. Weaklings together."

Her arm fell back down at her side and soon we were both distracted by the fragrance of something delicious.

"Are you hungry?" I asked Abigail as I started following the scent. My own hunger was drawing me in to whatever that sweet scent was.

A grumble came from her stomach. She nodded profusely. "Let's go see what it is." We began to walk, and both prayed it wasn't far.

As we had hoped, it wasn't far. Just around the bend was a small store with outdoor seating selling pies. Abigail and I looked at each other in unison. The hunger we shared was apparent in our eyes.

We sat down at a small wooden table with two well-padded seats that were somehow still uncomfortable. The store to our right had an open kitchen with pies cooling on a long windowsill showing off their goods.

She looked at the pies, then at me, then back again. "I wasn't sure what I wanted." Her eyes never left the pies as she spoke. "But this is definitely good."

"Agreed."

It wasn't long before a young woman came out from the kitchen. She brushed crumbs off the white apron protecting the plain azure dress underneath. Her blonde hair fell from her bun as she pulled out a small string that had tied it behind her head. She spoke in a voice that sounded as sweet as those pies looked. "Welcome! How are you guys doing today?"

"Hungry." We both said in unison.

The woman chuckled softly, "Well let's get you started then. Any clue what you want to order?"

Only then did I notice the thin paper menu on the table. "One moment please." I looked up at her and smiled, which she correctly took as my signal to give us time.

I scanned the menu looking for anything familiar to me before realizing that I'd never had pie before. I glanced at Abigail sheepishly and saw that she already seemed ready to order. "Hey Abigail," She turned to look at me and I continued, "I've never actually had pie before. Any recommendations?"

She cocked an eyebrow, "Seriously? Never? Well, I *guess* I can help you." She smiled down at her menu as her eyes soared across it. She leaned over the table and tapped the berry pie section with a slender finger.

"Berry pies?"

She nodded solemnly. "Berry pies."

I chuckled mildly, "Alright, I'll choose one." I scanned the page for anything of interest. Then something caught my eye, Oruje berry. It was the only thing on the page that I recognized. My sister and I used to climb a cliff near our house for Oruje berries. We would sit staring out over the thousands of miles of green forest below and gorge ourselves on the tangy purple berries until we could hardly walk. In retrospect, it was incredibly risky, but I was too young to realize it then. Besides, it was a few cycles too late to think about that.

I hadn't thought about those berries in cycles and was grateful we came here even just for the memory, even if the pie was horrid. I looked back up at Abigail, "I think I'm ready."

"Great! What'd you decide on?"

A faint smile tugged at my lips as memories surfaced. "Oruje berry pie."

"Oruje berries? I've never heard of them. How about splitting it?"

"Sure. It's probably more than I can eat anyway." I chuckled.

As if we had summoned her with just a thought, the waitress appeared again. "Ready to order?"

I grabbed Abigail's menu from her and stacked it with mine before handing it to the lady. "Yeah, we're going to split an Oruje berry pie."

Her eyes raised ever so slightly in surprise, "Oruje, huh? Unique choice, not many people like those. Are you perhaps ordering it because of the myth?"

Now it was my turn to be a little confused. "The myth?"

She nodded. "With King Optyr, Master of the Four Winds?" She searched my face for any ounce of recognition but was disappointed to find none.

"The title Master of The Four Winds sounds vaguely familiar?"

She sighed. "Well, I'll give you the bit of the myth that's relevant to Oruje berries as it's my job to give you pie, not *tell stories*." I hint of annoyance flickered into her voice before quickly turning placid again. "King Optyr was a born on the edge of the mountain, far out of the reaches of the clans. King Optyr used his powerful wind magic to crush any opponent he came across in his conquest to reach Anhalt. Eventually, he did make it here and peacefully took over. His descendants still rule today. It is said that he fed Oruje berries to his children every day to strengthen their body to be fit for rule as he did himself before coming to this mountain." She paused and took a breath before continuing, "The berries used to be extremely expensive, similar in price to high delicacies. After cycles of people trying, nobody was able to recreate anything close to the myths, so they just became normal berries. Most people now just believe his lineage is blessed."

She continued talking about some of King Optyr's feats, but they went in one ear and out the other. *Could my body be stronger then?* It was a silly idea. I would have noticed if something like that were true. Every battle I fought ended in a loss. If I really had gained some sort of physical enhancement from eating those berries for cycles, I couldn't tell.

I hadn't noticed the lady stopped talking until Abigail nudged my leg under the table. My voice rose to a slightly higher pitch in surprise as I rushed to say something. "A-ah! That was very interesting. Thank you."

She nodded politely. "I'll be right back with your pies!" And with that, she disappeared into the kitchen.

Abigail looked at me again. "What's up?" She smirked, "Either you were *so* invested in the story that you didn't say a word, or you zoned out."

"It was interesting to hear about the properties of the berries. I used to eat these with my sister for cycles. Maybe that's why she turned out like such a monster." My lips tightened to hide the bitterness slipping onto my face. *If they did so much for her, why am I so pathetic?*

Abigail's eyebrow raised slightly. "Sister? I didn't know you had one. Tell me about her."

I sighed. "Well, she's an ice elementalist. She took the same journey I'm on now when she was my age. It was easy for her. As if Iora herself had stepped down into a human body. The day she came back, she was much more powerful than my battle trained father."

She cut me off with a wave of her hand. "That's great and all. Now, tell me what she was *like.*"

I stared at her for a moment, stunned. All anybody cared about was power, or so I had thought. A warm feeling spread through my chest and a smile spread along with it. "She was kind, funny and ruthless. We wanted to be royal knights someday. We spent hours training every day. She would beat me every time we competed. Even still, she never gave up on me, she never let me get down on myself. She always pushed me, telling me this was an opportunity to grow. To be better. We would do extraordinary things to prove we could. She was always so warm. Despite when she left..." My voice broke and I wiped away a tear I hadn't realized formed. "D-despite how cold she was when she left... something is wrong. I can't afford to let her be alone any longer."

Abigail nodded slowly. "What do you think happened?"

Screams penetrated my mind. Flashes of blood. Glassy eyes. I shuddered. "I-I... I don't know. Even with how cold she was, what I wouldn't give to see her raven hair in the wind again."

"Raven hair?" Abigail tilted her head to the side. "How long ago was this?"

"A few cycles. Why?"

She touched her bottom lip in thought. "Huh. Sounded familiar."

"*What?*"

She muttered to herself for a moment. "It's probably nothing. Might've just gotten her confused with someone else."

"Ah." I wiped my eyes as the pie was placed on the table atop a wooden cutting slate with utensils on either side.

The waitress beamed at us. "Enjoy the pie!" She held her hand out and I started to rummage through my pocket for change, but Abigail was faster. Three silver coins clinked in the woman's hand, and she gave us a shallow bow before pocketing the money and walking away.

I shoved the money back into my pocket. "I could've gotten that you know."

She shrugged and gave me a grin. "Well, looks like you were too slow. Are you sure you're ready for a mission if you can't even pay for a meal faster than me?"

"Not in the slightest." I picked up a knife and absent mindedly cut the pie into sections. "Honestly, I sort of wish I could refuse. Ronhelm is forcing Hundri's group on the mission. Apparently, I've been lumped in with them, so I don't have much of a choice." It was only a little lie, but I hoped it gave the impression I wasn't purposefully leaving her.

"Ah." We sat in silence for a moment before starting to tentatively taste the pie that sat steaming before us. It was a strange sensation as the pie dissolved in my mouth. At first, it was painfully sour, then overly sweet before mellowing out into the familiar tangy taste I was used to. The part that made me really enjoy Oruje berries, however, was the aftermath of swallowing even just one berry. And this pie was filled with them.

Each time I swallowed a bite, it felt like an electric shock hit my limbs filling me with a sensation of power. It emanated a warmth from deep inside my stomach like I had swallowed fire. I had missed it more than I remembered and quickly shoveled bite after bite into my mouth. Between bites, I glanced over at Abigail in anticipation.

I almost spit out my food as laughter bloomed like an explosion in my chest. Her face shifted from disgust to enjoyment then to an expression of vague happiness but confusion. I could see the exact moment it felt like lightning struck her system. She visibly shuddered and a look of wonder and shock stretched across her face.

"Pretty good right?" I said between bites and laughter.

She stared at her piece of pie. "That... that is the weirdest thing I have ever tasted."

I smiled. "But it's good, right?"

"At first it tastes worse than a rotting rat, but that feeling at the end makes it all worth it. What a strange flavor." She took another bite and to my disappointment, reacted less extremely than she had the first time.

"Honestly, this is more intense than just the actual berry on its own." I paused for a second before a memory floated up. "Well, it depends on the age of the berry. But still, it always has the same effect feeling, just different intensities." She mumbled something I wasn't quite able to understand and continued eating.

Before long, the sky was shifting colors and the entire pie was almost gone after an evening of eating and joking. My body felt bloated and heavy as I stood from my chair, the electric feeling of Oruje berries still coursing through my veins.

Abigail and I waved at the lady who had served us the pie and began to make our way back towards Hundri's house through the winding city streets. "So, Rey," started Abigail as she stared up at the sky. "I've been thinking."

I glanced over at her and waited for her to speak again but nothing came. "About...?"

"Well, we're currently coming up on a break at the academy." She fidgeted her hands on the pommel of her sword. "Do you think I could... come with you... to Eiona?" She trailed off and looked me in the eye.

I hesitated for only a moment, and that moment was too long. She quickly began to speak again before I could open my mouth. "I mean, I wouldn't be too much of a burden! Not more than you, since you know, I'm stronger. I know Hundri would probably say no and that's okay! We can convince him. I just want a good chance to grow stronger and you're my friend and—"

My hand rested on her muscular shoulder, and she stopped, face flushed. "Abigail, if you want to come, I'm all for it." I gave her a warm smile. "It'll be nice having someone else I trust there because I don't know Hundri's team all that well. You will definitely have to work some things out with Hundri first, because I know for a fact there's no way he will let you follow us if he has a shadow of a doubt that you could betray him."

She looked back at the mystic sky and frowned slightly. "Hundri will be the hard part. I still don't know how I feel about him." She raised her hand up to the sky as if grabbing for something. "After seeing him be so... open, I don't know what to do with all this..." She clenched her hand into a tight fist. "All this anger." She sighed and dropped her unclenched hand back to her side.

"Well... I don't think Hundri is upset with you. I think he's more upset with himself." Now it was my turn to ponder the tapestry of light above us. "You should just speak what's true to you and he'll listen. Personally, I don't think there is a good place to put your anger. I think you should let it fuel you to grow, so you don't have to be in a situation like Hundri was." She stared at me thoughtfully and I scratched the back of my neck, suddenly uncomfortable.

"Thank you, Rey. You better catch up to me!" She gave me a smirk, "We can't both be weaklings forever."

I smiled up at the sky. "Yeah. Soon enough, we'll walk together as equals." I felt a pit forming in my gut. This was familiar. *Too* familiar.

She chuckled uncomfortably "So Rey, I probably should've asked this earlier... but what is the mission?"

I stared at her deadpan as we turned a corner. "You want to come, and yet, have no clue what it is?"

A sheepish grin spread to life on her face. "In my defense, you said it was going to be a long mission, so I'm guessing it'll be something tough or far away. Either way, it's a chance to grow right?"

"Yeah," I smiled. She had the same mindset and determination that I did. Well, almost. "Honestly, I'm excited. We're supposed to force out some bandits that have taken control of Eiona. They're going to be tough opponents, not a single one below steel. Their leader is as strong as Hundri."

She looked at me in mild concern, "Not a single one below *steel?* You've got to be kidding me. You're still going on this mission, knowing how weak you are?"

"Yeah. I need to fight and push myself to the limit if I want to catch up to my sister. I can't afford to die on some random *mountain*. I will fight until my last breath, for that is a brother's duty."

Abigail's brow creased ever so slightly. "Even against gold? You refuse to give up?"

"That's why we have Hundri and the rest of them right?" I smirked. "Not like it's just you and me."

She nodded slowly and we walked in silence for a few moments as we stared at the glowing sky. Abigail spoke without breaking eye-contact with the tapestry above. "I know it's far out, but what's next for you after this mission?"

"After this mission... well, I'm trying to find my sister, so whatever takes me towards that." I sighed. "I'll probably be leaving Iora and going into the Lower Greens."

She nodded. "I've never been off the mountain before, but the world below has always looked so interesting. Hardly anyone comes up or down with how rough the conditions are. For me, I'm not really sure what comes next." She shrugged. "More training I guess?"

I chuckled softly and we turned another corner, Hundri's home now in sight. "Fair enough. I mean it's the same for me too, just traveling while I do."

It was clear Abigail saw it too as her happy look withered. "Well Rey," She looked down on me with excitement. "I'll see you in the morning at...?"

I never told her where we were supposed to meet. How stupid of me. "Front gate is what I heard from Hundri. If you'd rather, you could probably catch me and Hundri leaving here."

She smiled again and brushed some loose hair from her eyes. "Alright. Sleep well Rey. See you tomorrow."

I smiled as well and waved goodbye as I entered Hundri's building. I could already tell it would be hard to sleep as every bit of me was filled with an electric tingle. My feet hammered the staircase of the building as I climbed up to his home and knocked on the door, only to find it slide open as my fist rapped against it.

My head stuck through the crack between the door and the frame. I looked around the dark living room. The curtains of the large floor to ceiling glass windows fluttered in a gentle breeze and revealed the reclined silhouette of Hundri on the balcony. The door slid shut with a click as I twisted the cool steel lock and made my way to Hundri.

A slight breeze made my hair dance and sway as I stepped out onto the balcony and took the chair next to him. The cushion sank below me as I made myself comfortable. We were silent. After a moment, I heard glass clink to my left —where Hundri sat— and turned, curious. Hundri drew a ball of ice from thin air with a pulse of cold air and took a sip from the now iced drink. His dimly luminescent eyes eventually drifted towards me, and he finally spoke, "How're you feeling about tomorrow?"

I let my gaze shift to the sprawling city around us. "I'm nervous, but excited." I smiled faintly but it slowly faded as I thought of my reason for climbing in the first place. "I hope we find something about my sister. *Anything.*"

He studied my face in the darkness, then sighed. "Listen, are you sure you want to know? What happened to her I mean."

"No," I said after a moment of thought. My voice hardened. "But it's my duty."

"Rey..." He hesitated, took another sip, and continued, "Just don't throw your life away becoming something you're not. Even if you feel like you have an obligation, it doesn't mean you have to change who you are for it."

I furrowed my brow in confusion. "I don't understand."

He sighed and went back to staring up at the sky. "You may be a brother and a son with all the care and loyalty in the world. That doesn't mean you have to do something like *this*. You can still be those things without throwing your life away. Hell, there's a thousand ways you could find your sister. Just make sure this is the one you *want* to take."

He met my eyes. "When I was your age," He took another sip. "No, even before that. I have always been in the footsteps of a legend. From before I can remember, I was told I would be a hero. I was a prodigy. I would be the one to inherit those... *stones*." He spat the last word with hate.

"I've never been that man, and the realization that I would *never* be tore me apart. Those stones never responded to me, and for cycles that tore me apart. I worked my whole life to *win*. To be the hero everyone said I would be. When everyone realized that I *wasn't* going to inherit that ability, I was regarded with contempt."

"Nobody saw the cycles of practice I took into honing my swordsmanship. Nobody paid attention to the fact that I had exceptional control over energy. Nobody had a care in the world that I saved lives time and time again. No. Instead, they said, 'Isn't he the son of Halvor? Why didn't he do *more.*'"

"So, I ran. I gave up on the military. I was no *hero*. I was always Hundri the failure, not Hundri the captain. I turned to the world of mercenaries and started to build my reputation there." He cracked a faint smile. "That's how I met the group you see today. I walked in that tavern full of naivety and determination and took the hardest missions they offered. Eventually, I even had a nickname," He chuckled. "Frozen Eyes."

I cringed.

He chuckled. "I know, it's terrible. I tried as hard as I could to stop it, but it stuck. I hate names like that. Worthless." He sighed. "Anyway, I was now a hero in the eyes of the people, with a list of exploits and tales longer than the list of bounties in Hell's Pavilion. And when I came back to the military, they finally acknowledged me as *me*. And I wasn't satisfied."

"Eventually I realized something. I had spent my whole life becoming something I thought I had to be, what I had been born into because of my lineage. I never once *paused* to think about what *I* wanted to be." He frowned, gaze trained on the sky again and went silent.

After a few moments, I asked the burning question. "And what did you want to be?"

He smiled a sorrowful smile before taking another sip. "I still don't know." He let the words hang for a moment. "But as long as I'm with my friends, I remain happy enough."

I frowned. "Then why do you stay in service of the military?"

"Duty my friend, duty. My cycles of working to become a hero have shackled me to the role. I am bound to fight, whether it's what I want or not." He smiled genuinely and met my gaze again. "But I am glad it led me to you, if for no other reason than to impart my story."

I smiled back. "Thank you, Hundri." Then all was quiet. Finally, I found the words I searched for, "I think, this *is* what I want. My family has been all I have had for cycles, and I refuse to let my sister be in possible danger. I refuse to *abandon* them after everything they've done for me. I know what that will lead to. The bodies, the death, the legacy and the hardship. But it's all I have ever wanted."

"Remember that." He sipped again, the ice clinking.

I frowned, confused. "What?"

I looked me in the eye with a sudden firmness. "Remember that you *chose* what's to come. Death and fighting seems glorious to all who haven't experienced the cost. Remember to do what I didn't, pause, and think about if this life is what you truly want."

I nodded. "I promise." He nodded back.

After another few moments of silence, he stood and placed the empty glass on a nearby table. His glowing eyes flicked down to me, "Get some sleep. We have a long trip ahead of us." With that, he disappeared inside. I sat there for a moment, mulling over his words. Eventually, I stood and wandered back in and shut the door behind me with a click. I headed off to bed with one final thought, *tomorrow, tomorrow is when my journey truly begins.*

CHAPTER EIGHTEEN

March for the Mountain

Reynolds Helphain

The morning was a blur. Hundri woke me up bright and early and hurried me to prepare. I washed myself in a large tub of hot water, which was a delightful new experience. After throwing together some simple black clothes and strapping on some black leather plates from Hundri's armory, I was ready to go. Hundri threw some supplies in a large backpack and after strapping it to his back, we departed for the gate.

According to Hundri, we had exited the military district and into one of its neighbors, an upper-class residential district. We were the first ones to arrive from the Blades of Iora. The only people at the gate at this time of morning was an official wearing lavish black robes embroidered with glowing purple runes, silver swirls and ornate details, two knights flanking the official, and Abigail who was wearing a fair amount gear herself.

Hundri and I bowed respectfully to the official before walking over to Abigail. I gave her a little wave which she returned with a nod before Hundri began to speak. "Abigail. What are you doing here?"

She took a deep breath and stared Hundri in the eyes, her determination clear. "I want to come with." She gestured to me. "I'm going to be less of a burden to you than he will at least. More numbers *are* better, right?"

Hundri didn't look convinced. Abigail took notice of this and shifted uncomfortably before speaking again. "And..." She gave me a nervous look. "While I don't forgive you, I can't hate you forever. I... I want to work things out. My parents trusted you, and so will I."

Hundri's face lit up. "I'm glad Abigail. Your parents were some of my closest friends. Everything I do is to honor their legacy."

He reached forward for a hug, which was met with Abigail's palm pressing him backwards. "Not there yet." She said flatly and Hundri immediately stopped.

"Sorry." He scratched his messy hair sheepishly. "You can come if you want, but I should warn you, you'll have to form a blood pact with the Grand Commander."

A range of emotions flashed on her face. "Sorry, I'll have to *what?*"

Before Hundri could answer the rest of the team showed up. They filed in from different streets roughly at the same time and gathered with me, Hundri and Abigail. They all wore different battle gear, backpacks, and the weapons I had seen at the bar. Each of them gave Abigail a strange look. She looked at me with an unreadable expression, so I just returned a sympathetic smile.

Hundri addressed the group when they all arrived, his voice raised. "Alright team. Now, before we leave, I'm guessing we will have to speak to that Pactmaster to form the contract. All this will do is bind us to completing the mission and keep us from deserting." He noticed the strange glances toward Abigail and added, "And as you all know, this is Abigail Deptheart. You all remember Madrigal and Kael. Well now their daughter wants to come with us and our friend Rey. Let's prioritize keeping these two safe."

Scattered greetings in the form of murmurs came up from around the group as they all acknowledged Abigail. There was a clear uncomfortable air surrounding the group, but it was quickly forgotten as the Pactmaster and his pair of knights walked up to the group. "Hello everyone!" He croaked, trying his best to be cheerful even though he looked gaunt enough to fall apart at a moment's notice. He brushed a curtain of long, curly platinum hair from his vision and smiled at us.

Something churned in my stomach at his smile, and I could see the rest had similar reactions. The Pactmaster's smile faded, and he produced a large wooden disc with golden runic inlays in the form of a script. "If you would all release a droplet of blood into the script. That will activate the contract."

He came around with a small knife and the tablet. Each person in our group pricked a finger and let the blood drop into the circle. Once we had all provided our blood, the man held his hand over the disc and began to mutter. The circle blazed with crimson light as he slowly clenched his outstretched fingers into a fist. The red light streamed together into a ball as he closed his hand entirely. After a moment, it split into one ring for each member of the team.

Each ring was a dark crimson metal with runes formed across the surface. He handed one to everyone and instructed us to put them on. The runes blazed for a second then went dark again before sinking below our skin like a liquid. "Each of these will act as a key to the city and keys in Eiona. With these on, you can open most doors and operate most lifts." With another gnarly smile, he wished us good luck and they marched back into the city.

I turned to head towards the rest of the group, but Kai stopped me. He still looked a little uncomfortable around me but produced a thinly wrapped package. "I managed to finish in time."

The paper tore away, and bundled up inside was a hooded black cloak lined with white bear fur that seemed to emanate a hungry power. I spread it out in front of me and was filled with excitement and gratitude. "Thank you, Kai!" I pulled it over my shoulders where it rested comfortably.

"Don't mention it." He muttered. "If you push energy into it, the bear's fur will conduct your power and reinforce itself temporarily."

"That's amazing!" I admired the fur inside. The thought of the bear I had killed without reason weighed on my conscious slightly, but this cloak was invaluable to me. With that out of the way, we turned back to the group who was waiting on the moving platform that hovered over the military track that led to Mount Eiona.

Hundri whistled as he saw me approach. "Looking good kid." He then turned to the rest of the group. "Is everyone ready to head out?"

With a resounding cheer, Hundri touched a similar pedestal to the one me and Hundri had used to get to Anhalt. Nothing happened. Hundri spoke with a sigh, "Well then. That must be the *real* reason Ronhelm isn't going."

"What?" I walked closer and noticed for the first time the lack of a platform.

Hundri walked towards a small doorway carved into the side of the mountain. "We'll have to go through here. Looks like the bandits stopped the platform from travelling."

Ogland groaned. "Yer tellin me we need to *hike?*"

"Yes Ogland, that is exactly what I'm saying! Let's get moving then, no time to waste."

Everyone groaned, but we marched quietly through the door. Our footsteps echoed in the dimly lit, stone brick staircase as we slowly descended. At the bottom of the climb, we found the familiar stone and bronze doorway. With a touch of Hundri's pendant, the inlays filled the dark room with azure light. With a loud grinding, the stone door pulled itself apart into triangular fragments and slid into the walls.

I grimaced and raised my hand to shield my eyes from the blinding sun as I stepped out into the frigid hellscape of a forest. A light wind whipped through the barren branches and lightly dusted us with snow. Hundri's boots crunched as he stepped out in front of the group.

"Onwards!" He yelled. He glanced upwards at the large bronze rails and began to walk beneath their supports.

I sighed and marched after him. After a few minutes of hiking through the snow-laden forest, I felt the pressure of a hand on my shoulder and turned.

To my left stood Syre. "How're you feeling?" Her deep golden eyes emanated a warmth of concern as she glanced at where my runes were beneath the layers of fabric. "Did my seal help?"

I gave her a confident smile. "I'm feeling much better, thank you." I tapped where the seal had been and chuckled. "I would probably be dead without your seal."

"Well, it's good that I was here then." We hiked through the snow in silence for a few moments. "Have you spoken to Ralteir yet?"

My smile died. "Not yet. Probably should before we get there, right?"

"Yeah," She nodded, "Don't want to fight with someone who has a grudge. You're begging to be stabbed in the back. That's probably not going to happen though."

"Probably?"

She smiled. "Probably."

I sighed. She was right, I knew it. "I'll go talk to him." I grumbled. With that, I turned and set my sights on Ralteir. I sped up to catch up to him, jogging through the crunching snow.

Ralteir wore gleaming steel pauldrons and leather plates over loose beige pants. His attire seemed unwise to me, seeing as it left his entire chest open, and we were hiking through freezing temperatures. He didn't seem to mind. Resting over his sternum were concentric rings of complex runes with his family crest in the center. Now that we were headed into real battle, he wore leather wraps over his hands. Even when heading toward a slaughter, he did his hair spiky and greased.

"Ralteir." I looked him in the eyes, "We should talk."

He grimaced and scratched the back of his neck as he glanced past me, "No, I should talk. You should listen." I raised an eyebrow in annoyance, and he started talking again. "I can get a little... crazed in the heat of battle. I shouldn't have driven you that far." He looked up again nervously but avoided my eyes, once again looking past me.

I turned around to see Hundri giving Ralteir a cold look while we trudged forwards. He noticed my gaze almost immediately and quickly dropped the cold expression and waved overenthusiastically. "The forest is gorgeous behind you two!" He called over.

I rolled my eyes and looked back towards Ralteir. Even if it was forced, an apology was an apology. "Thank you, Ralteir." I lightened my tone, "You fought well, from what I remember. It's a blur."

He cracked a confident smile, "Of course I did. You didn't do too badly yourself."

I raised my eyebrows. "Oh, 'not too bad' you say? I feel like I remember you saying I could've killed you with one of my punches."

He scoffed. "Exaggeration."

I rolled my eyes and added one final comment before walking away, "Looking forward to fighting with you."

"Likewise," And with that, I slowed and maneuvered towards Abigail.

She smiled at me and slowly, the chill of the softly gusting winds disappeared. I smiled back. After a moment of silent hiking, she gestured at the Blades. "Anything I should know about them, Rey?" Her head swiveled to look at me now, her gaze soft.

I scratched my chin lightly and felt the scratch of light stubble. I cursed internally. "I assumed your mother would have talked about them at least a little."

She shook her head. "Hardly. Only about how they were all cowards and lowlifes."

"Ralteir maybe." I chuckled softly and Abigail gave me an inquisitive look which I waved away. I gestured to Yaldrie, "She uses wind and a staff while generally keeping her distance." Next, I pointed to Ogland, "Fire mage. Uses a large great sword. I've never seen him fight before so I don't know how he behaves."

Abigail made a quiet noise. "Got it, avoid him."

"What? Why?"

"Unsurprisingly water and fire mages rarely get along. Just our temperaments."

I sighed. "That's a shame. He seems nice." I gestured to the next person, Syre. "Another wind mage, she uses a bow and wind magic. She also can use seals."

Abigail's eyebrows shot up and she immediately looked at Syre intently. "Seals, huh? That's impressive."

"Really? Hundri told me a little about them but nothing more than basics."

She laughed, "Basics? This is *the* most basic piece of information on seals." She formed a hazy aura of energy around the tip of her slender index finger. "Take the concentration to gather, shape and solidify aura to a density that could block an attack for example. After practice, it becomes like second nature, and the easiest part is that after its already formed, you barely have to focus on it."

She let the energy wink out and the blue glow disappeared. "Now for most steel practitioners, you barely have to *think* about an aura for it to spring to life. With the advancement, some say your willpower is reforged because your control over energy is stronger. Snappier. You get the point." She gestured to the rest of the group. "You've fought them, so I imagine you've seen runes or glyphs form when they manipulate energy right?"

I nodded. "It was a little strange at the time. I didn't understand why they would show the enemy so clearly an attack was coming, but I'm guessing you're going to tell me why now?"

A smile danced on her lips, "Oh, well *now* I'm not so sure." She sang. "But yes, yes, I will tell you. Take the runes on your chest," She ran her finger down my sternum, and I shivered. She smirked. "They help focus the energies of the world into *you*. Other runes on your chest help you change where the energy gathers, thus giving you the abilities you have. Your runes for converting the energy into a real element are extremely underdeveloped, and that's why you can hardly control your lightning."

I glared at her, "Oh be quiet with that. I'm working on it."

She laughed again, "I'm only joking, Rey. Come on, I know you can take a joke."

I rolled my eyes, "Whatever, just go on."

A satisfied look solidified itself in her eyes. "Well, steel warriors form those runes to help better channel the specific spell they want to use. It helps give form and direction, letting the user focus more on power. Most people at bronze can't form these runes for the exact reason we can't use seals; we don't have the control needed. It's as simple as that. Being able to form seals at steel is almost unheard of."

I blinked slowly and just stared at her. "That simple?"

"Yep!" She smiled.

"Well," I sighed, "Thanks for the lesson, I guess."

Her smile grew, "Of course!"

"I did have a question though." My pride stung.

She looked me in the eyes, her gaze turning from satisfaction to elation. "Really now? *Anything* for my lowly student." Her smile sent a shiver down my spine.

I cocked an eyebrow. "Lowly student?" I sighed, "Is there a danger in trying to form runes for my spells now?"

Her smile faded slightly. "In training, no. Anytime you're fighting, absolutely. The runes themselves take enough concentration that you'd hardly be able to defend yourself. Again, that's why it's something steels use. They have much better control."

I sighed, disappointed. "I can't say I'm surprised. Lightning is just such a pain to control."

"Again," She flicked my forehead and I winced. "Don't *control* the lightning. If it's anything like water, it wants to flow. You have to *guide* it. True control can come when you reach steel."

Syre popped up next to us out of nowhere. "Aw, you guys look so cute together!"

We both glared at her. "Hello Syre." I said, my voice dripping with annoyance.

She raised one eyebrow, "Woah, cool it. Just wanted to see what you guys were talking about." I looked up at the gorgeous, blue sky through the leaves of the massive trees around me. Abigail's voice slowly became unintelligible as I stopped listening and took in the scenery. I smiled. It felt good to be out in the forest.

Slowly but surely, time crept on. After a day of hiking, joyous conversation and beautiful forest vistas, we stood at the base of a mountain. The towering stone peak blocked the setting sun as we finally took our first break in hours.

Ralteir nodded towards to the steep inclining stone and looked at Hundri. "Want me to create a way up?"

"Yeah, please do."

Ralteir cracked his knuckles and stepped up to the wall of stone. He closed his eyes. Glowing runes began to form around his fists and forearms. Not long after they formed, the white snow was painted a deep orange. He placed his palms on the stone.

The ground rumbled and snow fell from the trees as a winding staircase formed leading to where the tracks disappeared into the cliffs.

He opened his eyes and flashed us a grin. "Handy, eh?"

Ogland patted him on the shoulder as he walked by, a simple silver ring catching the light. "Yeah, yeah. Let's move rock-for-brains."

Ralteir sputtered and chased after Ogland. Yaldrie chuckled softly. "Boys will be boys."

We hiked up the winding stone staircase silently, bathed in darkness. Nobody wanted any potential attackers to know we were coming. Each person treaded lightly, the only sound was the whistling wind outside the stone tunnel. After the final short hike, we reached our destination.

The mouth of the staircase opened up into a grand room made of white polished stone that was contrasted with dark black rock and deep brown wood. It was bathed in simple white light from countless gems that either hung from the ceiling or were mounted in various places. Large white pillars supported the domed ceiling. Where the bronze tracks met the large white tile, was the platform we *should've* rode over on. Large softly glowing chains engraved with runes held it locked in place. A chill went down my spine. The entire area was empty and eerily quiet. I looked around the group and it was clear everyone felt the same. After dropping our bags on the staircase, we slowly crept forwards.

I felt the team's auras spring to life around each person as they placed one hand on their weapons. Syre's strange handle blazed green, and with a quite click, a large, jagged black bow telescoped outwards. Abigail tapped her foot impatiently next to me as she waited for me to form my aura. I let the warm power flow through my limbs and out into the scaled armor around my chest, arms and legs. By the time everyone was forming into a ringed formation, I had finished. Me and Abigail hurried after them with our hands on our own swords.

We crept in, silent. The farther we got, the more decoration became visible and the more unsettled I was. Benches, withering bushes and hedges, small tables, and an imposing staircase that led up to a massive stone archway. It was decorated with symbols and pictures I was too far from to read, but I could feel my curiosity burning brighter with each step closer.

We walked next to Hundri, and I murmured to him, "What do you see?" His eyes blazed brighter than usual as he swept the area.

Without looking at me, he responded, "This place is *full* of the aura of death. It's blinding."

Every hair on the back of my neck stood up as Hundri whirled around, panic painted across his face. Suddenly, waves of energy exploded out from every direction. Our own group's power blazed as well, overwhelming my senses. I stood there, starstruck as I shakily drew my sword. When I came to my senses, a bald man in loose furred leather armor with a wild expression was diving at me with an awl.

I couldn't move. My blood froze. Every sense in my body screamed to move. I was going to die.

I was going to *die.*

Hundri's sword flashed out faster than I could see. A spray of warm crimson life splattered my face and I stumbled backwards. I watched in horror as his body fell away from his head and he toppled to the floor with a sickening squelch.

Hundri grabbed me by the shoulders, despite the battles breaking out around us. His eyes pierced my soul as he screamed. "*Fight!* If you don't fight, you *will die!*" And with that he charged off to help the blades. I looked at the battlefield and felt something churn in my stomach.

In a moment, my eyes swept the battlefield. Fire blossomed in one of Ogland's hands as he blocked a jab from a spear with the flat of his great sword. The flaming orb he held exploded outward in a cone of fire that seared through the woman's aura and blackened her shoulder.

Syre crouched in the background, loosing arrows with such force that the air seemed to pop the second her string released. A glowing green monocle decorated with runes caught the light as she swiveled from target to target, raining death.

Everywhere I looked, gruesome battle raged. Swords clashed, flesh was sliced from the bone and blood sprayed. I steeled my will and gripped my sword so hard my knuckles whitened. I couldn't afford to shake. It was life or death now.

I looked over to Abigail and gestured to a man charging toward us with a spear. I shouted over the midst of battle, "Together!" She nodded and we dashed to meet the man. Unlike the previous man, this one's aura was focused almost entirely on his spear, with thin plates of hazy glowing energy protecting their arms and legs.

His runes burst to life on his chest and the tip of his spear grew red hot. His maniacal laughter filled the air as his spear blurred right at my throat. Without time to think, I weaved right and threw a punch at the spear shaft. As quickly as it had shot forward, it was out of range. I stumbled forward slightly and felt my stomach drop as my fist failed to connect.

His spear streaked at my chest. With a flash of steel, the spear was knocked aside. Abigail burst past me with determination in her eyes and slashed in a lightning-quick arc at his legs.

The battle receded from me for a moment as Abigail and the man danced in combat, neither giving any openings. I recollected myself and brandished my sword. I willed energy into my legs and dashed forward towards Abigail and her opponent. The moment Abigail started to slip; my sword was there. I gave her a tight-lipped smile as I joined the fray again.

Together now, we began to push the man back. He backpedaled as we scored more and more glancing blows, leaving thin lines of crimson and shallow holes all over his body. Suddenly, the man threw himself backwards with a burst of energy. "You *worthless* bronzes!" He roared as he began to twirl his spear. The tip left a trail of bright fire in the air that writhed like a snake before coalescing into tiny blazing discs.

I shot Abigail a look and she uncapped a large waterskin on her waist. The water inside shimmered as it shot outward with the speed of an arrow. The man immediately fired the discs, and they streaked through the air like comets. Two were met by water and were doused into puffs of steam, but four made it through the clash of elements.

We dodged and weaved the blazing projectiles as we desperately avoided certain death. I regained my footing and panted from exhaustion. As much as I needed it, there was no time to rest. I searched for the man but found nothing. Fear grew in my chest and burned brighter than any fire.

I looked to Abigail, who screamed my name with a look of sheer panic. I whirled around to see a spearpoint descending inches away in a flaming arc. I felt the heat lick at my shoulder as it closed the distance in a matter of a moments. With an explosion of pure wind pressure, the man was thrown backward just before the grievous injury was dealt. As he stumbled to his feet, my eyes caught the forearm-length onyx arrow that stuck through his shoulder. The man screamed in pain as he clawed the arrow from his now crimson stained arm. It dangled uselessly at his side and his curses filled the air.

I pushed his screams aside. Now was not the time. I gathered all the energy I could muster into my sword, legs and arms. With a leap, I rocketed towards him. My sword planted itself firmly in his stomach with the sickening feeling of tearing flesh and breaking bones. The man stared at me in horror and disbelief as he winded back a punch with his good arm. It felt like time slowed down as I met his horrified eyes. I roared in desperation and fear as I twisted my sword and slashed upwards through the man's body without a second thought. Hesitation was defeat.

A wave of crimson arced out from the slash and splattered the polished stone in front of me. I stood still, stunned as I looked into the man's wide eyes. The light deep within was gone. All that remained was a glazed-over glassy husk. Emptiness. A deep, sick part of me was filled with immense conflicted satisfaction. I felt the pie I had the day before rising in my throat as a wave of sadistic joy washed over me. There was something surreal and twisted about taking another man's life. Every droplet of blood that dripped down my blade amplified my emotions.

Abigail grabbed me by the shoulders and shook me back and forth, pulling me from my thoughts. "-EY... REY!" She looked deathly pale, but still the tiniest bit composed. Maybe because it wasn't her hands that were stained with blood. "We need to help! *Come on!*" I blinked as I let the world stream back to me.

"Right." I mumbled as I flicked the blood off my energy-coated sword. All around me the battle was beginning to die down. It had been a small wave of soldiers that we cut through like grass. Every member of the Blades was stained with blood as they tore through person after person. Only a few remained fighting each member. After a glance around the battlefield, I quickly chose to go help Syre. Exhaustion had crept into all my muscles and each step was a struggle.

In a matter of seconds, I reached Syre. She fought three people in a mesmerizing dance of blades. Using only dual daggers she blocked and parried while scoring shallow slashes all over their bodies. However, after watching for a few moments, the outcome was clear. They were slowly overpowering her.

I approached a woman with dual axes from behind and focused my energy into my hand. After a few moments, I felt the voltaic power sparking to life within my palm. Syre met my eyes, and I gave her a determined nod before thrusting the electrified palm strike into the back of the woman's neck. Normally, this weak and uncontrolled burst of lightning could barely make someone twitch. But when the shock blasted directly into her neck, her entire body locked up. She shook and flailed with a howl. Syre noticed my attack and flicked her knife at the now spasming woman. The air rippled. Her screams of agony became gurgling gasps as she choked on her own blood and fell to the ground.

Now very aware of my presence, the other man and woman leapt backwards in a pulse of energy that kicked up dust. Syre smirked. She sheathed her knife in a fluid motion and grabbed her bow handle from her waist. With a snap, the bow telescoped to full size. Syre effortlessly yanked back a long, onyx arrow on the bowstring and aimed at the man who was rapidly closing the distance again. A single ring of green wind runes formed floating in front of the bow at first, then another, and another.

The man approaching made no move to dodge, his arrogance clear in every step. Syre's smirk grew to a manic grin. She released the arrow. With a boom, the arrow disappeared. In an instant, the man's head snapped backwards with a crack as the arrow planted itself firmly in his forehead. He collapsed in a heap and deep crimson trickled out in a small puddle. My stomach twisted.

Syre whirled around to find the other man who had been attacking her thrusting a sword at her gut. With one fluid motion she dodged to the side and retaliated with an energy empowered roundhouse kick into his ribs. The man twisted and put his aura-coated forearm in the way of the kick in a last second block. His sword clattered to the ground as the energy cracked and splintered with brutal force.

As he stumbled to his feet, I took my chance to go on the offensive. Energy blasted through my legs as I jumped forwards with my sword raised above my head. My blade flashed downwards in a shining vertical arc. He easily ducked under my stupidly telegraphed blow and the world slowed as I met his eyes. His eyes were wide with the look of a murderer. His fist met my aura protected chest with enough force to send me stumbling back. My scales shattered under the force as I tucked into a roll, narrowly dodging a kick.

My chest stung and my muscles ached as I pulled myself to my feet and glared at my opponent. *If it weren't for Syre, I'd be dead right now.* I thought as I started to form a new barrier over my chest, scale by scale. The man had picked back up his sword and was locked in a flurry of blows with Syre. I started sprinting over as I contemplated what to do when a voice spoke in the back of my mind. *You don't need them. Leave. What's the point? We can find power without these pathetic weaklings.* I shivered at its grainy voice and pushed those thoughts deep inside.

I brandished my sword in one hand and built-up electric power in my other. I waited, watching their clash intently. At the perfect moment, I joined the duel. I slashed at the man's gut in a feint. With the reflexes of a hardened warrior, he dropped into a block. His eyes widened when my blow never connected. Syre, seeing his mistake, rammed her knife deep into his forearm and slashed across it in a catastrophic wound. He screamed and his sword clattered to the ground.

I quickly landed a crackling palm strike filled with voltaic energy to his heart. He stood still for a second as his heart beat out of rhythm. His eyes grew wide in pain but there was nothing he could do. Syre and I's blades sunk into his chest in unison.

He fell to the ground without a sound, dead. Once again, I felt the color drain from my face. Syre patted me on the shoulder. "Thanks," she said with a smile.

I nodded weakly and scanned for Abigail. Worry flowed through my veins as I swept the battles. My eyes finally settled on her fighting with Hundri as they finished their last enemy. Relief crashed over me.

It didn't take long for everyone to finish off the last few bandits. Everyone started to move towards the center of the room, away from the lakes of blood and tens of corpses. To my surprise, Abigail was running directly at me.

I braced myself as Abigail practically leapt at me and wrapped her arms around me. "I was sure you were dead with how weak you are!" I stood there stunned for a moment.

"I'm glad you're okay too." I smiled weaky as I felt like my ribcage was going to crack.

CHAPTER NINETEEN

Morality

Reynolds Helphain

The battle was a brutal massacre. The voices of my teammates and friends were drowned out as I stared with unfocused eyes at the mangled corpses and crimson splatters. The thought that *I* had caused some of the deaths of these men and women churned my stomach like a cauldron. *They attacked me. It was self-defense. It's not my fault,* I thought to myself as I tried anything to stop the rising bile in my stomach. It would've been worse if Abigail hadn't cleaned the blood from us.

The weight of my actions made it hard to breathe. These people weren't just monsters or mindless obstacles in my path. They were each people —just like me— who were trying to make their own path. I had taken it away. *No,* I thought, *they lost, they had every chance to take my life, and failed. It was me or them.* My stomach calmed a little and I tuned back into the conversation.

"—'re going to have a brutal ascent so we should talk strategies, formations, and the like," Hundri said as he read our faces. I gave him a weak smile and he frowned slightly. Nevertheless, he continued, "I'd like Yaldrie and Syre to take the back, as they are our ranged fighters." They both nodded. "If you wouldn't mind ladies, I would also like to put Kai back with you. Sound good?" They nodded once more and Hundri smiled.

"In the front will be Ogland and myself, accompanied by our lovely little children here, Abigail and Rey." I saw a muscle twitch in Abigail's face, but she said nothing.

Ralteir echoed my thoughts, "What about me? Where do you want me?"

"Well buddy," He grabbed Ralteir by the shoulder. "No matter where I put you, I am almost certain you will just jump *headfirst* into a crowd of enemies."

The group chuckled and Ralteir flushed slightly. "Hey! I can follow orders alright."

"Uh-huh." Hundri said skeptically with a twinkle in his eye.

"Hundri, give me a position. I'll stay there."

Hundri cocked an eyebrow in surprise. "Really now? Well, thank the gods. Okay, then you'll be in the front with the rest of the close quarters fighters." His smile grew. "Now what do I get if you leave formation, hm?"

Ralteir scratched his head, "Well... how about a hundred gold pieces?"

Hundri nodded. "Alright, I look forward to being a hundred gold richer. Well, everyone, take a moment to gather energy, then we begin upwards."

It felt like something invisible and powerful began to shake lightly and tremble. With a feeling akin to a strong wind, the air grew stale as different aspects streamed into the members of the Blades. Ogland grimaced. "Not much fire energy 'round here."

Syre chimed in, "Wind is alright."

I focused on drawing the lightning energy around me and found nothing different than usual. The energy around me responded sluggishly before eventually trickling into my runes with a familiar warmth. Once my runes were full, I shot Hundri a confused look which he easily interpreted. "The energies of our world that we use are created by the things in it." He saw my frown deepen in confusion and continued, "Fire energy is thin up here because it's extremely cold, and there's no fire nearby."

I nodded. "That makes enough sense. I've never noticed a change in the lightning energy around me before though. Is that simply because of the nature of lightning?"

"Well," Hundri scratched his head before continuing, "Lightning is a less understood element because of the scarcity of its users. But from what we know, lightning energy is universally thin." He saw the disappointment in my face and quickly added, "However! It apparently is significantly stronger where lightning has just struck. There is also an idea floating around that lightning energy is like fire in the sense that it can be created by man instead of just by nature."

I perked up at the last piece of information, which I found extremely interesting. "Created by man? How?"

"Ah, sadly, that is just a rumor I heard from Kai." He gestured to the thin man fiddling with gears off to the side. "But anyway, energy in general will become easier to channel and absorb as your runes evolve through the stages."

"That reminds me, how *do* you evolve your runes?"

A familiar voice sprung up to my right and I turned to Abigail. "Gods Hundri, did you teach this poor boy nothing?"

"Hey, listen, I was going to get to it when he was closer to steel."

Abigail cocked a suspicious eyebrow, "Uh-huh. Well go on." A smile threatened to pull on my lips.

Hundri sighed deeply before explaining, "You can... almost feel it," his eyes seemed to drift away as he reminisced the feeling. "It's a feeling like every channel in your body is humming with power, your very soul feels like its trembling. You can feel this... this dam inside you. With little concentration, it blows apart and washes over your body and your runes, reforging it all." He smiled. "Then it feels a little *less* good. The burning feeling from when you first got your runes comes back in force as they get more complex and powerful. Those first few minutes after ascension, you feel... invincible."

"Interesting!" I focused on the feeling of energy in my runes and probed for that feeling of a dam. I was disappointed to find no such feeling, even if I knew it was unlikely.

I shook my head and Hundri nodded. "I expected as much. How about you Abigail?"

A faint smile spread on her face as she opened her eyes. "I can feel the beginnings of that 'dam' like feeling." I felt a pang of envy, then guilt. *I should be happy for her.*

"What even dictates whether or not we advance or not?" I asked.

Hundri spoke over Abigail who shot him and annoyed look. "It's not a science. Nobody really knows the 'trick' as you might call it. It's a mix of understanding energy, being able to manipulate it and practice."

Now it was my turn to sigh. "That is... painfully vague."

Abigail and Hundri nodded together. "As are most things with energy," Hundri replied.

My attention was drawn from the conversation as Kai tapped me on the shoulder. "Yes, Kai?"

He fidgeted with the gear exoskeleton covering his hand before speaking, "How'd the cloak hold up in battle?"

"Honestly," I wrapped the cloak around me again. "I didn't get the chance to use it." His face fell slightly so I quickly added, "But I can test it right now! Hundri, why don't you shoot some ice at me."

Hundri smiled evilly. "Gladly." The moisture above his palm solidified suddenly into a hovering foot-long dagger of ice. The second it left his palm I pushed a pulse of energy into the furs of the cloak. It felt heavier as a web of interlocking runes formed in between the fur and the weighty exterior.

The icy dagger crashed into the cloak with little force as it exploded into shards of ice, leaving me, and the cloak, in perfect condition. I stared down at the fur as the runes faded in wonder. "This is amazing Kai!"

"Thank you." He smiled as he walked away.

I turned back to Hundri and Abigail. "So Hundri, what *is* our plan to get up there anyway?"

"That," He raised his voice, "is a question that should be answered with the whole group!" We waited silently with a smile as the other members grumbled and walked over to our little circle. Hundri's smile radiated satisfaction as he began to speak once again. "Great. So! The plan should be pretty straight forwards."

Ogland raised an eyebrow. "Really?"

"Yes, really! Kai is the one with the complicated plans, mine are just... fun!"

"Fun?" Chimed in Ralteir. "What about the time you had us jump off a *cliff!*"

Hundri raised his hands sheepishly as my eyebrows shot up, "It was fun *and* it worked, right?" He chuckled.

"Excuse me but, *why* did you jump off a mountain?" I asked with a strong tone of concern.

"Well, we needed to catch a flying wind mage, and we had the high ground and a few wind mages ourselves so... I said why not!"

"'Why not'? *Because* we were *jumping* off a *mountain!*" Ralteir yelled while gesturing wildly.

Hundri shrugged. "You could've chosen not to."

Ogland raised an eyebrow. "If my memory serves me, I *did* say no to yer crazy plan and had got a firm shove to the back."

"Must've been the wind." A mischievous smile tugged at Hundri's lips.

Kai groaned, "You're still using that excuse? You know it'd be impossible and improbable for the wind to-," A snowball broke against his face as he stumbled backwards.

"Hush now," Said Hundri with a twinkle in his eyes. "Back to the original point; ascending the mountain. I was given a map that generally shows the layout of the pathways that lead up this mountain," He pulled out the map and made a show of unrolling it slowly, to which everyone rolled their eyes. "My guess is that they have the bulk of their forces in the main staircase and on its landings. Our first option is to push around the side paths and find weaker ways to the top. The second, which is *my* favorite by the way, would be to just rush through the middle."

As Hundri set the map on the ground, Syre knelt next to it and tapped the main path with her knife before talking. "Why would we ever take the main path? Wouldn't we be at a severe disadvantage there?"

"She has a point Hundri. I *know* you love a challenge, but this is downright foolhardy," agreed Yaldrie.

Hundri nodded. "Think about how fun it'd be! Though you are right to think about how and where we spend our energy. If we go through the majority of their forces, we eliminate the possibility of the leader getting major reinforcements in the middle of the fight."

This time, unexpectedly, Abigail chimed in, "And while we do get rid of the chance of reinforcements, we also would be exhausted and out of energy from fighting *a literal army.* To make things worse, their leader could come *down,* couldn't he? If he joined the army mid fight, we would have no chance." She gestured to Syre and Yaldrie, "I agree with these two."

His glowing azure eyes scanned each person before he sighed and deflated a little. "Alright, alright. I need someone to reel me in sometimes. Thanks guys." He forced a smile, "We push the side paths then!"

I surveyed the field of splayed out and brutalized corpses and felt the weight of my guilt slowly grow with each one. My eyes lingered on each person I had personally executed. My stomach tightened, I sighed and looked back towards where Hundri and the group were. Except, now I was alone. It was silent. I slowly turned to find myself alone with the corpses. I blinked slowly and rubbed my eyes. Still gone.

Sweat beaded on my forehead as I drew my polished sword. I slowly turned around the room as panic coursed my veins. My hands grew slick on the handle of my sword as I failed to see a single difference. Until my eyes locked onto one of the men I had killed. Or, at least where he should've been. I slowly backed away as I kept my sword in a guarded stance.

My back hit something a little too soft to be the wall and I turned slowly. Behind me stood the mutilated body of the man who had attacked me with an awl. My breath caught in my throat. I whirled around and leapt backwards in one fluid motion as I slashed open his throat. My gut churned watching the crimson blood pour, but it churned more to see the man advance toward me with a sickening, bloodstained smile on his face.

His eyes were glazed over, and dried blood covered his face in a horrifying mask. With each step, the crimson liquid poured from his throat and stained the rest of his body. I shivered. Impossibly, it opened its mouth and began to speak in a horrifying scraping noise, "Rey... look at what you did to me."

My eyes wanted to look anywhere else, to get this creature out of my sight, but the torn flesh of his throat didn't want to let my vision go. I choked out what words I could, "What... what do you want from me?!"

Its smile deepened and it growled, "To recognize, what you've become." It gestured around it to the bodies that lined the room. "A murderer. A *monster.*"

I ground my teeth together, "No! It... it was self-defense! I had to kill them, or they'd kill me."

My feet bumped into a corpse with a sickening squish as I looked down to see my boots soaked with blood. "Was it?" It hissed as it got closer. "You had a *choice.* Did you not?"

"No!" I screamed. "I had to come here, for Serena!" The sword rattled in my hands.

"Did you?" It roared through torn vocal cords, "Or did you come here for your own... *selfish* gain? Strength is *intoxicating*, isn't it?" It smiled wider than I thought possible.

I glared at it as I gripped my sword hard enough to turn my knuckles white. "You're wrong!" My voice trembled, "I came here for Serena! I love my sister and I refuse to let her be in danger! She needs me, and I won't let anything get in my way!"

It sneered, "You sure made that clear." Each corpse I had killed stood up and looked at me with the same impossibly wide grin.

I opened my mouth to say something, but no sound left my throat as I stared at each brutalized corpse. A tear ran down my cheek in silence as the first one continued to march towards me. "Each. One. Cut down for *your* ambition."

I grimaced and glared at it with every ounce of anger in my body. I steeled my will and responded with a voice as solid as steel, "I did what I had to for my family."

I could smell the stench of death and blood as it walked into my sword's range. Before I could open my mouth, it walked *into* my sword. The squelch of meat and blood filled my ears. It smiled down at me. "Sure, but you *enjoyed it*. You *liked* cutting them down." My guilt constricted my heart more. "You felt powerful tearing the life from their body, didn't you?"

I roared and slashed my sword through its body and sliced it in half diagonally. I glared at each of the standing corpses as they continued to smile at me. *Monster,* they hissed in my very mind. Nothing should've been able to speak in my mind, nothing except... "Show yourself!" I roared into the dark cave.

After a moment or two, a dry cackle filled my ears. The shadows of the cave flowed together to create the same form I had seen days ago, the one that had threatened Abigail. *If you're going to slaughter every person you come across, at least take their strength,* it hissed in my mind like a parasite.

"No." I muttered. "*You* only showed up after I took that bear's strength. I'm not going to make the same mistake twice."

It smiled wide and its scratchy cackles filled my mind. *You only deny yourself power. It is your gift to take from others what is improperly used. Do not waste it.*

My vision went black.

. . .

I woke up to a pleasant warmth against my cheek and a deep throbbing in my temples. I groaned quietly as the dim light of the cave streamed back into my vision. My tight muscles ached as I slowly began to sit up. A pair of hands jerked away from my head. I looked around. Abigail sat right next to me with a deep blush on her face as she looked away. My head was too foggy to figure out why and I muttered out in a slur of words, "What... happened?"

She cleared her throat and stood. "Your eyes glazed over, and you passed out on the ground. Before long you started twitching and shaking. We decided to wait here until you woke up, so I... watched over you while you slept."

I groggily rubbed my eyes and looked around. "Thanks then." I smiled. Hundri was leaning against a column and grinned at me with mischief in eyes. The rest of the group was playing some sort of game a little farther away. I pushed myself to my feet with a groan and Abigail rose with me, placing a steadying hand on my shoulder.

Hundri looked towards the group and gave a shrill whistle. They immediately got up and prepared to leave again, throwing the pieces back into their bags. I glanced over to Abigail, whose blush was almost faded. "How long was I out for?"

"You only *delayed* us a few hours, three at the most. I'd say let's hurry to make up the time, but your slow ass definitely can't keep up."

I raised my eyebrows. "You're being awfully rude to someone who could've died."

"Yeah, well, you deserve it." She looked away.

I frowned slightly and sighed. "Fair enough."

"And if you died from that, I would've killed you."

"I'm sure you would've." I chuckled and began to walk toward Hundri.

Hundri pushed himself off from the pillar and brushed his curly mess of black hair to the side. "Welcome back."

"Hey."

He frowned. "What happened there? Was it those stones?"

I opened my mouth to respond but felt the cold hand of fear grip my heart like a vice. The vivid memories of those *things* surrounding me... their smiles... I couldn't find the words. A bead of sweat formed on my forehead as I plastered a fake smile and mustered all the confidence I could into my voice. "It was nothing."

His frown deepened and his faintly glowing azure eyes seemed to dig into mine. "Alright." He rubbed the stubble on his sharp chiseled chin. "This won't happen in the heat of battle, right?"

"It won't," I lied with uncertainty. He nodded once and began to walk away, the contents of his bag clanking with each step. I hurried after him. "So, what happened with Abigail?"

He flashed me a grin. "Well, when you passed out, she watched over you."

"Yeah, I know that, but why was she so flushed?"

"You were sleeping on her lap."

My face heated. "Ah."

Hundri stifled a laugh as he watched the expression on my face. "You slept like a baby."

I sighed. We reached the other members of the group and Abigail quickly joined us. She threw a weak, shimmering punch at the back of Hundri's head before he could talk to the group, and he easily ducked it. He slowly turned and cocked an eyebrow at her.

"Do you have eyes in the back of your damn head?" She asked.

He waggled his fingers. "It's magic," he sang with a smile.

"It's 'is damn bloodline eyes," grunted Ogland.

Hundri puffed out his cheeks. "No need to spoil the trick Ogland." I smiled. "Everyone all ready to continue on up?"

"Guessing we can't finish our game of Olpindal?" Asked Syre.

Hundri shot her a look. "What do you think?"

She groaned. "Yeah, yeah. Important mission I get it. Let's go."

We walked up the large set of chiseled stairs that stood opposite the platform. I hadn't noticed when we first entered, but every inch of this place was an artistic feat. The fronts of each step were carved into long swirling patterns, each tile in the floor arrayed in a way that somehow felt artistic and each column carved with weaving stylish runes.

The staircase led to a tall room with beautiful white arches that supported a domed ceiling. Even more so than the room below —even before we had painted it with blood— this one was dazzlingly white in every regard, without a hint of dark accent. Similarly, there was another long staircase that led higher in a clear path, with two small arches on either side that lead to areas unknown to me.

Hundri promptly turned right and began to walk down a long corridor with the Blades in close step. "So, I thought this place was for prayer, but it seems like there's a lot more here than just religion," I said.

"Aye. Normal people come once a week to pray to some god. But them higher up members of the church and those truly devoted *live* here." Responded Ogland.

My stomach churned. "Does that mean these bastards slaughtered innocent priests?"

Ogland shrugged. "Is possible. Most likely—"

Yaldrie cut him off with a stern look. "What my husband is *trying* to say is that they are hopefully alive."

We walked through a large, less ornate arch into a simple, but giant training room and I felt my stomach threaten to send back my breakfast. The walls and ceiling were made of the same white stone as the rest of the building. Glowing white crystals inlayed in the walls and ceiling painted the room with a peaceful light. All around the room were various kinds of training equipment. Thick wooden logs lined the room with wooden rods sticking out of them for hand-to-hand training. Large wooden benches surrounded four sparring rings made of packed dirt. Every surface was splattered with blood.

Littered around the room were tens of corpses. Some wore white combat robes and looked between ten and twenty cycles old. Others wore similar robes, but more trimmed and refined with golden lining. Surprisingly, there were also tens of bandit corpses. The room reeked of iron.

I shivered and looked at Hundri. His face twitched in anger as he grimaced at the gruesome sight before him. Yaldrie recoiled in horror as she surveyed the room. "They... they slaughtered *children*?" Her voice quivered as she grew more paled.

Hundri's voice was firm and grim as he gave us an order. "Fan out. Look for survivors."

We split off and began to slowly comb the room. It took everything I had to not throw up as I passed each mutilated child. It seemed like these trainees had put up quite the fight, however. The older ones, the ones who looked to be just younger than twenty were surrounded in bandit bodies. For each of their bodies I found, there were at least five dead bandits around them.

This was something I knew would never stop haunting me. Maybe it would've been tolerable if they weren't starting to decompose. It was clearly a fight that was days or even weeks old. After combing through the bodies for what felt like too long, something caught my eye. One of the tiled walls nearby looked... warped, as if it had frozen while rippling.

I raised my voice and called over to the rest of the group. "Guys I think I found something!" They all hurried over.

Ralteir wrapped his knuckles against the wall with a hollow echo. "Looks like signs of earth magic. I can feel the excess energy still in the stone. This was recent."

"Can you open it?" asked Kai.

Ralteir rolled his eyes. "Of course I can, Kai." Orange light and floating runes flared to light above the back of his hand as he pressed his palm into the wall. It melted away to reveal the form of a teenage boy, cowering in a small stone room he had clearly formed in the wall. It had a small table, food, a stone platform with a bedroll and a small candle. Before we could say a word, the boy exploded out of the wall fist first.

His white robes blurred as he slammed a punch into Ralteir's gut that sent him stumbling backwards. Before he could make another move, Hundri dashed forward in a blur. He positioned his leg right behind the robed boy's front foot and reached across his body with his arm. With a twist the boy was thrown to the floor. As he tried to get back up, Hundri flicked his wrist and ice exploded outward from that ground, surrounding the boy in a cage of icy spikes.

Ralteir growled and dashed forward with a stone gauntlet forming around his fist. With another flick of the wrist, ice exploded around him too. Hundri glared at him, then the boy.

Hundri's voice boomed out, "Enough." The words swept the room with a wave of chilling pressure. Both the boy and Ralteir suddenly looked unnerved. Slowly, he dropped the cage around Ralteir.

The boy looked about my age, with a blocky chin and short cropped black hair sticking up from his head. He wore the same attire as the slaughtered boys and girls around us. Hundri gestured to the corpses. "You survived?"

The boy nodded, his face hard with determination. "I did what I had to," he said in a gruff voice that sounded like it had been without water for days.

Hundri nodded and let down the icy cage. "We are not your enemies; we're working to get rid of the bandit scum here."

The boy's face loosened and he dropped his guard. Slightly. "I am going to the lift," The boy growled in a gruff voice, "You will not follow me. Understood?"

Hundri nodded and the boy slowly inched towards the door we had entered from, then sprinted away. After he had gone, Hundri sighed. "We couldn't even ask him any questions, damn it." A smirk crept onto his face, "but he did get you pretty good, Ralteir."

Ralteir flushed slightly, "I was caught off guard. That kid would get floored in a duel."

Hundri's eyebrow slowly raised. "You're sure about that? You have heard how terrifying their fighting style is though, right?"

I perked up slightly, suddenly paying more attention and I heard Abigail stifle a chuckle as she watched me. "Yeah, yeah," Ralteir sighed, "But I'm like twice the kid's size, have more experience *and* to top it off more runic strength."

"That's true," Hundri nodded, "But you know who I would love to see fight him?" Slowly and steadily, his face turned towards me.

I chuckled nervously, "Well, luckily for me he left."

Hundri's grinned, "I get the feeling we'll see him again."

I groaned. "Let's just move, this room is making me feel sick."

Everyone nodded weakly and a resounding agreement went up from the group as we started towards the arch on the opposite side from where we had entered from. *I'm going to need new boots.* I thought to myself as I watched the blood of children and adults cake the bottom.

As we walked up another impossibly tall staircase, Abigail slugged me in the arm weakly. "How're you doing Rey? You looked a little... shaken back there."

I shuddered. "How could I not? They killed *children* Abigail. Some of them couldn't have even had runes yet." I shook my head, my hair falling in my eyes. "It's barbaric."

"I know." She sighed. "But this is what life is like for people like us. We have to learn to move past the deaths, no matter who they may be."

I looked into her deep hazel eyes. "How can you be so calm about death?"

She smiled with a deep sadness in her eyes. "I've grown up with my parents constantly going out every day, not knowing whether they're coming home again. Death means a lot less to me as I expected it to come for my family every day." She clenched her fist. "But that doesn't mean seeing what they did to those kids doesn't make my blood boil."

I nodded solemnly and we walked in silence for a minute before I heard someone call back from above that we were about to enter the next room. It was a large rectangular room, similar in size to the training room, with large tables and benches for dining. Off to the left and right were doors to what I presumed to be kitchens. The wooden tables had been flipped over to form barricades blocking the other side of the room where a group of bandits stood guard.

Immediately upon seeing us, they began to shout. Energy pulsed, and weapons were drawn on both sides as tens of bandits hurried to the barricade.

After a few moments, a tall, muscular man with long, curly greasy hair came to the front of the group. A sneer formed on his blocky face as he started to *walk* on the air and came to a stop floating a few feet in the air above his barricade. His black cloak fluttered out around him revealing his lean body wrapped in bloodstained bandages. With a flick of his wrist, he brandished two, long serrated knives from the depths of his cloak. "May I know the names of you cretins before I *gut* you like pigs?" He licked his knife.

We brandished our weapons and our auras blazed even stronger. My heartbeat filled my ears as I steadied my footing. I looked at Abigail and nodded in an attempt to silently say we should work together. She nodded back.

I took a deep breath and looked back to the floating man, only to see a dark blur. Every alarm in my body went off as I hurriedly raised my cloak and activated the shield. An impact like a cannon smashed into me and threw the sword from my hand as I rocketed away. I flew backwards and rolled across the floor for a second before I slammed into the wall. Pain exploded across my back. My vision swam as I pulled myself to my feet and released the cloak's spell.

The man slowly walked towards me, emanating the aura and the energy of a high steel. "You shouldn't have survived that." He hissed. I clumsily put up my hands in a dazed guard and willed as much energy as I could into the scaled-aura gauntlets. I glared at him, and he pointed a knife in my direction. "There's ferocity in those eyes. I love a struggle." He grinned unnervingly.

Suddenly, he shot to the side in a burst of wind magic. A spike of ice erupted from the ground where he had been standing and I heard Hundri curse. I looked up to see him walking over from the middle of the newly raging battlefield with his sword drawn and covered in blood. Behind him were several corpses impaled on frozen spikes.

I felt my confidence return as Hundri clamped a hand on my shoulder. "You okay kid?"

"I'm fine." The man swiped at us with his knife and an almost invisible blade of wind rocketed towards us. Before I could react, Hundri slashed through it with his sword, and it dispersed. Hundri glared at the man and brandished his sword before beginning to walk toward him slowly.

The man matched his pace at first, spinning his knives in anticipation at his sides. With a sudden explosion of wind, the man rocketed forwards. His blades glowed green with wind magic as he swiped at Hundri with inhuman speed. Hundri easily ducked the blow and slashed at the man's gut as he dropped.

The man's other knife flashed downward and blocked the swing with a resounding clash. Hundri dashed to the side as he flicked his other hand towards the man. An icicle flashed outward towards the man's shoulder with a burst of energy. He grimaced as he tried to twist out of the way. The icicle ripped through his aura and slashed open a small wound on his shoulder. The man stumbled backwards but quickly used a burst of wind behind him to regain his balance.

Normally, with the length of a longsword, Hundri's opponent shouldn't have gotten anywhere close to him, however with the speed of his wind energy he could close the gap easily. They traded tens of blows in a matter of seconds, but it was clear Hundri had the advantage. Wind and ice magic flew back and forth as they clashed in a mesmerizing dance of steel.

I forced myself to look away from the beauty of their duel. I needed to find my own blade. I locked my eyes onto it... in the hands of one of the bandits. A burly man with greasy, short brown hair brandished it, obviously getting a feel for its weight. He grinned with blackening teeth as he saw me eyeing my sword. I steadied my breath, pumped energy into my legs and dashed forwards at break-neck speeds.

His eyes widened as he saw me running at him with my cloak billowing out behind me. He stepped forwards and my sword hummed with energy as he slashed at where my neck was about to be. I dropped into a slide and glided between his legs. He whirled around, obviously coming in for a follow up strike. I turned, planted my feet, and pumped even more energy. With an explosion of power, I leapt up towards his head.

His sword flashed below me —where I was moments before— and he looked up at me in shock. I clenched my aura-clad fist as tight as I could and slammed my fist into his jaw with a devastating right hook. His head snapped to the side as he stumbled from the blow of my strike. *Not enough.* I gritted my teeth and dropped to the floor. In his moment of shock, I grabbed his beefy left shoulder and brought my knee up into his groin. His eyes went wide as he screamed and dropped my sword.

I grinned and spun to catch my sword. In the same fluid moment, I pumped energy into the blade, whirled around and slashed through the aura protecting his chest as he lost the concentration to maintain it. Blood spilled from his chest like a waterfall, and he locked eyes with me, dumbfounded. My face twitched as I regained my footing and drove the point of my blade into his throat.

He fell to the ground, gurgling in his own blood as I withdrew my sword. Something inside me felt... satisfied. I hated it. I pushed the thoughts away and flicked the blood off my sword while scanning for my next opponent. I let the energy around me fill my runes as a man lumbered up to me with a large war hammer. The balding man grunted and scratched at some facial tattoos as we studied each other.

He used the same energy reinforcement technique as the others, all on the arms and legs for maximum strength. A risky choice considering they wore mostly cloth or were simply bare chested.

I blinked and he was suddenly much closer. My instincts screamed as I rolled to the side. The air churned beside me as a massive hammer splintered the floor where I had been standing moments before. My eyes darted back to him as I bounced to my feet only to find the hammer flying upwards in another swing. I sidestepped the blow and felt the wind tear beside my ear as it flew by.

I released one hand on the grip of my sword and slammed it into the front hand holding the hammer. He grunted, unaffected. Pain exploded across my cheek as my head snapped to the side. My vision swam and my thoughts were fuzzy as I hit the ground. I started to desperately crawl away as I struggled to regain my senses and heard his footsteps approaching one after the other like crashes of thunder. The darkness faded from my vision as I started to push myself to my feet. His foot slammed the ground like an earthquake as a pillar of earth shot up beneath my chest and into my ribs. The energy protecting me cracked and splintered as I was thrown upwards.

Before I could react, his energy-clad beefy hand wrapped around my throat like a vice and began to tighten. "Damn rat." He grumbled. Panic exploded through my body as my vision began to fade along with my remaining strength. My hands slowly began to go limp as I struggled to breathe one last time.

Something slammed into me, and I stumbled to the cold tile below. I coughed and heaved helplessly as I let my sight return to me for the fourth time this battle. Slowly, I managed to regain the strength to push myself onto my hands and knees. I looked up to see Abigail extending a bloodied, trembling hand towards me. "Rey! We need you! Get *up!*" It sounded like she was speaking through cotton, but I got the message and took her hand.

By the time I was on my feet my senses had returned and my neck hurt like hell. I winced as I rubbed it and looked to Abigail, who was scanning the ongoing battlefield like a predator. She was lit in the bright orange light of several nearby fires that made her eyes seem to glow. Her hair was tied back in a messy bun and her face and body were painted with splatters of blood. Panic welled in my chest as I saw gashes in her clothes and minor cuts all across her body.

I clenched her hand, which I hadn't realized I was still holding. "Abigail, are you okay?"

She turned back to me with a look of surprise on her face that morphed into confidence as she smiled. Even her teeth were stained a light pink. "Of course. You think I can't handle some bandits?" She gestured to some of the cuts, "These are nothing. I'll be fine. I've taken about five of them out. How about you?" She returned her eyes to the battlefield, looking for her prey.

"Two or three." I groaned as I shifted my weight and felt a bruise on my chest where the stone pillar had broken my aura.

She nodded, "Not bad." She smiled wide, as if proud. Her eyes finally settled on something across the room, and she drew her blade again. Aura shimmered brightly around her as she charged a small woman standing on a table with a bow. I stepped over the body of the man with the hammer— whose neck had been almost entirely slashed through and shuddered at the gruesome sight.

I turned back to Abigail to go help, only to watch her spin under a dagger slash and counterattack with a blast of water to the face. In one fluid motion, she rose from her crouched position and slashed upwards through the woman's hand. I winced but it was already over. Reeling from the shock and unable to defend herself, the woman quickly found her head split from her body.

Never get on Abigail's bad side, I guess. I weakly chuckled to myself as I picked up the sword I hadn't realized I'd dropped. Just in time for bolt of fire to soar towards my face. I pumped energy into my sword quick enough that it made my channels hurt as I flicked my wrist to have my sword intercept the flaming projectile.

It blew apart into wisps of fire energy as I scanned for my attacker. Barely out of the corner of my eye I noticed the flash of steel and quickly weaved to the side. But not enough. A sharp pain exploded to life in my thigh as a dagger skimmed my flesh leaving a shallow cut. I grimaced slightly and swung downward to find my opponent gone. Every instinct in my body screamed an attack was behind me and surely enough, when I ducked, I felt the swish of a blade fly straight overhead.

CHAPTER TWENTY

Ascension

Reynolds Helphain

My eyes snapped open, and my heart boomed. I sat up and my eyes darted around, alert and frenzied. The calloused hand of Hundri landed softly on my shoulder and I felt my adrenaline begin to fade as I took a deep breath. Pain flared from where I had been stabbed. I winced and touched where I had been stabbed lightly. Bandages wrapped around my waist and a few places on my arms, where in the heat of battle, I hadn't even noticed the small gashes.

The chilly mountain air bit at my skin as I shivered. Hundri chuckled and handed me my sliced shirt which I gratefully accepted and put on. "What happened while I was out?" I groaned as I rubbed my face, noticing the splatters of blood and the dirt had been rinsed off.

Hundri studied me with a look of concern that he was dreadfully failing at hiding. "Well, we finished off the bandits. Well, except for that one." He pointed a finger toward the wind dagger user he had fought. The bandaged man was stuck to the wall with large spikes of ice that stabbed through his hands and protruded from the wall. The other members of the Blades and Abigail rested near him, with a small pot that surely sizzled wonderfully, though the sound was drowned out by the bandit screaming and cursing at us.

I winced at the sounds and raised my eyebrows. "No gag?"

He shrugged. "We were just talking to him. Must've forgotten to put it back." He flicked his wrist in the direction of the man and his screams stopped. "Better?"

I chuckled. "Much."

Hundri smiled and scratched his head. "By the way, Kai asked me to tell you, he gave you a healing elixir while you slept. The more energy you cycle around the wound, the faster it will heal."

After a few moments of concentration, energy flowed through the world, into my channels and out into the rest of my body. I focused on the wound, letting it pool and gather. Sure enough, a tingling, warm sensation flared to life around the wound. I smiled. "That feels much better already. I never took Kai for an Instiller too. Handy."

"Oh, he isn't. His main practice is an Artificer, but he dabbles a bit in all fields." He smiled. "As you said, handy." The pain creeped away as the elixir did its work and I took that as a sign to start to climb to my feet. "Woah," Hundri said as he stood up quickly, "Here." He extended a hand which I gratefully took as I rose to normal height.

"Thanks," I grunted. We walked towards the others, who cheered when they noticed my approach, each of them cleaned and bandaged.

"Ay lad welcome back." The short, stout man stood up with his bowl of stew and clapped me on the back. Hard.

I winced. "You know I'm the victim of a stab wound, right?"

Ogland scoffed and responded in a jovial tone, "And the dealer of a cracked skull." He gestured to the woman who had stabbed me. I shivered as the sound of her skull breaking played again in my mind. "Besides! Coulda been worse! Ya coulda been *slashed!*" He gestured slowly, as if there was some mystique to being cut.

A gust of wind swept Ogland off his feet and a look of surprise blossomed on his face. The wind lowered him sprawling on his back as Yaldrie sighed. "I do apologize for him, Rey." She glared at her husband. "Go easy on the poor kid, it's his first stab wound!"

"Sorry! Sorry." Grumbled Ogland. "Sit, have some of this fine stew."

I sat down next to Abigail, who gave me a smile and patted me on the back, *lightly*. I returned her smile and picked up a wooden bowl. "Where'd you get the bowls? No, actually, where did you get any of these things? I know for sure we didn't pack them."

Syre smiled gleefully and pointed a thumb in the direction of the captured man. "He graciously donated these supplies after," she gestured to some cut marks on his waist that still bled through his bandages, "we asked nicely!"

I paled slightly. "I-I see." Abigail shot me a sympathetic look. I dipped the bowl into the pot and filled it with the brown stew. The warm liquid flowed down my throat and burned in my stomach. The meaty flavors popped on my tongue, and I raised my eyebrows. "Surprisingly good. What's in it?"

Hundri's face darkened. "That's the question. Nobody here recognized anything in it. Even Kai has never seen these ingredients, and he's been everywhere on this mountain."

I blinked, confused. "What's that mean? Maybe they're just rare?"

Kai sighed quietly. "Why would these *bandits* have high end materials?" He paused as if waiting for someone to answer, then answered his own question, "They wouldn't. And that hints that these are probably not from this area meaning. Meaning—"

I finished his sentence, "These people came from the lower greens." Hundri nodded solemnly. We sat in silence for a moment, eating the warm stew. "Has he confirmed that?" I gestured to the greasy man.

Hundri shook his head. "No, no matter how much we... ask nicely, he just curses us."

I sighed and took another sip of stew. "Do we tell Ronhelm this?"

Hundri shifted at his name. "I don't know. We're under a lot of pressure, with the Wings, now these bandits from the outside the mountain?" He shook his head solemnly.

"But, if he doesn't know, he can't prepare, and that will mean the downfall of Anhalt." Countered Kai.

We sat in silence again. Then, Ralteir finally joined the conversation, "So, how many did you all get?"

"Get?" I tilted my head slightly in confusion.

"How many did you *kill*. What else would I mean?" He grinned.

My gut twisted, their gruesome deaths flashing in my mind one by one. "Three or four."

Hundri raised an eyebrow. "More than I expected honestly. Good job."

Abigail joined him in raising an eyebrow, as if to say that one of those was technically her kill, but she said nothing.

Hundri gestured to the man on the wall, "Restraining that slippery bastard took a bit, but I got about ten or twelve myself." More than I expected.

Ralteir nodded slowly. "Makes sense. I got eight." He looked a little annoyed about being outdone but didn't mention it.

Slowly, we went around the group treating the lives of people like score. I tuned them out as they slowly went around. Eventually, Abigail grabbed me by the shoulder, "Hey," she muttered quietly while the others talked and laughed. "Are you okay? You look a little... out of it."

I sighed and relaxed the tension in my back I hadn't realized was building. "I'm fine. I just... even with their atrocities, it feels wrong to disrespect their lives by turning them into scores."

"I get it." She nodded. "This is what a lot of mercenary groups do. It's a hard job. I think they don't have the same regard for human life that an honorable knight like you does." She smiled playfully.

I smiled back. "Thanks."

"If you're feeling tense, try cycling energy. That usually calms me down." With that, she turned back to pay attention to the conversation. I did as she said and felt the soothing warmth running through my veins. As I concentrated on the flow, I felt my worries slipping into the tide of the warm power. I mindlessly sipped my stew.

Time slipped away slowly as I cleared my mind into a meditative state, only to feel a firm hand clamp on my shoulder. Every muscle in my body tightened in response. Ogland looked down at me in concern. "We're about to get movin' lad. Get ready."

I nodded and faked a smile. "Thanks." I paused. "Ogland... how do you get over the death?"

He shook his head and looked away. "Ya don't." His eyes swept the piles of bodies until he finally said, "But eventually ya learn to shove it away for the right times." With that, he got up and started to look through his bag.

Most of the group was standing over by the captive, ready to go. My wounds ached as I stood but thankfully, they didn't reopen. Luckily my little meditation had done wonders for healing. I broke into a light jog and caught up to the group.

Hundri turned his head as I approached. "Welcome back."

I looked at the captive who was muttering curses under his breath, frozen tears stuck to his gaunt face. "What's going on with him?"

Hundri's face darkened as he turned back to the man. "We're giving him *one* last chance to give us anything useful before we head up." The energy in the air around Hundri seemed to flare as he spoke, putting a terrifying strength behind his words.

The man went silent. Slowly an eerie smile spread across his face. Spittle flew from his mouth as he began to rave. "You *fools* don't know what you're getting into, Grulvin will pound you worthless pieces of trash into—" A frozen spike exploded out from his shoulder, spraying crimson.

The air was filled with screams.

"You are all *done for*! After training with the monks of the great Pohn Tree, he's unstoppable!" He cackled maniacally.

Hundri smiled. "And what skills did this Grulvin fellow attain there?"

The man's face paled. "Absolute strength! No matter what happens to me, you're already dead—"

Another spike exploded through his throat.

It was silent once again.

"We'll see about that." Hundri sighed "Well, at least we have a name. Grulvin. Let's get moving." The dead man wore the same eerie grin as the corpses from my dream. My stomach churned, and I tried everything in my power to push that memory out of my mind.

With a flash of steel, Hundri drew a small knife from a sheath on his thigh. I cringed as he cut a small circle of runes into the man's sternum. With a pulse of ghostly green light, tendrils of energy writhed around a small crystal Hundri held in his palm. In a matter of moments, the light faded.

"What was that?" I walked over and inspected the faceted jewel. "It looks like—"

"Yeah. Crystallized the energy left in his body. Same thing I did with the bear." He tossed it towards me, and I scrambled to catch it. "You and Abigail should use that. It should help get you closer to ascension."

I hadn't noticed Abigail had walked up next to me, but we both nodded. I turned to her and looked into her hazel eyes. "You know how to do this?"

Tapped a finger to it, and a chain of floating runes connected to the ghastly gem. "Of course."

I formed my own connection to the crystallized energy with a simple thought and watched the chain form. "Ready?"

"Ready."

The air rippled with energy as the green glow grew brighter. The satisfying heat of raw power filled my body as we drained the crystal. She smiled at me as the glow began to die.

"I can definitely feel the dam now." She took her hand off the gem and touched her leather breastplate, just above where her runes would be. A large, genuine smile spread on her face. "How about you?"

After letting the energy settle into my runes, I probed mentally for a dam-like feeling. Sure enough, I felt a loose barrier of energy —more like a ball in shape— floating deep within. It was faint, but there.

I smiled gleefully. "I feel it too!" My gaze wandered to the grinning corpse. The excitement died.

Yaldrie patted us on the back and gave us a warm smile. "Good job you two!"

Hundri smiled as well. "Now that that's out of the way, let's get a move on." He gestured to the white polished staircase. "Shall we?"

We quickly hiked up the staircase, and each of the Blades came by me and Abigail one by one to talk a little about ascension, life, and other random topics. After we finished the climb, we reached a crossroads. Going forward led to another staircase like the one we had just climbed. The left led to a large, reinforced door made of metal, the right had a simple wooden door. Ralteir spoke up. "I think we should keep going straight."

Ogland turned to him. "Ya see a large, *reinforced, metal door* and think, 'we should ignore it!' Is something wrong with yer head?"

I chuckled as Kai spoke up. "I agree with Ogland. This door could have untold treasures behind it with such reinforcement."

"And if it has enemies?" Asked Ralteir.

Syre cocked an eyebrow. "We kill them. Shouldn't that be obvious?"

Hundri clicked his tongue and waggled his finger. "Kids, kids, let's stop arguing and—" He weaved a punch from Syre. "—go through the big door."

Syre grumbled something about not being a kid anymore and the group begrudgingly moved toward the large door. It was a block of steel with a small hole for a crystal to be placed, like other doors I had seen in Anhalt. Just like every other door in this place, there wasn't a hint of a label on what could be on the other side. Hundri looked around the group, took off his pendant and let the casing fold away.

He slotted the glowing stone into the door and with a hum, lines of energy traced the doorway in complex, rigid, geometric patterns. With a groan, the door slid into the ceiling. Hundri smiled wildly. "I didn't think that'd work!"

Everyone glared at him.

We moved cautiously in. It was a large cylindrical room, with a short walkway leading to a large disc of dark grey stone inlayed with bronze floating in the center. On either side of the walkway were two staircases, leading up to a semicircular room with large, curved windows looking down on the dark stone circle. As we walked into the room, runic crystal lights lit up, bathing the area in white light.

"Oh Rey, you are in for a treat." Hundri smiled ecstatically. "This, my friend, is an Ascension Chamber. If we're lucky, it *might* have enough power in its crystals to push you to steel. Abigail too, as the energy crystals are divided by element."

Energy flared around his right foot and he stomped the floor, soaring in a precise arc to the top of the steps. He waved down, "Come up!" Then disappeared into the room. The group exchanged confused looks before following him up the carved, white stone stairs.

Kai gasped upon seeing the interior. The wall with curving paneled windows had a large array of bronze knobs, levers and buttons on a stained dark oak control panel. Opposite the windows were a dozen glass tubes reinforced with bronze and supported with beams of the same dark oak. Inside each were massive, man-sized energy crystals. All glowing and releasing auras of different types and intensities. Hundri walked to a large crystal that crackled and sparked with lightning that looked like a frozen bolt from the heavens.

He turned to me with a wide grin. "Kai," He called to the man drooling over the controls, "Do you think you could figure out how this works?"

"Gladly!" He called back with fervor in his voice.

"Splendid." Muttered Hundri as he led Abigail and I back towards the staircase. "Do you youngins know what an Ascension Chamber is?"

"No," we both responded.

He grinned widely. "Well, they're very expensive, time-consuming pieces of complex technology that gather energy from the atmosphere, *very* slowly to charge those large crystals. Then, we can focus *all* the energy gathered over very painstaking cycles on one person for about five seconds." We reached the bottom of the stairs. "Rey, go meditate in the center of that fun looking stone tablet."

I looked him in the eye, deadpan. "It looks like a sacrificial altar."

"Problem?" His smile remained, unwavering.

I sighed. "Never mind."

I walked onto the large stone disc and sat down. Hundri and Abigail watched from the other end of the walkway. "Now, Rey, ascending to the next stage can be strange, and a little painful but let it happen. When you feel the energy entering your body, focus on that dam. Try to break it."

"What?" I called over.

"Focus on dam! Break dam. Energy flows through you! Reborn! Got it?"

I sighed. "Yeah." I shut my eyes. I heard Hundri call out, "Kai! Whenever you're ready." The air began to hum. Every particle of energy around me began to vibrate and shudder. "Now, focus!" The bronze inlay beneath me grew hot as I felt the electric energy begin to arc to my body.

In a matter of moments after I felt the energy begin to seep into me, I felt the dam powerfully, a dominating presence in my mind. I pulled with all my willpower and felt the orb collapse inside me. An overwhelming amount of raw power roared through me like a tidal wave of molten lava. My screams were drowned out by the hammering of my heart in my ears. I felt the power burn through my channels, widening and reinforcing them. The runes on my chest seared my flesh as they grew more complex, and at the same time I felt my reserves deepen. Wherever the burning feeling touched my body felt reborn. The stab wound knit itself back together in a matter of moments as an incalculable amount of power washed it. After a few seconds, it was over. The pain was gone, but the feeling of newfound strength remained.

I stood and wiped the tears from my face. The ground spun as I stumbled and took a step forwards, still delirious from the pain. Abigail rushed forward and grabbed my face, concern in her eyes. "Rey! Are you okay? You sounded like a dying animal!"

I laughed weakly. "Thanks."

Hundri sauntered over behind her. "How're you feeling?"

I grinned. "Reborn."

"Good." He mimicked my expression. Then he turned to Abigail, with a cheery tone he said the words she clearly dreaded, "Your turn!"

"I don't know..." She turned to me, "Did you really advance that far?"

I nodded. "Yeah, I bet I used the *whole* damn crystal though."

"It shattered, actually!" called down Kai.

I raised my eyebrows. "I hope that wasn't too expensive."

Hundri shook his head. "Replacing one of those crystals probably costs more than this whole temple."

I paled. "Well let's forget we used them then. It was the bandits!"

Hundri chuckled, "Sure, sure."

"Alright. I'll go." Abigail's face was firm with determination as she walked onto the stone disc. Hundri raised his hand, a few moments after Abigail sat and closed her eyes. He lowered it quickly. The air began to hum like I had felt, though the feeling was almost negligible compared to sitting in the middle of it.

It became obvious that she began her ascension as her skin began to glow faintly. "How's it feel?" asked Hundri.

"Like nothing else." I said simply.

"Yeah." He smiled wistfully. "There's no feeling like fresh ascension."

"I bet."

The glow began to fade from Abigail's skin as the humming grew quieter. She stumbled as she stood. I smiled. After a moment, Abigail reached us, drenched in sweat and with puffy eyes. "Abigail! How was the ascension?"

She looked him in the eye with a look of exhaustion and irritation. "Fine."

Hundri clicked his tongue. "You seem so sour! Cheer up! You're a lot stronger now! No need to be like that."

Abigail cracked a smile. "Fair enough."

He turned back towards the way we entered the chamber. "Aren't you going to use it? Even if you can't ascend, shouldn't it still help?" I called after him.

He shook his head, "Not worth it. Steel is a much longer stage than bronze." He signaled to the rest of the group to come down and went to lean against the thick metal door.

"I didn't hear a single sound from you." I turned to Abigail.

She wiped some sweaty strands of hair from her forehead and tucked them behind her ears. "Yeah. I'm just tougher than you." She smirked.

"As tough as you may be," after a second of thought, scales blossomed out. They weaved a thin gauntlet of energy that hummed with an intoxicating strength. "Now, we're equal."

She slugged my arm. "In terms of raw power, sure. But technique wise? You've got a while to go."

I scoffed, turned back to the door and walked away with Abigail close behind. I waited patiently beside Hundri as the group slowly trickled down. All except for Ogland, who appeared last, holding Kai like a sack of potatoes.

Kai flailed and kicked in Ogland's arms, but Ogland held him strong. The group broke into laughter as he descended the staircase with a Kai acting like a child. "Didn't wanna leave the controls," He smiled with yellowing teeth. "So, I grabbed 'em."

Hundri chuckled, "Thanks Ogland."

He scratched his large beard and nodded. Once we had exited the Ascension Chamber and locked the door behind us, Ogland placed a disgruntled Kai back down. "You know," I started, "I'm surprised a room like that wasn't already stripped to pieces for the salvage."

Yaldrie rapped her small knuckles against the door. "This type of door, with this lock," She gestured to the hole that Hundri had placed the crystal in, "is inordinately expensive and impossible to break into. I would've been stunned if they could've."

Syre nodded. "Not even our good pal Hundri here could break in."

"You haven't seen me try! Maybe I could!" He gave a confident smile.

"Go ahead, try, please." A sly smile spread on Syre's lips, "I'd like to see you try."

Hundri scratched the back of his head, "Well, you see I need to keep my energy for that Grulvin. It'd be a waste!"

"Great! We can try on the way down." Satisfaction and victory lit up her eyes as she began to walk down the hallway.

Hundri sighed and followed after, muttering curses. I chuckled to myself as we walked to the wooden door. The contents were rather uninteresting. As the door slid open, it revealed rows upon rows of bunkbeds, stretching into the darkness. Ogland peaked around me and into the room. "Are we gonna botha lookin' in 'ere?"

Hundri shook his head. "Use your nose. I don't think we want to see what lies in the dark." The scent of iron wafted into my nose, and I recoiled.

"Let's just move on." I said solemnly, the images of the mutilated boys and girls flashing in my mind. I shivered and struggled to push them away. A guilt pulled at my chest with each face that flashed by. We should've come faster, maybe then they wouldn't have had to die.

We turned back and walked towards the stairs. If it weren't for the strength of an energy enhanced body, most people would've collapsed after climbing so many flights. Hundri walked next to me. "You don't forget them."

"What?" I turned to him, pulled from my thoughts.

"The bodies. The cost of ambition."

This time I pictured the smiling corpses as they walked toward me. I shook my head sending a few strands of hair into my eyes. "I wish I couldn't remember them." I said quietly.

"They won't leave you. Think of it this way. They lacked the strength to overcome the challenges of life. Now, it's up to you to take them with you, to use them and their memory to overcome what they couldn't." He was silent for a second, "You couldn't have helped them, so don't get caught up wishing you could've done more for them."

It was as if he had read my mind somehow. "I—" I stopped speaking. I didn't know how to say this without him thinking I was crazy. "When we fought the first group, at the base, I... passed out because of a vision."

He cocked his head to the side. "A vision?"

"Yeah, I saw... their bodies, they got up and stared at me and started to walk toward me and told me I was a murderer and a monster and—" I realized I was rambling and shut my mouth with a snap.

He stared at me cool and collected, "Rey, you are not a monster. If you're a monster, I'm Demon King Daelgeth himself."

"Who?" I asked.

He sighed, "He was a mass murderer, general, demi-god level person who wiped out cities, anyway, doesn't matter." He gestured to the Blades walking up the steps in front of us. "Without a doubt these people have killed hundreds of times more people than you. Sure, we might be monsters in combat, but we do the things we do to help people, to support the people we love. And most importantly, we have morals. We don't senselessly slaughter children like these... calling them people is too nice but it's the best I've got right now." He grabbed me by the shoulders and looked deep into my eyes. "You fight for your sister, for your family and for yourself. You kill not because you enjoy it, but because you have to. You are leagues apart from them, and are already a much better man than I." He smiled at me.

My face grew hot, and my vision fuzzy as uncontrollable tears ran down my face. As I heaved, Hundri wrapped his arms around me and pulled me in close. We stayed there until my tears stopped. Finally, I pulled myself out of his embrace and smiled at him. My voice broke as I wiped the tears from my eyes. "Thank you. I needed that."

He smiled, broad and genuine. "Never forget your reason to fight. It's what gives you strength." He held a white knuckled fist in front of his face and pounded his heart with it twice. I mimicked the motion and found a strange solace in it. "Now, on the topic of those visions, this isn't your first one, is it?"

I shook my head slowly. "Sorry."

He sighed. "It's fine. My guess is they're coming from the stones. My father never truly told me much. Despite what you may think about those stones, they only seemed to help my father. I bet deep down; they're trying to help you somehow."

I raised my eyebrows. "If you'd have seen these visions, you would not believe that so confidently."

"Well, that's just what my father told me." He shrugged. "He never once complained about them or even tried to be rid of them."

I sighed. "I'll be more open-minded then. Try to look for any hidden wisdom and the like."

He grinned widely. "That's the spirit!" His expression died a little as he continued, "I'm glad you got the stones Rey. *Finally*, I am free of them. Explore them at your own pace. I'm certain they will grant you great strength in the future."

I smiled. "I will. Thank you, Hundri."

He gave me a thumbs-up. "No problem. Now, let's get moving, they seem to have left us behind."

I looked up at the seemingly infinite staircase and was shocked to find Hundri right. The Blades of Iora were growing smaller and smaller with every step. "In good news, I needed a chance to see how strong my aura is now."

He grinned. "Be careful, it's a bit hard to control after an ascension." With that he blasted off the ground and arced higher every passing second until he had easily cleared forty of the polished stone steps.

"Here goes nothing." I muttered to myself as I let a pulse of my energy into my feet. I judged my trajectory quickly and pushed off the ground. The air whistled in my ears as I shot upwards... and into the ceiling. My eyes went wide as my back slammed a stone arch. With a quick redirection of energy, I stopped any real damage from happening to my body as I hit the ground.

Hundri's guffawing laughter echoed from high above. I could've sworn I heard the words, "I told you so."

I glared up the staircase and pulsed energy downwards again, this time with more of an emphasis on going forwards. The air whistled as it accommodated my high-speed travel. With the satisfying feeling of my foot meeting another solid stone step, I pushed off again. The feeling of flying was so... freeing. In that moment, I envied wind mages.

After a minute or two of bounding up the steps, I reached the group. Hundri was already walking alongside them. I landed with a stumble and quickly looked around, hoping nobody had seen. Abigail smiled at me. I sighed. "Hello Abigail."

"Nice landing."

"Why don't you try jumping like that then?"

She grinned wide. "I heard the noise of *something* hitting the ceiling, then the floor. Care to explain just *what* that was?"

My face flushed slightly. "Nope."

"Exactly. Well, if you find out, maybe I'll try jumping like you did."

Finally, the staircase opened up into a large domed room, similar to the ones we'd come across before, only this one had four archways. One opposite the staircase we'd climbed and two much larger ones on either side of the room. In front of the archway to the left, and what I guessed was the largest staircase, were wooden barricades in the form of large spikes. Two men with bows stood looking down the stairs atop raised platforms. Behind them, was a large group of sleeping men and women. They were laying on bedrolls arranged in circles around smoldering campfires that blackened the pearly tiles.

Something pulled at the back of my mind. A familiarity.

Hundri looked me in the eyes, curled his fingers into a fist, and pounded his heart twice. "Stand back everyone. I'll deal with this myself." They nodded solemnly.

I tried to protest but Ogland shook his head. "Yer bout to witness the power of a gold."

Hundri clenched his fist at eye level with his palm pointing at his face and grabbed the back of his fist with his other hand. He closed his eyes and began to chant. Kai placed a set of stones in the doorway's corners. The air seemed to distort between them.

I looked at Kai and before I could ask, he answered. "They'll keep the guys over there from sensing Hundri's power. Think of it like a seal on the air." I nodded and watched Hundri again.

Light leaked from beneath his fingers and cold air seemed to gravitate toward him as frost formed at his feet. The effects grew more pronounced as he chanted. After almost a minute of chanting, he released his stance and opened his eyes. Instead of just his iris glowing, now even the whites of his eyes were glowing an icy blue. On the back of his right hand was a complex glyph that seemed to suck the heat from the air.

"Drop it." He looked at Kai, who nodded weakly and grabbed the stones hurriedly. The second the distortion disappeared, Hundri exploded outwards from the mouth of the staircase. Almost immediately the archers spun and trained their arrows on him. A bell began to ring and the people below him stirred quickly into action with practiced efficiency. He spun in the air and energy coiled around his legs as he prepared to land in the center of the waking bandits.

Hundri's feet touched the ground with a thud, and I could've sworn I saw the hint of a smile on his face. The air seemed to swell as he wound back his fist and, with a wave of power, his knuckles touched the ground.

Sheets of ice exploded out across the ground with an accompanying wave of freezing air. Frost exploded across every surface in crystalline webs. The fires were snuffed out. Men's faces were frozen open mid speech. Everything around Hundri in a circle was coated in ice and frozen solid. The room was filled with a deathly silence.

Hundri's wavy mess of hair fell back into place as the light in his eyes rapidly dimmed and returned to normal. My mouth gaped. We slowly walked into the room. I yelped and jumped back as I bumped into a man who was frozen in place as he was clambering from his bedroll. Even the cloth was frozen solid. His unsettling dead eyes seemed to stare up at me.

As I jumped back, I hit another with enough force that his frozen head cracked off his body and fell the floor, shattering into pieces. I quickly averted my eyes and did the salute that Hundri had taught me. It helped.

I quickly moved to Hundri, deftly maneuvering through the field of once-living sculptures. He stretched his back and gave me a smile. "What'd you think?"

I surveyed the decimation. "Terrifying."

He frowned a little and held up his index finger. "I prefer my friends to think of it as *awesome* and my *enemies* to think of it as terrifying."

Abigail walked over next and whistled. "This is... a little ridiculous. Why haven't you been doing this every time?"

"Oh, Abby—"

She glared at him. "Don't call me that."

"Sorry, sorry. Anyway, where's the fun in doing this," he gestured around, "every time?"

"The *fun* is that we don't have to risk our lives."

He waggled his finger. "But if you don't *fight* you don't *grow.*"

She opened her mouth to respond, closed it, then finally found her words. "I... can't argue with that. I think we can all agree that attack is disturbingly powerful. I vote it should be used more."

Ralteir sauntered over. "I know right? His Subzero Wave is crazy—"

Hundri sighed. "You know we don't need a name for *every* attack I do, right? I thought I said to stop calling it that."

"But... it gives them so much more power!"

I blinked. "What? How?"

"It gives it an *emotional* impact. Nobody is afraid of an unnamed punch, but something called the *Ultimate Kerfuffle-Ender* will strike fear in the hearts of all."

The small group collectively burst into echoing laughter. Ogland, Kai, Yaldrie and Syre walked over, looking confused. "What's so funny?" asked Ogland.

Hundri looked over at Ogland with teary eyes and said between laughs, "Ralteir suggested I should name the giant, *gold-level* attack I just did, *Ultimate Kerfuffle-Ender.*"

With that the laughter was rekindled and echoed across the large room. After we all finished laughter and caught our breaths, Ralteir spoke again, "I mean not *specifically* that version! Maybe your single target version of that is better?"

I perked up. "Single target version?"

Hundri winked at me. "That one's a secret for next time."

Ralteir continued, "I could live with parting with its previous name—"

A groan escaped Hundri, "Don't. Don't say it."

"—Absolute Zero Strike," finished Ralteir.

I cringed slightly. "Subzero Wave is tolerable... but Absolute Zero Strike?" I shook my head.

A smile lit up Hundri's face and he waved at me excitedly. "Ha! See? He gets it!"

Abigail interjected. "He *also* said Subzero Wave is tolerable."

Hundri's face dropped. "Silence. You are *clearly* imagining things."

I smiled as I watched them bicker. A warm happiness bubbled up inside me watching them fight. They both glared at me. "What're you smiling at!?" They both yelled.

I stepped back. "Sorry, sorry. It's nothing."

After a little longer, Syre interjected. "Alright, alright. You two can bicker later. We need a plan to take down Grulvin."

Hundri looked over to Syre. "Well, if he's as strong as reported, with all of us it shouldn't be too much of a problem."

"What if things don't go our way though. We should have some *real* plans."

"Fair enough. Well, like our usual roles then. I will take the frontal attack with Ogland and Ralteir. Syre and Yaldrie, you guys stay in the back and try to pin him down with ranged attacks. Kai, you focus on laying traps and the like. Abigail and Rey, you guys are going to be backup for the frontal attack squad, as I don't trust your experience enough to handle a gold." He looked at each of us. "Understood?"

We all nodded, and he continued. "Backup plan is, of course, run the hell away. The last resort is the same as previous battles with golds."

He started to move, and I quickly chimed in. "Wait, me and Abigail have no clue what that is."

He sighed. "I hope we don't have to do this, but, if need be, I will remove my spiritual heart for you to infuse in your weapon." Me and Abigail looked at each other, equally confused. Hundri sighed deeper. "Quick lesson on energy theory then. Runes are sort of like an anchor that ties a 'heart' to your body. That's what gives you the ability to gather and use energy. If very specific runes are carved into the body at very specific places, it opens something like a door to your spiritual heart, and you can disconnect it from your body."

He gestured by clenching a hand over his chest, slowly pulling away and holding his hand to the side like he was holding a fruit. "You can then *temporarily* infuse my heart into your weapon. The benefits of that, are that your weapon will generate a gold level aura *on its own.*"

Me and Abigail looked equally stunned. "If this... 'spiritual heart' does what you claim, why don't they teach that in the academy?" Abigail asked.

"I'm not surprised they don't. It's very frowned upon. It's basically sacrificing lives to forge a weapon. It's both unethical and extremely dangerous."

"Woah, wait. Will this *kill* you?" I exclaimed in a worried voice.

"No, you can survive without it. Not forever though. Your lifespan drops drastically the more time you spend without it. Humans *need* primordial energy to survive." He smiled. "I'll be fine." The rest of the group looked uncomfortable but said nothing. It was clear they hated the idea of using Hundri's life as a weapon, but they said nothing.

Ogland broke the silence. "I'm thinking we're ready to go then, yeah?"

"You've got that right. Everyone remember to gather energy while we go up, I need you guys in peak condition." He turned away from the hundred or so men he had easily slaughtered and toward the other large archway. Inside was a large platform that followed the same design I was accustomed to seeing now. White stone, black accents and bronze inlays in the form of runes.

A familiarity itched my mind.

Hundri dropped his bag onto the floor of the platform as we gathered on it. The platform could've easily fit a hundred people. With a pulse of energy from Hundri's feet, the runes lit up and gears began to whir. Slowly, the platform began to ascend. "Why do they have all those stairs if they could've just done this?"

"It's to show your *determination* and your 'unrelenting faith in Iora.'" Hundri said mockingly as he gestured grandly.

I chuckled and raised an eyebrow. "For a group literally named The Blades of *Iora*, you all seem rather disconnected from the religion that worships her."

"Who do you think came up with the name?" He raised his eyebrows at me. "Have you ever known *me* to want to name anything?"

"That makes much more sense. I didn't think Ralteir worshipped Iora."

"He doesn't." Hundri chuckled. "I still, to this day, do not know why we're named that. He started calling us that around other people before approving the name with the rest of us and it just kind of... stuck."

A wry smile played at my lips. "Maybe if you named something yourself, you'd get a name you actually *like*. If you don't call that Subzero Wave anything, it makes sense someone will name it for you."

"I guess that makes sense," he sighed, "but do I really need to name a simple punch infused with Iora's energy something grandiose like Absolute Zero Strike?"

I folded my arms. "That's the beauty of naming it—surprise, surprise— yourself."

"That's fair." he said begrudgingly.

Light began to stream through a doorway above us as the platform approached its destination. Perhaps as I reached my final destination. I tied part of my hair back to prevent it from falling in my eyes while I fought and let the rest droop over my shoulders. The rest of the members with long hair did the same.

Finally, with a thump, the platform slotted into place. The light on the other side of the arch was blinding compared to the almost pitch black of the lift's shaft. Hundri exited first and one after another, we followed with our hands on our weapons.

The room I entered was not what I expected in the slightest. It was a large domed room with walls made of ice-looking crystal that emanated a faint blue glow. The ground was covered in a color that was unfamiliar to me in such wide swathes; bright green. Thin grass covered miniature hills that swept the ground of the glowing room. The faint trickle of a river filled the air. As we walked, we found the stream. It ran through the ground cutting up the green hills. A small, ornate wooden bridge spanned the gap.

Each footstep forwards made the overbearing weight energy in the air more palpable. Across the bridge was a field of white flowers with a path cut through them. After another minute of walking, we reached a large clearing in the field. A lifelike and life-size statue of a woman with a blue glowing crystal in her bosom stood with arms outstretched to the sky. Around the lady was a series of stone black obelisks of different sizes with azure glowing runes carved into them.

The clearing was shaded by a ring of white leafed trees. Slowly a shadowed man rose from a kneeling position at the statue's feet. Leaves lazily fell from above, dancing and twirling through the light before meeting the cold hard ground. He stepped out from the deepest of the shadows slowly. He oozed confidence. The energy in the air around us pulsed and I felt every muscle in my body tighten as he cracked his knuckles. Sweat rolled down my brow.

He had a long scar running down his left eye and it cut through his bushy eyebrow like a ravine. His long, curly, greasy, black hair danced in the wind before settling down on his back and spilling over his bulky shoulders. He wore sparse leather armor lined with black fur over his massive, tanned muscles that were a collage of scars. The light caught the tapestry of runes on his ornate bronze knuckledusters as he sauntered towards us.

He grinned a toothy grin. I reflexively stepped back and pulled my sword from its sheath. Syre drew back her bow. Yaldrie's staff began to hum and glowed a deep emerald. Hundri flared his own aura and drew his sword. We all had instinctively prepared for a battle, the only one who looked remotely calm was Hundri, everyone else was more tense than taut rope.

"So," Grulvin said in a jarringly smooth voice. "I give you this chance. Flee." His aura pulsed violently. Before a single leaf could touch his skin, they burst into flames and were reduced to ash.

Hundri pointed his sword at the man and hardened his face into a mask of determination. "Not a chance."

Grulvin nodded. The pulses of his aura slowed to a heartbeat-like rhythm as a spectral orange shell formed around every limb of his body. "So be it."

CHAPTER TWENTY-ONE

Atop Gods' Peak

Reynolds Helphain

Hundri nodded almost imperceivably and Ogland and Ralteir leapt diagonally to either side. They flew through the air and pulsed with energy as they drew back their weapons. Hundri's aura flared as he blasted forwards, kicking up dust. With a crack, an arrow exploded out from Syre's black longbow. Syre began to rise slowly into the air as she manipulated the wind below her. Finally, Abigail and I began to charge in, making sure to stay behind the front liners.

Grulvin effortlessly backhanded the arrow from the air, and it dug into the ground with a thump. Ogland's sword began to trail fire as he descended on the monster of a man in a downwards slash. Grulvin met his blade with an aura-clad forearm and was left... unharmed. Ogland paled as he quickly twisted his sword and blocked a punch with the flat of his blade.

His sword rang like a bell as Ogland rocketed backwards and slammed into a tree. Blood flew from his mouth and the bark behind him cracked and splintered from the impact. With a shrill scream, Yaldrie released a barrage of wind blades. In a gust, she flew towards Ogland.

Grulvin dashed backwards, weaving between the blades as they slashed into the grass and sent up puffs of dirt. An amber rune glowed on Ralteir's stone gauntlet, and the dirt halted in the air, then blasted towards the beefy man like shrapnel. Through the cloud of dirt, Ralteir dashed forwards with a punch in a surprise attack.

The real surprise was when Grulvin's fist pierced the dirt cloud — much faster than Ralteir's— and flew towards Ralteir's face. He desperately raised his arms in a clumsy block and was blasted backwards, arms outstretched as his cross-guard was destroyed along with his stone gauntlets. Left wide open, Ralteir quickly twisted his wrists and a wall of earth jutted from the ground just in time to intercept a jet of blue-tinged fire.

Grulvin frowned. "Not bad." Ralteir flicked his wrists towards the ground and the stone pulled itself apart, forming gauntlets again along with plates of stone armor that reinforced his aura. Another arrow snapped through the air and Gruvlin twisted to the side, caught it, and snapped it in his hand effortlessly. A web of complex orange runes tinged with blue formed above his hand. Even from where I stood, frozen, the air began to warm.

A large orange fireball flickered to life, solidified into a globe of incinerating heat, then compressed into a ball of blue fire in a matter of moments.

He wound back his arm and prepared to toss it, only for a blade of wind to slice it in half. It detonated with a roar and the air itself seemed to burn. Grulvin was consumed in the spherical ball of white-hot energy. When the smoke cleared, Grulvin was gone. My heart soared, only to drop again as his fist slammed into the flat of Ogland's great sword. Again, Yaldrie stood behind him, surrounded by floating green runes. Blood ran down Ogland's chin as he skidded backwards from the impact. Before a surely lethal roundhouse kick could connect with Ogland's neck, a spike of ice burst from the ground in the path of his leg.

Unconcerned, Grulvin's kick continued. It cracked the point of the spike off without so much as piercing his aura. Something was wrong. The kick continued until it lost its momentum deep in the spike. He pulled it from the broken spike and ducked as Hundri's sword flashed above his head, slicing off strands of hair.

In a matter of moments, they had exchanged twenty blows. Flashes of steel deftly dodged or blocked. As they fought, rings upon rings of green runes circled the arrow pulled back on Syre's bowstring. With a boom, it rocketed forwards at Gruvlin's head. Instantly, he sidestepped the arrow and simultaneously caught Hundri's blade in an iron grip.

Hundri paled and screamed, "There's a pattern! *Watch closely—*" Grulvin's fist slammed into Hundri's ribs. Blood spewed from his lips as the man grinned wide. Hundri skidded and rolled across the grass before springing to his feet, with no sword in hand. A crack filled the air. Grulvin effortlessly snapped the unenhanced sword in his fist.

Hundri's eyes glowed brighter as he swept his arms forwards and countless spikes of ice the size of my body erupted from the ground. Grulvin dashed between them as he approached Hundri. He weaved and smashed through each one, eliciting a grimace from Hundri. The aura around Hundri swelled and pulsed. He was charging the glyph I had seen before.

Grulvin picked up the pace and closed the distance in a matter of moments as he tore up grass with every step. Ralteir caught a speeding right hook with a grunt as he dug troughs in the ground with his feet from the sheer force. Ogland swung his flaming great sword in a horizontal arc at Gruvlin's thighs. It dug into the monstrous man's aura less than an inch before stopping.

I started to count.

Grulvin grunted, unclenched his fists, wrapped his meaty hand around Ralteir's forearm and *pulled.* With a cry of surprise, Ralteir was lifted from the ground and was slammed into Ogland.

Ogland stumbled backwards in surprise and was met with a side kick to the chest. He was once again lifted from the ground from the sheer force and slammed into the same tree as before. Yaldrie fired a few blasts of wind that buffeted harmlessly off Gruvlin as she maneuvered towards Ogland.

I felt helplessness pull at me. Nevertheless, I counted.

In one smooth motion, Ralteir was slammed into the ground, over and over as the stone plating slowly crumbled away. Aura swelled from

Hundri, and he swung at Grulvin with his fist glowing empowered by the glyph. Absolute Zero Strike. Grulvin sneered, twisted and placed Ralteir in front of the blow. Hundri paled again as his fist connected with Ralteir's shoulder. The energy of the attack immediately cut itself off as Hundri tried to save his friend, but the damage was done and Ralteir's shoulder and left arm were frozen solid.

Grulvin grabbed Ralteir by the back of his neck and tossed him away. Hundri stumbled back in horror before regaining his resolve. Ralteir's arm shattered like glass as he slammed into the ground and went limp.

Ogland roared in rage and charged forwards behind a wall of fire. Gruvlin sighed and extended his hand. He clenched his hand in a grabbing motion and a wave of nauseatingly powerful formless energy overtook Ogland's wave of fire. Grulvin sneered as it collapsed and compacted into a tiny blue marble.

It jetted forwards at Ogland's face and he closed his eyes, accepting his fate. The air rippled and it snuffed away without a trace. Ogland deftly ducked under a following left hook, only to have his head grabbed like a fruit the next moment. Grulvin smiled wildly as he pounded Ogland headfirst into the ground, blowing away chunks of grass with each blow.

Yaldrie screamed in horror and fired another barrage of wind blades as she rushed to Ogland's aid. Before Yaldrie could reach him, Hundri swiftly jabbed at the behemoth's back with an icy dagger. It shattered against his back and chipped away at the man's aura but did no substantial damage. Grulvin dropped Ogland to the ground, turned, and kicked Hundri in the knee with a devastating crack.

Hundri's leg caved inwards in a sickeningly unnatural way. He screamed in agony as he began to fall to the ground, unable to support his weight. The air cracked again and he was hit with a backhand. Grass flew up behind him as he skidded over to me. His screams were bloodcurdling. Yaldrie reached Ogland and started to activate a glyph on her fist, the sound one I presumed, only to find Grulvin ready for it. A crack echoed through the air as his fist hammered her temple. She crumpled to the ground next to Ogland as blood dripped from the hit.

Grulvin hit her over and over and blood flew like a fountain. "Stop... *please!*" cried Ogland as he watched his wife be beaten repeatedly.

Grulvin placed his foot on her dented skull. "I... love... you..." Yaldrie smiled as the pressure grew.

With a sickening crack and splatter, her head blew apart. I averted my eyes as I began to feel faint. A wave of emotions washed me. I looked back to see the bloody splatter of meat covering the grass and Ogland's face. He screamed and tears poured from his face as he tried to wipe the pieces of his wife off his face. Blue fire danced on his skin, and he began to pull himself to his feet. With a quick punch to the head, he was out cold a moment later. Before Grulvin could hit him again, three arrows cracked through the air.

Aura flared next to me, and I immediately flinched backwards, turning my attention next to my right. Hundri's eyes met mine with unrelenting determination. In his hand was a ghostly green sphere that pulsed and glowed in the rhythm of a heart. His chest was covered in glowing bloody runes from where I guessed he'd removed it.

"Are you sure?" I asked, my voice cracking. He nodded and pounded his heart twice with a tight fist. I returned his salute and gripped the freezing cold orb, feeling the true weight of life in my hands. I gritted my teeth and thrust it into my blade. The air rippled in resistance. I poured energy between them as a binding and felt the two slowly merge. After a moment, they were one.

The sword pulsed in my hand slowly and rhythmically as it radiated an aura as strong as the man before me. *This is no time to hold back.* I pumped energy through my body, and into the bear's rune without limit. I felt my aura spike and grow violent, hateful even. I cracked my knuckles and let the energy form the scaled aura I was familiar with over every inch of my body.

It gave a new meaning to power. The combined strength of a gold-powered weapon in my hand and my new abilities as a steel were like nothing else. It was time to fight. My golden-scaled aura began to crackle like lightning as I exploded forwards. The world blurred for a moment, then my eyes caught up. The world seemed to slow as I soared towards him. I watched another of Syre's arrows catch up and pass me.

He swung a punch —faster than an arrow— and I dropped to my knees. I swiped at his knees with my blade that now shined a magnificent blue. It sunk into his aura and stopped just before drawing blood. He grimaced and whirled around —carried by the momentum of his punch— and unclenched his fist into a palm strike. A jet of azure fire blasted outwards, lighting the grass on fire as it traveled.

With an upwards slash, I split it in two and jabbed through the screen of flame. He somehow managed to weave the surprise attack and planted a kick on my aura-protected chest. The scales cracked and splintered as I skidded backwards. Grulvin beckoned me towards him with a stone-cold expression of determination. Just like the one plastered on my own face. Out of the corner of my eye, I saw Kai. He nodded and gestured to the trees. *The traps!*

I dashed towards Grulvin again and channeled lightning to a point in my palm. He dropped into a battle stance to intercept me. The lighting concentrated until it felt like it would burn through my hand.

I released it.

I guided it with my thoughts, focusing my will on knocking him backwards. The lightning exploded through the air in an instant. My momentum stopped midair from the sheer explosive force. It snapped at him in an instant and took him square in the chest. The crystalline aura on his chest shattered and smoked as he stumbled backwards. To my own sick delight, his flesh sizzled and popped where I had hit him.

His back hit the bark of the tree and a smile spread on my face, the anger and hatred I felt for him bubbling brighter with every second. Energy spiked behind him, and tendrils of glowing blue and white light wrapped themselves around his arms and legs. They drew themselves tight enough to cause cracks to spiderweb out across his aura. As he strained and roared against the restraints, I hit him in the face over and over alternating punches and slashes until his aura cracked and crumbled away.

With one final flex, his aura flared with power and the restraints exploded. I stepped backwards and found fire behind me from the grassfire he had started. A massive globe of water drifted overhead before splitting in two. One half burst apart and doused the fire. Abigail dashed next to me a moment later.

"Hey, I've got your back, okay?" I nodded without looking away from Grulvin. My heart was burning nothing but rage and determination. My channels had started to burn from the strain, even past the dulled senses the bear's rune gave me. Time was short.

I rocketed forwards and dirt exploded upwards as I soared. We collided in a flurry of blows, neither of us losing ground. I could feel the pattern Hundri had talked about. We dodged and blocked in a tornado of flashing steel. Our blows met and traded over and over as time seemed to slow. Blood trickled from my mouth and bruises covered my body. Cuts and slashes began to sprout over his taut muscles. We kept fighting.

I feinted a swing to his head and whirled into a right hook. His aura was thinning across his body from the prolonged battle; however, I was suffering from the same issue. He dodged my punch, grabbed me by the wrist, pulled me in and delivered a devastating knee to the ribs. Blood spewed from my lips as I stumbled backwards, only to be met with punch after much to my face. My aura cracked and split as he kicked me *hard*. I felt my ribs crack with dulled agony as I flew backwards, digging into the earth.

I regained my footing in a matter of moments and saw through my swimming vision Abigail pelting him with projectiles. I cursed myself.

I clenched my jaw tight and began to charge, when I saw him grab her by the ponytail. I froze. She screamed as she was yanked backwards.

Grulvin wrapped his hand around her throat and squeezed. The color began to drain from her face.

"*Stop!*" I screamed desperately in a hoarse voice. "Please."

Grulvin considered me from behind his cracked aura helmet and smiled. "Lay down that *DAMNED* sword. Then we have a deal." I grimaced. There was no chance that he'd let her go.

"Alright." I said slowly as I pretended to put down the sword. In a last-ditch effort, I began to obviously gather energy in my left hand. He sneered as I thrust my hand forward, and placed Abigail in the way of whatever attack would be flying towards him.

The perfect opening.

The air exploded with a deafening boom. Blood sprayed from his neck and his eyes widened in surprise. *Thank you, Syre!* I held the energy in my palm until Abigail was out of his grasp and released. The lightning tore through the air and through his failing aura. His skin blackened and sizzled as he was blasted backwards by the voltaic bolt.

I charged him one last time, pumping as much energy from Hundri's heart as I could. *For Hundri.* I kicked him in the knee with all my strength and felt the tendons in his leg tear as it caved in. *For Ralteir.* I swiped up with my sword, carving his arm from his body. *For Yaldrie!* I fell to my knees over his dying body, dropped my sword, and began to beat him relentlessly. Blood flew from each punch, my knuckles began to stain red. *For Serena.* I stood and picked up my sword before looking the dying man in the eyes one last time. Without a second thought, I flicked the sword across his neck and effortlessly carved his head from his body.

I stood over his body and relinquished my hold on the bear's rune as my face flushed. I felt something snap deep inside me; the runes on my chest burning. Tears ran down my face as I heaved from the pain of it all. The loss, the wounds and the relief were too much to bear. Abigail wrapped her arms around my waist, turned me around and pulled me tight against her chest.

Every inch of my body burned from the agony of hundreds of blows. My heart ached from the loss of Yaldrie and the guilt of not doing anything until we'd already truly lost. I wept for what felt like hours before I pushed myself away from Abigail. "Thank you." I murmured in a broken voice.

She smiled. "Good job, Rey."

Another tear rolled down my cheek.

My face slowly returned to a normal shade as we walked back towards Hundri. He was pale and covered in sweat. Syre had left his side and was tending to Ogland and Ralteir with Kai. He smiled weakly at me. "You fought wonderfully."

My eyes swept from Hundri's leg to Ralteir's arm, Yaldrie's... head. What little food I had eaten lurched up and out of my mouth as I slumped over; the reality of the death of a friend striking me suddenly. I wiped my mouth and looked back at Hundri. "What does it matter? Look at what victory cost."

His eyes danced across the charred and bloodied field as tears welled. "'You die once when you take your last breath, you truly die the last time someone says your name.' That was something my father used to say to me," he pounded his heart twice and raised his fist, "the sacrifices of those we love and have lost join our reason to survive. To fight, and to live in their stead."

I nodded as another tear dripped from my face. I returned the salute. He solemnly took a swig from a small, faceted glass vial, emptying it. "Help an old man to his feet, will you?"

He took my hand as I held it out. As hard as I tried to smile at his humor, I couldn't bring myself to. I supported Hundri as we walked towards the rest of the group, who were either giving medical care, or receiving it. After I sat him down with my sword so he could regain his spiritual heart, I walked towards the statue of Iora. Slowly, I dropped to a knee at her feet. I clasped my hand over my heart, put a tight fist to my forehead, and closed my eyes.

For the first time in my life, I prayed.

I had never believed the Gods heard or cared about the prayers of the common person; the world was too cruel to have merciful Gods. But more than anything, I desperately needed something, anything to believe in. I prayed for my sister and my friend's health with everything I had. Finally, I opened my eyes. I stared up at the effigy of Iora. My stomach clenched in horror. Sweat beaded across my skin as I shot to my feet. I looked at the statue in its carved eyes and felt like throwing up again. The familiar features, the kind eyes... no, this was no god. It was a statue of my sister.

Energy poured out of me in response to my emotions. My mouth felt dry, and the world seemed to spin. The air wavered with my trembling hands as I fell to the ground. My words echoed my thoughts. "That's... impossible..." The sound of my own voice was dull as my heartbeat pounded louder and faster every second.

Abigail grabbed me by the shoulders, her hair growing in volume as the electrical energy in the air spiked and shook violently. "Rey..." She seemed to shout. "Breath...! Slowly." I nodded weakly as I focused on drawing in and releasing air. I focused on the feeling of the grass against my palms. Slowly, the world felt clearer.

"Abigail..." I said slowly. A tear rolled down my cheek.

She looked down at me, concerned. "Rey? What happened?"

"It's all wrong." I still felt sick as I fixed my eyes back on the contours of the statue's face.

"What happened?" Abigail followed my gaze. "Was it something with this statue?"

I nodded weakly. "Do you... remember this being built?" I asked slowly.

"Yeah, I do. It was a few weeks after a rumor spread about this place being attacked. It was halfway done when I visited for one of the few times I was here." She cocked her head to the side slightly, "Why?"

I shook my head and rubbed my eyes as I rose to my feet again. The statue remained the same. "It... looks just like my sister."

Her eyebrows shot up. "*What?*"

I stepped closer to it and placed my hand on the glowing crystal resting in its chest. "The body is more matured than I remembered, but this face..." I moved my hand, brushing its cheek in horror. "It's hers. I'm certain." I placed my hand back on the gem and probed my energy inside it. I recoiled in horror again, taking a step backwards. "This crystal... it's energy feels... so familiar."

Hundri limped next to me and placed a hand on the crystal. His brow furrowed. "This is a spiritual heart. Of a steel at best from the amount of power it gives off."

I rubbed my forehead slowly as a headache set in. "This... can't be her spiritual heart, right? She'd be *dying* then. I... I don't understand."

Abigail shook her head. "I don't think any of us do."

"You should take it with you," Added Hundri. "If you end up finding her, she will definitely need it back."

I nodded slowly and stepped up to the statue that resembled my sister. Energy pulsed out of my hands into a gauntlet. Pain seared my channels and the aura trembled, threatening to burst apart. My fingers wrapped around the ice-cold crystal. I hesitated. "You don't think... this is her body, right?"

Hundri shook his head. "Not a chance. Abigail said she saw it being built, remember?"

I nodded slowly. "Right. That's obvious." I pushed my feelings of stupidity away and yanked the crystal free. The glowing crystal ceiling immediately dimmed to a dark grey and the trees began to wither and die rapidly.

I grit my teeth and the energy around me moved erratically. "Sick *bastards*," I muttered.

Both Hundri and Abigail turned to look at me. "This is why the spiritual heart isn't common knowledge. People use lesser people as... fuel."

My eye twitched. The grass flattened as energy roared into the bear's rune without limit. "Lesser?" I gritted my teeth. "*Lesser?*" I spat.

Abigail grabbed me by the shoulder and looked into my eyes deeply "I'm sure that's not what he meant." Her eyes softened.

I felt tears brim in my eyes once more. "You're right." My voice broke slightly as the anger from the bear's rune receded. After a moment of silence, I tried to change the topic to anything but my sister. "I'm sorry about Yaldrie, Hundri." My voice quavered.

He sighed and tossed me back my sword before looking up at the dying light of the crystal ceiling. "I should've done better. Though it doesn't seem like I'll get the chance now."

I stopped, mouth open. "What?"

"I pushed my spiritual heart too hard." He winced as a flimsy aura formed around his finger. "It's like a hand crushing my heart when I try to gather energy."

My mouth opened and closed for a second as I processed what he had said. "Is that... my fault?"

He smiled sadly and looked at his friends. "I'd have given my spiritual heart and ruptured my channels a thousand times if it meant saving even one of their lives." He turned to me. "You saved their lives with my power. Never regret saving a life." He pounded his heart twice and raised his fist to the sky. With a smirk he looked back to the Blades. "Besides. Now we're all broken in one way or another."

I clenched my fist and blood trickled from my palm as my knuckles went white.

"Rey, he's right." Abigail walked in front of me and smiled. "And besides, I'm fine! You protected me! Unless..." She frowned. "Unless my life means nothing to you..."

I smiled weakly and slugged her on the arm. "Wouldn't have saved you if it was worth nothing."

She clicked her tongue. "Fair."

We walked over to the group of our wounded friends and upon arriving, Abigail pulled Hundri to the side, so I talked to Syre, who was dressing Ralteir's arm in a myriad of bandages and salves. "How's he doing?"

They had moved them under the dwindling shade of the dying trees. She wiped sweat from her brow as she turned her attention to me. "Better." She grimaced.

The stump of Ralteir's missing arm was blackened and dead from the freezing temperatures. Bandages finally wrapped the remaining decaying skin and Kai poured a vial of liquid down Ralteir's throat. "Why didn't you guys use your family crests?" I felt anger bubble up as I asked the question but pushed it down.

Kai sighed. "Not all of them are as useful as Hundri's and yours. Mine lets me know what materials something is made of if I push energy into them. Doesn't work if I haven't seen the material before though."

Syre glanced up at me with sorrowful eyes before going back to tracing glowing runes in a path from Ralteir's runes to his destroyed arm. "Mine isn't very useful for this sort of fighting either. A taste of their blood lets me see a glowing outline of the person if I focus on them, no matter how far."

"That makes sense." I sighed and the anger left me. "I... I just still have all this anger still. I'm sorry for assuming you guys could've done more."

"It's fine, Rey," said Syre, "we all have more emotion than we know what to do with right now. After years of doing this... we all have learned not to show our pain."

Kai nodded slowly before tapping me on the chest. "Speaking of family crests, can I see something?"

"Sure, go ahead."

He put on a small bronze mechanical monocle, and it lit up with runes. With the whir of gears and the clattering of pistons, the bronze exoskeleton on his right arm extended a small claw of glowing white crystal. Kai pressed it into my sternum with almost enough force to break the skin. Luckily, the throbbing from hundreds of bruises drowned the pain. My channels seemed to tingle inside my body as a wave of unfamiliar energy washed through me. I pulled back instinctively and looked inquisitively at Kai's brown eyes.

Gears clicked and spun on the monocle and the runes pulsed as they shifted rapidly. Kai grimaced. "It's just like I predicted. That bear's rune is destroying your channels."

I froze. I knew it put a strain on them, but *destroying* them? A freezing hand gripped my chest at the thought. "What... do you mean?"

He sat back down as the mechanics clattered together on his arm. After a moment, a blue crystal wrapped in bronze supports popped up above his palm with a hiss. A quiet hum emanated from the skeletal armament and a dim, flickering image of my body appeared. As the gears clattered and the bronze hummed, the image revealed the network of channels within my body.

"This," He pointed at my hands and arms on the spectral model. "Is where most of the damage is. That rune is leaving a web of cracks on your channels. If you hadn't ascended recently, they would probably be bigger."

I frowned. "I guess this power really wasn't meant for the human body." I flexed my fingers and stared at my hand, the feeling of indomitable strength still lingering among all the pain.

Syre smiled weakly. "It turned you into a true monster. I agree with Kai though. As amazing as your bear rune is, the power supporting that is even more impressive." She pointed at the mutilated corpse of Gruvlin. "Go rob that bastard of his strength."

I recoiled slightly staring at the broken body of the behemoth I had felled. "Why must it be him? I'd rather anyone else." I grimaced.

Hundri —supported by Abigail— limped over to us and chimed in. "They're right, kid." He frowned deeply. "He took so much from us. Take one last thing from that *plonthent*." He spat the last word with malice.

I chuckled weakly and my ribs burned like magma, quickly stopping my laughter. "Plonthent?"

"It's a word in the city's mercenary community," Kai explained. "Think of it like calling someone stupid, horrible and revolting at the same time."

I nodded, still smiling. "I mean I could just hold onto this rune, in case of emergencies." The truth was, I didn't want to take a new power. That... *thing* might grow stronger, and that wasn't something I wanted to risk.

"Rey... I hate to say it, but you've demonstrated it will act in accordance with what's in your heart. I don't think you can stop it if you get angry, and that could cripple your ascensions for the rest of your life." He furrowed his brow in anger, "As much as you hate that bastard, I hate him more than you could imagine. He *murdered* my close friend," the energy around us swelled with his emotions and he coughed in pain. The air stopped humming. "But he could give you a spectacular amount of power. I think it's necessary."

The whole group nodded, even Abigail. I took a deep breath and walked over to the body of Grulvin, the man whose life I'd taken. My chest hummed as I stood over his bloody corpse and extended my hands. I placed my hand against his muscular chest. His runes heated and my hand burned as my runes blazed brightly through my armored shirt.

I focused as hard as I could as darkness threatened my eyes. I struggled against the feeling of unconsciousness tugging at my brain. *NO. I WILL NOT. TAKE. HIS MEMORIES.* I screamed and shakily drew my sword and ran its blade against my forearm in a desperate attempt to stay conscious. A wave of lucidity crashed over me as I opened my eyes wide in shock. I gritted my teeth and focused on drawing the energy into my body. The searing pain of runic power blazed where the bear's rune had sat, morphing and changing.

And just like that, it was over.

I stood there, stunned as the pain of my bruises rejoined the cut on my arm. The ground below me swayed and moved. No, *I* moved back and forth with a nonexistent wind as I struggled for footing. The ground spun out from under me as I fell backwards and landed in the soft embrace of Abigail.

She grinned at me. "Heya, how're you feeling?"

I groaned and slowly pushed myself from her arms as I finally found my footing. "Like I got a mountain dropped on me."

Hundri chuckled. "Any idea what power you grabbed from him? Do you even control what you take?"

I sat there thoughtfully before responding, "You know, it would *probably* be a good idea to figure out which I'm taking before moving to action."

"Plonthent," Abigail playfully slapped me on the head with her palm and I winced. "Sorry." She smiled. She didn't look sorry.

"Well, I would find out, but my channels feel like they're going to burst with one pulse of energy, so maybe when we descend this hellish mountain."

"That's fair." Hundri chuckled. "Let's rest here for the night before descending."

We agreed and spread out to find different areas to sleep. Ogland, Ralteir and Hundri stayed with Syre and Kai for medical aid while Abigail and I wandered under the ring of trees. The rough dark brown bark pressed into my chest uncomfortably as I slumped down, exhausted. I let my head rest against the tree and stared up at the grey crystal sky that had been once lit by the energy of my sister.

I missed her. This whole ascent had left me with nothing but a burning sense of panic. I had been *right*, something was terribly wrong. As I vowed to myself once more that I would find her, Abigail sat next to me.

"Hey," she said.

"How're you feeling?"

She sighed, "Fine." After a brief pause, "I talked to Hundri about my parents."

I turned to look into her brown eyes. They reflected the dim ghostly light that my sister's crystallized spiritual heart projected. "Are you okay?"

She looked up at the grey ceiling. "I don't know how to feel," she finally said. "I feel like I got robbed of a parent, and the other one left broken. I hardly had a mom. And it's because of that man. That's how I've felt my whole life. But now that I'm older and have seen so much more, heard more, I just can't feel the same way. They made the choice to go. I told Hundri I can't hate him anymore. I don't think I can ever truly like him, but I don't think he's a bad guy. I can see that with how much he cares about you." She smiled sadly.

"At the same time... I just don't know where to direct this... anger." She grabbed her tunic and clenched her fist hard. "It's like a fire that's burnt up my soul." She looked deep into my eyes. "I don't know where to put it. I told Hundri I needed some time before I could talk to him again in any depth, and I intend to find where to place this... hate."

I nodded slowly. "Why don't you come with me? To the Lower Greens. I could always use a travel buddy, especially now that Hundri is... crippled. Maybe along the way you'll find something to quell your hate."

She stared at me, looking starstruck. I stared at her, confused. "What? Did I say something weird?"

Her face seemed to deepen in color as she quickly looked away. "No." She smiled wildly. "I would love to, Rey."

I grinned back. "Then, let's make a promise. Together, we venture out. To fight fate, to find purpose and to find ourselves."

I leaned forwards and extended my hand. I saw her roll her eyes in the dim light. "Together, we fight." She smiled. "And by the way, you have *got* to stop cutting yourself, I mean really, what am I supposed to do with you?"

I smiled and looked up at the grey ceiling. After a few minutes of silence, she finally spoke. "Today... I felt so useless."

I looked at her, startled. "What do you mean?"

"You and everyone else worked so hard to take out Grulvin. I felt like I was only getting in the way." She frowned and looked at the grass. "I hated it."

I watched her for a moment before comforting her. "You weren't useless. Without you, I would've never had the opening to finish him."

She didn't look up. "That's true."

"How about we make that part of our promise too. I know we said we'd be weaklings together, but I know we both aren't satisfied with that. Not forever."

"Not forever." She echoed and looked up, smiling weakly. We both went quiet for a minute, staring off into empty space. "By the way, I know this is a little random, how *did* you know something happened with your sister here?"

I glanced at her. "A vision." I said simply as I recalled the dying memory of fighting from my sister's perspective.

"Huh." She said while simply looking up at the ceiling, "Well tell me about it some time, in case I forget. I'm going to pass out." She shot me a sly smile, "Don't get any weird ideas."

My face flushed. "I would never. I'm going to sleep too."

"Good. Sleep well Rey."

"Sleep well."

CHAPTER TWENTY-TWO

Descent

Reynolds Helphain

I awoke with a start, my hands trembling as I jolted upwards to a sitting position. My breath came out in ragged heaves and sweat rolled down my brow. My dreams had been plagued with flashes of brutality, sensations of slaughter. The memories of Grulvin. I stared down at my bloodstained hands and screamed. With a blink it was gone. The sensation of crushing skulls and pounding ribcages, the feeling of such immense bloodlust still lingering.

I shivered.

Abigail sat up next to me, looking tired and concerned, but mostly tired. "What... what's wrong?"

"Nothing. Sorry Abigail." I muttered. I picked myself up as I grabbed my sister's crystal and felt a dull throb from across my body. Everything still burned and ached, the cuts remained on my limbs, pulsing with fiery pain. I wasn't in fighting condition, but I could at least think clearly now. I pushed energy through my body and felt a dull pain. Still, I smiled.

I extended a hand to Abigail, who smiled playfully and slapped it away. "Oh, I don't need your *help*." With a pulse of energy, she flew upwards, onto her feet.

I rolled my eyes. "Whatever. We should go to Hundri and the rest of the Blades."

"Agreed." She nodded and rubbed the sleep from her eyes before marching away.

We walked in silence over to the group. They stood at the base of the now black and dying trees, with Ogland over Syre's shoulder and a bright aura around her. Hundri wore a large bag where he had consolidated the group's things. The largest surprise, however, was Ralteir standing next to Hundri.

I rushed over. I hadn't been the best of friends with Ralteir, but he was still someone who I had fought with. That was a strong enough bond for me. "Ralteir! You're awake! How're you feeling?"

He turned and looked at me slowly. His eyes looked... broken. He raised the one hand he had to eye level, then looked at his bandaged shoulder. "I...I can still feel it. It hurts. Where is my arm? Why didn't you save it? It hurts, Rey. It hurts." He began to yell. "Where is it?! I can *feel* it. Where did it go? It hurts so bad!" Tears dripped down his face as he slowly collapsed to his knees at my feet.

I stepped back in horror. My mind raced as I stared down at the form of my broken comrade. Hundri's calloused hand clamped my shoulder, and I jumped in surprise. "He's in shock. He only woke up a few minutes ago." Hundri's face was grim and tight.

"It's not your fault." I said, meeting his luminescent eyes.

He looked back with surprise that slowly faded to sorrow. His eyes looked puffy, and raw. "It feels like it is. I... I don't know if I can handle Ogland waking up." His face hardened back into a grim mask. "But I will, because I must." Kai hurried over and began to talk quietly to Ralteir in an attempt to calm him down.

Abigail spoke from behind me, "Also Rey, what rune did you get from that *Plonthent*." She chuckled at the last word.

I stepped away from Ralteir and pulsed energy through the rune tentatively. My mind felt as if it were breaking in half. Searing, jabbing pain burst to life in both of my temples as my concentration faltered. Slowly, I regained control of myself despite the pain. Something about this felt familiar to the fragmented sensations I had felt the night before.

I said through gritted teeth, "Hit me!"

Abigail smiled. "Thought you'd never ask." She swung a punch at my shoulder, and just before it hit, I *felt* it. A jolt and a tingle in my mind as it passed through the air next to me. The bruises flared to life in my shoulder as it connected and with that final wave of pain, my concentration broke.

I slumped down and placed my hands on my knees as the world spun. I heaved heavy breaths and sweat poured down my forehead and out over my body. My head's throbbing slowly faded away with each breath and passing second. Both my channels and mind stung from the use, even though it had only been for a few fleeting moments.

Abigail leaned down to my eye level. "Is your new rune letting me hit you? Because that sure is a good ability." She smiled devilishly.

I pushed myself up and took a deep breath. "I have no clue what it does. Maybe I shouldn't have pushed away his memories."

She raised an eyebrow. "Didn't realize you could see their memories too. Remind me to never let you take my runes."

I chuckled and wiped the sweat from falling into my eyes. "I wouldn't."

Kai and Hundri approached with Ralteir slowly shuffling after them. Kai spoke first, "Let me see it. Maybe I could tell you something from reading it."

"Alright." After removing my leather plates and putting my sister's crystallized spiritual heart on the ground, I pulled up my shirt and showed the new rune to Kai and Hundri.

They both leaned in and whistled. "Now that," said Hundri, "is a glyph."

I looked down in surprise to find that they were indeed correct. A solid black glyph sat imbedded onto my chest like a tattoo. "Well now the pain makes sense."

They nodded. "Glyphs require a lot of practice to use, just like everything else related to energy. Just keep using it and you'll figure out how to use it effectively." Said Kai with a twinkle in his eye. "An inscribed glyph at steel... this is unprecedented..." He muttered to himself.

Hundri scratched his stubble and gestured towards the glyph. "If I had to guess, it makes some sort of bubble."

"Bubble? Why do you say that?"

He raised an eyebrow, and said in a slow voice, "I can see energy, *remember?* It was around Grulvin the whole fight."

I heard Abigail sigh from behind me and mutter, "Idiot..."

With that, I pulled back down my shirt, reattached my leather plates, grabbed my sister's crystal, placed it in a pocket within my cloak, and turned back to Hundri. "Is it time we descend the mountain then?"

He nodded and we began our descent. We quietly moved through the dying chamber. An oppressive sullen energy had blanketed each person. I let my thoughts wander, the feeling of my sister's crystal being the only anchor that kept an ounce of my attention on the world around me.

After a few minutes of walking, we had passed the wooden bridge and reached the large white stone arch that led to the lift. We slowly shuffled one by one onto the stone disc, and with one pulse of energy from Syre, it began to descend. As it clicked into place, the tens of men that Hundri had turned into statues came into view. We stepped out into the freezing room. I shivered. Not from the temperature, but from the terrified frozen faces as their lives were taken without even a fight.

Hundri sighed as he swept the room with his eyes. "I will certainly miss this."

I stepped next to him. "Miss what? The slaughter?"

"No. The feeling of... *power*. I never thought I'd miss it but now that it's gone...?" He shook his head. "Maybe this is for the best. I was growing tired of the slaughter anyway."

I smiled slightly and raised my voice so the rest of the group could hear my question, "What will you all do when we get back to Anhalt?"

Hundri took one last look at the point where his fist had impacted the ground the day before. The beautiful, horrifying sheets of ice coated the ground. He started limping back towards the doorway we had come from and answered, "I don't know. I will need a new hobby, that's for sure. I don't think I'll ever fight like I used to."

We began to descend the steps when Syre answered. "I'm thinking I might re-enroll at the academy. It wouldn't hurt to take my experience to somewhere I can learn." She looked to Abigail, "How about you, Abigail?"

Her face flushed slightly, "Well, I'm thinking of adventuring outside of Anhalt actually."

Hundri waggled his eyebrows. "Really now? You know Rey is doing that too! Maybe you should travel together."

I sighed and glared at him. "That was the plan."

"Really?" He feigned a look of surprise. "Curious!"

Syre elbowed him and smiled at me. "That sounds nice!"

"Yes," I smiled and imagined hiking through the forest and cracking jokes. "It does."

After a few minutes of silence, we reached the offshoot hallway that led to the Ascension Chamber. I glanced at the large metal door and an idea came to mind, "Hundri, could the Ascension Chamber heal your spiritual heart?"

He glanced at the chamber before it disappeared behind the polished white corner as we continued our descent. "I wish it could." He frowned slightly. "It would probably do more harm than good. The only way it could be of any use would be if it could push me to ascend. Other than that, the energy would just dissipate, and that's still only if it doesn't destroy my broken heart."

"Ah," I frowned as well. "I see."

He formed a weak smile. "Thanks for the thought though. Do remember that this isn't your fault. I chose this. Don't worry about it."

"Right." I still felt guilt tug at my chest.

We continued our descent in silence, passing by room after room of mutilated corpses that reeked of death. Each polished room stained red with the stolen life of others placed a heavy weight on us, as if each of us were regretfully thinking, "If only I could've been there."

Reynolds... A deep, gravelly voice in my head echoed.

I froze.

Slowly, I turned to look behind me. The shadow of my descending group had grown deeper, darker, almost pitch black. Slowly a pair of dark inky hands extended as a pair of large eyes opened. The hands reached for me, groping at the air as if begging. Sweat rolled from my brow as I lowered my hand to my sword.

I blinked, and it was gone.

"Rey?" I heard Syre call. I turned to find the rest of the group had stopped and were staring at me.

I shook my head. "Sorry, it's nothing."

"Are you sure?" Abigail looked at me in concern as she put a warm hand on my face. "You can talk to us."

My face grew hot. "I'm fine. Really."

She withdrew her hand and nodded. "Alright. Just remember, it's okay to mourn. We all feel the same."

"Yeah." Even though I hadn't really known Yaldrie, the guilt I felt surrounding her death seemed to pull harder. I pushed it down again, bottling it up.

We walked in silence for a while, occasional halfhearted conversation sprung up around the group but died as fast as it began. Nobody felt up for the normal light-hearted banter. Finally, we reached the bottom where we had begun the ascent.

The tall pillars that supported the large, tiled room cast long shadows in the golden light of the morning sunrise. I breathed in the cold morning mountain air, thankful that the stench of iron had been blown away. Abigail walked up next to me and looked out of the opening where the platform passed through. To my surprise, the platform was gone. *I hope that kid got away.* I frowned, looking amongst the bodies of the bandits we had slaughtered for his face.

I breathed a sigh of relief and looked back to Abigail. "The platform is gone; do you think the kid got away?"

Her eyes reflected the golden light as she stared out at the horizon. She tucked her swaying hair behind her ear. She smiled, and my face heated slightly. "I'm sure he did."

Hundri stepped up next to us, the golden light contrasting his luminescent eyes. "Well, either way, we must call it back." He stepped over a crimson-stained corpse and placed a hand on a small gem embedded in a dais. It flickered with light for a moment. He winced and turned to me. "Forgot. Rey, would you mind?"

"Yes, right. Of course." I pressed my hand on the gem and sent a pulse of energy into it. It glowed brightly and hummed to life, resembling Hundri's eyes in color and brightness. "There," I smiled. "You're going to have to get used to that."

He frowned and dropped his bag at his side before he sat down, resting his back on the chiseled column-like base of the dais. I sat down with him, and the rest slowly joined us aside for Ralteir. He numbly stared into space and paced back and forth, droning under his breath restlessly.

Abigail followed my gaze. "Is he going to be alright?"

"It depends," Syre traced a glowing rune in the air idly, "He will heal physically, but his mind is something else. I can't guarantee he will ever be the same." She saw my lips curl into a frown and quickly added. "But someone more trained, it's much more likely."

"Will he fight ever again?" His bandaged stub of a shoulder moved wildly as he gestured with his other arm to nobody.

Kai spoke up, "When I finish my artificial limb, maybe. But as it stands, it leans more towards no."

Hundri sighed. "Besides, I have no clue what will happen when we get back to Anhalt. Ronhelm very likely will be furious that we didn't finish all of their forces."

"What's the worst he could do?" A bead of sweat rolled down my forehead. "We still did the hard part."

"At the very most, execution, but more likely banishment." He looked at the ground, sullen. "However, my guess is as good as yours. Just in case, Syre should be able to seal the blood pact for a time, and you can escape. I advise you two to spend as little time as possible in Anhalt."

Syre nodded. "I can seal them, but it won't last forever. You will have to find someone to remove them or figure it out yourself."

"What can he do with the blood pacts?" Abigail interjected.

"Well," Hundri looked up. "The ones he gave us, in theory, should only let him track you."

I sighed. "So, we get a head start. Great." I glanced back up the stairway. "Is it worth it to try and rest? Give it another go?"

"We don't have the supplies, or the manpower anymore." Syre fiddled with the retracted form of her bow as she thought. "We're only four steels now, and even worse, two *inexperienced* steels and a non-combatant. It's not worth the risk."

"Not that inexperienced." I grumbled. "But anyway, I agree."

Abigail frowned. "Wait, but I have family there." Her voice slipped into desperation, "What's going to happen to them? I need to say goodbye at least."

Hundri grimaced. "It's a risk. I doubt Ronhelm would extend punishment to your family. That would be ridiculous... but saying goodbye might be too much of a risk."

Her voice raised, now tinged with anger, "Too much of a risk? Are you serious?"

"Your family lives outside the military district, right? Most of the exits out of the city are in the military district or guarded." He looked her in the eyes with a stone-cold serious expression. "If Ronhelm finds out you aren't with us, he very well might hunt you down for questioning. If you value your freedom, you should run."

He sighed. "Besides, I needed to talk to your mother either way. I can send her a message for you if that helps."

Abigail looked clearly upset but spoke slowly, and carefully. "Alright... I'll write something." She breathed deeply and slowly, calming herself. Hundri rummaged around in his bag and pulled a piece of parchment and a feather quill. He handed it to Abigail, who began to write.

"So," I cleared my throat. "What's the exact plan?"

Hundri pulled out his steel cube necklace and it unfolded to reveal a glowing box. "I'll give this to you and claim I lost mine. You show this to the guards for the lift that leads back to your home, ride it back, and find someone to remove the pact."

I nodded. "Alright." I heard the rattling of the tracks and the clanking of gears as the platform approached rapidly. "Are you sure you guys will be alright?"

Syre nodded. "Yeah, we have more than enough of a reputation to survive this. You two are nonexistent compared to our exploits." She smiled at my feigned hurt. "Sorry, but it's true. One day I'll be excited to hear tales of you two."

A loud series of clanks and hisses filled the morning air as the platform came to a stop in its slot. We all scrambled to our feet and Hundri grabbed the large bag, slinging it over his shoulder. Abigail handed him back the parchment with a small block of black characters scrawled onto it. We stepped onto the platform, and I once again pushed energy into a crystal. The familiar bubble formed, gears clattered, and we were off.

The light flared as my eyes adjusted and we were bathed in a golden light. I sucked in my breath slowly, staring at the jaw dropping view. "Wow..." I muttered. The golden light painted the trees, snow and rocky cliffs in a gorgeous way. The track dipped down just above the tree line, its long metal supports digging into the ground several hundred feet below.

I smiled, trying to make the most of the moment despite the tragedy of the past day. Abigail walked up behind me and wrapped her hands around my waist, standing behind me. My face reddened. "Abigail?" I said in surprise, my voice pitching up.

"I'm cold."

"Ah." I acted as casually as possible. "Feel free to use me as a heater then, I guess." I let as much sarcasm as I could enter my voice.

"I think I will." I could *hear* her smile.

The rest of the ride blurred together until Syre walked over to us. "Hey idiots. Seal time."

Abigail let go of me and turned to Syre. "So how does this work exactly?"

"Give me your hands that have the rings for a moment." We both raised our hands and the rings bubbled up from our flesh like blood from an open wound. "Now, this might hurt a little."

She traced green glowing runes onto the air above our rings. Her fingers danced in the air and traced green light. Slowly she wove characters and lines together in a tapestry of power. Finally, she pressed her palm against the seal, and pushed it into the ring. Red lightning crackled off the ring and I grit my teeth as it scorched my skin in explosions of pain. Finally, the clash of green and red light ceased, and the pain along with it. The ring's runes glowed the same green as Syre's energy before sinking back into my skin.

"Not too bad?" Abigail looked at me with a teasing smile.

"Not too bad." I repeated.

With that, Syre repeated the process. Almost immediately after finishing, the shadow of the mountain Anhalt sat within washed over us, snuffing out the dying morning light. Hundri grimaced. "It's time." We all nodded. "Quickly, let me say something I forgot to mention. They will definitely be waiting for us. Syre, me and Kai will rush out with Ogland and Ralteir to draw their attention. In the confusion, you two make a run for it. I suggest you gather energy."

Hundri walked over to Ralteir and stretched. "Been a while since I lifted anything without an aura." With that he squatted and whispered in Ralteir's ear. He responded with something slurred and groggy before trying to climb on Hundri's back, only to scream as he realized he couldn't use his missing arm. With a little wind magic support from Syre, Hundri lifted Ralteir onto his back.

He turned to me and smiled weakly as we entered the mountain. "Rey, it was a pleasure to meet and train you. Remember what I said, don't let expectation and duty consume you. Take some time to stop and smell the roses." He winked at Abigail.

I nodded and smiled. "Thank you. Goodbye, Hundri."

As I said goodbye, the bubble dropped. My eyes rapidly adjusted to the bright city lights and glowing starry sky above. A few guards stood waiting and their eyes widened as Hundri, Syre and Kai sprinted at them with the wounded members of the blades. Hundri looked back one last time and gave me a firm nod.

The guards stumbled backwards in confusion as Hundri crashed into them. Abigail and I flared our auras to life and darted around them. We broke into an energy-enhanced sprint as we leapt into the sparsely populated morning streets. People cried out in confusion as we barreled down the street, each step carrying us tens of paces. We practically flew through the streets as the terraced stone buildings blurred around us.

Our footsteps pounded like thunder as we whirled around corner, the hub of military gates coming into sight. We burst into the stone semi-circle and hundreds of soldiers looked at us in surprise as we barreled towards the gate we wanted, gate number four. We dug our heels into the stone and slowed to a stop with stone chips flying from the ground. I pulled out Hundri's keystone and showed it to the bewildered guard, who upon seeing it, let us through.

From that point on, we lost our breakneck pace and simply strolled down the long hallway. Abigail looked at me and smiled. "Looks like we made it."

"Don't say that yet. You never know what could happen." Neither of us had broken a sweat sprinting here. The power of a steel was truly wonderful. "How are you feeling about your mother?"

She looked off into the distance and frowned slightly. "I'm worried about her. I don't think she'll be upset with me leaving like this, she's told me stories from when she did the same thing. My whole family were wanderers, except for me. I think she'll agree that this is a great chance for me to get stronger. I'll need it." She clenched her fists at her sides and energy leaked out of her slightly before dispersing suddenly. "But Ronhelm could be unpredictable. I just hope she stays safe."

I nodded slowly as the large cave opened up around us. The effigies of the heroes stood familiarly in the center with bronze channels carved into the floor that spiderwebbed out from them. We walked past the images of the heroes and found the large platform waiting for us. I stepped onto the platform and looked out along the tracks and at the large snowy landscape beyond. Abigail stepped up next to me and slung an arm around my shoulder. "Where to first?"

I smiled and pressed my hand on the large crystal, giving it a pulse of energy. "Home."

. . .

The snow whipped through the trees with increasing fervor as Abigail and I burst out into a clearing. I adjusted my cloak and felt it billowing out behind me. Abigail gestured to the shadow of a structure ahead of me. "This is where you lived?"

I smiled, meeting her hazel eyes. "Yeah. Let's head in."

She rolled her eyes. "Alright. Can't believe I'm meeting your parents already."

"Parent. Singular." I sighed. "You make it sound so much more than it is."

She smiled with teeth as bright as the snow. "It's my job as your travel companion after all."

I rolled my eyes and marched through the white powder; the crunches of my boots drowned out in the whistling wind. "My father is a... strange man, so be ready for that."

She caught up to me. "Strange? How so?"

"Think Hundri but... sillier and not involved in the deaths of your parents?"

"That sounds like a Hundri I can like."

Orange firelight streamed through the shuttered windows as we reached the wooden door. With a quick knock of the fist against the old wood, I pressed down on the handle and the door swung open. The silhouette of my father sat in a chair at the hearth, watching the flames. His aura flared to life as he slowly turned.

I met his eye, and I could see the tension drain from his posture. "Son!" he shouted, rocketing up from his chair and charging across the room.

"Father—" His full weight slammed into me as he wrapped his arms around my chest.

After a moment, the burly man pulled himself off me. "Sorry son. Welcome home! I've gotta say, I did not think you were coming home."

I smiled weakly. "No way. I wouldn't die that easily."

He took a step back looking me up and down. "God's boy! Look at you! You're a man now. I can see it in your posture." He met my gaze. "The death in your eyes."

My smile faded. "Yeah."

His aura flared as he shoved me aside. "Never mind my own son! Who are you?" I stumbled and looked back at him in disbelief as he inspected Abigail slowly.

Abigail looked at me with wide eyes and I struggled to contain a chuckle. "A-Abigail."

"Look at that! Finally managed to get a girl, eh?" He smirked at me.

"We're not like that." Our words stumbled over each other as we tried to speak at the same time.

He raised an eyebrow skeptically. "Oh? Really?" He narrowed his eyes at me. "Well, how about both of you take a seat? I'd love to hear your stories."

He walked away from the two of us and pulled out two chairs at the dining room table. With a gesture to sit, he took his own seat across from us. The chairs creaked under our weight, and I unclasped my heavy cloak before setting it on the table.

"So!" He smiled. "Strength! Runes! Feats! I want to hear it all."

I gestured to myself, "I've ascended once, and used our family crest a few times."

"I've also completed the first ascension, but don't have a flashy family crest like Rey's." Abigail fidgeted in her lap with a small knife. "I'm definitely better at hand-to-hand combat though."

"Hey!" I elbowed her. "She's lying. Don't mind her."

Gaelin chuckled. "You got a girl who can kick your ass?"

I felt my face heat. "If anything, it's an even match."

Abigail rolled her eyes. "Uh-huh. Sure."

Gaelin smiled wide. "So, what element are you working with, Abigail?"

"Water, how about yourself?"

"Fire."

Abigail gave me a look. "Fire? I've known plenty fire users and you don't seem a thing like them."

He smirked. "I know," before I could say more, he continued, "anyway, stories! Tell me tales of your adventures!"

Time seemed to slip through my fingers as I recounted my adventures, with Abigail jumping in every once in a while to fill in details I missed. A warmth filled my heart as the conversation went on. Words could not describe how relieving it felt to be home, with my father, with the warmth of the fire at my back while I told stories.

Finally, we finished with the fight with Grulvin, and our journey here. Gaelin whistled. "Now that, that was quite the story." He touched his sternum gingerly. "I had no idea our family crest was so powerful. Good for you for getting it under control."

I smiled. "Thanks, father."

"I'm guessing you're off to the lands below then?"

"That's the plan."

He sighed. "Don't know how to take a break, do you?"

"Not in the slightest." I grinned.

Abigail slugged me on the arm. "Don't worry, I'll keep him alive."

Gaelin looked at the ceiling in thought. "I wonder what the statue meant."

I grimaced. "I intend to find out."

He flicked a wrist at the door. "Go wait outside for a minute son. I want to talk to Abigail for a moment. I'll give her some supplies too."

I pulled myself up from the chair and Abigail gave me a pleading look. I smiled. "See you outside."

She gave me a fake smile that seemed to say, "I'll kill you."

With that, I threw my cloak over my shoulders, clasped the two sides together, and stepped out into the cold. The wind had died down and the stunning view of the world below stretched out in every direction. I smiled and took in a deep breath of cold mountain air.

The hair stood up on the back of my neck. Heavy footsteps crunched in the snow behind me. I whirled around, hand on my sword.

Darkness.

What stood before me was the smoky, wispy form of a knight. Its armor was made of interlocking plates of inky black metal that oozed liquid shadow. Brilliant white light leaked from the joints and visor. The dark knight was easily three heads taller than me, and each step seemed to shake the snow from the trees.

Its voice came out, cold, echoing, and deep. Yet somehow familiar. I clenched my knuckles white. I couldn't move. Panic flooded my veins. "Reynold Helphain. Bearer of emptiness, container of the Void. Spiritwielder. We meet at last."

"W-what are you?" My voice came out small, meek. Terrified.

Its armor was soundless as the plates shifted over one another with each step. It pressed a dark armored figure into my sternum. "You," it gestured to the mountain, "the void," he gestured to the Lower Greens, "everything," it pointed at me once again, "nothing."

I stared at it blankly. "Was that purposefully vague?"

It was silent. After a pause, "Perhaps."

I sighed. "I'm guessing you the voice in my head? That... shadowy figure? Spirit?"

"No," it clasped its hands behind its back, "not entirely."

"Not entirely?" I looked up at its glowing white visor. "What are you talking about?"

"My... malice. My bloodlust. Hate." It let out a noise I interpreted as a sigh. "It is not an easy concept to explain. I am... fractured. In many ways. This," it gestured at itself, "is my mind. Pieces of me lay dormant across these lands. It is a long story. You simply were not ready for my full mind and a fraction of myself nested in your mind. Now, you are ready."

I swept my gaze across the horizon. "So... you're not some... great evil? Guess I thought wrong."

It chuckled in a rasping voice. "The opposite. I was once a great hero. No longer."

"Really now? Well, as a part of me, do you have any fun abilities to offer? Hundri said you might."

"In time." Its arm slowly disintegrated into a mix of pitch black and glowing white smoke. "And it appears my time is limited."

"Wait! What do you mean 'in time'?"

It turned to me again. "Abilities untouched for generations will dance at your fingertips. I fear the power you will soon discover you have. Use it wisely."

"What?" Confusion riddled my mind.

"Find my fragments. You will know when they are near." Half of its body had slowly turned into mist. "We shall speak again. In your mind utter my name, and I shall descend to you."

"Wait! What *is* your name?" I cried out as it billowed into smoke.

Its voice filled my mind. **Utekimeth, Voidbearer.**

Footsteps crunched behind me. "Who were you talking to?" Abigail said in my ear.

I jumped slightly. "Abigail! Hello! Nobody."

She raised an eyebrow. "You better not be going crazy on me. I need that head of yours."

"I'm perfectly fine." I chuckled.

"Well," she toted a large bag that *looked* heavy. "Your father bid us farewell and good luck."

"Not going to come out here himself?"

"No, he said he'll talk to you when you come back."

I smiled. "That sounds like him."

"For a fire user," she smiled, "he's surprisingly nice."

"Yeah. You *have* to tell me what you two talked about." I smiled and looked out at the rolling green hills. The trees coating the lands below like hair. In the distance, a massive, sprawling city. Our next destination.

I could hear her smile, "Maybe." She pointed at the city in the distance. "You ready to head out?"

A wild grin formed on my face. "I've never been more ready." I pulsed a glowing shell of energy around my body and gave her a smile. "Let's go."

I leapt off the cliff. As the wind whistled around me, I looked towards the rising orange sun on the horizon.

I'm coming for you, Serena.

EPILOGUE

The Head

Darkness clung to the room like an oppressive blanket. The only light to find my eyes emanated from a small, glowing, crystal lamp that sat beside me as I worked. Rolls and rolls of parchment sat sprawled out across the polished surface of my desk.

With a sigh, I placed a long, raven feathered quill tip first into a small pot of ink. Contemplation filled my mind. The almost silent imperceivable footsteps of someone entering the room broke my concentration. I slowly pulled myself up from the beautifully carved, ornate chair I had been sitting in and rose to confront the silent person.

A long billowing cloak fluttered out behind me as I shot into the air with a pulse of energy. Its black feathers caught the light, reflecting a prismatic sheen. I slowed my descent with a quick application of gravity magic and landed gracefully. Not a need to even adjust my mask.

A man in similar —but less decorated— robes knelt before me.

I filled my vocal cords with energy, giving my words a powerful weight. "Raise your head."

The man looked up at me, his twisted, black metal mask rippling in the light. The curved beak opened as he spoke, "Greetings, Head."

"I have no time for games. Deliver your message." My gauntleted hand twitched at my side in impatience.

The man rose to his feet. My face twitched. "The King is displeased. He heard your hired men failed to capture their holy mountain."

My knuckles went tight. "He heard of this before even I. Do we know what happened?"

"The son of their hero killed your mercenaries. They say his name is—"

"Hundri. Hundri Tracgan." Energy roiled off my skin like smoke.

The man hesitated. "You are aware of this man?"

"Yes." I grinded my teeth. "Too well."

"Well," The man sauntered towards me, slowly, confidently. "The King has asked me to inform you, that you have one, final chance to *finish* these mountainfolk, or he will send you yourself."

Arrogance.

The man continued. "Despite being our leader, I *doubt* you want to go back to—"

My face twitched and my anger boiled over. I thrust my hand forwards in a pushing motion. Energy pulsed. The man yelped in surprise as the direction that had been *backwards* became *down*. He tumbled through the air before slamming into the stone brick wall on the other end of the large room.

The lantern on my desk flickered. I wrapped a shell of energy around myself and was now unaffected by mortal constraints such as gravity. I was something more than these... fools. I floated through the air towards the man.

He struggled and squirmed as I clenched my fist, increasing gravity five-fold. "Y-you can't do this!" He gasped for air. "I'm the King's messenger!"

I tightened my fist again and the stone behind him cracked. "*King?* What *King?* You serve that damned *woman* and nobody else! I *created* you! And yet, you have the *NERVE* to stand before me?"

I took a deep breath. Slowly I let myself lower to the ground along with the man. I kept him in a tight grip of suspended gravity. "Tell your *god* it shall be done. She needn't worry."

With that, I released the man.

He scrambled across the floor like a wounded animal before disappearing into the shadows with a gust of wind. *Useless.* I cursed to myself.

I pulsed energy around myself and let *forwards* become *down*. People always thought I could fly, but the reality was that all it is, is falling in a different direction. Let people believe what they want. People need to see a God as divine.

I settled back into my chair and scratched my patchy beard beneath my liquid mask. *Too much to do.* With a flick of the wrist, I withdrew the quill from the ink, and began to write a new set of orders.

Reynold's journey shall continue.

About the Author

Finn Douglas is a new, young author from Kirkland, Washington. Finn aims to craft interesting and gripping fantasy narratives that captivate audiences. After consuming ludicrous amounts of media across many genres, he puts the essence of his life and all he's experienced into thought-out worlds.

Aside from writing, Finn spends his time listening to music, spending time with his friends, playing video games, reading, walking through the wilderness and drawing.

Finn will continue to write books into the future as he experiences new things and moves through the next stages of his life. Long live the Birthright Tomes!

On the off-chance you would like to contact Finn, feel free to send him an email at finndouglasauthor@gmail.com. You can also find him on Instagram @finndouglasauthor for book updates and various shenanigans.

Made in United States
Troutdale, OR
08/27/2023

12398660R00170